"Within the panoramic backdrop of historically accurate figures and events of the Korean War, Nurse Jennifer Haraldsson experiences love, loss and renewal. The remarkable contributions and innovations of nursing in caring for wounded warriors is nothing short of inspirational!"
Nancy Ridenour PhD, APRN, BC, FAAN
Dean and Professor
University of New Mexico College of Nursing

"*Forever We Serve* begins five years after the wrenching ordeals of World War II, so vividly recounted in R.S. Baty's acclaimed military thrillers *Footsteps to Forever* and *Darkness into Light*. Haunted by memories of love lost in the violence of that war, army nurse Jennifer Haraldsson hopes to find happiness with Colonel Jack MacLaine, even as the Korean conflict draws them inexorably into its bloody web. Baty deftly interweaves their imperiled romance with riveting depictions of battlefield action between the numerically superior North Korean army and woefully untested UN forces under the magisterial command of General Douglas MacArthur. With an historian's keen eye for dramatic detail, Baty meticulously revisits the bold decisions, legendary personalities and seminal engagements of that brutal conflict, ultimately rewarding his captivated readers with an unpredictable but most satisfying conclusion."

Marty Fleck
Playwright

"Sam Baty brings readers another non-stop adventure in *Forever We Serve*. Jennifer Haraldsson and Jack MacLaine return along with a cast of characters that includes Gen. Douglas MacArthur, Winston Churchill and Presidents Truman and Eisenhower. With his knowledge of military history and the intricacies of military life, Baty skillfully guides the story, keeping the reader guessing until the end, wondering how Jennifer will make the decision that will impact her life forever. *Forever We Serve* is an unforgettable read."

--Paula Paul
author of Sins Of The Empress

"An exciting blend of fact and fiction — *Forever We Serve* is an easy read that provides an excellent history lesson about the events leading up to and through the Korean War. Through the characters, the reader experiences the emotions and thought processes of not just the military characters, but those of their wives and lovers. Realistic and enjoyable."

-- Circe Olson Woessner, Executive Director,
Museum of the American Military Family

"Sam Baty has done it again. In his Korean War thriller, *Forever We Serve*, Baty has crafted a novel which will have the reader eagerly turning pages. Whether you are someone who has read the first two novels in the series and want to be reunited with old friends, whether you are steeped in history, or whether you are a true patriot at heart, you will not be disappointed. There is something in *Forever We Serve* for everyone."

Sam Smith
Retired AT&T Engineer and U.S. Navy Veteran

"A forgotten war, a "proxy" war--the Korean War impacted a generation of men (and a few women) from 1950 to 1953. Mr. Baty's story, *Forever We Serve*, shows us soldiers and nurses from World War II developing their personal lives as they are compelled to bravery in the stress of wartime. The best of the book is the fictional study of MacArthur's aggressive behavior and President Truman's insistence that he must not use atomic weapons or pursue the enemy with American Troops beyond the 38th Parallel. Truman's decision to relieve MacArthur, the hero of another time, is a turning point. This war between the forces of democracy and those of communism is little known today, but very important in our time. To revive it in fiction is a service."

--Publisher of works by Peggy Pond Church--
Accidental Magic, and Shoes for the Santo Nino"

"For those of you who were entranced by Sam Baty's WWII account, *Footsteps to Forever,* starting with the attack at Pearl Harbor in the fall of 1941, December 7, to his continuing novel, *Darkness into Light* of postwar-Cold War Berlin, you will want to continue Nurse Jennifer's fantastic novel of novels action ride. This she gives us in her living account of the dynamic and dramatic action in the US Police Action in Korea along with MacArthur, Truman, and Eisenhower in Baty's latest page turner novel, *Forever We Serve!*"

Dr. Ray Bruce
Fulbright Senior Specialist,
Adjunct Professor
Embry-Riddle Aeronautical University and the
Universiy of Electrical Science and Techonogy China, Chengdu,
China

"Forever We Serve is one of those tales you hate to see end. But perhaps it doesn't, as Sam Baty has brought people out of his earlier Footsteps to Forever World War II thriller to weave their lives into the Korean War and all the intrigue associated with it with a promise of more to come. Baty's books show a very human side to military conflicts, to include Presidents, Prime Ministers, generals, and a beloved Army nurse. An enjoyable and informative read."

Allen Dale Olson, Editor, the QUARTERLY of the American
Overseas Schools Historical Archives

Forever We Serve

Korean War Thriller & Third Novel in Series

R. Samuel Baty

iUniverse, Inc.
Bloomington

Forever We Serve
Korean War thriller & Third Novel in Series

iUniverse books may be ordered through booksellers or by contacting:

iUniverse
1663 Liberty Drive
Bloomington, IN 47403
www.iuniverse.com
1-800-Authors (1-800-288-4677)

ISBN: 978-1-4759-3516-5 (sc)
ISBN: 978-1-4759-3517-2 (e)
ISBN: 978-1-4759-3518-9 (dj)

Library of Congress Control Number: 2012912063

Printed in the United States of America

iUniverse rev. date: 7/17/2012

Dedicated to my wonderful wife, Linda, who has always been and will always be my inspiration.

Prologue

Footsteps to Forever started in the fall of 1941. On December 7, the attack at Pearl Harbor plunged America into the Second World War. Two young U.S. Army lieutenants – Jennifer Haraldsson, a beautiful nurse, and Jonathan Partude, who fell in love with her almost at first sight – received a secret assignment from Army Chief of Staff General George Marshall to rescue a top U.S. nuclear physicist from Norway, which had been occupied by German forces.

President Roosevelt, warned that the Germans might be on the verge of developing terrible new atomic weapons, had asked the elderly physicist, James Flannigan, to spy on a plant in Norway believed to be producing the "heavy water" needed by the Germans for the manufacture of such weapons.

Haraldsson and "Dude" Partude, who were fluent in Norwegian and excellent skiers, had to find Flannigan and help him escape across treacherous mountains to the seacoast, where they expected to be picked up by a waiting submarine. All three were fully aware that the ailing Flannigan must not be allowed to fall into enemy hands.

Chased by the enemy, hampered by the physicist's deteriorating health, impacted by a blossoming romance, and faced with harsh winter conditions, the two young Americans and their allies struggled to avoid disaster. An epic battle occurred at the water's edge, and neither Dude nor the professor survived the mission. Jennifer had to fight through her despair and somehow cope with this terrible loss.

The explosive action of *Footsteps* soon expanded to use the whole war-torn world as its stage, with action scenes involving the doomed Allied raid at Dieppe, the Russian Front, the D-Day invasion of Normandy, and ferocious air battles in the Pacific.

In addition to Roosevelt and Marshall, the cast of characters featured Winston Churchill as well as other historical figures who were among the most important leaders of that most crucial era (of course, the need for a desperate attempt to prevent an enemy from developing nuclear weapons is as relevant today as it was then). Fictional characters with significant roles included an American fighter pilot, a British Special Operations officer, overworked medical personnel, and a pair of German officers – one cruel, the other surprisingly tenderhearted.

As World War II raged on, human emotions smoldered, clouded by issues of ethics and morality. Jennifer met her old foe – the wounded German officer Otto Bruner – in an American field hospital in Normandy. At first, she was attracted to him. When she found out that he had participated in the Norwegian action that resulted in Dude's death, she was outraged. She requested an immediate transfer to get as far away from Otto as possible. She spent the rest of the war in the Pacific Theater.

After the war, friends convinced Jennifer that Otto was only doing his duty. Did she love him? She wasn't sure, but she knew that she had to find out. Europe was in a mess, so she had to find him and find him fast. She previously thought that her greatest adventure was behind her. Now she realized that it was only just beginning.

The sequel (*Darkness into Light*) picks up where the original (*Footsteps to Forever*) leaves off. The horrific World War II is over, but the world is not a safer place. The Soviet Union, in the words of Winston Churchill, has dropped an iron curtain in front of Eastern Europe. It is almost universally accepted that the Soviet dictator, Josef Stalin, has world domination as his ultimate objective. It will be up to the United States and its allies to stop him.

Against this backdrop, two people – on opposite sides of the iron curtain – must risk everything to find out if they are in love. One is the American Nurse, Jennifer Haraldsson, and the other is Otto Bruner, her former patient and a German Prisoner of War. Now that the war is over, each has returned to their former lives with unfinished business. Jennifer is back in the United States, and Otto has returned to East Berlin and is near the remnants of his family. Both know that they cannot live with the status quo.

In a desperate attempt to rendezvous, the two young people throw caution to the wind. They link up with Intelligence Agencies and take unmitigated risks to cross into the other's territory for what might be a moment of ecstasy. The results are sobering. In the final analysis, both realize that the obstacles to spending their lives together are overwhelming. In an emotion-packed scene and one that has been fraught with violence, the two say goodbye as they plan to return to their more traditional lives. But first, Jennifer has to get her critically wounded Intelligence partner, Jack MacLaine, to a U.S. Army hospital in West Berlin. It is a life and death situation that Jennifer does not intend to lose. At this stage, Jack is her best hope for romance.

Part 1

Chapter 1

Aftermath

For Jennifer Haraldsson, time was passing at an alarming rate. It was early June, 1950. She had finished her tour with the Intelligence Agency and was now working as a nurse at Walter Reed Hospital. Jack MacLaine had fully recovered from the wounds he received in Europe, but he was dragging his feet on asking for her hand in marriage. With her biological clock ticking, she was – to say the least – getting nervous. She did love him, but she couldn't wait forever. She would confront him on the issue when they met for dinner this evening.

She still thought about Otto Bruner regularly. There was no doubt in her mind that he would have jumped at the chance to marry her if she had given him the chance. But it still was true that the problems would have been daunting. How could he have ever left his mother and sisters in East Berlin, or would it have even been possible for her to somehow sneak in there to be with him? After all, the Soviets would have made it extremely difficult if not impossible.

Fortunately, her other friends were all doing well. Francis Dunbar and his wife were the proud parents of a son. Winston Churchill, although now nearly eighty, was more-than-likely being brought back for another run as Prime Minister of Great Britain, and both Molly Davis and Jacob Partude were settled in to family roles. Molly had married Bill Summerfield and was expecting, and Jacob was back with Sandy. Now if only she could get Jack MacLaine to propose!

Jennifer was monitoring a patient's vital signs when Dr. Brad Taylor stuck his head in the door. This was the same doctor that Jennifer had worked for in Normandy, and she was sure that he had been instrumental in getting her the nursing position at Walter Reed. They had renewed their relationship as best friends and confidants.

"You have time for a cup of coffee?" he asked.

"Give me a minute to fill out this chart."

She quickly filled in the required information. "Let's go."

"You'll be back soon, won't you?" her young patient asked with a hint of urgency in his voice.

"I'll be back before you know it," Jennifer replied with a smile.

Jennifer and Brad sauntered down the hallway to the coffee shop. They each ordered a cup of coffee (black) and went to a table and sat down.

Something was obviously bothering Brad.

"A penny for your thoughts," Jennifer said.

"Well, for starters," Brad said after a momentary lull, "things couldn't be much worse in Asia. Generalissimo Chiang Kai-shek has been forced to withdraw to Formosa. The Communists have taken over the China mainland, and MacArthur has removed the last of his troops from Korea."

"So?" Jennifer asked.

"Well, in Korea, you now have the North and the South. The North is dominated by Communists, and the South is supposedly our ally. If the North decides to attack, we would undoubtedly have to go to their aid."

"Militarily?"

"Yes, militarily."

Jennifer had been so engrossed with her own problems that she hadn't given any thought to the global picture. Now she could see the gravity of the situation.

"Do you think North Korea would attack the south?" she asked, her voice reflecting alarm.

"I think they very well might do it. The Communists want to dominate the world, so Korea would be a very likely spot to initiate military action."

Jennifer was stunned. *The world did seem to be unraveling. And here just a few short years ago, a terrible World War was fought. Had the human race not learned anything? Apparently not.*

"Do you think that this will have an impact on us?" Jennifer asked.

"It could. Since you and I were in field hospitals during the last war, we could be called up to serve again if war breaks out in Korea."

Whoa, she thought. Up to now, her primary concern had been whether or not Jack MacLaine would pop the big question. Now she realized just how insignificant her problem was.

Brad shook his head. "Just a few short years ago, the United States was the premier military power in the world. Now our military is essentially an empty shell."

"Couldn't we build up again pretty rapidly?" Jennifer asked.

"Perhaps, but it's not for sure. Everything changes. Take, for example, General Patton. He's no longer living."

Jennifer nodded. *Old 'Blood and Guts' George Patton might really be needed in the days ahead. But he was dead and no longer a consideration. Hopefully, there would be someone around who could take his place.*

"Thank goodness, we have General MacArthur in Japan." Brad continued. "He probably understands the situation in Asia as well as anyone."

"I agree, "Jennifer replied. "I'm meeting Jack MacLaine for dinner tonight. Perhaps he can shed a little light on things."

"I doubt that he can tell you much, even though he may know a great deal. As I recall, your security clearance was lifted when you got out of the Intelligence business."

As usual, Brad was right. Jack MacLaine was now in the Central Intelligence Agency (CIA), and from everything Jennifer knew about it, security was very tight.

Brad looked at his watch. "We better be getting back."

Jennifer nodded. The two got up and started back to their duty stations.

That evening, Jennifer prepared to meet Jack MacLaine at *Hogate's,* a fish restaurant in the nation's capital that was on the Potomac River. *Hogate's* was known for its fine food and affluent atmosphere. Jennifer put on a black, silky dress, wanting to make a very good impression on the elusive Jack MacLaine. She would try and pin him down tonight. After all, he had stalled long enough (actually too long). She finished dressing and went out to get in her car. She would meet Jack at Hogate's, as they lived quite a distance apart.

As she drove up to the restaurant, Jack MacLaine was standing outside waiting for her. He motioned for her to pull into the parking lot and started walking in that direction. Jack was puffing on a cigarette, and he looked more nervous than usual. *Something must be up,* Jennifer thought as she pulled in to a parking space next to his car. Hopefully he would be able to tell her.

Both Jack and his boss, Bill Summerfield, were now civilians. Bill, who was a colonel in the U.S. Army just a few short years ago, had retired from the Army and transitioned into the CIA. *Would they stay civilians,* Jennifer wondered, *or would they be recalled to active duty?* She just might find out tonight! For Molly's sake, she hoped that Bill would be able to stay a civilian and remain in the D.C. area. For her own sake, she didn't want to be separated from Jack.

Jennifer got out of her car and closed the door. The couple greeted each other and kissed. "Do you have a reservation?" Jennifer asked.

"Yes, fortunately. The place appears crowded tonight."

MacLaine went to the front desk and gave his name. The receptionist checked his name off the list, picked up two menus, and escorted the couple to a corner booth. "Is this okay?" she asked with a smile.

MacLaine looked at Jennifer, got her approval, and then told the receptionist that it was fine. The receptionist put the menus on the table and left. Jennifer slid into the booth followed shortly by MacLaine. He smiled at her as they both glanced at the menu.

"Do you know what you want?" he asked.

"Yes, I'll have the Fisherman's Platter."

"Same here," he replied.

Soon, the waiter came for their order. They ordered a drink as well as dinner. Jennifer ordered a glass of white wine, and Jack ordered a Scotch and water. Jack pulled out another cigarette.

"I have something to tell you," he said as he lit a Chesterfield.

He put out the match and continued. "I am being recalled to active duty and transferred to Tokyo. I will be going back into the Army as a colonel."

"I was afraid of this," Jennifer replied. "What about Bill Summerfield? Is he being recalled also and being shipped overseas?"

"Yes. He will be serving in the temporary rank of brigadier general and going to Tokyo with me."

"That's impressive," Jennifer said. "But what about the fact that Molly is expecting? Doesn't that impact the brass's thinking?"

"I'm afraid not. And it's probably the right decision for them to make. After all, it's when the kids get up to grade school and beyond that they really need both parents. And, if war breaks out over there, many folks will be recalled to active duty just when their kids need them the most."

"Do you think there will be war?"

MacLaine shrugged. "I have no idea."

I'll bet he does, Jennifer thought. *No use pushing it, though. He'll just deny it.*

Jennifer stared at Jack, not knowing how to broach the subject that was foremost in her mind.

"Oh-oh," MacLaine said with a pained expression on his face. "I know that look. What is it you want to ask?" By now, their drinks had arrived, and Jack took a healthy swig of Scotch.

Jennifer swirled her wine glass and then started in. "You remember when I wheeled you on that cart to the U. S. Army Hospital in West Berlin? I wasn't at all sure that you would make it, but I prayed with all my might that you would get well and that we would spend the rest of our lives together. You got well, but we still aren't together. What is it now – four years?"

Jack took another gulp of Scotch. "I know," he confessed. "But you are the only woman in the world for me, and we will be together. I promise!"

"But when?" Jennifer pleaded. "I'm not getting any younger, and I can't afford to wait much longer."

"We'll be together soon," MacLaine replied as he took Jennifer's hand. "I can't marry you immediately, because I will be leaving for Tokyo very shortly. But I can get an engagement ring to solidify our relationship. Will that suffice?"

Jennifer pulled her hand back and thought for a moment. Then she sighed. "I guess it will have to do. But I'm warning you -- we better set a wedding date soon and stick to it. And I mean soon!"

MacLaine obviously got the message. "I will get the engagement ring tomorrow, and tomorrow night we can decide on a tentative time and place for the wedding."

The two clinked their drink glasses as their meals arrived. Jennifer smiled at MacLaine, and there was a special sparkle in her eye. *Mission at least partially accomplished,* she thought.

"I'm starved," Jennifer said as she viewed her sumptuous meal.

"Me, too," MacLaine replied. They both dug in.

7

The realization that she might – finally – become Mrs. Jack MacLaine in the near future was sinking in. The feeling was warm and pleasurable. She hadn't experienced anything like it since Dude had proposed to her on that fateful day in Norway. Would MacLaine really come through? She thought – and hoped – so.

They finished their dinners, and both seemed very content and relaxed. It was as if a heavy burden had been lifted from their shoulders. MacLaine asked Jennifer if she wanted dessert, and she shook her head. "I couldn't eat another bite," she groaned. MacLaine nodded. Obviously, he felt the same way. He took out a cigarette and lit it. This time, however, he didn't exhibit the nervousness that he had before. They gazed at each other, oblivious to anyone else in the room. *Perhaps he is as happy with the commitment as I am,* Jennifer speculated.

"I guess we better go," MacLaine said, "even though I really don't want to." He motioned the waiter over and asked for the check. The waiter reached into a pocket and pulled it out. MacLaine pulled out his wallet, took out some bills, and returned the wallet to his rear pants pocket.

"Do you need some change?" Jennifer asked. MacLaine shook his head, and the twosome got up and headed for the exit. Soon, they were at Jennifer's car.

"I can cook the dinner tomorrow night," Jennifer said, "if you want to come to my place."

"I don't want you to have to go to all that trouble. Would you meet me at the Fort Myers Officers' Club at – say – seven p.m.? They have a dance band tomorrow night, so it should be very special."

"Sure," Jennifer replied. "I think that would be the perfect spot."

The two kissed, and Jennifer thanked MacLaine for a perfect evening. "I'll never forget it," she said as she looked longingly into his eyes.

"It was perfect for me also," MacLaine replied. "I'm only sorry I took so long to get serious about us."

"Don't even think about that," Jennifer responded softly. "All of that is in the past." She got in her car, started it, and drove off. She looked in the rear view mirror to see Jack MacLaine for as long as she could.

The next morning, Jennifer got to work a few minutes early. She was walking to her work station when Brad Taylor came into view. He was deeply engrossed in a patient's record. He looked up just as the two were about to bump into each other.

"I don't ever recall seeing such a big smile on your face," Brad said in amazement. "Did something special transpire last night?"

"Yes, it did. After tonight, I should have an engagement ring and a tentative date to be married."

"That's wonderful," Brad replied, giving Jennifer a big hug. "Do I know the lucky fellow?"

"Of course you do," Jennifer said, trying to hide her exasperation. "It's Jack MacLaine."

"My congratulations to you, and please pass it on to Jack." The two hugged again, and then Taylor hurried off. Looking back over his shoulder, he said to meet him for coffee at 10: a.m. "I want to hear all about it," he added.

"I will if I can," Jennifer shouted. "I have to see what's on my schedule." Taylor nodded. *If anyone should understand, it should be him,* Jennifer mused.

Jennifer arrived at her duty section and checked her schedule. She was on the docket for surgery at 9:45 a.m. Thus, she wouldn't be able to meet Taylor this morning. Looking at her watch, she decided that she should proceed to the washroom and scrub up. After the surgery, she would try and find Taylor and reschedule their meeting. Perhaps he could join her for lunch.

The surgery was intensive, but it was over by 11:30 a.m. If she hurried, she might be able to meet Brad Taylor for lunch, as he usually went about noon. Thankfully, one of the other nurses agreed to cover for her. Jennifer rushed to the dressing facility, washed up, took off the special gown, and changed back into her normal work clothes. She then hurried to Brad's office. Thankfully, he was still there.

"Thank goodness you're still here," Jennifer exclaimed.

Brad looked up and smiled. "We can go in a minute, but first I have a question to ask."

"Oh? What's that?"

"Do you know Monica Davis, Molly's sister?"

"I've never met her, but I've heard Molly talk about her. I know she's just finishing up Nursing School. Why do you ask?"

"She's applied for a nursing position here, and I've got to make a recommendation to the Director as to whether or not we should hire her. I do have the latitude to bring her in for an interview."

9

Jennifer stroked her chin and thought for a moment. "I'm scheduled to go to Molly's for dinner tomorrow night. Would you like me to ask Molly about her?"

"If you wouldn't mind, I would certainly appreciate it. While I would be willing to give a positive recommendation based solely on her being Molly's sister, I would feel a lot better if there were some concrete information on her."

"I certainly understand," Jennifer replied. "Let's go to lunch."

Brad straightened the pile of papers containing Monica's application, and the two headed for the hospital cafeteria. Once in line, they selected their lunches and went to a table in the corner.

"Okay," Brad said. "I want to hear all about last night. Don't leave anything out."

Brad's enthusiasm delighted Jennifer. "Well," she replied, "Jack is getting me an engagement ring today, and tonight we're going to set a tentative date for the wedding."

"Will I be invited?" Brad asked.

"As if you didn't know!" Jennifer retorted. "Of course you will!"

Brad turned serious. "I can't begin to tell you how happy I am for you. Of all the people I know, you more than anyone else deserve a rich and fulfilling life."

"Thank you," Jennifer said softly as tears welled up in her eyes. "Your saying that means the world to me."

They finished their meals saying little. Just being together was very comforting.

That evening, Jennifer felt excitement and exhilaration as she drove to Patton Hall – the Fort Myers Officers' Club. The club had been renamed in honor of the great World War II General, whose picture hung in the lobby. She felt that it was a well-deserved tribute.

As she approached the gate to Fort Myers, she passed Arlington Cemetery on her left. The setting was breathtaking, as she could see the Washington Monument and other D.C. landmarks as she looked in the rear view mirror. *Too bad so many brave souls had to give their lives at early ages,* she thought. There was no time to dwell on it, though, as she reached the Fort Myers gate. She took out her identification, and the guard waved her in. She pulled in to the Officers' Club parking lot, where Jack MacLaine was waiting for her. He was beaming, and he looked much more relaxed than he had the previous night. He waved her in to the parking space next to his car.

"I can't tell you how good it is to see you," Jack said as Jennifer got out of her car.

"I feel the same way," Jennifer replied. They put their arms around each other as they walked to the entrance of the Officers' Club. Once inside, they went directly to the dining facility.

"Can you put us at a corner table where we will have some privacy?" MacLaine said to the receptionist.

"Absolutely, sir. Please follow me." The receptionist led them to a corner of the dining room.

"Is this satisfactory?"

"Absolutely," MacLaine replied with a smile. The receptionist walked back to the front, and MacLaine held the chair for Jennifer as she slipped into it. He then sat down and reached into his pocket. He pulled out a little box and opened it.

Jennifer was speechless for a moment. "That is the most beautiful ring that I have ever seen!" she said after she had somewhat regained her composure.

"Then I guess now is the perfect time to pop the question. Will you marry me?"

"Yes! Yes! A thousand times yes!" Jennifer replied, as tears trickled down her cheeks. By now, others in the restaurant had heard the commotion, and they applauded and cheered. MacLaine smiled and waved.

Jennifer was intent on putting the ring on her finger and was oblivious to the activities around her. She reached over and planted a big kiss on her fiancé. The others in the restaurant applauded and cheered even louder.

Looking intently into MacLaine's eyes, she asked if he were happy. "I've never been happier," he replied. "The only thing that makes me unhappy is that Bill Summerfield and I have to leave for Tokyo tomorrow."

"Oh no!" Jennifer replied, obviously stunned. "Is there any way you can delay it?"

"I'm afraid not. We are scheduled to meet with General MacArthur shortly after our scheduled arrival. We have a transport plane that is presently sitting at Andrews Air Force Base waiting to take us."

"Well," she sighed, "at least I will have my ring to keep me company while we're apart. And how can we set a wedding date under these conditions?"

"Well," MacLaine replied, "I think we could tell folks that the wedding will be in about six months. That will give me time to settle in to the new job and to look into housing and hospital situations and report back to you."

That seems fair, Jennifer thought. *I don't really like it, but it's the best that can be done under the circumstances.*

The waiter came to take their orders, bringing with him a bottle of champagne. "The management sends their congratulations along with this gift."

"Please thank them for us," MacLaine said. Jennifer nodded.

They ate a steak dinner and then danced to some Glenn Miller music. "What a great band!" MacLaine said.

"I couldn't agree more," Jennifer replied. The two snuggled tightly as waltzes were played by the band.

MacLaine paid the bill, and the two walked to their cars. *Should we go to a hotel?* Jennifer asked herself. *Better not suggest it.* She could tell that Jack was thinking the same thing.

"I would love to go to a hotel with you," MacLaine said slowly, "but it has been a perfect evening, and I think it is perhaps best to let it end here."

"I agree," Jennifer replied, "but can I see you off at Andrews tomorrow?"

"Absolutely, and I would be very disappointed if you weren't there."

"I wouldn't miss it for the world," she whispered softly in his ear. "See you tomorrow." The two kissed and exited the Officers' Club parking lot.

Chapter 2

Something New and Something Old

Jack MacLaine and Bill and Molly Summerfield were seated in Base Operations at Andrews Air Force Base by the time Jennifer arrived. Jack and Bill were in their uniforms, complete with the ribbons they had earned while in the Service. *How handsome Jack looks,* Jennifer thought as she strolled across the room to join them. The three got up and waved as she approached. Jennifer and Jack kissed, clinging to each other as both realized that very shortly they would be separated.

"Should we let the two of you have some time alone?" Molly queried.

"That won't be necessary," Jennifer replied as she held her gaze steadily on MacLaine. The two remained in an embrace.

Bill Summerfield looked at his watch. "Well," he sighed, "we only have about ten minutes before we have to get aboard our plane. I see some of the passengers are already boarding."

"Oh," Jennifer said as she reached into a sack she was carrying. "I brought you some reading material and some cookies that I baked. I hope they will taste good on your long flight."

"Do I get some?" Summerfield quipped.

"Only if you're very good," Jennifer replied.

MacLaine and Summerfield picked up their duffel bags, and the four headed to the tarmac. Jennifer and MacLaine clung tightly together as did Molly and Summerfield. By now, there was no doubt but what Molly was well into her pregnancy. The four reached the staircase leading into the passenger section of the airplane. Tears started flowing from both women. The men maintained their military bearing, but both were trembling slightly. The upcoming separation was obviously very hard on all of them.

MacLaine and Summerfield went up the steps, turned and waved. The two women returned the waves and blew kisses to their loved ones. *What an eerie feeling,* Jennifer thought. She couldn't help but be reminded of when Dude and she boarded the airplane for Norway. From the same terminal! Hopefully, it would turn out differently. She sure didn't want anything bad happening to Jack MacLaine, or, for that matter, Bill Summerfield.

Jennifer and Molly watched the airplane carrying their loved ones as it moved onto the runway, sped up, and lifted off the ground. Turning to Jennifer, Molly asked if she would like to get a cup of coffee before they departed. Jennifer nodded, and the two went inside to a little coffee bar. They each got a cup and then went to a small table in the corner. They sat down.

"You're still coming to my house for dinner tonight, right?" Molly asked. "My kid sister, Monica, is here and will be joining us."

"Perfect," Jennifer replied. "As I'm sure you know, Monica has applied for a nursing position at Walter Reed, and I told Brad Taylor I would talk to you and try to find out something about her."

"Sounds like a plan," Molly retorted. "Ordinarily, I would expect you to just take my word that she would be a perfect addition to the staff." She rubbed her stomach and then continued. "But with this new little person about to arrive, I will let you interact directly with Monica and come to your own conclusion."

Jennifer thought for a moment before responding. "I still trust your judgment totally, so any insight you can give me would be greatly appreciated."

Molly sighed. "You know I will have to give you my best opinion, so here goes. Monica is a lot like I was or am. She speaks her mind, marches to a different drummer, and always does what she thinks is right. She is a tireless worker, and I know she would be a super addition to the Walter

Reed staff. And tell Brad Taylor that, if he doesn't hire her, I'll never forgive him!"

Jennifer chuckled. "I'm sure he knows that."

The two finished their coffee, hugged, and went their separate ways.

"I'll expect you at 1800 tonight," Molly shouted over her shoulder.

"Roger that," Jennifer replied.

Jennifer went straight to work and arrived before her shift was to start. She decided that now would be a perfect time to catch up on paperwork. She picked up a pile of charts and went in to a small office that had been set aside for just such a purpose. No sooner had she begun than Brad Taylor stuck his head in the door.

"How are you doing?" he asked, obviously sensing how traumatic the situation must have been.

"I'm okay, but just barely. I figure I'll be best off if I bury myself in my work."

"You're probably right," Brad replied. "And how is Molly taking it?"

"About like I am. But I did find out that I'll be meeting Monica tonight. She is here in town, probably sensing that you may want to meet her."

Brad chuckled. "Always ahead of the game. Just like her sister."

"And Molly told me some sparkling things about her sister," Jennifer related. "She thinks she would be a great addition to our staff."

"I'll bet," Taylor responded. "What else could she say?"

Jennifer grinned. "She said she would never forgive you if you didn't hire Monica."

Taylor smiled and walked off.

"I'll give you a much more detailed report tomorrow," Jennifer shouted after him.

Taylor waved without looking back and proceeded onward.

Jennifer was not scheduled for surgery this day. Instead, she made the rounds of patients who had already been through the surgical process. She kept looking at her watch, as she was eager to see Molly at dinner and to meet Molly's sister. Finally, her shift ended. She hurried home, showered quickly, and changed into evening clothing. She went to her car, got in, and headed for Molly's house.

Molly and Bill Summerfield lived in MacLean, Virginia, fairly close to the Pentagon. MacLean was a substantial distance from Jennifer's apartment in Maryland. However, the drive was very pleasant, and the time went by quickly. Jennifer parked in Molly's driveway, went to the front door, and rang the doorbell. Soon, the door opened, not by Molly but by someone who was the 'spitting image' of her. Jennifer was momentarily taken aback.

"You must be Monica," Jennifer said, somewhat stunned. "I guess you know how much you remind people of Molly."

Monica sighed. "Yes, I've been told that often. And you must be Jennifer."

Jennifer nodded, and the two shook hands. Monica motioned for Jennifer to come in.

Molly yelled in from the kitchen and told Jennifer to have a seat. She added that she would be in shortly. Jennifer and Molly sat in two chairs close to one another.

"So," Monica said, "I understand that Dr. Taylor wants you to spy on me."

"No, not at all. But he is interested in me finding out what I can about you."

"In that case," Monica replied, "I should tell you that I sowed some fairly wild oats when I was younger. I never got in trouble with the law, but I did some things I'm not proud of."

"You and me, both," Jennifer responded. "I doubt that there are many – if any – young people who are totally proud of their past."

"Amen to that," Molly piped in from the kitchen. Soon, she came into the dining room carrying bowls of hot food. "Dinner is served," she announced as she peered into the living room.

Jennifer and Monica got up and went to the dining room. "Where do you want us to sit?" Jennifer asked.

"Anywhere is fine."

The three sat down, with Molly at the head of the table and the other two on each side of her. They passed the food, and Molly offered up a short prayer. They then dug in.

"Is Monica passing so far?" Molly asked.

"With flying colors," Jennifer replied. "I do have two more questions, though. What made you become a nurse and how dedicated are you?"

"I became a nurse because Molly is a nurse. That is as straight an answer as I can give you. After I went to nursing school, though, I guess I got the bug. Now I love helping people who are sick or ill."

"I couldn't come up with a better answer, myself," Jennifer responded. "I will give you a sparkling recommendation when I see Dr. Taylor tomorrow. I'm sure, though, that he will want to interview you himself."

"That's part of the reason why I'm here," Monica replied.

The three finished their dinner and had coffee in the living room. The more Monica and Molly talked, the stronger their resemblance seemed. It was actually uncanny. The resemblance cemented Jennifer's belief that Monica would make an outstanding addition to the Walter Reed nursing staff.

It was getting late, and Jennifer told the others that she had better go.

"On one condition," Molly retorted. "And that is that you come here often."

"You can be sure of that," Jennifer replied. The three hugged, and Jennifer headed out. She got in her car for the substantial drive to her quarters.

The next morning, Jennifer headed directly for Brad Taylor's office.

"Come in," he said as he looked up from the pile of papers he was studying. He pointed to the vacant chair, and Jennifer went over and sat down.

Jennifer excitedly told him about how much Monica reminded her of Molly and that, in her opinion, Monica would make an excellent addition to the nursing staff.

"Great," Taylor replied, "I'll invite her in for an interview. It will just be a formality, of course. Then it will be up to her. Either she will accept my offer or not."

"Oh, I suspect she will. Here is the phone number where you can reach her. She's staying with Molly."

"I'll call today and make the appointment," Taylor said. He paused and added, "With Bill gone, it's good that Molly has her sister to lean on."

"I agree," Jennifer replied. "She has the two of us, but having a family member here is even better."

"Well," Jennifer added, "I better get going."

"See you for lunch?" Taylor said.

"You bet. I'll be here about 1130 if I'm not otherwise tied up. I will let you know if I am."

She got up and walked out, eager to find out what her assignments would be for the day. Arriving at her duty station, she had a message to call a Bill Thomas. *The only Thomas I know is the one that I went on the Santo Tomas raid with in the Philippines. Could it be him? Mustn't speculate, though. Bill Thomas is a very common name.* Since she was not scheduled for surgery, she could call at her 1000 break.

Jennifer spent the early part of the day making rounds. She recorded the patients' vital signs and monitored the pain medication. All of the patients were very happy to see her, but she was consumed wondering who the Bill Thomas was that had called her and what he wanted. She tried not to be obvious about it, but glanced regularly at her watch. Finally, her 1000 break was at hand and she could make the call. She hurriedly went down the hall and into an unoccupied office where she could have some privacy. She dialed the number.

"Hello?" came the response.

"Hi. This is Jennifer Haraldsson. You called?"

"I certainly did. This is a voice from your past. I was on the Santo Tomas raid with you."

"It is you!" Jennifer squealed. "I was hoping so! Where are you?"

"I'm in your neck of the woods. I'm getting treatment at Walter Reed for an old Army injury.

"Nothing serious, I hope."

"No, I don't think so. I have some stiffness in my right leg that your specialists are starting to treat."

"They're the best, and I hope they get it straightened out for you."

Jennifer asked what he had been doing since the end of the war. Thomas replied that, along with millions of others, he had been discharged in the fall of 1945. Since then, he had been drifting. He had spent some time working on his parents' ranch in Texas, but that wasn't really fulfilling.

"I'm afraid that the adventure and the excitement of the war have ruined me for a civilian endeavor," Thomas moaned. "Anything in civilian life seems too tame."

"I can sympathize with you," Jennifer replied. "It certainly is a different world."

"Are you free for dinner tonight?" Thomas asked.

"Yes, I am. But I must tell you that I am now engaged."

"I was afraid you would be by now, but I do want to offer my congratulations and tell you that I won't interfere."

"Good," Jennifer replied, obviously relieved. "My fiancé is on his way to Tokyo and not here to defend himself." She asked Thomas what type of food he would prefer.

Thomas laughed. "Being from Texas, I have had my share of steaks. I guess seafood would be my first choice."

"In that case," Jennifer replied, "I suggest we go to Hogate's.

"I've heard of that restaurant, and I wholeheartedly agree."

Thomas was staying near the Pentagon, so Jennifer said she would meet him at 6:30 p.m. at the restaurant. She was secretly thrilled about seeing her old comrade in arms. She periodically checked her watch during the rest of her shift.

As her shift wound to a conclusion, Jennifer briefed the oncoming nurses on the status of the patients. She was hurrying off the floor when she saw Brad Taylor coming down the hall.

"Whoa," he said. "Why the big rush?"

Jennifer explained that she had gotten a call from Bill Thomas, who she had worked with in the Philippines. She was meeting him for dinner.

A sly smile came over Taylor's face.

"Why the grin?" Jennifer asked inquisitively, not knowing if Taylor thought that she shouldn't be going to dinner with Bill Thomas.

"I received a query from Thomas shortly after you had left our field hospital in Normandy. He wanted an appraisal of your character."

Jennifer was relieved. She considered Brad and Molly her two best friends. She did not want to disappoint either of them, and, apparently, she had not disappointed Taylor. When she tried to explain that her dinner with Thomas would be entirely on the up-and-up, Taylor waved her off, saying that there was no need for her to explain anything.

"Incidentally," Taylor added, "I got ahold of Monica, and she will be coming in for an interview tomorrow." He added that it was just a formality.

Jennifer nodded and said that she had to run. They waved and bade each other goodbye as Jennifer hurried down the hall.

Jennifer could not help but think of her night there with Jack MacLaine as she drove to Hogate's. Did she make a mistake by suggesting to Thomas that they go to dinner at Hogate's? She didn't think so, but she knew that she would have to be careful. After all, things could easily get out of hand!

As Jennifer pulled up to Hogate's, Bill Thomas was waiting out in front. She motioned that she was going down into the underground parking lot. He nodded and started walking in that direction.

He looks as good as ever, Jennifer thought. She had to admit that it was good seeing him, even though she was engaged to another. *What could it hurt to see him?* After all, they were old friends, and she couldn't just ignore him. They had been through hell together.

Jennifer pulled into a parking space, stopped her car, opened the door, and got out. Bill Thomas came up just as she closed her door. "It's so good to see you," he said. The two hugged and then went to the elevator. They pushed the button to the main floor. Soon they were at the front desk.

"I have a reservation," Thomas said to the receptionist. He gave her his name, and she crossed him off the list.

"Please follow me." The receptionist led the two to a table overlooking the water. "Is this okay?"

Thomas looked at Jennifer. "Perfect," was the reply. The receptionist smiled and returned to the front desk.

Soon, a waiter came over and asked if they wanted a drink. Jennifer ordered her usual glass of white wine, and Thomas asked for a Jack Daniels with one cube of ice. *Hmmm,* Jennifer thought. *That is exactly the way Dude liked his bourbon.* In what seemed like no time at all, the waiter returned with their drinks. The two took a sip, and the waiter took their dinner orders. They each specified the Fisherman's platter.

"I know that you were in Intelligence work," Thomas said after the waiter departed, "but why?"

"It's a long story. But basically it was because of my former patient, the German Officer Otto Bruner. Friends convinced me that I had to find out if I loved Otto."

"And did you – or do you?"

Jennifer shook her head. "After meeting, we decided that there were too many obstacles to pursue a relationship."

"Such as?" Thomas asked.

"The remnants of his family – a mother and two sisters – were in East Berlin, behind the iron curtain. The Soviets would not allow me to come into East Berlin, nor would they allow Otto and his family to come out. It was a totally impossible situation."

"I can see that," Thomas said softly. "I must say that I'm very happy that we did not lose you."

Jennifer nodded. "And what about you? I'm very surprised that you aren't married."

Thomas smiled. "Maybe it's because I'm more attached to you than I realized at the time that we were together."

"I'm flattered," Jennifer replied, "but I intend to become Mrs. Jack MacLaine."

"So that's his name! You know, I think that I've heard of him. From all that I know, he's a fine man."

Thomas took Jennifer's hand and looked at her ring. "I must admit that I noticed your ring earlier. It's a real beauty."

Thomas hoisted his glass and proposed a toast. "To you and Jack. May you live in eternal bliss." Jennifer raised her glass and clinked his. Each took a sip. She smiled and thanked him.

Well, Jennifer opined, *everything is working out splendidly. Now I can enjoy the rest of the evening.*

The rest of the evening went by quickly, with each recounting some of the humorous events that had occurred during their Philippines mission. They both laughed easily. *I always knew he was a great guy,* Jennifer thought. *I just didn't know how great!*

Jennifer looked at her watch. "It's getting late, and I have surgery in the morning. I hate to break up this fun evening, but I think I had better go."

"I certainly understand," Thomas replied. "Can I see you again?"

"You certainly may. Call me when you have time."

Thomas said he would. He paid the bill, and the two walked out of the restaurant.

The next morning, Jennifer scrubbed for surgery. She would be assisting Dr. Brad Taylor, who was also scrubbing at a sink nearby.

"How did it go last night?" he asked.

"Splendidly," Jennifer replied. "I got everything out in the open. He knows that I'm engaged and to whom. He indicated that he would honor my engagement."

"Great," Taylor responded. He looked at his watch. "We better get this surgery underway." Jennifer nodded, and the two walked into the operating room. The rest of the support personnel were already there.

Later that day, Jennifer asked Taylor how his interview with Monica Davis had gone. He said that it had gone very well and that he had offered

Monica a job on the spot. She had until quitting time tomorrow to accept or decline the position.

"I'm glad to know this," Jennifer said to Taylor. "I'm having dinner at Molly's tonight."

"Good," Taylor whispered. "If you find out anything about her decision, please let me know first thing in the morning."

"I will," Jennifer replied in muted tones.

At 6:00 p.m. sharp, Jennifer rang Molly's doorbell. The door opened, and Molly motioned for her to come in. Monica was standing nearby. The three were obviously glad to see each other. They greeted each other enthusiastically and hugged one another.

"Okay," Molly said to Jennifer, "tell us all about last night, and don't leave anything out."

"Well, the main thing is that Bill Thomas now knows that I am spoken for, and he says that he will respect this fact. Other than that, we just had a really good time rehashing old stories and being together."

Molly shook her head and was obviously disturbed. "Well," she sighed. "I have to trust that you know what you're doing. But if you plan to see him again, my advice to you is to be careful. Things can get out of hand very easily."

Jennifer nodded and turned to Monica. "I understand that your interview with Brad Taylor went very well and that he offered you a job. Do you know if you will accept it?"

Monica shrugged. "I'm not sure, but I don't have to give him an answer until late tomorrow."

"Oh, she'll take it," Molly replied, with a hint of exasperation in her tone. "At least she better!" The two sisters glared at each other momentarily.

Oops, Jennifer thought. *Perhaps I shouldn't have brought it up. There is obviously more here than meets the eye.*

The conversation at dinner was pleasant. Controversial subjects were not brought up, and everyone seemed to enjoy the atmosphere. There were problems aplenty, it was true. But perhaps time would take care of them.

Chapter 3

View from the Top

General Douglas MacArthur, Supreme Commander of U.S. Forces in the Pacific, was poring over papers on his desk in Tokyo's Dai Ichi building. The scowl on his face indicated to MacArthur's Chief-of-Staff, Major General Ned Almond, that all was not well. Since the end of World War II, MacArthur had been in Japan with the purpose of rebuilding the Japanese nation into a democratic entity. He also had the task of keeping Communism from spreading in Asia.

He looked up to see his Chief of Staff, Lieutenant General Ned Almond, standing patiently in front of his desk. "What is it, Ned?" MacArthur asked.

"Sir, I've brought some more Intelligence data, hot off the press." He handed the papers to his boss.

MacArthur flipped through the papers and shook his head. "I hate to say it, Ned, but the situation in Korea is – to say the least – grave. When South Korea was under my jurisdiction – after the war ended – I had General Hodge beef up the defenses clear up to the 38th parallel. Now South Korea is under the auspices of our State Department, and, if you ask me, Secretary Acheson depends too much on that fellow John Foster Dulles. Dulles looked at the South Korean defenses recently and thought everything was fine. But what does he know? The South Koreans only have small arms, while North Korea has been armed mightily by the Soviets. The North Koreans have tanks, planes, heavy artillery, and numerical superiority. It will not be a fair fight if the North attacks."

General MacArthur got up and paced as he continued. "I have to wonder just what the American policy in Asia is. In a few short years, the United States has gone from the premier military power in the world to a mere shadow of its former self. Could we stop an attack if the Communists do decide to throw their weight around? I don't know."

Whenever his boss became dejected, Ned Almond knew just what to do. "But, sir," he stated, "look at all that you've accomplished. You've turned Japan into a bastion of democracy. You brought in enough food to feed the people properly, women now have the right to vote, you fixed the education system, and – perhaps most importantly – you were the force that got them to adopt a new, democratic constitution."

"I suppose you're right, Ned. After all, there is only so much I can do. I can't help it that our war ally, Chiang Kai-shek, has been pushed out by the Communists and is now on the island of Formosa. The present administration made the decision not to support him the way the Soviets supported Mao Tse-tung. And I certainly can't help it that President Roxas of the Philippines – a gifted leader – died of natural causes."

General MacArthur was obviously feeling better. He looked more relaxed, and he went back to his desk and sat down.

But he also seemed melancholy. "You know, Ned, George Marshall was just here. It's sad to think of his decline. I remember when he visited me at the front in New Guinea. He was very alert, decisive, a real military leader. Now he is worn out. I guess the Second World War really did him in."

All Almond could do was nod and then move on. "General, not to change the subject, but your new Intelligence head – a Brigadier General Summerfield – and his second in command have just arrived. Should I set up a meeting with them?"

"By all means. Intelligence is going to be vital as we go forward."

General Almond was pleased to get his bosses' mind off of the depressive topic of age and onto more relevant subjects. "Good, sir, I'll get ahold of Summerfield and then put the meeting on your calendar."

MacArthur nodded, and Almond saluted, turned, and started to leave the room.

"Ned," MacArthur called after his aide, "get these Intelligence boys an office nearby. I have a feeling that I will be meeting with them often."

"Yes, sir," was the response. MacArthur returned his attention to the documents on his desk.

Bill Summerfield and Jack MacLaine looked around their spacious new Tokyo quarters. They would be sharing a two bedroom apartment that was on the top floor and reminiscent of a penthouse. Their staff included two Japanese cooks and two Japanese housekeepers. The four staff members stood over to the side and bowed any time Summerfield or MacLaine looked in their direction.

"Pretty nice," Summerfield said.

"Pretty nice, indeed!" MacLaine replied, parroting his boss. "I'm sure glad you made general."

"Me, too." was the response. The apartment and amenities were definitely better than if Summerfield had remained a colonel.

A knock was heard at the door. One of the staff started walking toward the door, but MacLaine waved him back. "I'll get it," he said. MacLaine opened the door and saw a sergeant standing there. The sergeant said that he had a message from General Almond to General Summerfield. MacLaine thanked the sergeant, took the envelope, and handed it to Summerfield. MacLaine then closed the door.

"We just got here," Summerfield said under his breath. "Couldn't this have waited?" He ripped the envelope open and quickly read the message.

"I guess it couldn't have waited," Summerfield said after reading the dispatch and looking in MacLaine's direction. "We have a meeting with General MacArthur tomorrow morning at 1000.

"That should just give us time to meet the boys in the Intelligence Unit," MacLaine replied. "The Intelligence offices are in the Meiji building, which is very close to MacArthur's building. Right?"

"Yes," Summerfield said, stroking his chin. "But I wouldn't count on us being in the Meiji building – MacArthur may have other plans for us."

After a short pause, Summerfield continued. "I imagine his Chief-of-Staff, General Almond, will be able to tell us. The message said that we should meet at Almond's office in the morning at about 0945. That should give us time to get to know Almond – at least superficially."

MacLaine nodded. "From what I know about it, I'm sure glad that Almond took over for MacArthur's former Chief-of-Staff – what's his name."

"You mean the infamous Richard Sutherland?" Summerfield asked somewhat facetiously.

"Yes. I don't think Sutherland was liked by anybody but MacArthur."

"Now, Jack, I wouldn't say that too loudly. I'm sure there are still some Sutherland supporters around here."

"Besides," Summerfield continued, "I wouldn't take Almond lightly. "He certainly isn't a 'yes' man, as many on MacArthur's staff in the past have been."

"I certainly won't take him lightly," MacLaine replied. "I checked his record before we came, and he has been outstanding in every regard. He is indeed a fighting man's general."

Summerfield nodded. "Let's query the people here and find out about our Japanese help."

The two men talked to the staff members and found that two of the four – a cook and a housekeeper – spoke English. "You'll have to relay messages to the others," Summerfield said, "as we don't speak Japanese." The two staff members acknowledged the direction.

"By the way," MacLaine added, "it would be very helpful if the other two learned English. And I can't speak for the general, but I'll try and learn Japanese."

"Don't leave me out," Summerfield injected. "I'll try and learn Japanese also." The two staff members were obviously very pleased.

Summerfield and MacLaine spent time with the English-speaking cook telling him of their likes and dislikes food-wise. The cook made notes as they went along, and he didn't indicate that there was any dish that he couldn't make.

"You can make all these dishes?" MacLaine asked.

"Yes" was the response. "I worked at U.S. Embassy after war, so I have had lots of practice making dishes that Americans like."

"How about the other cook?" Summerfield inquired. "Is he as accomplished as you?"

The cook smiled. 'Almost' was the reply. Both Summerfield and MacLaine said that they should get along splendidly.

Summerfield told the cook that the first meal they would need would be in the morning. The two officers were obviously tired and would be going to bed shortly.

The Americans called the English-speaking housekeeper over. He was as impressive as the cook was. "At home," Summerfield quipped, "I have to fold my own clothes, but I guess I won't here!"

"Poor Molly," MacLaine groaned. "I can see that you're going to be spoiled rotten."

"And how about poor Jennifer?" Summerfield countered. "What goes for Molly goes for Jennifer."

MacLaine laughed and nodded. The two Americans joked that they better pitch in from time to time with the housework just so they wouldn't get too out of touch.

The next morning, Summerfield and MacLaine looked rested as they came to the table in their crisp uniforms. Summerfield asked if his second-in-command knew anything about their new boss, five-star General Douglas MacArthur.

"Not much," MacLaine replied. "I know he is a brilliant strategist and tactician, as his losses from New Guinea through the Philippines were less than the American losses at the Battle of the Bulge. Other than that, the only thing I know is that he didn't want us OSS types involved with his campaigns."

"I wonder what changed his mind," Summerfield muttered.

Before MacLaine could respond, the Japanese cook brought in a piping hot tray of food. He set a large dish down in front of each of the Americans. There were eggs, bacon, hash browns, and toast on each of the dishes.

"This looks perfect," Summerfield said. "By the way, what is your name?"

"It is Tamotsu," the cook replied.

"And what is the name of the housekeeper that we spoke with yesterday?" MacLaine added.

"It is Tetsuo."

"Tamotsu and Tetsuo," Summerfield parroted back. "I'll have to practice these."

"So will I," MacLaine chipped in.

The two men devoured their breakfasts without saying anything further. As they finished, they looked at each other. "That was delicious," MacLaine said as he patted his stomach. He was very careful not to muss his uniform!

"That it was," Summerfield replied. "We're going to have to be careful that we don't get fat!"

"I agree," MacLaine responded.

Shortly after breakfast, Jack MacLaine called for a staff car to take them to the Meiji building. The car arrived shortly, and the two officers got into the back seat. After a short drive, they arrived at their destination.

The Meiji building was indeed just a stone's throw from the Dai Ichi building. The two admired the tall, white Dai Ichi structure through the window of the staff car. As they got out of the car, the driver asked if they wanted him to wait.

"That won't be necessary," Summerfield replied, pointing at the Dai Ichi building. "Our next appointment is there, and we can walk."

"What exactly is the function of the Dai Ichi building?" MacLaine asked after the driver had driven off.

"Dai Ichi is an insurance building," Summerfield replied with a grin. "Maybe General MacArthur is providing more than military assurances in the region."

The two officers strolled into the reception area of the Meiji building. Seeing the rank on Summerfield's shoulders, a sergeant called the area to attention.

"As you were," Summerfield said. "I'm looking for the man in charge. Where can I find him?"

"You found him, sir," a colonel said as he walked over. "I'm Joe Thompson." The three men exchanged greetings and shook hands. "We've been expecting you," Thompson said, "and your offices have already been set up. Would you like to see them?"

"That's fine, Joe," Summerfield replied, "but we have a meeting with MacArthur mid-morning, and he may perturb things."

"You're right," Thompson sighed. "The general does like to impact decisions."

"But we'll take a look at them, anyway," Summerfield countered. "After all, we may end up with two offices, one close to MacArthur and the other close to our Intelligence people." The three started walking down the hall. Thompson motioned for them to turn in at the first opening.

"This is your set of offices, General," Thompson said as they entered an outer reception area. A master sergeant at a desk facing the entrance popped to attention.

"As you were, Sergeant," Summerfield commanded.

Thompson introduced the sergeant as Tom Sweeney. Summerfield and MacLaine shook his hand and said that they were very happy to meet him.

Sergeant Sweeney replied "welcome aboard, sirs." The three exchanged pleasantries about working together, and Thompson led Summerfield and MacLaine into the general's office.

"Very nice," Summerfield said as he looked around. "This is more than adequate. By the way, where are the encryption devices and the analysis staff?"

"Right down the hall," Thompson replied. "We'll go down there as soon as I show you Jack's office."

Summerfield nodded, and they went back through the reception area and across the hall. The two men were obviously impressed. MacLaine sat down at his desk. "It has just the right feel," he said as a smile crossed his face.

MacLaine looked at his watch and then back toward Summerfield. "We better head over to General MacArthur's. Our meeting with him is in a few minutes."

Summerfield concurred. "We'll have to meet the rest of our people and tour the facilities after our meeting. Thanks for everything, Joe."

Thompson was obviously pleased. "We'll take up where we left off when you return," he said.

"Fine," Summerfield replied. Summerfield and his second-in-command started walking toward the lobby.

It was a short walk to the Dai Ichi building. When they entered the building, there were three Japanese in formal suits standing in the lobby. They came over immediately when they saw the Americans. In broken English, one of the three asked what they could do for them. Summerfield said they needed to meet with General Almond. The three Japanese nodded and motioned for Summerfield and MacLaine to go to the elevator. One of the Japanese accompanied them. The three got on the elevator, and their Japanese guide pushed floor #6. Soon, the door opened, and the men exited.

Their guide motioned for them to follow him. He stopped at the doorway to what appeared to be a reception area. Inside was a tall, erect, distinguished-looking gentleman. It was Ned Almond.

"Good morning, gentlemen," Almond said, "I've been expecting you." The three exchanged greetings punctuated with a quick handshake, and Almond motioned for them to have a seat in the comfortable-looking chairs to the sides of long tables. He then sat down across from them and pulled out a cigarette. "Feel free to light up if you so desire," he said as he flicked the rotator on his lighter. Summerfield abstained, but MacLaine lit up.

"We just about have time to finish these cigarettes before we're due in General MacArthur's office," Almond said as he glanced at his watch. "Let me be brief. First of all," he continued, "MacArthur wants you in this building, so I've gotten you offices on the second floor. I think you'll find that they will suffice. Next, the general wants a short briefing from you daily at 1000. Keep them short and to the point, as he easily becomes bored. Finally, if something big happens, such as North Korea invading South Korea, call him – and me – at any time of the day or night. Any questions?"

"Just one," Summerfield replied. "I would like for the two of us to maintain an office in the other building so we can be close to our operation. Is that acceptable?"

Almond nodded. "It's time for us to go into the general's office." Almond put out his cigarette, and MacLaine followed suit.

The three walked over to the doorway leading into MacArthur's office. The general was seated in a beat-up leather chair that was pulled up to a table without drawers. He was intently studying a document.

"Is that his desk?" MacLaine asked under his breath, somewhat in shock. Almond nodded and held a finger to his lips. *Mustn't interrupt the great man's train of thought,* MacLaine guessed. Soon, the general looked up.

"Well," MacArthur said, "I've been expecting you, and I'm delighted that you are aboard." He came over, shook hands, and told them to have a seat in chairs that had been brought in. All three quickly sat down as the general started pacing and talking.

"I guess you know that I never liked Intelligence Personnel, be it OSS or CIA or whatever you call yourselves now. I always preferred to have my own G2 filled with people that I trusted." He stopped to light his corncob pipe. "However," he sighed as he continued, "times are changing, and I realized that I had to establish a more professional Intelligence operation. Hence, I brought in you two."

MacArthur relit his pipe and continued. "I don't have to tell you the gravity of the situation in Korea. It is, of course, because the country is divided north and south instead of east and west. Look at our own civil war. It was the north versus the south. The same thing is happening in Korea, with results that could be catastrophic. But the powers that be don't

30

listen to me, and, of course, they should. I have spent a great part of my life learning about the Asiatic mind. I think this makes me an expert."

All agreed, with Almond vocally substantiating the general's position. "Sir, I think I speak for all of us when I say that we consider you the foremost expert on this topic."

No wonder he's MacArthur's Chief-of-Staff, MacLaine mused. *He knows exactly what to say!*

MacArthur nodded and dove back in. "Well, enough of the philosophy and now for my plan." He unfurled a map of Korea, and Almond helped him mount it on the wall. "I believe that the North Koreans will spill over the border at any time. When they do, there will be very little to stop them. Our South Korean Allies have only rifles and machine guns, while the North Koreans have tanks, heavy artillery, and planes. I believe that the North Koreans will roll until they reach the southern tip of the peninsula. And, by then, I believe that I will be given permission to move in and stop them, which is exactly what I intend to do. I will establish a perimeter around Pusan with the Eighth Army. It won't be easy, but I have been in tight spots before."

There he goes again, MacLaine thought, *using 'I' when it'll be other people who sacrifice their blood to achieve his objectives. No wonder there are people who aren't in his camp.*

The map started to come down, and Almond rushed to the wall to pin it back up so that his boss could continue. "Any questions?" MacArthur asked.

"Sir, I have just one," Summerfield said. "I doubt that you would be satisfied by a stalemate such as this. What are your plans for pushing the North Koreans back to the 38th parallel and possibly further?"

"I'm glad you asked. The Marines don't like me, and – quite frankly – I don't have much use for them. But I must admit that they have a lot of experience with amphibious operations. Therefore, I think they would be perfect for what I have in mind."

MacArthur puffed on his pipe and pointed to Inchon, a city almost directly to the west of Seoul, the capital of South Korea. MacLaine couldn't help but notice the twinkle in MacArthur's eyes. *He looks ten years younger,* MacLaine thought, almost gasping.

Summerfield interrupted, obviously flabbergasted. "Inchon, General? That, in my estimation, is too risky. From my study of the area, the tides are very strong there most of the time. And I would expect the North Koreans to have a heavy troop concentration there."

"Exactly!" MacArthur responded. "They wouldn't think we would attack there. So we would have the element of surprise."

Summerfield shook his head. "I don't like it. You could lose your whole invasion force."

"Let General MacArthur finish," Almond chided.

MacArthur looked at Summerfield with a hint of pride in his expression. He smiled. "I didn't want a 'yes' man, and I guess I got my wish. But back to the subject at hand, I have contacted the Chief of Naval Operations and the Marine Commandant to ask if they would put the Marine First Division under my command. I should hear from them shortly."

MacLaine figured it was time for him to get into the discussion. "Sir, with you no longer in charge of South Korean defenses, won't you need the President's permission to put your plan into action?"

MacArthur glared momentarily at his questioner. "I'm way ahead of you. I have drafted a letter to be sent immediately to the President if South Korea is attacked. It requests that American ground, naval, and air forces be sent to Korea to stop the act of aggression and that I be put in charge. I, of course, believe that the President will have no alternative but to accept my request."

"Summerby," MacArthur said looking at Summerfield, "I will need you to put some Intelligence people into the Inchon area. I will need information on tides, where we can land troops and material, and other pertinent data. Can you do it?"

"Yes, sir."

Summerby? Jack MacLaine was obviously amused. There was no doubt that General MacArthur had more important things to worry about than people's names.

General Almond was obviously concerned. "Sir, are you going to let the Marines have all the credit?"

"Absolutely not. I will break – what I will call X-Corps – off from the Eighth Army and have them go ashore with the Marines."

"And who will lead them?" Almond asked.

"You, of course. You will be in charge of all landing forces."

Chapter 4

Clandestine Preparations

The three departed General MacArthur's office, and it was obvious that Ned Almond was consumed with planning for his future takeover of X-Corps in the likely chance that South Korea was invaded. The three stepped on the elevator, and Almond pressed the button for the second floor.

"I'll show you your offices," Almond said, "and then you are on your own until tomorrow morning. I've got a lot of work to do."

Summerfield and MacLaine nodded. The three got off on the second floor and walked across the hall. They entered what appeared to be a reception area. Almond nodded at Summerfield before turning to MacLaine. "Your office is to the right, and yours is to the left." The three entered Summerfield's office first and then went into MacLaine's.

"Very nice," Summerfield said. "These will certainly be more than adequate."

MacLaine concurred. The two bid farewell to Almond, who went to the elevator and pressed the up button.

MacLaine grinned after the two-star was no longer in sight. "I'll bet he won't be any bother."

"You're probably right," Summerfield sighed. "He has a potentially very hard job ahead of him. I can't help but feel sorry for him."

MacLaine shrugged. "Well, another way to look at it is – if he does well – he'll probably get a third star."

"Can't argue with that. Now, let's go meet the rest of our people."

"Before we go," MacLaine said. "I'd like to volunteer to go to Korea and act as a spotter."

Summerfield was stunned. "If something happened to you, Jennifer would never forgive me. Neither would Molly. I can't let you do it."

"But Bill," MacLaine argued, "I'm an expert at guerilla warfare and not being captured. I spent years in the jungles of the Philippines avoiding the Japanese. And besides, I don't think your operation here is big enough for both Joe Thompson and me."

"Summerfield sighed. "So that's it. You don't want to play second fiddle to Joe."

"Or have him play second fiddle to me. After all, he's been in charge over here, and I feel for the guy. With you coming in, he's being relegated to a lesser position – probably a much lesser position."

Summerfield looked pensive. "You've given me some things to think about, but mind you, I won't make a decision for a while. I've got a pregnant wife and her best friend to consider. That, of course, is off the record."

MacLaine nodded. The two departed their offices in the Dai Ichi building, got on the elevator, went down, and headed for the Meiji building. Both were very interested in meeting the rest of the people in the Intelligence Operation.

When they reached the lobby, Joe Thompson was waiting for them. "How did your meeting with General MacArthur go?"

"Fine," Summerfield replied. "We'll tell you about it when we get to an area where we can discuss classified material."

Thompson said that Summerfield's new office was secure.

Summerfield nodded. "Good. Let's go." Soon, the three were in Summerfield's office, and he motioned for the other two to have a seat. He went over and sat down at his desk.

Summerfield reviewed MacArthur's plan for an Inchon landing if the need arose, and he said that MacArthur wanted someone to go to Inchon and start gathering crucial data on tides, landing zones, city layout, and other pertinent data.

Thompson was awestruck. "Who but General MacArthur would plan a landing at Inchon?"

"No one in their right mind," MacLaine said. "But maybe that is exactly what it will take to make it work. After all, no one will be expecting it." The others shrugged and agreed.

Summerfield returned to his previous point. "MacLaine here has volunteered to go to Inchon and accumulate the necessary data. Joe, regardless of whether or not I approve him to go, I will need you to recommend someone to accompany him. Someone who is smart, brave, and knows how to survive in a harsh situation."

Thompson smiled. "I think I have just the man for you."

"Good," Summerfield replied. "We will also have to have a Korean contact in Inchon. Someone we can trust and who can hide the Americans that we send in. The person will also have to help obtain the necessary data."

"That won't be a problem," Thompson injected. "I can have names of a Korean and the American officer that I have in mind first thing in the morning – and the name of anyone else that we need to get the information back here."

Summerfield was obviously pleased. "Great. I can pass that information to General MacArthur at our 1000 meeting tomorrow. Now let's meet the rest of our people."

The three left Summerfield's office and went through the analysis section. They viewed the cryptographic gear and met the people that were busy deciphering intercepts. Thompson patted the shoulder of a sergeant sitting at a machine. "General Summerfield, this is a very important man. He will encrypt and transmit messages that you need to send to Washington."

Sergeant Gary Lockman sprung to attention. Summerfield smiled. "At ease, soldier. It's a pleasure to meet you." The two shook hands, and Thompson introduced the sergeant to Jack MacLaine after the first introduction was complete.

Shortly, they came to a tall, lanky major who was bent over a teletype machine. Thompson tapped the major on the shoulder. "This is Jim Sherman, the man I alluded to in our earlier discussion." The major turned around and stood up. Introductions were made.

"I'm glad to meet you," Summerfield said.

"And I'm very happy to meet you," MacLaine said enthusiastically. "You and I may be going on an adventure." Summerfield just scowled.

"Oh?" Sherman replied with a grin. "It's gotten rather boring here, and I would look forward to some excitement."

"You can save that until later," Summerfield injected tersely. "No decisions have been made – yet." The boss said that he had seen enough and that they should go to his office to discuss priorities.

Summerfield, MacLaine, and Thompson started to head for Summerfield's office when Sherman called after them. "If you want to go out tonight for some entertainment, I know exactly where to go."

"We may do that," MacLaine replied, covering for his boss. The three arrived back at Summerfield's office. They sat down, with Summerfield once again seated at his desk.

"That was very impressive, Joe," Summerfield started in. "You obviously have the situation well in hand here. How often have you sent a report to General MacArthur?"

"About once a week," Thompson replied, "more often if the situation dictates."

"Starting now, we will have to send a report to him daily. We will have to have it completed and over to his office by the time he arrives in the mornings – at approximately 1000. The report will go out over my signature." Thompson nodded and busily made notes.

"Then we will have to decide who will go to Inchon," Summerfield continued. "I personally liked Sherman and think that he will definitely go. As for MacLaine here, I am not sure yet. I have some personal things to consider." Thompson kept writing.

"Is there anything else?" Thompson asked.

"I need the latest intelligence estimates. Can you have them here within the hour?"

Thompson said that he could. Summerfield then asked if there was a good place for MacLaine and him to get a quick lunch. Thompson replied that there was a sandwich shop in the basement. They could either eat at a table down there or bring their sandwich back to their offices.

"That sounds perfect," Summerfield said. "By the way, Joe, you've been doing a super job here, and I appreciate it."

"Thank you very much, sir," Thompson replied. "I'll start rounding up those reports for you."

Thompson departed the office, and Summerfield and MacLaine headed down to the sandwich bar. They each got a sandwich and a cup of coffee and headed to a table. They sat down and started eating. Soon, Jim Sherman appeared in the doorway. He smiled at them and headed to the sandwich bar. After getting a sandwich and a drink, he headed toward their table.

"Mind if I join you?'

"Not at all," Summerfield replied. "Please have a seat." MacLaine pulled out a chair.

Summerfield continued. "I take it that you consider the Intelligence operation here to be efficient but boring."

"That I do. But you have to realize that I was in combat during the war. Others who haven't been in combat may consider the assignment challenging rather than boring."

"Where were you in combat?" MacLaine asked.

"The Philippines and Okinawa. In the Philippines, I served with General Krueger's Sixth Army."

"I was in the Philippines, too," MacLaine said softly.

"I know you were," Sherman replied with a grin. "I looked both of you up when I found that you were coming here."

"By the way," Sherman added. "I know a great place for some entertainment tonight if you're interested."

"Sorry," Summerfield replied, "but I have to write my wife. We are expecting our first child, and that is huge for me. After all, I'm in my forties."

"I might take you up on it," MacLaine said. "But mind you, I'm engaged, and I don't want to be involved in any hanky-panky."

"There won't be any. There is a Geisha entertainment center where the ladies perform classical Japanese music and dance. They are also wonderful conversationalists."

"I'm glad to know that," MacLaine replied. "I had heard differently about these ladies."

Sherman nodded. "There are Geishas and then there are other Geishas. One has to be careful, especially if new bosses are involved." The familiar grin came over his face once again. "I wouldn't want to get off on the wrong foot."

Both Summerfield and MacLaine chuckled. The three finished eating and headed back to their work spaces. By the end of the long work day, Summerfield had reviewed the documents that Thompson had placed on his desk. He shipped the ones that he felt pertinent over to Jack MacLaine for his review. He also drafted and signed the Intelligence report that would be on General MacArthur's desk the next morning when he arrived at work.

Feeling that he had done all that was necessary, Bill Summerfield straightened his tie, put on his hat, buttoned his coat, and went over to

Jack MacLaine's office. "Are you ready to go?" he asked. "I think I've done all the damage I can do for one day."

MacLaine nodded. "Just let me take these documents down the hall to be locked up. Be back in a jiffy."

Soon, MacLaine reappeared. "Do you owe Jim Sherman an answer regarding whether you're going with him tonight?" Summerfield inquired.

"I took care of that just now. He gave me an address, and I'm to meet him there at 2000 hours. I'm also to come with a good appetite."

The two rode the elevator down to the first floor and exited the building. The staff car was parked right outside the entrance, and the driver was leaning against the side. He promptly came to attention and saluted smartly. He opened the door, and the general slid in. Jack MacLaine walked around to the other side, opened the door, and got in. The driver got in, started the car, and off they went. Soon, they were at their living quarters.

The time on his watch registered 1945 as Jack MacLaine waited for a taxicab outside of the quarters that Bill Summerfield and he shared. Soon, a rickety taxi cab pulled up. MacLaine got in and handed the driver a paper with the address that Sherman had given him.

At 1955, the cab pulled up to the address of interest and stopped. *Made it with five minutes to spare,* MacLaine mused as he looked at his watch. He walked up to the front door of what looked like a night club. He entered and found Jim Sherman waiting for him.

"Greetings," Sherman said. "I hope you're hungry, because I've ordered a nice spread for us."

"Yes, indeed," MacLaine replied. "In fact, I'm famished."

The two went to a table that Sherman had staked out for them. Sherman asked if MacLaine had ever used chop sticks, and MacLaine answered in the affirmative. "As a matter of fact, I'm quite good with them if I do say so myself."

MacLaine looked at his dinner mate with a critical eye. So far he liked what he saw. Sherman was obviously very comfortable with himself. He was relaxed and seemed to enjoy every minute of his life. He also seemed adept at taking things in his stride, and he was comfortable around his superiors. *These are characteristics that will serve him well in a combat situation,* MacLaine thought. *Must remember to look up his background and check out his military service.*

MacLaine didn't want to make any snap judgments, but he couldn't help but like Sherman. He thought that going on a dangerous mission with a man like Jim Sherman wouldn't be bad – and perhaps as good as it could get. *But I've got to get away from doing instant analysis!* he warned himself. After all, he was going to be a married man very shortly, and he didn't want a judgment made on the spur of the moment to cut short his future.

Soon, waitresses brought out the food. It looked so good that MacLaine's mouth watered. There was fried shrimp, rice, chicken, noodle dishes, and mixtures of meat and vegetables.

"Do you recognize any of it?" Sherman asked.

"Yes. When I was in the Philippines during the war, I subsisted by taking food from the Japanese."

"Okay, then," Sherman replied enthusiastically. "Dig into anything that appeals to you."

MacLaine responded by taking some of everything. The manner that he wielded his chop sticks gave away the fact that he was ravenous. After all, a mere sandwich at lunchtime hadn't held up for very long.

"The entertainment will start before long," Sherman said between bites. "They will start out with a Geisha singing and doing traditional Japanese dances. She will be playing a guitar, called a Samisen in Japanese."

MacLaine nodded and wiped his mouth with a napkin. He would be interested in watching the performance, but right now he was more interested in eating.

Soon, a woman appeared from behind the curtains that were at the front of the establishment. She was carrying a guitar and was dressed in a traditional kimono. Her face held the familiar makeup of a Geisha.

"That's Aika," Sherman whispered. "It means 'love song' in Japanese."

MacLaine nodded. There was something about Aika that commanded his whole attention. Much to his own surprise, he put down his chop sticks and prepared to listen.

Aika began playing the guitar and singing. MacLaine found that he was mesmerized, as were all of the other guests. Aika was so feminine, so cultured that it was as if he had been put under her spell.

Sherman looked at MacLaine and grinned. "Would you like to meet her?"

"No, not tonight. Maybe later."

MacLaine planned to be loyal to Jennifer, no matter what it took. Tonight showed just how difficult that might be. He would have to renew his efforts – perhaps even more vigorously – to convince Summerfield to let him go on the journey to Korea. That would be one way to head off what might be a huge problem in his personal life.

Aika finished her routine and went behind the curtains. Sherman had an amused look on his face as he glanced at MacLaine. "Are you getting enough to eat?"

"Yes." MacLaine replied. "I'm stuffed!"

"Good," Sherman said. He then turned more serious than MacLaine had seen him previously. "I know better than to ask you about our adventure in these surroundings," Sherman continued, "but suffice it to say that I would be glad to accompany you anywhere."

"I appreciate that," MacLaine replied. "But please remember that no decisions have been made yet as to who may or may not go."

Sherman nodded and motioned for the check. MacLaine scrambled for the bill, but Sherman wouldn't hear of it. "This is my treat," he said in no uncertain terms. He paid the bill, and the two departed the establishment.

The next morning, Summerfield was eating breakfast when MacLaine walked into the dining area of their quarters. "Good morning" Summerfield said looking up.

"Good morning to you, sir," MacLaine replied. He told his boss about the previous night's events. As he was finishing, Tamotsu came in and asked what he would like for breakfast. MacLaine replied that he wanted the same as his boss was having: two eggs over easy, bacon, hash browns, and toast. Tamotsu hurried off in the direction of the kitchen. Soon, he returned carrying MacLaine's order. MacLaine dug in, as he didn't want to hold his boss up.

"I'm more convinced than ever that I should go on the mission with Sherman, MacLaine said between bites and softly so that the others wouldn't hear. "He and I really hit it off, and we could greatly aid one another." He looked at his boss, not knowing how he would respond.

Summerfield looked around to make sure no one was eavesdropping and then replied slowly. "I thought it over last night, and if you really want to go, then I shouldn't stop you. After all, the mission comes first, and everything else is secondary."

40

MacLaine nodded, and Summerfield continued. "When we get to the office, tell Sherman that he is going and brief him on the generalities of the mission. Tell him that he will be given the details shortly.

"Yes, sir!" MacLaine replied, trying to hide his enthusiasm. He quickly finished his breakfast, and the two went back to their bedrooms. They soon reappeared at the door leading out of their quarters. They went out of the building, and the staff car was there. After a short drive, they arrived at the Meiji building. The car stopped, and the two officers got out and went in the building. Colonel Joe Thompson was in General Summerfield's office when the two arrived.

"Jack, go find Sherman and tell him that he is going," Summerfield said as he turned toward his subordinate. MacLaine hurried off, and Summerfield related to Thompson that MacLaine would also be going.

"Sir, isn't that a bit of overkill?" Thompson said, frowning. "A colonel and a major?"

"Under normal circumstances, yes. But MacLaine doesn't think that this office is big enough for both him AND you. And a final note impacting my decision is that MacLaine has a lot of experience with guerilla warfare and clandestine operations."

"I understand now," Thompson replied. "Is there anything I can help you with to prepare for your meeting with General MacArthur?"

"Not unless things changed during the night." Thompson said that they hadn't. MacLaine returned, and the colonel and his boss set off for their meeting in the Dai Ichi building.

Chapter 5

Calm before the Storm

General MacArthur was intently studying Summerfield's report from the previous afternoon when the three officers walked into his office. General Almond had joined Summerfield and MacLaine a few minutes before in the waiting area.

MacArthur looked up and shook his head. "Just when I need them, they are nowhere to be found. I'm of course talking about my old Army commanders, Walter Krueger and Bob Eichelberger. They've both retired and gone home. That's probably what I should have done." He lit his corncob pipe.

It was time for Ned Almond to bolster his boss' ego. *This should be good,* MacLaine mused as he tried mightily to suppress a grin.

"Sir," Almond countered surprisingly gruffly, "you're nothing like the other two. You're a hero to almost every American, and Americans sleep much better at night knowing you're over here and in control."

Almond's input seemed to have done the trick. "Ned, I suppose you're right," MacArthur said, puffing on his pipe. "When one has done as much as I have for their country, one cannot simply walk away from a challenge."

Oh, please, give me a break, MacLaine thought. His disdain was more obvious than he'd thought, as Summerfield was glaring at him. *Better straighten up in a hurry,* MacLaine told himself. Otherwise, he might find himself out of a job. He plastered an expression on his face that exuded proper admiration and respect for the five-star general.

"Sir," Summerfield interjected, "I believe you now have General Walton Walker as your Eighth Army commander. He was one of General Patton's corps commanders, and I know that Patton thought a lot of him."

"You're right," MacArthur replied. "I know 'Johnny' Walker is a good man, but he fought in the European Theater in the war. He knows little about the Oriental mind and how the North Koreans will fight. That is why I want the Marines to lead the assault at Inchon. After all, they are masters at amphibious landings and fighting in this part of the world."

"But will they do it?" MacLaine queried.

MacArthur's sharp glance indicated that he was not happy with the question. "They will if I ask them to!" he snapped.

MacArthur's mind now jumped to a more pleasant subject. He went to the map that was still mounted on the wall and pointed to Inchon. "We will land here, and I will crush the enemy. You can count on it." The five-star general had obviously regained his swagger, as he was once again totally confident.

"Sir," Almond stated. "There's one thing I should mention. It's been five years since the Marines were in the war. I hear that they are now emphasizing Staff work rather than combat training. Are you sure that the Marine's First Division will be up to the task?"

"Good point, Ned. I will ask the Marines to use combat-hardened veterans. That fellow Lewis Puller comes to mind. I will ask for him by name and request that he be put in charge of a regiment. He is, after all, a colonel if my memory serves me correctly."

"Old Chesty?" MacLaine inquired.

"That's the fellow," MacArthur replied. "If the Marines put the right men in charge, I'm sure that they can get the job done.

Summerfield briefed the general that he had selected Colonel MacLaine and Major Sherman of the Intelligence Staff to go to Korea and get the necessary information regarding Inchon. MacArthur simply nodded. He was obviously off in his own little world thinking about the days ahead.

"Sir, is there anything further?" Almond asked.

The general shook his head, and the three men saluted before departing MacArthur's office. Almond headed for his own space, and Summerfield and MacLaine went back to the Meiji building.

"We really have our work cut out for us," Summerfield said as they entered the Meiji's lobby.

"No doubt about it," MacLaine replied.

They walked down to Summerfield's office. The general rang for Joe Thompson. "Joe, get Sherman and come to my office. We need to put the plans in motion."

"Yes, sir." Soon, the two men walked in. Summerfield and MacLaine were sitting at a large table as MacLaine wrote out notes.

Summerfield motioned for Thompson and Sherman to have a seat. "I'll get right to it," Summerfield began. "Jim, you and Jack here will be going to Korea – Inchon specifically – to get the data that will be necessary if a landing is to be made there. I can't begin to tell you how important your work will be. But I can tell you about the preparations that were made before the D-day landings in Normandy. Samples of sand were taken and shipped back to England where extensive tests were made. We had to be sure that the sand could support the weight of our tanks and other heavy vehicles. Unfortunately, we didn't have this crucial information when the failed raid was made at Dieppe in 1942. We also had to know of the obstacles that were placed by the Germans on the beaches, and we had to get data on the tides and currents."

"That is all well and good, sir," Sherman interrupted. "But what will we do with this data once we get it? From what I know of Inchon, there are no beaches – the Marines will be landing in the city itself."

"Good question," Summerfield replied. "I'll let Joe Thompson address it."

Thompson was obviously pleased to be able to show his knowledge to the new boss as well as the others in the room. "We have some undercover agents working at the U.S. Embassy in Seoul that will be a big help. We also have South Koreans who are on our payroll. And, yes, Jim, you are correct that Inchon doesn't have beaches, but there is other information that is critical that these folks will help you get – information on the tides and where the enemy can be expected to have gun emplacements, for example."

"Can we bring our chief contact to Tokyo?" MacLaine asked. "It would be a big help to have eye-to-eye contact with him and to be able to do some preliminary planning."

"That we can do," Thompson replied reassuringly.

At that moment, Sergeant Sweeney knocked on the general's door. "Sir, I have a message marked urgent for you."

"Let's have it." Summerfield said. He tore open the envelope and a broad smile came over his face. "Gentlemen, I'm the proud papa of a baby boy – Todd Allen."

Pandemonium spread over the room, and everyone passed their congratulations to the new father.

"Where are the cigars?" Sherman queried in a half-joking fashion.

"I'm glad you asked," Summerfield replied. "I have them right over there." He went to his desk, opened a drawer, and pulled out a box of fine Cuban cigars. He returned to the table and passed them out.

Soon, the room was filled with the aroma of cigar smoke, and the only one who didn't seem to be thoroughly enjoying himself was Jack MacLaine. *He needs to go home and see his baby. I'll have to broach the subject with him in private.* MacLaine hoped that his expression wasn't giving him away.

"Okay, MacLaine," Summerfield said as he looked at his friend and deputy. "What is it?"

"You could always read me like a book," MacLaine said under his breath. "I'll tell you later."

The men finished their cigars, and Sergeant Sweeney returned to the outer office. Of the four left in the general's office, all but Bill Summerfield threw themselves into the task at hand. But Summerfield was obviously wondering how his wife and baby were doing. Who could blame him?

Summerfield looked at his watch, and it was now 1700 hours. "I need to send a telegram to my wife," he said. "Let's reassemble here tomorrow morning at 0800 and continue the planning." All agreed, and the meeting was adjourned.

The ever-trustworthy staff car was parked out front, and Summerfield and MacLaine got in and headed for the nearest Western Union office. Eyebrows in the office were raised when the people saw a staff car with a one-star general's flag attached stop in front. Summerfield and MacLaine got out of the car and went into the office.

Summerfield told the clerk manning the counter that he needed to send a telegram to his wife. The clerk gave him a pad, and Summerfield started writing:

> *Molly Dearest*
> *Excited beyond words. Congratulations on the birth of our son – Todd Allen. Can't wait to see both of you. More in a letter tonight.*
> *All my love,*
> *Bill*

Summerfield paid the bill, and the two officers went out and got in the car. "Where to now, sir?" the driver asked.

"Our quarters," Summerfield replied. He then turned his attention to MacLaine. "Now what was it you wanted to talk to me about in private?"

"I'll tell you when we get into our quarters," MacLaine said under his breath. Summerfield knew not to press the issue further. Soon, the car stopped and the officers got out. They thanked the driver and went inside.

"Now can you tell me?" Summerfield said in an annoyed tone.

"I think you ought to go to Washington and see your wife and new son. It's as simple as that."

"But I just got here," Summerfield complained.

"If anyone should be sympathetic to your situation," MacLaine countered, "it should be General MacArthur. If I recall right, he was in his late fifties when his son was born."

MacLaine's logic gave Summerfield pause for thought, and he started to pace. "Perhaps you're right," he said after what seemed like a considerable amount of time. "And it would be wonderful to see Molly and little Todd."

He thought a little longer, commencing his previous pacing. "By golly, I'll ask the general first thing in the morning."

"Boss, I'm on a roll, so I might as well continue. If I were you, I would call Almond right now. I wouldn't wait until tomorrow morning. Start the ball rolling now."

Summerfield glared at his deputy for an instant. Then he sighed. "Perhaps you're right." He went to a phone and called General MacArthur's Chief-of-Staff.

After hanging up the phone, Summerfield turned to his assistant. "You won't believe it, Jack, but Almond told me to go! The only restriction is that I should return in a week."

46

MacLaine smiled and nodded. "It doesn't surprise me. You had told me that Almond wasn't a 'yes' man, and that appears to be the case. I must say that now I have even more respect for him."

"That you should," Summerfield said as he dialed a number that Joe Thompson had given him. "Hello, Joe? This is Bill Summerfield. I'm going to Washington to see my wife and new baby. You'll be in charge here."

Summerfield told Thompson that he would be back in a week. Pleasantries were exchanged, and Summerfield hung up the phone.

"You better call base ops and find out when you can get a flight out," MacLaine advised.

Summerfield nodded and dialed the phone once again. He made the necessary inquiries, scribbled some notes, and hung up the phone once again. A big smile came over his face. "I can get a flight out first thing in the morning. I'll fly to Guam, Wake Island, Hawaii, and then to San Francisco. After that, I can board a flight to Washington."

"How long will all of that take?" MacLaine said with a scowl.

"About two-and-a-half days – if I'm lucky," Summerfield sighed.

"If it takes the same amount of time to return, you'll only have two days with Molly and Todd."

"I know," Summerfield replied. "But at least I will get to see them. And that's more than I had dreamed of. Besides, I may be able to squeeze an extra day in there."

"I'll call and get a staff car to take me to the air terminal in the morning. It will be early – oh dark thirty."

"I've had plenty of those myself," MacLaine said with a grin. "But I know it will be well worth it for you."

"That it will," the boss replied. "I better go get packed. I'll tell Tamotsu we'll be ready to eat in about an hour if that's okay with you."

"Fine," MacLaine said.

It was still dark when Jack MacLaine got out of bed. Quickly, he put on his robe and left his bedroom. He walked to the dining area and found Bill Summerfield eating a hearty breakfast. Summerfield looked immaculate in his uniform, and MacLaine could tell that his boss was eager to start on the long trip to Washington.

Summerfield looked up and smiled. "I want to thank you again, Jack. You were absolutely right. I should have thought of asking the head shed myself, particularly since MacArthur started his own family late in life."

47

"And I want to thank you again for letting me go on the mission with Sherman. Being separated from Jennifer is hard enough, and the least I can do is to get involved in something useful."

Summerfield nodded. "Just don't do anything to get you killed. I don't think Molly and Jennifer would ever forgive me."

"I'll try not to," MacLaine replied, "but there are no guarantees in life."

Before Summerfield could respond, Tamotsu came in carrying MacLaine's breakfast. It was the same as Summerfield's.

"Looks delicious," MacLaine said as he dug in.

Soon, the two had finished their breakfast. Summerfield checked his watch. "The driver will be here shortly, so I better get my bag."

MacLaine nodded. His thoughts turned to the upcoming mission, and he thought that the first thing he should do would be to bond with Jim Sherman. *That shouldn't be hard to do,* he mused. After all, he had taken an instant liking to Sherman.

MacLaine was still sitting at the table when Summerfield stuck his head into the room. "I'll see you in a week," Summerfield said.

"If I'm still here in a week," MacLaine said with a grin. He stood up and shook hands with his boss. Amenities were exchanged, and Summerfield scurried out the front door.

MacLaine walked down the hall to his office. Waiting outside was Joe Thompson. "Hi, Jack. Will you accompany me to the old man's briefing this morning?"

"Sure," MacLaine replied.

Thompson nodded and continued. "I want to thank you for making the transition to a new boss very easy for me. To tell you the truth, I was concerned."

"I know that it was difficult for you. But you've done a super job here, and I had hoped for the opportunity to tell you so. I also want to say that I'll stay out of your way as much as possible."

Thompson was obviously relieved. "If there's anything I can do for you, just let me know."

MacLaine nodded. But right now, he had other things on his mind. He had jumped from the frying pan into the fire by volunteering to go to Inchon. He didn't want to get seriously hurt or – God forbid – even killed. After all, Jennifer was waiting for him, and a new chapter in his life was about to begin. But he had volunteered to do something useful,

48

and his survival would be dependent on working well with Jim Sherman. Thus, he would have to get to know him well enough to react with him like a well-oiled machine.

"I need to talk to Jim Sherman," MacLaine said as he looked Thompson directly in the eye. "We're going to need to figure out exactly what data we need to get and how we're going to get it."

"Good thinking," Thompson replied. "By the way, I'm having two people from Seoul fly in this afternoon. They will provide necessary support. Can you meet with them about 1600?"

"Sure. I'll also plan to come here about 0935 so we can head over to brief General MacArthur."

"Great," Thompson said. "I'll let you tell the General what you and Sherman are planning."

The two colonels went their separate ways, Thompson to make preparations for the MacArthur briefing and MacLaine to start the planning process with Sherman. During the planning, MacLaine hoped that he would find out a lot about the inner workings of Jim Sherman. After all, it wouldn't be long now until they started on their magnificent journey.

Time passed quickly. MacLaine had met with Sherman, he accompanied Thompson to the MacArthur briefing, and now he was waiting in Bill Summerfield's conference room to meet with the two support people from Korea. Thompson and Sherman would also be in the meeting.

Thompson arrived, and Sherman came in shortly thereafter. Thompson sat at the head of the table, and Sherman took a seat next to MacLaine's. Only Thompson had a notepad, as it was obvious that the other two didn't feel it would be appropriate to take notes. After all, this meeting was clandestine to say the least.

Thompson got up, closed the door, and then returned to his seat. "The two men coming from Korea are Clint Phelan and Junsuh. They should be here any minute."

"How do you spell Young-Soo?" MacLaine inquired.

"Good question," Thompson replied. "It's spelled J-U-N S-U-H."

MacLaine nodded, and he looked at Sherman. His second-in-command smiled. It was obvious that Sherman either had known how to spell the name or that he had just learned. MacLaine wasn't sure which it was.

A knock came on the door, and Thompson scrambled to get it. In walked the two who would obviously serve as the support personnel. Introductions were made, and the five each took a seat at the table. MacLaine learned that Phelan's rank was that of a major.

Thompson looked at Phelan. "It's your nickel, Major."

Clint Phelan started in. "I understand that you two will be going to Inchon. Is this correct?" MacLaine and Sherman nodded, and Phelan continued. "I have made plans for you to be flown to Seoul early tomorrow morning. From there, Junsuh will take you to Inchon. As you get data, Junsuh will get it to me, and I will send it on to Colonel Thompson. Any questions?"

MacLaine looked at Sherman, who shook his head. "I guess not," he said. "Oh – one thing – what time do we leave in the morning?"

"You leave at oh dark thirty," Junsuh said with a grin.

That settles that, MacLaine thought. *He speaks perfect English.* But it didn't answer the question!

Phelan quickly covered. "Be at Base Ops at 0530."

The meeting broke up, and MacLaine and Sherman stood outside the conference room. "Want to go out tonight?" Sherman asked, grinning.

MacLaine thought for a moment. "Well," he sighed, "I have to write Jennifer, and I have to pack. But what the heck, it's our last night here for a while. If we don't meet until 8:00 p.m. tonight, I think I can get everything done, so let's do it!"

Sherman grinned and patted his new friend on the shoulder. Tomorrow they would be heading out on a new grand adventure, but tonight they would have some relaxation and enjoyment.

Chapter 6

Quick Trip Home

Bill Summerfield raced down the hall of Walter Reed Hospital to see his wife and newborn son. *Imagine,* he thought, *I'm now in my forties and having my first child– a son no less! It must not get any better than this!*

It was true that he had flown almost half-way around the world non-stop, but he didn't feel tired. The exhilaration that came from just thinking about seeing the two most important people in his life washed away any feelings of fatigue. He came to Room 240, skidded to a halt, and peeked in. There they were, both seemingly asleep, the baby in his mother's arms.

Molly opened her eyes and squinted toward the doorway. She gasped when she recognized her spouse and burst into tears. "I was so glad to get your telegram that you were coming," she wailed. Summerfield walked over hurriedly, bent down, and gave her a big kiss on the lips. She hugged him tightly and obviously didn't want to let go.

"I'm so glad to see you," he said.

"Are you sure you didn't come to see this little guy?" Molly replied.

"Well, him too," was the response.

Molly handed the baby to his father, who held him very gingerly. Summerfield carefully sat down. "He's so tiny," the new father whispered.

"That's what you think," Molly replied. "If you'd had carried him all this time in your stomach, you'd have thought that he was anything but tiny."

Summerfield nodded. "I suppose you're right."

"Did you tell anyone else that I was coming?" Summerfield inquired.

"Not a soul. I want you all to myself." The two laughed softly. Summerfield started to get up to go to his wife, but Molly motioned him to sit back down.

"You have your hands full right now," Molly said as she proudly looked at their son.

Presently, Molly's sister Monica, in her new, crisp nurse's uniform, came into the room. "Oh, my God!" she squealed. "I must be seeing things!" She raced over, bent down, and gave Summerfield a big kiss on the cheek.

Summerfield smiled, returned her kiss, and gave her a pat on the back. "I'm glad to see you, too," he said as he kept a firm grip on his newborn son. He certainly didn't want anything bad to happen to this new blessing in his and his wife's life.

"Well, I'll let you two talk," Monica continued. She scooped up the baby and left the room.

Summerfield noticed the disappointed look on his wife's face. "Is everything okay between you two?"

Molly shook her head. "I don't know what the problem is," she sighed. "Maybe it's jealousy that I have you and the baby. Maybe we're too much alike, and she resents that I'm so close by. I just don't know." Summerfield saw the tears welling up in Molly's eyes. He tried not to make the situation any worse.

"I'm sure everything will work out. You just have to give it time." *What a lame response!* he thought. Under the circumstances, though, it was the best he could do.

"Enough about me," Molly said as she brightened up. "I'm so glad to see you, and I want to hear all about your relationship with General MacArthur. Is he as difficult as I've heard?" She had pulled her legs up and was now resting her arms on them.

"No, not at all. I've found him to be quite affable and eager for my input."

"I'll bet," Molly mumbled. "You've always looked on the bright side of everything."

"I can't deny that," Summerfield replied. After being in deep thought for a moment, he continued. "I'm concerned with how serious the situation is over there, and I hope he'll thoroughly evaluate the Intelligence data we give him in the future. After all, I wouldn't want World War III to start over there on our watch."

"That bad, huh?"

"I'm afraid so."

"Not to change the subject, but how is Jack MacLaine working out?" Molly asked. "I know that Jennifer will be asking about him."

"He couldn't be working out better. He has taken a lot of the burden off of me, which will allow me to do a better job of seeing the big picture."

"And he's staying true to Jennifer?" Molly asked with a slight smirk.

Summerfield nodded. "With him being my roommate, I can say that he is being straight arrow all the way."

Just then, Jennifer stuck her head in the door and did a double-take when she saw Bill Summerfield seated in the chair by Molly's bed.

"Omigosh, I must be seeing things!" She quickly walked to him and gave him a "peck" on the cheek.

"I'm glad to see you, too," Summerfield said with a chuckle.

Jennifer patted Molly on the shoulder and sat down on the edge of the bed. "Tell me all about your assignment and about Jack."

Summerfield reiterated what he had told Molly and filled in the details. A slight scowl came over Jennifer's face.

"What?" Summerfield asked inquisitively.

"Well," Jennifer started slowly, "I know you're a general, but you only have one star. Do you think MacArthur may want someone of higher rank to head his Intelligence operation?"

Summerfield sighed. "That's a distinct possibility. I hope it doesn't happen, but I have to be aware of the possibility. I also have to tell you one other thing."

"What's that?" Jennifer asked apprehensively. Summerfield realized that she was anticipating something bad, so he started off trying to put her at ease.

"I don't want you to worry, but Jack has volunteered for a mission that could be somewhat dangerous."

"And you approved it?" Jennifer asked with dismay in her tone.

"Yes. I didn't have a choice. With his background, he is the best man for the job."

Jennifer sat silent for a moment and then responded. "And knowing Jack, I'm sure he pushed mightily for his selection."

"He did, but the decision was mine and mine alone."

Jennifer smiled. "I know better than to ask for the specifics, and I understand your decision. I really do."

"Thank you," Summerfield replied. He wasn't sure that Jennifer was actually letting him off the hook, but he genuinely appreciated her response.

Jennifer turned her attention to the new mother, patting Molly on the leg and looking her squarely in the eyes. "Since we're clearing the air, I have something I want to run by this young lady."

"I don't think I'm going to like this," Molly muttered.

"I'll get right to the point. Bill knows how serious the situation is in Korea. Talking to Brad, I'm almost certain that the two of us will be recalled to active duty if war breaks out. With your approval, I would like to ask Monica if she would go with us."

Molly appeared stunned. She started to shake her head when Summerfield interceded. He took her hand as she looked directly at him.

"Molly, dear, I know you would hate to have Monica go into a dangerous situation. But I think it would be good for her. She needs the opportunity to spread her wings without being in the shadow of her big sister."

Molly kissed his hand and asked, "How did you get so smart?" She then turned toward Jennifer and shook her finger. "Okay, you can ask her, but I'm warning you. I will expect you to get her back here safe and sound."

"Understood," Jennifer replied. She started to continue, but Molly cut her off.

"Cut the small talk! This is serious business, and I won't tolerate you running off the way you did in Normandy when you found out about Otto's past. Understood?"

"Yes – completely!" Jennifer was obviously miffed that Molly was leaving out some of the key facts of the case, such as Dude having been killed in Norway. Jennifer got off the bed and shook hands with Summerfield. "I'll leave you two alone, as I imagine you have a lot to talk about." She quickly exited the room.

Summerfield whistled softly. "You were rather hard on her, weren't you?"

"Yes, I was. But it's better to lay all of the cards on the table now than after something bad has happened."

"I couldn't agree with you more," Summerfield said as he took Molly's hand in his.

The two talked softly, laying out their hopes for their son's future.

"By the way, how long can you stay?" Molly inquired. "I hope it's forever."

Summerfield said that he had a week's leave before he had to be back in Tokyo. "That should be enough time to get you and Todd settled at home."

Summerfield could tell that the wheels were turning in Molly's head. "If you have to be back in Tokyo after you've been gone a week, that means you will have to fly out of here in just a couple of days! Terrible!"

Summerfield nodded sadly. "I just have tomorrow and the next day here. Then I will have to go." He asked when she and the baby would be going home.

"The day after tomorrow if everything continues to be okay," Molly replied. "That means we will just have the day to settle in before you depart."

Summerfield nodded. "But, thankfully, I did get the week off." Molly had to agree.

Jennifer was still bristling over the rough treatment she had gotten from her best friend. *Oh well, if it had been me, I would have probably reacted in the same way.* She continued making rounds to check on patients just coming out of surgery. As she walked out of the Intensive Care Unit, she saw Monica coming down the hall in her direction. *Now is as good a time as any,* she told herself.

"Hi Monica. Can you join me for a cup of coffee?"

"Sure," was the response. The two walked down to the hospital cafeteria, got their drinks, paid for them, and went and sat down.

"I doubt that this is a social function," Monica started in. "But if you think you can get into my personal business ---"

Jennifer cut her off before she could continue. "Oh, no! You're absolutely right. Your personal business is your affair. I want to ask you about an entirely different matter."

"Sorry. I shouldn't have been so abrupt. Please continue."

"You don't have anything to apologize for," Jennifer said softly. "But I do want to ask you a question about what you would consider as your future line of work. As I'm sure you know, the situation in Korea is rapidly deteriorating. Brad Taylor thinks that he and I will be called back to active duty if war breaks out. My question to you is this – would you consider going with us if there is a war? I won't kid you, it would be dangerous.

Better not tell her that I ran the idea past Molly. There's obviously some friction there.

Monica thought for a minute and then turned her gaze toward Jennifer. "Can I have a day to think it over? I'm pretty sure I know my answer, but I don't want to make a hasty decision."

"Certainly," Jennifer replied. "We really don't need to know your answer until war breaks out and we're recalled." The two laughed half-heartedly. "Besides," Jennifer confessed, "I still have to run the idea past Brad Taylor."

Monica looked puzzled. "Do you think he would object to my going with you?"

"Absolutely not. I think he would love to have you come with us."

Monica looked relieved. "I certainly hope he would. I have given this job my very best, even if I've been here only a short time."

"I know you have, and I should say that you have impressed all of us. I know that Brad thinks highly of you."

"I'm glad to hear that," Monica replied. "I know that Brad really likes my sister, and I can understand why. But I have to tell you, Molly and I are entirely different people, and I hope that people would evaluate me for who I am and not as someone's sister."

Jennifer smiled. "You won't have any worries there. Molly did a fantastic job for Brad from the African Campaign through the end of the war in Europe. But a conflict in Korea would be a whole new ballgame. Past performance won't be a consideration. It is only the present and thoughts about the future that will carry any weight."

The next morning, at the start of her rounds, Jennifer went into Molly's room. The baby had been fed and was asleep in his mother's arms. Molly looked up and started right in. "Jennifer, I'm so sorry that I was less than polite to you yesterday. Please forgive me."

"If anyone should apologize, it should be me. I should have had more sense than to bring up a potential conflict when you and your husband have such a short time together."

The two hugged, and Jennifer asked what Molly's plans were.

"The hospital says I can leave today. This is good, as it will leave a day for Bill to help get Todd and me settled in."

"I'll be only too happy to help in any way that I can," Jennifer replied.

Molly thought for a moment. "The best way you can help is to lead the way through the maze of red tape. I'm hoping that Todd and I can leave the hospital with Bill at about noon."

"I'll get right on it," Jennifer said. She quickly walked to the door. Looking back, she said, "I'll tell Brad to come down and check that everything is okay with you and the baby and that it is okay for you to leave. In the interim, I'll get the paperwork moving." Smiling, she added, "It helps that you are married to a general!"

"Roger that," Molly replied, motioning for her friend to get going.

As Jennifer was leaving the room, Bill Summerfield was coming in. The two acknowledged each other, and Jennifer gave him a quick update on what she was doing. Summerfield thanked her and told her to contact him if she ran into any resistance. She responded that she would.

Summerfield walked to the bed, kissed his wife, and gently stroked their newborn son's head. Molly could tell that something was bothering her husband. "What is it?" she asked.

Summerfield sat down on the bed and sighed. "Apparently, I'm no longer in charge of the Intelligence Operation. My second in command sent a telegram saying that MacArthur has brought Major General Willoughby in to head the operation."

"I'm so sorry," Molly replied, almost grief-stricken. "Do you know this man?"

"No, but I've heard a lot about him. From what I hear, he likes to please his boss, and this is a quality that is very important to MacArthur. MacArthur rates loyalty as more important than anything else."

"Uh-oh," Molly said softly. "What do you intend to do?"

"I really don't have a choice. I'll do as I've always done, giving it my best shot."

"I'm so very proud of you," Molly said softly. "I've never been more proud of you than I am right now."

Summerfield smiled. "That means everything to me." He reached down and gave his wife a long, meaningful kiss.

Jennifer saw Brad Taylor talking to a nurse in the hall. She stopped and quickly relayed the data to Brad. He whistled softly. "Good grief!

If Summerfield has to leave the day after tomorrow, I can see why they're anxious to get out of here. Let me know if you need any help with Admin. In the meantime, I'll go and give Molly and the baby the once-over."

Jennifer nodded and darted off. Soon, she was at the Administration Office. She told the lady behind the window that she needed to walk the paperwork through to get Mrs. Summerfield and her baby released from the hospital. The lady seemed unimpressed. "I'll do the best I can," the lady said nonchalantly.

"You'll have to do better than that," Jennifer fumed. "General Summerfield has to leave the day after tomorrow for Tokyo, and he wants to have his wife and baby settled in at home before then."

The woman shrugged, and Jennifer asked who her supervisor was. The woman pointed to an office with the nameplate Major Tom Burton attached to the outer wall. Jennifer had to squint to see the sign, but when she could read it, she walked directly to the major's open door. She knocked, and the man behind the desk looked up and told her to come in. They exchanged greetings, and Jennifer explained the problem.

"If the doctor gives her and the baby a clean bill of health, it won't be a problem," the major said. "Please come back and see me with the doctor's signature, and I'll walk the paperwork through myself."

Jennifer thanked the major and walked past the lady at the window. She thanked her for pointing out the major's office. *No need to get anyone down here mad at me. I may need them in the future!*

Jennifer raced back to Molly's room to see if Taylor had been there yet. When she got there, she saw the doctor talking to Molly and Summerfield. "If you will sign off on them, I will take your signature to a Major Burton. He will personally walk the paperwork around to get Molly and Todd released.

Brad Taylor smiled as he applied his signature to the form. "I know Tom Burton. He is very helpful."

Jennifer took the form. "I should be back shortly," she said as she dashed out of the room.

True to his word, Major Burton walked the paperwork through with Jennifer tagging along. "Now all I have to do is get a wheelchair to take Mrs. Summerfield to her car." This activity proved to be no problem, as the sergeant in charge said that a wheelchair would be up in the room in about 15 minutes. "Good," Burton replied appreciatively. He turned to Jennifer. "Is there anything else I can do for you?"

"Nothing I can think of. I greatly appreciate your help."

The two shook hands, and Jennifer headed back to Molly's room. When she arrived, Brad Taylor was just departing the room.

"Brad, I need to talk to you for a moment," Jennifer said in muted tones.

"What is it?"

I asked Monica if she would go with us if war erupted in Korea and we were recalled. She said that she would give her answer tomorrow."

"Good," Taylor replied. "I can't think of anyone else that I would rather have – except you."

Jennifer smiled. "Thank you. I'll let you know as soon as I get her answer."

Taylor departed to see other patients, and Jennifer went in to Molly's room.

"We're all set," she said, obviously relieved. "Thanks to Major Burton, a wheelchair will be here any minute now."

"We can't thank you enough," Summerfield said to Jennifer. "Since it will be pretty hectic from now until the time I leave for Tokyo, I should ask if there is anything you want me to tell Jack?"

"Just tell him that I love him more than anything and can't wait to see him again."

Summerfield nodded and smiled. "Thank you for keeping it simple and to the point."

True to her word, the wheelchair arrived shortly. Molly was bundled in a robe, and with Todd held tightly in her arms, the sergeant wheeled mother and baby toward the doorway.

"I'll say goodbye now," Jennifer told Summerfield and Molly. She hugged the two and started to walk down the hall.

"Don't be a stranger," Molly called after her.

"You don't have to worry about that," Jennifer said looking back over her shoulder. She waved just before turning out of sight.

The Summerfields arrived at their quarters shortly before noon. By late afternoon, everything was squared away. Molly and Summerfield spent the evening sitting by the fire that Summerfield had built. They talked quietly. At 10:00 p.m., Molly said that they should turn in.

"Our son will expect to be fed in a few hours," his mother said with a sigh. The father just nodded and smiled.

The next morning, Summerfield went out to get the paper. It was June 24, 1950. He was stunned as he read the headlines of the Washington Post: "North Korean Troops Pour over the Border." He took a moment to read the article, and then he went inside. He quickly relayed the information to Molly, who was caught off-guard.

"I didn't expect this – at least not so soon," Molly said softly.

"I'm the same way," Summerfield exclaimed. "I knew it was coming, but I thought later rather than sooner. I guess that shows you how little I know."

"I'm surprised that you didn't get a telegram – or a call – from your unit."

"They probably have their hands full about now. But I expect there will be a message for me when I arrive at Base Operations." Summerfield looked at his watch. "We better eat, as the staff car will be here to whisk me away in about 20 minutes."

Molly nodded and went to the stove to take up the scrambled eggs, bacon, and hash browns. She then took the toast out of the toaster, buttered it, and added jam. She took the plates to the table and sat them down.

Molly brought over the coffee pot and poured the coffee into two oversized cups. She took the coffee pot back and then returned to the table.

The two ate breakfast in silence. Todd was asleep in a bassinet nearby. Summerfield finished his breakfast and then went to put on his blouse and hat. He came out of the bedroom carrying his suitcase.

"You look mighty handsome," Molly said as she went over to kiss him. Looking very serious – especially for her – she added. "The most important thing is that you come home safely to Todd and me. Don't take any unnecessary risks."

"I won't – I promise." Summerfield went over and gently kissed Todd on the forehead. He gave a long, impassioned kiss to Molly and then headed out the door. He turned around and waved goodbye as the staff car was approaching. His great adventure was about to begin.

Part 2

Chapter 7

The Onslaught

It was 4:00 a.m. when MacArthur's wife Jean gently nudged the general awake. She informed him that it was Ned Almond, the general's chief-of-staff, on the phone. "What is it, Ned?" the general asked as he tried to shake off the mist of having been awakened from a sound sleep.

"It's not good news, sir," Almond replied. "The North Koreans have attacked South Korea en masse. I'm starting to get my X-Corps plans into motion, but is there anything else you would like me to do?"

The general was lurched wide awake. He thought for a moment. "Nothing right now. I'll get back to you." The general handed the phone back to his wife and asked her to get his bible. She obviously knew that something big was up. She also knew not to ask about it. MacArthur would tell her in his own good time.

This is hauntingly similar to when the Japanese attacked Pearl Harbor, the general thought. *But it is an opportunity for me to show once again my value to my countrymen and to the rest of the world. I mustn't let them down!*

Jean handed her husband his bible and sat down close to him. "Go back to bed, Jeannie," the general instructed, "it's going to be a long night." After dutifully asking if there was anything she could do, Jean MacArthur went back to get some more sleep.

As he had done after the Pearl Harbor attack, MacArthur started reading his bible. This time, however, he didn't experience the paralysis that he had before. As he read, his mind darted to steps that he must take.

While he hadn't received marching orders from the President or the Joint Chiefs or the Army Chief-of-Staff for that matter, this had never stopped him before. He called for his wife to get Ned Almond back on the phone. Moments later, he realized that his wife had gone back to sleep, and he apologized as she went to the phone and dialed Almond's number.

"What is it, sir?" Almond asked.

"Ned, get "Johnnie" Walker and the highest representative of my Intelligence Unit to meet me at the Dai Ichi Building in one hour. Also get someone in Transportation over there for the meeting."

"Yes, sir!" was the response. Almond was obviously raring to go.

By the time he arrived at his office, MacArthur found that Walker, Willoughby, Thompson, and Brigadier General Sturgis from Transportation were already there. Almond was also present.

MacArthur glanced at the men in attendance. Walton "Johnnie" Walker was a three-star General in command of the Eighth Army. While short and rotund in stature and not particularly looking like a general officer, Walker had served honorably in Patton's Third Army in World War II. Patton had taken a liking to him and admired him for his fighting ability. After the Second World War was over, he was selected for prestigious assignments and ended up as the Eighth Army Commander.

Willoughby was a favorite of MacArthur's from the last war. He had been part of the small group of officers who had accompanied MacArthur during the escape from Corregidor on a PT boat. MacArthur smiled when he looked in Charles Willoughby's direction. Willoughby had proven to be very loyal to MacArthur, a trait that MacArthur valued above all else. Willoughby had brought Thompson with him, since Summerfield was not yet back and Thompson was next in command. Sturgis was in charge of the Transportation Office.

"Let's first get an update from my Intelligence Staff," MacArthur said, looking in Willoughby's direction.

"Since I'm new in this job, I'll let the number 2 man, Colonel Thompson, take it from here."

"Thank you, General Willoughby," Thompson replied as he moved to the lectern at the front of the room.

"Reports that we've received indicate that the North Koreans are moving quickly down the peninsula. The South Koreans are breaking and running, as they only have rifles and small-arms weapons, whereas the North Koreans have Soviet-made tanks and heavy artillery pieces. The North Koreans even have air cover!"

MacArthur shook his head. "I warned Washington, but no one would listen. Please continue." He lit his corncob pipe.

Thompson nodded and said that the North Koreans would soon overrun Seoul, the capital of South Korea, and that they would reach the southern tip of South Korea in a matter of a few days.

MacArthur got out of his chair and walked to the lectern. "We can't let that happen," he stated emphatically. "Thank you, Thompson, you may be seated."

MacArthur took another puff on his pipe and started in. "Johnnie, I will need the Eighth Army to hold, approximately here." He walked to a map of Korea attached to the wall and made a hand gesture, ringing the city of Pusan near the southern end of the peninsula. "I shall call it the Pusan Perimeter."

"But, General!" Walton 'Johnnie' Walker fumed, "I don't have any troops in Korea – or equipment! This, to me, is an unattainable goal."

MacArthur just smiled as he once again lit his pipe. "Why do you think I invited someone from the Transportation Office to this meeting? What's your name – Sturgis? I invited you, Sturgis, so that I could personally tell you to move every piece of military equipment and all of the military personnel – except my staff of course – from Japan to Pusan as expeditiously as possible."

Walker again was obviously unhappy. "But General, that will leave the whole of Japan open to invasion by the Soviets or Mao or whoever else may be interested – for whatever reason!"

MacArthur smiled once again. "Johnnie, you let me worry about Japan. You have enough to worry about."

Walker shook his head and clammed up.

MacArthur looked back at Sturgis. "My Eighth Army Commander is very concerned, and rightfully so. I need you to start shipping men and material to Korea immediately. I need them there in a matter of hours, not days. Do you understand?"

Sturgis nodded. "With the General's permission, I would like to leave and start the ball rolling now."

"Absolutely," MacArthur replied. "And, Sturgis, if you do a good job, there is a promotion waiting for you."

Sturgis nodded and threw a salute in the general direction of MacArthur as he rushed out of the room.

"That's the dedication I like to see," MacArthur said under his breath. "Any questions so far?" he asked the remaining officers.

"No questions," Walker responded. "But I can tell you this. I will be living for the next few days with Sturgis by my side."

"You do that, Johnnie," MacArthur said, concurring and moving rapidly on to the next subject. "Now I will go into what will be done after our line around Pusan has stabilized. I must tell you not to mention this plan to anyone. Its success hinges on the element of surprise." He looked at each of the attendees to emphasize the point.

MacArthur faced the map of Korea hanging on the wall. He picked up a pointer and placed the tip on the port city of Inchon. "This, gentlemen, is where we will make a landing after Johnnie has stabilized our line further to the South. We will cut off the enemy and throw his operation into complete disarray. I believe that the war will end shortly after that – in a matter of days."

MacArthur puffed on his pipe and let the idea sink in. He could see the skepticism in Walker's expression. "What is it, Johnnie?"

"Well, for one thing, you will need to land tanks and heavy artillery pieces there if we are to fight the enemy on equal terms. I have heard that Inchon only has piers and seawalls – no beaches. Can we land what we need to at Inchon, realizing that we will be right in the city? More importantly, I have heard that the tides in that area can be overwhelming. Is there a window when the tides will be such that landings can be made?"

"Good questions," MacArthur said. "I'll let our Intelligence representative answer them." He pointed to Thompson, gesturing that he could remain seated.

"Two of our best people, Colonel Jack MacLaine and Major Jim Sherman, have been in Inchon accumulating the data we need. We have received their initial material, and we now know that the enemy has not laid any mines in the area. Hence, we should be able to land what we need at will. The tides could be a bigger problem, but we are coming up with windows in which we think the tides will be acceptable and we can make the landings."

"I'm glad you said 'we think'," Walker grumbled under his breath.

MacArthur looked at Walker. "Well, what do you think, Johnnie?"

"It could be doable," Walker had to admit, "but Inchon is about 150 miles north of Pusan. It is risky at best."

MacArthur smiled. "What is it your old Commander, George Patton, used to say? That one had to take risks in war?"

"You've got me there," Walker conceded. He then looked at the Intelligence men. "Start checking dates for the Inchon landing after the first of October."

"Make that from the first of September," MacArthur countered. Walker knew better than to argue. MacArthur then told Walker that he could leave, as he was sure that his Eighth Army Commander had numerous plans to make. Walker nodded and left the room.

"I want the rest of you to stay," MacArthur said. "I have some questions for you."

MacArthur took the initiative. "Remember, gentlemen, the Japanese landed twice at Inchon – 1894 and1904, I think – and were successful in capturing all of Korea. So it certainly can be done. Having noted these successes, I want to find out what they learned and what they should have done differently."

Willoughby looked at Thompson, who indicated that he wanted to say something. "Go ahead," Willoughby said, somewhat impatiently.

Thompson nodded and started in. "Apparently, the North Koreans don't think that anyone would be foolish enough to attempt a landing at Inchon. As I mentioned before, according to MacLaine and Sherman, no mines have been laid. If the North Koreans had thought that a landing was possible, common sense would have dictated that mines be placed at the appropriate spots."

"Go on," MacArthur said, bored at the repeat of previously stated facts.

"Since there are only piers and seawalls rather than beaches, we will essentially be attacking the city itself. Unless the attack is made at high tide, the port will be nothing more than mud flats. These flats would be unusable by and hazards to moving boats."

The last statement got MacArthur's attention. "What dates would be acceptable for amphibious landings?"

"Sir, starting with the middle of September, we have come up with three dates so far – September 15, September 27, and October 11."

MacArthur turned to his Chief-of-Staff. "Ned, plan for our Inchon landing to be on September 15. That is all, gentlemen." MacArthur got up and walked to the door. Turning back, he motioned for Almond to come with him. The other attendees came to attention.

MacArthur strode into his office with Ned Almond directly behind him. There was a communique lying on his desk. He took off the cover and started reading.

"About time," MacArthur muttered. He looked at his Chief-of-Staff. "I'm finally getting some direction from the powers that be. They are telling me to evacuate the Americans in Korea, cover the evacuation with fighter planes, and send available ammunition and equipment to the South Koreans. Now why didn't I think of that?" His last statement was obviously facetious.

MacArthur continued reading the communique. He finished perusing the document and sighed. "Well, Ned, they're doing one smart thing. They're putting all U.S. forces in Asia under my command." His Chief-of-Staff nodded his approval. MacArthur added that his new title would be Commander in Chief, Far East (CINCFE).

"Ned, take a message for President Truman. Tell him that the South Korean Army is unable to hold off the North Koreans. The primary reason is that the North Koreans possess tanks and planes."

"Yes, sir" was the response. Ned Almond saluted and left to get the message transmission under way.

Jim Thompson sat dumbfounded next to his superior, Charles Willoughby. "Did I hear what I thought I heard? That we are to consider that September 15 is the firm date for the Inchon landing?"

"That is exactly right," Willoughby replied. "And you better give that date to General Walker. He had left by the time General MacArthur made his decision."

Thompson started to stand. "With your permission, sir, I'll do that right now."

Willoughby made a corroborative wave with his hand, and Thompson left the room.

Jim Thompson arrived at Eighth Army headquarters finding the Commanding General, Walton Walker, barking commands to his assembled staff. "What do you want?" he said, looking at Thompson.

"Sir, can we speak in private?" he asked.

Impatiently, Walker told the others in the room to 'get out.' He shut the door. "Now what is it?" he asked in an annoyed tone.

"Sir, General Willoughby wanted me to tell you that the Inchon landing is set for September 15. He felt you should know that, since you had left by the time General MacArthur made his decision."

He started to make a terse comment, but then held back. "Colonel, I appreciate your telling me. Right now, though, I have other things of a higher priority to worry about."

"I certainly understand, sir." Thompson saluted and left the Eighth Army headquarters.

By early July, the situation in Korea looked even more desperate. The North Koreans had captured Seoul and were rolling southward at an alarming pace. General Walton Walker was doing everything he could to stop the advance, but even MacArthur was becoming alarmed. MacArthur paced endlessly, deriding the fact that America's Army, which only a few years earlier had been considered to be the most powerful in the world, was just a shadow of its former self. "How could this happen?" he asked no one in particular.

Bill Summerfield was now back at work after having visited his wife and newborn son. He had met with General Willoughby, his new boss. He was kind of in limbo, as there was nothing much for him to do. This suited him fine, as he could direct all of his attention to getting Jack MacLaine and Jim Sherman back home safely. Not an easy task.

Summerfield moved into Jack MacLaine's office in the Meiji building, as his old one was now occupied by Willoughby. He was deeply engrossed in reading Intelligence reports when he heard: "What are you doing in my office?" He looked up to see a smiling Jack MacLaine followed closely by Jim Sherman. Both were in need of a shave, shower, and change of clothes. This didn't bother Summerfield. He went over and warmly greeted both of them.

"Thank God you're back safe and sound!" Summerfield exclaimed after the bear hugs were finished. He reached in his pocket and pulled out a letter for MacLaine. "Before I forget it, this is for you. I've had it with me every minute since I left Washington." It was a sealed letter from Jennifer. "You can read it now. Jim and I won't bother you, right Jim?" Sherman grinned and nodded.

After moving to the side of the room, MacLaine eagerly ripped open the envelope and pulled out the letter. He read the letter intently and relayed some of the content to the other two after he had finished. "She still loves me, and she wants me to be careful. I'll have to write her tonight and tell her I've arrived safely back in Tokyo. And – of course – that I still love her."

Both Summerfield and Sherman eagerly endorsed what MacLaine had told them. Then the conversation turned to the business at hand.

"Bill," MacLaine said, "we're very sorry to hear you're no longer in charge. But it appears to me that I have become expendable, particularly since you have moved into my office!"

"Jack, you and I have worked together for quite some time, and it pains me to have to say it. But I think you're right. Thus, I talked to General Willoughby and General Almond about it, and Almond assures me that he has a good spot for you. After you have rested up – and cleaned up – I think you should talk to him. I would suggest that you do it soon, and I will make an appointment for you with General Almond in the morning if that is acceptable to you."

"Absolutely," MacLaine replied. "The sooner we get it resolved, the better."

The next morning, Jack MacLaine was rested and had regained all of his strength. He looked at the spit shine on his shoes and the sharp crease in his trousers as he waited in General Almond's outer office. Soon, he was called in. He saluted, and Almond motioned for him to sit down. He slid into a chair and pulled it close to the general's desk.

Almond looked him over closely before speaking. "I've read your reports on Inchon, and I'm impressed. Obviously, there is no one in our Army who knows the spot better, so I have the perfect assignment for you."

Almond cautioned MacLaine not to reveal the content of their conversation to anyone outside of Willoughby, Summerfield, and Sherman. He reiterated MacArthur's comment that surprise would determine whether or not the operation was successful. He also stated that General MacArthur had said that the Inchon landing would take place on September 15.

"You may recall that General MacArthur is placing me in charge of the landing force. My title will be X-Corps Commander. We will have both Army and Marine units in the Corps. My job for you is to interface directly with the Marines. Your job won't be easy, but I think that you will handle it splendidly. Any questions?"

"Just one, sir. Can I bring Major Sherman with me?"

"You will have to clear that with General Willoughby. If he can spare Sherman, it's fine with me."

Jack MacLaine got up, saluted, and left General Almond's office. He might be jumping from the frying pan into the fire, but it was okay with him. The only thing he really feared was becoming a fifth wheel.

Chapter 8

Dark, Early Days of the War

After the first few days of fighting, even MacArthur's optimism was definitely decreasing. Reports that were arriving back from the front stated that the situation was hopeless. He decided to see for himself. "Get the 'Bataan' ready," he told Almond. "I'm going to Korea."

MacArthur would take the plane that had carried him to Tokyo at the end of World War II. The C-54 was aptly named the 'Bataan,' in honor of the men and women who had served and sacrificed immensely for the General and for their country at the start of World War II.

None other than General Sratemeyer, MacArthur's air chief, came in to try and talk him out of this very dangerous idea. "I'm going," MacArthur said, "and that's all there is to it. Stratemeyer did manage to round up four P-51 Mustangs to fly cover.

The ceiling was zero, and the 'Bataan' should have been grounded. However, it wasn't. MacArthur overruled those who were in opposition to the plane taking off. On board with him were Willoughby, his trusted Intelligence Chief, and Colonel Jack MacLaine. MacArthur, who didn't say so at this time, was impressed with the work that MacLaine and Sherman had done during their stay at Inchon. Soon, MacArthur and his staff were airborne.

The relatively short flight over to Korea was mainly without incident. At one point, a Communist Yak did try to intercept the 'Bataan.' However, the P-51s broke off and quickly repelled it. The 'Bataan' was now approaching the pocked airstrip near the South Korean Capital of Seoul. By MacArthur's order, they would be landing not in the middle of harm's way, but close to it.

The landing was rough, not unexpectedly. Syngman Rhee, the President of South Korea – now called the Republic of Korea or ROK – was there to meet MacArthur. Rhee looked haggard, as recent events were telling on him. Rhee mainly let the Americans on MacArthur's Korean staff do the talking. After hearing the views of these men, MacArthur said that he wanted to go to the front and have a look. From previous experience, he knew that his own opinions would be the best.

The motorcade consisted of MacArthur in a black Dodge followed by a number of jeeps. Willoughby was in MacArthur's car, but Jack MacLaine didn't quite make it. He was in the jeep immediately behind the Dodge. Mortar shells were exploding in the near vicinity, and MacLaine marveled at MacArthur's bravery and fortitude. He could see MacArthur chatting casually in the car up ahead. MacArthur was not paying any attention to the danger that surrounded them.

MacArthur was, however, amazed at the columns of soldiers and civilians retreating along the road. There was agony and grief everywhere. Interspersed among the masses of people were ambulances carrying the broken men. "This is worse than anything I've ever seen," MacArthur muttered. He got out of the car and stood erectly on a small mound at the side of the road. Personal safety was obviously of no concern to him. *What a magnificent figure,* MacLaine thought. *I will certainly have something to tell my grandchildren if I'm lucky enough to have them.* MacLaine could tell that MacArthur was already planning to drive the North Koreans back where they belonged. *He is the best,* MacLaine told himself.

After eight grueling hours in the combat zone, MacArthur and his staff boarded the 'Bataan' for the flight back to Tokyo. MacArthur paced up and down the aisle even during takeoff. When someone tried to get him to take his seat, he simply waved him off. MacLaine could tell that something big was brewing. MacArthur motioned for Willoughby and MacLaine to join him at the back of the plane. He was seated next to a window. "You can see why my plan for a rear-echelon attack is so important," MacArthur declared in muted tones. "I desperately need the First Marine Division. I

---

only hope that they're as good as they used to be." CINCFE sat down on an inside seat and gazed out the window. He might be downcast, but he would only show it to those he felt most comfortable with.

Suddenly, MacArthur lurched in his seat. He called after MacLaine. "Inchon! You can see why your upcoming assignment is so important." MacLaine looked down, and, sure enough, someone would have to storm the land from naval ships! And who better to do it than the U.S. Marines?

Well I'll be darned, MacLaine thought. *And here I was thinking that he didn't even know I would be interfacing with the Marines. Obviously he did. Guess my job will be more important than I thought. Better make sure when we get back that Bill Sherman will be coming with me.*

"Yes, sir!" MacLaine replied to the big boss.

The next day when MacArthur arrived at his office, the reports were no rosier. He held his usual staff meeting, and General Willoughby, General Summerfield, Colonel Thompson, and Colonel MacLaine were in attendance. The few American troops that were dispatched from Japan broke and ran as quickly as the ROK troops did. "Why don't they stay and fight?" he asked no one in particular.

MacLaine spoke up. "General, very few of these troops were in the last war, and all of them that were sent to Korea from here have gotten soft from duty in Japan."

"I know they're soft," MacArthur replied icily, "but they're *MY SOFT TROOPS*, and I shall always protect them." As usual, MacArthur declared no responsibility for the shape of these troops – only that they were his troops.

Oh no! I've gotten on the wrong side of the big boss. Better think of something in a hurry. Got it! "Sir," MacLaine replied, "I think these men will toughen up in a hurry. It won't be long until they're first rate troops. You'll be proud of them. I guarantee it!"

"I hope you're right."

MacLaine's input was the correct one, but MacArthur was skeptical.

MacArthur's dubiousness was warranted. Reports coming back from Korea indicated that field hospitals were crowded with American soldiers, some with self-inflicted wounds. The situation was totally unsatisfactory, and MacArthur called in the Eighth Army Commander. He was bound and determined to get to the bottom of it.

"Johnnie, what's the meaning of this?" MacArthur slid the hospital report over to General Walker after the general had reported. The general was seated at a table in MacArthur's office. Walker looked at the report and slid it back.

"I've seen the report, and I don't like it any better than you do. But you can't blame the troops. This isn't a declared war, and the men feel that they are risking their lives for nothing."

MacArthur nodded. "I know it's a difficult situation, but I expect you to impress upon your men that it is their duty and responsibility to stand and fight. I told your predecessor – Bob Eichelberger – in New Guinea to either take Buna from the Japanese or not come back. I am now telling you the same thing – either hold the Pusan perimeter or don't come back. That is all." MacArthur took another document from the pile on the table and started reading.

Walker shook his head, got up, gave a half-hearted salute, and walked to the door. It appeared that MacArthur was deeply engrossed in the document and oblivious to anyone else in the room. For Walker, it was a do or die situation. Failure was not an option.

On July 14, General "Lightning Joe" Collins, the U.S. Army Chief of Staff, arrived at the Dai Ichi building in Tokyo. Perhaps the Joint Chiefs felt from MacArthur's dejected messages that CINCFE needed some cheering up and perhaps a pep talk. After all, he was now in his seventies.

MacArthur and Collins warmly greeted each other. "I have brought you a little gift," Collins said. It was a United Nations flag. He presented it to MacArthur. "This will be a first. You will be the United Nations Commander, and you will soon have troops from 13 countries under your control. And your new title will be Supreme Commander Allied Forces in the Pacific, or SCAP."

"I've had similar titles before."

"So this will be a United Nations effort," MacArthur continued. He laid the flag on his desk. "How many troops will these countries send?"

"We've heard that Great Britain may send as many as 40,000."

MacArthur whistled softly. "Impressive!"

Collins relayed that MacArthur had two sources to thank – one was the hard work of U.S. Ambassador to the U.N., Warren Austin, and the other was the walkout of the Russians from the Security Council.

MacArthur chuckled. "I guess the Soviets didn't approve."

"Correct," was the response. "I guess you probably know that Truman replaced Johnson as Secretary of Defense with George Marshall."

"No, but it doesn't surprise me. He has to have a scapegoat for his failure in Korea, and Johnson is the stuckee." MacArthur shook his head and continued. "Now I have Dean Acheson at the State Department and George Marshall at Defense to contend with."

Collins looked somewhat shocked. "Don't you like George Marshall?"

"Not particularly. And I know that he doesn't particularly like me. But the move will let Truman wave his sword and talk about our military might when in fact it doesn't exist."

Collins had to agree. "I know you're a busy man, so I'll let you get back to work. Please know that the Joint Chiefs are behind you all the way."

The two men shook hands, and Collins departed. While Collins was technically MacArthur's superior, there were five stars on CINCFE's collar and only four on "Lightning Joe's."

By the end of July, Walker and his Eighth Army as well as the ROK troops were putting up strong resistance. Perhaps it was because the soldiers had learned that the North Koreans didn't like to take prisoners. Instead, they preferred to bayonet them. Or perhaps General Walker had gotten through to the men about duty, honor, and country. Whatever the reason, it now looked like the North Koreans would not be able to throw the opposing armies into the sea. It looked like the Pusan perimeter would be held by friendly troops.

While the onslaught had by no means stopped, it was now being readily repelled. Sturgis was still cannibalizing anything and everything he could to support the Korean operation, even using ships from the defunct Japanese Navy to transport items deemed critical.

And there was now a sizeable presence of U.S. naval and air power in the area. But in addition, troops and material from the U.S. homeland as well as from other U.N. countries were arriving at Pusan in massive size. Even the most negative of the skeptics was being converted. Not only light weaponry was being received, but tanks and heavy artillery pieces were in the mix. Thus, the playing field was being evened. While MacArthur would obviously – and perhaps rightfully so – be given the lion's share of the credit, it was undeniable that others should be given their fair share.

Jack MacLaine, through a substantial amount of pleading and maneuvering, had obtained the services of Jim Sherman. *It will be great to have Jim at my side through the harrowing days to come.* MacLaine now used his office in the Dai Ichi building almost exclusively, as it was only a few floors below that of MacArthur and his new boss, Ned Almond. Sherman had an office right next door to MacLaine's.

MacLaine knocked on Sherman's open door. Sherman, who was just moving in and getting settled, looked around. "What can I do for you?" he asked his boss. His usual smile lit his face.

"It looks like the Pusan perimeter is stabilizing, and I think it is time we meet our Marine friends. I am particularly interested in meeting this fellow, Chesty Puller. If he's half as good as I've heard, we will be in good shape."

Sherman nodded and beamed. "I'm with you on that, boss."

Part 2

Chapter 9

Joining Forces

Jennifer Haraldsson opened the front door of her apartment and stooped down to get her morning newspaper. The huge headlines on the front of the Washington Post blared out that North Korea had just attacked South Korea. While it had been expected, Jennifer was still in a state of mild shock after quickly digesting the headlines. *This can only mean one thing,* she thought, *a lot of young American boys are probably going to lose their lives in throwing the North Koreans back where they belong.* Up to this point, she had not really considered the consequences.

Jennifer hurriedly showered, dressed, and fixed some toast and coffee. *No use reading the rest of the paper,* she convinced herself. *After all, any news after this would be anti-climactic.* She finished eating and dashed to her car. She climbed in, started the motor, and headed for Walter Reed Hospital.

After arriving at the hospital parking lot, Jennifer went to the area reserved for the nurses. It was still early compared to when the next shift began, so she had no trouble finding a spot close to the hospital entrance. She nosed in, brought her car to a stop, got out, and turned her key in the lock on the exterior of the door. She took the key out and raced in the hospital entrance and up to her duty section. Fortunately, Brad Taylor had his office on the same floor. Since he always arrived early in the morning, she planned to see him first.

Just as Jennifer suspected, Taylor was at his desk reading the entries that the night shift had compiled. She knocked on his open door and he looked up. He was obviously glad to see her. "Come on in and have a seat."

"I guess you read the morning paper," Jennifer said.

Taylor nodded. "I don't know anything yet, but I should hear shortly. And, as I said before, I'll want you to be my head nurse if I go to Korea."

"I'll be honored to serve with you," Jennifer replied. "My first action will be to find out if Monica will go with us."

"Please do. And the sooner the better."

Jennifer nodded and Taylor continued. "From what I've been reading in Army medical journals, the Army will be trying a new approach. You and I will more than likely be serving in a MASH – Mobile Army Surgical Hospital. The concept is to get experienced medical personnel closer to the front lines. I have to tell you that it will probably be riskier than what we've been accustomed to in the past."

Jennifer just smiled. "Remember, I was shot at in Norway and at Dieppe. How can it possibly be any more risky?"

"Touché" was Taylor's response. He continued by saying that he would probably go back in as a lieutenant colonel – colonel if he were lucky – and that Jennifer would go in as a major.

"Fair enough," Jennifer replied. "Now, if there's nothing further, I will try and find Monica."

"No, there isn't. And by the way, you'll be closer to Jack MacLaine."

Jennifer looked back and smiled as she left Taylor's office. The idea had crossed her mind.

Looking at her watch, Jennifer thought that Monica should be in by now. She went down the hall, keeping a close lookout for Monica. Sure enough, she found her in the second room that she peered in, taking the vital signs of one of the patients who had been in surgery the day before.

"Can I speak to you after you finish?" Jennifer asked.

"Certainly. I have something I want to tell you, too."

When Monica finished checking on the patient, the two went to the coffee bar. "It's a little early for my break," Monica said, "but I'll just forego one later." Jennifer smiled and nodded. The two women got a cup of coffee and went to a table and sat down.

Before Jennifer could speak, Monica said that she had decided to go to Korea.

"I'm very happy that you have," Jennifer said. "But I have to add some information that may negate your decision. I just talked to Brad, and he tells me that we will be part of a surgical unit that will be located closer to the front than in previous wars. It will be more dangerous."

"I don't care," Monica replied. "I want the adventure."

"Don't you want to discuss your decision with your sister?"

The question obviously exasperated Monica. "Of course not! I make my own decisions."

Uh-oh. I shouldn't have asked that. I better change the subject in a hurry.

"I'm glad you'll be going with us," Jennifer replied, ignoring the controversy she had raised. "I'll keep you completely involved when we hear anything more."

"Good. I didn't mean to tear your head off. It's just that I'm tired of Molly always being crammed down my throat. Ever since we were little, my parents have held her up as the shining example. I want my own space so that I can have my own achievements – and, yes – my own failures."

Jennifer looked at Monica with admiration. "I certainly understand, and I very much appreciate your explanation. All I can do is promise that you will be your own person. And I should add that I'm very happy – upgrade that to delighted – that you will be going with us." Monica nodded.

She doesn't seem to realize, Jennifer mused, *that a big part of the problem is that she is just like her sister. She is a hard worker, talented, and very dedicated. She is also very trustworthy – her word is her bond.*

Thinking further, Jennifer was hit with a sobering thought: *Perhaps my sisters feel the same way about me!*

Jennifer asked how everything at work was going. Monica answered with one word – 'fine.' The subject then changed to lighter topics, such as the fact that there would be a lot more men than women in Korea. This statistic was obviously one that pleased Monica!

The two ladies finished their coffee and went back to work. Jennifer saw Brad Taylor in the hall and passed on the good news that Monica would be going with them. He was obviously pleased.

After a long day at work, Jennifer returned to her apartment. She no sooner had dropped her purse on the living room couch than the phone rang. It was none other than Jacob Partude!

"Jacob! How good to hear from you!" she squealed. "How is everything in the great state of Louisiana?"

"Fine. Sandy's teaching is going well, and your Goddaughter, Jenny, is growing like a weed. I can't believe that she is now two-and-a-half."

"Is she talking yet?" Jennifer asked.

"She never stops! I'll let you say hello when we finish, but I wanted to tell you right off that I'm being recalled to active duty. I will be re-trained to fly the P-51, but eventually I will be upgraded to fly jets. What's new in your life?"

Jennifer quickly reviewed that she is now engaged to Jack MacLaine, and that she expects to be recalled any day and sent to Korea.

"Where is Jack now?" Partude asked.

"He is stationed in Tokyo, but I know he's on a special assignment, so I don't know exactly where he is right now. I hope to hear shortly, though."

"Maybe he's in Korea," Partude replied softly. "That's where all the action is right now. Oops!" He obviously knew that his musing was a mistake.

"I hope you're wrong," Jennifer said, "but your reasoning is sound. In any event, if he is in Korea and if I'm sent there, I might get to see more of him."

"Correct. And as the old saying goes, there is a silver lining under every cloud."

In any event, Jennifer could hope so.

The two exchanged pleasantries, Sandy got on the phone, and then Jenny was put on. Jennifer greatly enjoyed talking to both Sandy and her goddaughter. Her maternal instincts were definitely aroused, and perhaps she would have her own child in the not-distant future.

Jennifer could tell that Jacob did not want to hang up. However, long distance phone calls were expensive, and the two eventually said goodbye. "Hopefully, I will see you in Korea," Jacob said right before hanging up the receiver. Thinking further, he added, "But not as your patient!"

"I hope not, too!" Jennifer replied as she signed off.

Jennifer wasn't very hungry, but she knew that she had to eat to keep her strength up. She went to the kitchen, opened some cans, and heated the contents. She also got a bottle of wine out of the refrigerator, as it was the only thing that really appealed to her. She quickly ate and then decided to write Jack MacLaine. Perhaps writing to him would cheer her up! She went to the desk and got pen and paper.

My Dearest Jack

I miss you more than you will ever know! It was great seeing Bill Summerfield, but the one I really wanted to see is you!

Bill told me that you volunteered for a dangerous mission. I totally understand. I really do. You have always been very honest with me, and I know that you are not one to live a sedate life. Therefore, I won't chastise you for going on the mission. Just know that I love you more than anything, and I pray every day for your safe return. If God will just grant me this one wish, I won't ask for anything further.

With the trouble in Korea, it looks like I will be called back to active duty. I'm sure you remember Brad Taylor. Brad tells me that he and I will probably be called up any day now. If so, I will be his head nurse once again, and I think that Monica, Molly's sister, will probably go with us. It would be a godsend, as Monica has proven to be an exceptional worker here at Walter Reed.

If we do go to Korea, we will probably serve in what's called a MASH Unit. MASH stands for Mobile Army Surgical Hospital. I don't know if you've heard of it, but the idea is to get the surgical team closer to the front lines. By doing this, the brass think that more lives can be saved.

The only other news I have is that I just got off the phone with Jacob Partude. He has already been recalled, and he will be getting some refresher training in the P-51. He thinks that he will be upgraded to jet fighters in the near future. While I was on the phone, I got to talk to his wife and my goddaughter, Jenny. Jacob says that Jenny is growing like a weed! I believe it, as she speaks very clearly, and I was able to have a nice conversation with her. Believe it or not, she will be three years old in a few weeks!

Well, my darling, I better go for now.

All my love forever and ever,

Jennifer

Getting the letter written was a big load off of Jennifer's mind. She went to bed and slept soundly. The next morning, she would put the letter in a mailbox on her way to work.

Jennifer arrived at Walter Reed Hospital the next morning feeling quite refreshed. She walked by Brad Taylor's office and there he was. He was intently pouring over some mail. She knocked on the door. He looked up, smiled, and motioned her to come in and have a seat.

"I've got our orders right here," he said. "They've put us on together." He handed Jennifer several copies from the stack.

She quickly read them. "They don't waste any time, do they?

"No they don't," Taylor's replied. "I'll also have to get some brand new uniforms, as I've put on a few pounds."

We're supposed to report to Andrews Air Force Base for deployment in five days!" Jennifer gasped. "Luckily, I haven't put on any weight. However, I'll have to go to Clothing Sales to make sure the uniforms haven't changed. If they have, I'll also have to get new ones."

"Oh, well," she added, "it would be nice to have some new ones, anyway."

Taylor nodded and thought for a moment. "You better take Monica with you, as she'll need to get uniforms. And by the way," he said grinning, "I have something for you." He reached in his drawer and pulled out some Major's leaves.

"Thank you very much," Jennifer replied. "I'll be honored to wear them."

"By the way, what rank is Monica going in with?"

Taylor reached into another pile and got the orders for her. "She'll be going in as a second lieutenant. Unfortunately, she won't be going with us. First, she'll have to go down to Texas for some officer training. You remember that, don't you?"

Jennifer nodded and took the orders for Monica that Taylor passed to her. *I guess it was too much to hope that she would go in as a first lieutenant,* Jennifer thought. *Oh well, I'm sure Brad will promote her as soon as he can.*

Jennifer asked how Brad's children would get along without him. He said that he was very fortunate, as his wife was very strong. Not wanting to take any more of his time, Jennifer said that she had best get to work.

"Let's keep in close touch until we deploy," Taylor said as Jennifer reached the doorway. She turned and gave him a thumbs-up signal. She would keep a close watch for Monica as she completed her rounds.

Jennifer stopped at the Nurses' Station and got a pen and paper. There would be a lot to do in the next few days. She would need to train completely the new staff that was arriving in the next twenty-four hours. She would also need to either lease her apartment or give it up. The trouble with giving it up is that she would have to store a lot of possessions or get it shipped to her parents in Idaho. Neither was an attractive option. There was also the question of her car. What would she do with it? *Better call my best friend Molly to see if she has any suggestions. I'll call her now to find out if we can get together tonight. I'll even offer to bring in dinner!*

Jennifer picked up the phone and started to dial. Out of the corner of her eye, she saw Monica coming toward her. *Uh-oh,* she thought. *Oh well, I better tell her now. Otherwise, she'll think I'm doing things behind her back.*

"I was just coming to look for you," Jennifer said. "Brad received your orders this morning, and you'll be going to Texas for some training to become a second lieutenant in the Army. Then you'll join us in Korea."

"Wow," Monica said, obviously shocked. "I can't believe things are working this quickly."

Jennifer smiled. "When I told Brad that you were willing to go with us to Korea, he obviously didn't waste any time. He knows what strings to pull to get things done in a hurry."

"I'll say," Monica replied, shaking her head.

Jennifer asked if Monica would help her train the new staff that would be coming in during the next 24 hours. Monica eagerly replied in the affirmative. The young lady also said that she would like to go with Jennifer over the noon hour to get some uniforms. *The preliminaries are out of the way,* Jennifer thought. *Now I have to tell her that I am going to ask her sister for some advice.*

"When you were coming up," Jennifer started in, "I was just calling your sister to ask her for some advice."

"Oh? What advice do you need?"

"Well, for example, I was wondering if I should put things in storage, sub-lease everything that I have, or ship it to my folks in Idaho."

Monica thought for a moment. "If I were you, I would ask the folks coming in tomorrow if anyone needs a furnished apartment to rent. I'll just bet that someone in the group does. And these are very reliable people. They would pay the rent on time and take very good care of your possessions."

Jennifer was astonished. "Here I was almost ready to panic, and you have just made some outstanding suggestions. I guess I should have planned to ask you in the first place."

Monica was obviously pleased. "Are there any other issues bothering you?"

"Just my car. I don't know what to do with it."

"Now that is a good question for Molly," Monica replied. "I suggest you ask her opinion on it."

"You've been a huge help, and I'll ask Molly as you suggest."

The two nurses hugged and agreed to meet back at the Nurses' Station at noon sharp. Monica turned to go see her next patient, and Jennifer resumed calling Molly.

"Hi Molly?" Jennifer. "You'll never guess what!"

"Okay, I'll bite. What?"

"Monica and I are being called up, and she gave me some good advice concerning personal belongings. She actually suggested I call you and ask you what to do with my car!"

"Will wonders ever cease?" Molly said under her breath. "Maybe the ice is thawing now that she will be going thousands of miles away from me."

"Maybe so," Jennifer interrupted. "What if I bring dinner over tonight so we can discuss things? How about Chinese?"

"Sounds good. And Monica likes Chinese."

"Settled then. See you about 6? Our normal time?"

"Perfect," Molly replied. "Todd should be asleep about then, and we can have a nice, quiet evening."

The two hung up, and Jennifer continued with her duties. At noon, she walked to the Nurses' Station. Monica was waiting for her.

Monica looked none-too-happy. "I have a question for you. What if the North Koreans push the friendly troops off of the peninsula? What then?"

"I've been thinking the same thing," Jennifer replied. "Obviously, we can't go in if South Korea is in occupied hands. But I'll ask Brad about it. Your question is very valid."

The two got in Jennifer's car and headed for the Clothing Sales Store at Fort Myers in Virginia. It was about a 30 minute drive on the beltway around the nation's capital. During the drive, the two avoided playing the "what-if" game. There was nothing that could be done if fate dealt a terrible blow to the people in South Korea.

"What type of uniforms and how many should we get?" Monica asked as they walked down the isle of the store.

"As I recall, they'll furnish your uniforms in your Officers' Training Class. Therefore, what I'm telling you applies to after you've received your commission."

"What exactly does my officer's training consist of?" Monica asked.

"It's been a while since I've been there, but as I recall, they will instruct you in leadership, the Army Health Care System, and – perhaps most importantly – the Army way-of-life. You won't have to undergo the rigorous physical training that the soldiers have to go through."

"Thank goodness," Monica muttered.

Jennifer continued. "I suggest you get one Class A uniform with tie, insignias, and etcetera. Then if you get three sets of fatigues, you should be in good shape. And, of course, you'll need your rank for the fatigues. Any questions?"

"What about surgical gowns?"

Jennifer smiled. "You're full of good questions, but don't worry about surgery. We'll furnish plenty of clothing for the operating room."

Jennifer could tell that Monica was satisfied. She looked at the new, crisp uniforms. While her old ones would probably suffice, she couldn't control herself. She ended up buying the same uniforms she had advised Monica to purchase – one class A with all of the paraphernalia and three fatigue uniforms, complete with rank!

Both found the right size, and no alterations were necessary. They carried their packages of clothes to the car, put them in the trunk, and got in. Jennifer started their car, and soon they were on their way back to Walter Reed Hospital. "Let's grab a sandwich that we can take up to our duty floor," Jennifer said. "As soon as we finish, I'll look for Brad to ask him your million dollar question."

After eating, Jennifer scurried off to find Brad Taylor. She spotted him just coming out of surgery. He looked tired.

"Brad," she hollered after him, "do you have a minute to talk?"

"I always have a minute for you. Let me get out of these clothes, and then let's go grab a cup of coffee."

They were soon seated in the snack bar. Brad had gotten a cup of coffee, but Jennifer had iced tea.

After taking a sip, Jennifer related the question that was posed to her. "This question was asked by Monica this morning, and I didn't have an answer. I told her that I would ask you."

Jennifer related that, with the bad news coming out of Korea, Monica wanted to know what they would do if the friendly forces were pushed into the sea.

Taylor smiled. "That young lady sure knows how to get to the crux of the situation. I don't think that even the brass has thought of that possibility yet, but I can assure you that we won't set up shop behind enemy lines."

Jennifer wasn't completely satisfied. "I hope I haven't encouraged Monica to take a big risk. Maybe we should have let her stay here."

Taylor launched into his pep talk. "I know how you feel, but we need the best people with us. And please remember that losses of medical personnel will always be a lot lower than those sustained by our troops on the front line."

Jennifer was momentarily embarrassed. "Please forgive me, Brad. What you say is the absolute truth, and I should never let personal feelings get in the way."

"No need to ask for an apology. You're the very best in my book, and you always will be."

It was comforting to Jennifer to know how her boss felt about her. He followed up by telling her that they would land in Pusan and set up their surgical unit to the South of the front lines. "We will be in a position to be evacuated if the need arises," he assured her. "But knowing you," he continued, "you will want to be the last one out!"

Jennifer could only smile.

Near the end of her shift, Jennifer received a telegram. It was from Jack MacLaine. She quickly tore it open.

My Darling Jennifer
Summerfield told you I was on a dangerous mission – stop – I was, but I'm now back in Tokyo safe and sound – stop – I think of you every minute of every day.
All my love forever,
Jack

"He's safe – he's safe!" Jennifer yelled as she skipped up and down the hall waving the telegram. Brad Taylor stuck his head out of his office, smiled, and gave her the thumbs-up signal. Visitors of the patients stuck their heads out of the doors and softly applauded. Jennifer, realizing that she had made too much of a ruckus, whispered "I'm sorry!" in different directions. No one seemed to mind!

At 6:00 p.m. sharp, Jennifer steered her car into Molly's driveway. She gathered up the Chinese food that she had ordered from a carry-out, got out of the car, and walked to the front door. She rang the doorbell.

The door opened, and Molly – holding Todd – beamed. "Let the good times begin!" Molly gushed enthusiastically. The hostess pushed open the screen door, and Jennifer walked in. Monica was seated on a living room chair but stood up when she saw who it was.

"Where do you want the food?" Jennifer asked.

"Just set it on the kitchen counter," Molly replied. "I'll be out in a minute to take it up." Molly handed the baby to his aunt and walked to the kitchen. The two women hugged.

"I got a wonderful telegram from Jack telling me that he's safe," Jennifer said.

"Oh, no!" Molly replied in mock disappointment. "I got a telegram from Bill saying the same thing, and I was going to surprise you with it. It was going to be a 'going away' present."

"It's still the best 'going away' present you could give me."

The two women hugged again, realizing that they would be separated for the first time in a long time. These two women had been through a lot together, and calling them best friends was putting it mildly.

Molly put the baby in his crib, and the three women went to the table and sat down. Some pressing items concerning Jennifer's and Monica's upcoming deployment were discussed. But overall, the conversation was pleasant, and Jennifer sensed that past frictions between Molly and Monica were just that – in the past. At least, she hoped so.

The dinner came to an end way too soon. "I'll let you two say your goodbyes," Monica said, obviously appreciating the sensitivity of the situation. She went down to her bedroom.

"I'll miss not having you there," Jennifer said as the tears welled in her eyes. "But I know that you have better things to do now."

"Not better," Molly responded, "but necessary. Now about your car. If you leave it here, I will take good care of it. I promise."

Jennifer nodded, and the two hugged once again. Molly assured her that she would be at the plane to see them off.

The next few days went by quickly, and Jennifer was very impressed with the quality of the newcomers who were coming in to take their place. One of these people wanted to sublet her apartment, so everything was working out satisfactorily.

The fifth day arrived, and Brad and Jennifer said goodbye to friends and family who had come out to see them off. They boarded the plane, and soon they were on their way. Who knew what the future had in store for them? They certainly didn't!

Chapter 10

Chesty

Since July, 1948, Colonel Lewis Burwell (Chesty) Puller had been stationed at Pearl Harbor, Hawaii as commander of a Marine barracks. *A Marine barracks!* What a way to end an illustrious career, but he thought the end was definitely coming. His outstanding service in Haiti and Nicaragua during the banana wars and at Guadalcanal and Peleliu during World War II didn't seem to matter. He could feel that the end was in sight, and he feared that he would never see a star on his shoulder.

What concerned him even more was the sad state of the Marine Corps. Even the Secretary of the Navy was now in the loop, decreeing that no officers would be selected for promotion unless they had staff duty showing on their records. "What about combat duty?" Puller moaned. "They're pushing out experienced officers to make way for these young pups as platoon, company, and battalion commanders. I'm afraid that the Marine Corps will pay dearly for this mistake in the coming years." He was making these remarks in the confines of his kitchen with only his wife, Virginia, in earshot. However, all of the officers up the line, including the Marine Commandant, General Vandegrift, knew just how he felt.

His own situation didn't faze him a bit as far as his job performance was concerned. When he arrived at Pearl Harbor, he found that no one was training gunners. This situation changed shortly, and one could soon hear the *rata-tat-tat* of machine guns on the firing ranges. With Puller in charge (at least of the Marine barracks), the Hawaiian Islands were in good hands. He inspected them as if national security were at stake!

And his efforts didn't go unnoticed by his immediate superiors. Puller continually received "outstanding" on his performance reports, and his family received the perks of being related to a high ranking Marine Officer. He, Virginia, and their three children lived in a spacious, well-staffed home with a swimming pool.

Thus, Puller had to secretly admit that life wasn't so bad here. But he yearned for the adventures that could only come with combat and the chance to excel and to be promoted. After all, he had been a Colonel for most of World War II, and this situation was unpleasant – if not detestable – to him. It seemed, though, that he would just have to grin and bear it. If he had to retire as a Colonel, so be it.

On June 25, 1950, Puller's world changed. As was his normal ritual, he walked out to get the morning paper before sunrise. He could barely read the headlines, but was able to make out the word "Attacked!" He hurried in to the kitchen, where his wife was sitting having a cup of coffee. A cook was hunkered over the stove making breakfast. Puller excitedly read the front page article.

"My dear," Puller said to his wife, "I think our luck is changing. There is a little war starting up in Korea."

"Oh, no!" Mrs. Puller exclaimed. "Lewis, I was hoping you would stay with me from now on. And when I think of those poor American boys who will probably have to serve – my God!"

"I agree with you there, but this will probably be my last chance to get a star."

"I know how much that means to you, and I hope it works out."

Puller scanned the front page article again. "I see," he chuckled, "Where President Truman says that men, ships, and planes are on their way to Korea. Oh, and he says that a small number of U.S. Marines are being sent in to help the Army stop the onslaught. I can agree with the word 'small.' He chuckled again and got up from the table. "I've got to get into this," he said to his wife, turning serious. "I'll send a telegram to everyone – including the Marine Commandant – if I have to. I'll see you later." He kissed his wife, put on his blouse and hat, and started to leave the room.

"Aren't you going to eat your breakfast?" Virginia called after her husband.

"I don't have time. I'll get a bite on the way to the office." Puller slammed the kitchen door on the way out. He was on perhaps the most important mission of his life – to get to go to Korea!

The Western Union office appeared at the side of the road as he drove along. *What the heck. I'll send a telegram to the Commandant, Vice Commandant, and to my old Division Commander, Oliver Smith. I know I'm jumping the chain of command, but it's a lot easier to get forgiveness than permission.*

Puller pulled into a parking space at the front of the Western Union building and got out of his car. He went inside and quickly drafted a message. He related how he had served in Haiti and Nicaragua and later in the Pacific Theater. He reminded the brass how helpful his experience would be in Korea. He then pleaded with them to activate his old first Regiment of the First Marine Division and to let him once again serve his country in combat. He gave the message to the man behind the counter, told him it was urgent, and paid him. He went outside and got into his car. *That's the best I can do,* he thought. *Now I have to wait for the response. It won't be easy.*

Puller decided to stop and inform his boss of his activities. He stopped his car and went in to the Headquarters Building. He nodded at the Seaman sitting near the door to the office of Rear Admiral C. H. McMorris. He didn't bother to have the Seaman announce him but went up to the closed door and knocked. "Enter," barked the Admiral,

who looked up and smiled when he saw who it was. "Well, Lewie, I was wondering how long it would take you to get here. I imagine you want to go to Korea."

"That's it in a nutshell, sir. I've already wired the Marine Commandant and the First Marine Division Commander to see if I can head up the First Regiment again."

The admiral motioned for Puller to have a seat. "I'll level with you, Lewie. You're one of the best officers I've ever known, and I reflected this on your performance reports. But, quite frankly, there are those in key positions who think you're over the hill and should retire. I don't happen to be one of them, and I think you did the only thing you could – go right to the top. I hope it gets you what you want."

Thank you for your understanding, sir."

"I'll do anything I can to help you," the Admiral replied. "After all, if we're to win this thing, we have to have our best men leading the charge." Puller thanked the Admiral again, saluted, and left.

Waiting to see if he would go to Korea was grueling for Chesty. He read the papers daily and fumed as the North Koreans pushed southward almost at will. He was alarmed but not surprised that the first American troops to be thrown into the battle were pushed aside as readily as the South Korean troops had been. It appeared to him and others in Hawaii that the Communists might achieve total victory.

Finally, in July, his orders came. He was to report to Camp Pendleton, California. It was Saturday, and he called his wife, Virginia, from work. "Our luck is changing, dear. I'm to report to Camp Pendleton as soon as possible. Can you leave for our home in Virginia Monday morning?"

"Impossible!" his wife screeched. The normally stoic Virginia Puller had lost her cool. But who could blame her? She had three children as well as numerous household items that she would have to prepare for instant movement.

"If I have to prepare to leave immediately," she said tersely, "I don't have time to talk. Goodbye!" She slammed down the receiver.

"That's my girl," Chesty said softly, smiling. He hung up the receiver and started drafting a list of items that must be accomplished prior to departure.

Monday morning came around, and Virginia Puller and the three children were with Chesty Puller at the Pearl Harbor air terminal. "You did it, dear," Chesty said admiringly. "You are the most reliable woman that a man could possibly have for a wife."

"Humph," was the response. But Virginia Puller's mood was brightening. "I hope everything goes just the way you want it to." She obviously realized that her husband was going back into combat, and it would be a long while before she saw him again – if ever.

Chesty kissed his children, said his goodbyes to them, and then turned his attention to his wife. He gave her the commercial airline tickets that would take her and the children from California to Virginia. He was feeling melancholy.

"It gives me comfort to know that you will be waiting for me in the home that we plan to grow old in together."

Tears welled up in Virginia's eyes. "I feel in my bones that you will eventually get your star – way, way after it is due."

A look of sadness came over Chesty's face. "Unfortunately, it will probably come after a lot of young American boys have given their lives. You were right the other day when you said it."

"I was only partially right. Having good men like you leading them will save a number of lives."

The two hugged and kissed passionately. The call came for passengers to board, and soon the airplane was hurtling down the runway. Puller watched the airplane until it was no longer in sight.

Chesty Puller arrived at Camp Pendleton in late July. The camp was really bustling. Men and machines were arriving from all over. It reminded Puller of the military buildup at the start of World War II. He went directly to see the Commander of the First Marine Division, Major General Oliver P. Smith. Puller had known Smith from their student days at Fort Benning, Georgia.

"Great to see you, Lewie. Please have a seat."

Smith said that the First Division was being built from scratch. "And, Lewie, the Commandant himself is rebuilding your old First Regiment, and he is placing you in charge. You're getting everything you want!"

"I only hope it isn't too late," Puller sighed. "The papers say that the North Koreans are now down to a perimeter around the southern port city of Pusan. And I'm afraid that the U.S. Eighth Army and the few Marines who are there won't be able to hold."

"Don't worry about that, Lewie. From what I hear, men and material are arriving every day at Pusan, and I believe they'll be able to dig in and stay put. The big problem will be pushing the North Koreans back where they belong."

The General lit his pipe and continued. "I don't have the foggiest idea how the North Koreans will be pushed out, but I do know that General MacArthur desperately wants the First Marine Division. A man of his strategic ability undoubtedly has a plan. And the Marines will be big players, so it is up to you and the other Regimental Commanders to be ready. Any questions?"

"Sir, I wouldn't know where to begin, so I'll just say 'thank you' and shove off. I have a lot of work to do." The two shook hands, Puller saluted, and then he walked to the door. His big chance was coming, and he wasn't about to botch it.

Puller went directly to the Quartermaster's office. He would have a large number of troops arriving in very short order and would have to have housing facilities. Puller and the Quartermaster, along with a Supply Officer, went to the grassy area that had been set aside for the First Regiment Marines. Puller looked over the area in disgust. The place was a mess. Weeds had grown up all over. Obviously nothing had been done since the end of the last war!

Puller turned to the Supply Officer. "Old man, I need you to send over all possible equipment – stoves, that sort of thing – by nightfall. If my men are going to live in tents while they're here, they deserve to have the proper amenities. Do I make myself clear?"

"Yes, sir! I'll get right on it." The Supply Officer saluted and left in a hurry.

Puller's three battalion commanders and their men arrived from Camp Lejeune, North Carolina the next day. All three were motivated and appeared eager to make their new boss happy. Puller asked about the status of weapons, and the three responded that they were 'fair.' Puller, however, was skeptical. "I'll meet you at the firing range at daybreak. We'll see if your description is accurate."

Chesty Puller was shocked when he found out the actual condition of the men's rifles. He declared that over half of them were unfit for use, and he ordered new ones from the Marines' supply base. When these arrived, a lot of them were also broken. "I won't have my men going into battle with weapons that don't work," he fumed. Somehow, he was able to provide satisfactory weapons to every man going to combat with him.

Puller spent most of his waking hours with his men on the range. He wore old fatigues most of the time, and this led to his being mistakenly called "Gunny" a good deal of the time. He didn't mind, as he was in his element. He simply smiled and waved.

The 16-hour work days were paying off. The men were rounding into shape, and those who were new in the Corps were getting the hang of it. *None of these boys will die due to a lack of training*, Puller thought. *They are turning into a fine fighting machine, and I am proud to call them 'Marines.'*

Puller knew that the call to war would come soon. He had a few last details to take care of. He would need a driver, an adjutant, and someone to ride 'shotgun' when he visited the front. He found the three, and two of them he didn't know. But he looked for and obtained the best available.

The third – the adjutant – was someone Puller had known clear back to his time in Nicaragua. He was happy to have someone in his inner circle that he had previously known and felt comfortable with. Major W. C. Reves filled the bill. His only remaining chore now before shipping out would be to write his beloved wife.

My Dearest

I have been very busy here, but I want you to know that you, Virginia Mac, Martha Leigh, and Lewis are constantly in my thoughts and prayers. I sense that we will be shipping out shortly, so it will be awhile before I can write again. However, I wanted you to know that my command has shaped up nicely, and I feel that my Regiment is now thoroughly trained and ready to go into combat.

Wherever I go, you will always be with me. Please know that you are the most important thing in the world to me. While I hope to finally get a star, the thought of a promotion pales in comparison to thinking of being home with you and the children.

I know that you will always encourage the children to do their best. If they do, we can be very proud of them.

At age 52, I can say that having you as my wife has made me the luckiest man in the world. I love you more than you will ever know.

Yours forever and ever,

Lewis

The order to Puller's First Marine Regiment to board ships finally came. He didn't know where they were going, but he could sure speculate. Korea! That was where the fighting was, and that was the overwhelmingly likely spot. But where in Korea was the question of the hour.

Shortly after boarding the ship, Puller gathered his battalion commanders to pour over maps of Korea. Most came to the conclusion that MacArthur wanted them for an amphibious landing. Several predicted that the most likely spot was Inchon.

"I don't know," Puller said haltingly. "The tides there are unfavorable most of the time, and there are no beaches. But it is the most likely spot, and I hope the Eighth Army can hang on at Pusan until we get there." He adjourned the meeting and let his commanders go back to dealing with personnel matters in their units.

After a long and tedious journey, the First Marine Regiment finally disembarked at Kobe, Japan. It was somewhat of a surprise to end up in Japan. After all, Korea was where the fighting was taking place. But the Marines had to have a place to organize and make preparations, so Kobe was as good a place as any.

Puller called some trusted sergeants in to his temporary office and asked them to scout around town. He was interested in any scuttlebutt that may give them more information on where they would deploy! In the meantime, he planned to talk to the Division Commander, Major General O. P. Smith.

Puller walked the short distance to Smith's office. The door was open, so Puller knocked and walked in. The General looked up. "Come in, Lewie. I was just getting ready to call for you."

Smith related that General Almond, MacArthur's Chief-of-Staff, was on his way to see them. "I think we're going to find out shortly what our mission is. Please have a seat. I want you in the meeting."

Puller nodded and sat down. Shortly, the no-nonsense Ned Almond appeared at the door. The two Marines stood up and shook hands with the visitor.

Laying his briefcase on Smith's desk, Almond hurriedly opened it and took out a map of Korea. "Gentlemen, here is your destination." He thrust his index finger at Inchon. "You will be part of my X-Corps, and we will land there on September 15. Do you have any questions?"

The ever-blunt Chesty Puller said that he did. "To start with, what is your X-Corps?"

"Simply put, X-Corps will have responsibility for the Inchon Landing. I am in command of X-Corps, so the Marines will be working for me."

Both Smith and Puller were flabbergasted, but both knew that there was nothing they could do about it. Both men clammed up.

"If there are no more questions," Almond said, "just be ready to land at Inchon on September 15. I will have members of my staff work closely with you." He shook hands and departed the office.

"I've heard about this Almond," Smith said, shaking his head. "He knows nothing about the Marine Corps. I hope his staff does."

"I wouldn't count on it," Puller replied. "But more importantly, we will be landing at Inchon in just a few days. I hope we can pull it off."

At this instant, Jack MacLaine stuck his head in the doorway. He smiled. "Gentlemen, I'm on General Almond's staff, and it is my duty to interface with you and allay any fears that you may have. Please call me Jack."

Both Smith and Puller unloaded on poor Jack MacLaine. Through it all he continued to smile and nod affirmatively. He said several times that he was in complete agreement with the views of the Leathernecks!

After Smith and Puller had finished venting, MacLaine told them that the landing would take place at 5:00 p.m. on September 15 and that they would have a narrow window to complete the landing. The tides would then recede and would be too low for an amphibious assault. He added that he had been in Inchon recently and helped to accumulate data that were critical to the landing.

After MacLaine departed, the two Marines looked at each other with astonishment on their brows. "I think MacLaine is someone we can work with," Smith exclaimed.

"I hope so," Puller replied with some skepticism. "It just depends on whether he knows enough to stay out of our way."

Puller had his work cut out for him as did other members of the landing party. They would be shoving off in just a few days, and there was no time to waste. Would they be ready? Only time would tell.

Chapter 11

The Brits

Major General Francis Dunbar reached down for the copy of the London Daily Telegraph that was lying in his driveway. *I was afraid of this,* he told himself. The headlines screamed in huge print of the massive amounts of North Korean soldiers and equipment that had poured over the border into South Korea. He felt sure that he would be going to Asia, so he hurried into the house to tell his wife, Carol. His children, Jonathon and Molly, were too young to understand the significance. All they would know was that 'Daddy' was not around.

Francis Dunbar was very sentimental. Thus, he and his wife had named the children after two of his best friends in the previous war. His daughter would have been named Jennifer, but that honor had gone to Jacob Partude's first-born. Through it all, Carol Dunbar was very cooperative. She was just thankful that the two children were healthy!

Dunbar handed the paper to his wife. She glanced at the headlines and looked at him with great concern. "This is just what we thought," she said under her breath. The children were playing nearby, and she didn't want to alarm them.

"Are you sure you'll have to go?" Carol asked quietly.

"Pretty sure. Bill Slim, our Field Marshal, warned me that I would be the one to lead our troops if the catastrophe happened. I'll go see him first thing this morning."

Dunbar ate his breakfast hurriedly. He spent a few minutes playing with the children and then kissed his wife goodbye. "I'll call you as soon as I find out what's going on," he shouted over his shoulder as he walked to the car. She nodded and waved to him. He got in, started the car, and was soon on his way to the Ministry of Defence. He had to watch the speedometer so he wouldn't exceed the speed limit!

Field Marshal Slim was seated behind his desk with the always-serious expression on his face as Francis Dunbar was escorted in. General Slim had been the only British General coming out of the Far East in World War II who hadn't been stained by poor performance. He hadn't been part of the fiasco at Singapore that resulted in the surrender of many thousands of troops, and his performance in Burma was exemplary in every regard. A slight smile came over his face as he looked up and saw who it was.

"Come in, Frank. Always good to see you." The Field Marshal got up and shook hands after the normal military courtesies were extended.

"Sir, I won't bother you for long," Dunbar replied. "I did see by this morning's paper that the North Koreans have done exactly what we expected them to do. Am I still expected to be in charge of the British contingent?"

"You're exactly right, old boy. We have a meeting later this morning with Prime Minister Clement Attlee, and he will let you know what's politically acceptable and unacceptable. Do you have any questions before we see him?"

"Yes, sir. How many troops will I have, and where will they come from?"

"I have been in contact with Hong Kong, and they have about 2,000 British Bobbies that they can make available. I'm now trying to get about 38,000 more troops for you, so you'll have about 40,000 under your command."

Dunbar whistled softly. "That's a serious number. But I suppose I'll be under the thumb of an American General, correct?"

"Yes. From what I know, General MacArthur will be given the overall responsibility for the United Nations troops. Therefore, when our troops are ready and over there, you'll probably report directly to him – or whoever he says. I'll keep you abreast of any news that I receive."

"Oh, and there's one more thing I should tell you," Slim added, "we're having our aircraft carrier 'HMS Triumph' head for the area. We will at least be giving aerial support at the start of the conflict. Naturally, the Navy will have the 'Triumph' skipper report up their own chain of command."

Dunbar nodded. "Just one last question, sir. What time is our meeting with the Prime Minister?"

"1100 sharp. Be here 20 minutes ahead of time, and we'll go together." Dunbar saluted and walked out of the office. He had plenty to do!

Dunbar headed down the hall toward his own office. His mind raced to all that needed to be done, as the British Army – much like the American's – had fallen into disrepair after the last war.

The first thing he needed to do was to select those officers who would be in charge of the various units. He wouldn't accept just anyone into positions of leadership. Instead, he would be quite selective. Then, once this process was completed, the leaders could get down to the serious business of checking weaponry. It had been about five years since some of these weapons had even been fired. They couldn't expect a lot of these to be in combat-ready condition. He would have to make this point clear to Prime Minister Attlee and – to a lesser extent – Field Marshal Slim. The Field Marshal was already aware of the situation, but Dunbar would have to make sure that Slim wouldn't be overwhelmed by political expediency. It would be awhile before the British were ready to tangle with anyone, particularly a well-trained group such as the North Koreans.

Dunbar stuck his head in the office of Major Brian Hawkins. "We need to talk." He motioned for the young Major to follow him. Soon they were at Dunbar's office, and Dunbar motioned for Hawkins to have a seat. Dunbar then went around his desk and sat down.

Dunbar looked at the major for a moment. *How fortunate I am that he's on my staff.* At moments like this, general officers wanted men that they could trust. And, over the years, Brian Hawkins had proven himself to be quite trustworthy. Dunbar was indeed fortunate to have him.

"I suppose you know that the North Koreans have attacked." Hawkins nodded and Dunbar continued. "We'll be getting into the fray very shortly. I'm going with Field Marshal Slim this morning to talk to the Prime Minister. After I get back, I'll need you to work with me to decide who will be in charge of the various units and what the conditions of the weapons are. We will have to get those that are out of shape into shape in a hurry."

"Very good, sir. "Do you know the number of men who will be sent from the U.K.?"

"Slim thinks it will be about 40,000."

Hawkins looked amazed. "We do have our work cut out for us, don't we sir?"

"I can't argue with that, but we don't have a choice. We have to get it done."

"I'll make some calls and be ready to talk when you return," Hawkins replied.

"Great! I knew I could depend on you."

Hawkins saluted, and, after his salute was returned, he left the office. Dunbar checked his watch, and it was time for him to return to Field Marshal Slim's office. Soon, they would depart for their meeting with Clement Atlee. Dunbar knew that the Prime Minister would not want to get into the military details. Rather, Dunbar expected him to be consumed with how they would pay for the operation!

Field Marshal Slim and Major General Dunbar were led into the Prime Minister's office by the secretary. The Prime Minister was gazing off into space, definitely deep in thought. He finally looked at his visitors. "Let's sit at the table." He motioned for the two to sit at the side. He got up from his desk and went to the chair at the head. He plopped down.

"Sir, I think you know General Dunbar," the Field Marshal commenced.

"Yes, good to see you again," the Prime Minister answered. He stuck out his hand, and Dunbar grasped it firmly. The two shook hands, and Dunbar eased back into his chair after the greeting was concluded.

"I have to tell you," the Prime Minister stated, "that this is uncharted territory for me. During the last war, when I was Deputy Prime Minister, Winston took care of the military issues, and I handled the economy. Now I guess I will have to do them both."

"Not necessarily, sir," the Field Marshal replied. "Dunbar here will lead our military effort, and he is a very capable officer. He is well versed in all of the military aspects."

"I'm sure he is, which is all well and good. That means I can go back to worrying about how we'll pay for it!" The Prime Minister shook his head, and his two visitors nodded in agreement.

Just as I thought, Dunbar told himself as he tried to hide the amused look on his face. *The Prime Minister will work the economic issues and leave the fighting to us. Not bad!*

"By the way," the Prime Minister asked Dunbar, "how is Winston? You're good friends with him, are you not?"

"Yes, sir. I haven't seen him in a while, but I plan to in the next few days."

"Please tell him hello for me."

"Will do."

Slim and Dunbar gave an overview of how they planned to support the United Nations war effort. It was very 'sketchy,' but it was all they could do at the present time.

"Keep me filled in as your plans firm up," the Prime Minister said. Field Marshal Slim said that they would. The three shook hands, and the Prime Minister went back to his desk, sat down, and gazed off into space.

"I wouldn't want his job for all of the money in the world," Slim said after they were out of earshot range.

"I wouldn't either," Dunbar replied.

It was early the next morning when General Dunbar headed for Chartwell, the country estate of Sir Winston Churchill. Dunbar was authorized a driver but – as he did this time – he usually drove himself. *It will be good to see the old boy again,* he thought. *How long has it been? Two years? At least!*

Dunbar pulled onto the mansion grounds and up to the main home. He looked out over the sloping grounds and there he was – Winston Churchill with paint brush in hand and the ever-present cigar in his mouth. Churchill was painting the vast grounds that adjoined the sprawling home. Dunbar got out of his car and briskly walked to where the old man was seated.

"Good morning, Sir Winston," he called out, barely able to hide the glee he felt in seeing his comrade from the previous war. Churchill slowly looked around, obviously not as agile as he once was.

"Good morning to you," Churchill replied, extending his right hand after shifting the paintbrush to his left hand. The two men shook, and Churchill started to get up. Dunbar reached down to help him, noticing that the old man was somewhat feebler than when they were last together. They walked to the house, where the butler swung the door open for them.

"Let's go to the study where we can have a good chat," Churchill said.

"Right behind you," Dunbar replied.

The two men walked down a hallway to the spacious study. Churchill motioned for Dunbar to take a seat in a chair next to his.

"Whiskey," Churchill clamored. An aide brought two glasses and a bottle, pouring a glass for his boss. Churchill took a big gulp and motioned for a glass to be given to his guest. Dunbar declined, asking for a cup of tea instead.

"What brings you here, my boy?" Churchill asked.

"For one thing, sir, it's been too long since I've seen you. Another is that I wanted to bring you up to speed on the Korean situation."

"Ah – the real purpose of your visit. I suppose that my old deputy, Clement Attlee, suggested you brief me. After all, he is astute enough to realize that I will probably replace him as Prime Minister in the near future."

"And the Prime Minister said to give you his best."

"I'll bet he did," Churchill grumped.

Talk about being between a rock and a hard spot. Better be careful. I don't want to upset either my present boss or my potential future one!

"I don't know about the Prime Minister's intentions, Sir Winston, but I have been told to let you know what we're intending to do. Please keep in mind that what I am going to tell you is for your information only."

Churchill nodded. "Okay, let's hear it." Churchill relit his cigar and settled back into his chair.

Dunbar went over estimated troop levels and approximate shipment schedules. He was surprised to find that Churchill's mind seemed to wander as the briefing transpired. *What a difference from when he was last Prime Minister!* Should he have retired from public life after the last war as some people thought? Maybe so.

Dunbar finished the briefing. "I have to ask, Sir Winston. Do you really want to be Prime Minister again?"

"A good question, and to tell you the truth, I don't have a good answer. My writing is going better than it ever has, and I am not in arrears on any of my debts. Better yet, I am building up enough money to give my family security. When I go back into public office, I will have to give up my other income sources. But, of course, if my country calls, I must answer."

Dunbar marveled at the depth of the answer. "Well put, sir."

The rest of the meeting was spent on lighter subjects. Churchill gave the status of his family members, and Dunbar responded with how his family was doing. Dunbar showed pictures of his wife and children, and Churchill seemed genuinely interested.

Dunbar prepared to leave, and Churchill said to come again but at a much smaller interval. "Besides," Churchill added, "I will need you in my Administration if I am re-elected."

Dunbar nodded and smiled, shook the older man's hand, and started to walk out of the study.

"And remember," Churchill called after his guest. "Our fate hangs with that of the Americans!"

Dunbar indicated his agreement, even though he wasn't so sure. But if Churchill once again became Prime Minister, Dunbar would have no choice but to go along – at least if he wanted to remain in the military.

Churchill rose partially out of his chair. "Oh, and one other thing – tell that American nurse hello for me if you're ever in contact with her again!" The former Prime Minister obviously hated to see his guest leave.

"Jennifer?" Dunbar asked as he neared the exit to the study. "I sure will." Dunbar also felt a pang of sorrow as their meeting was now in the past.

The butler bid Dunbar farewell as the general walked to his car. *The meeting went well,* Dunbar told himself. And he felt that he definitely had job security, even if the leadership changed!

It was mid-afternoon by the time Dunbar arrived back at the Ministry of Defense Building. He quickly updated Field Marshal Slim on his meeting with Sir Winston Churchill. Then he headed directly for the office of Brian Hawkins. When he got there, Hawkins was pouring over material on his desk.

Hawkins looked up, smiled, and stood up. "How was your meeting with Sir Winston?"

"About as I expected," Dunbar replied. "Sir Winston was definitely interested in what we will be doing, but – I hate to say it – I am concerned about him. His mind seemed to drift at times."

"But how old is he now?" Hawkins countered. "Seventy-five? At that age, most of us will be pushing up daisies!"

Dunbar laughed. "I can't argue with that. What have you got for me?"

Hawkins enthusiastically shared his progress. "I have contacted the commander of the Royal Marines, and he is all for them being in the fight.

I firmly believe that we need them to head up our effort. After all, we want to make a good showing, and they're the best we have."

"I couldn't agree more," Dunbar replied, "but Field Marshal Slim tells me that our folks in Hong Kong have agreed to send 2,000 military police, and they are going to arrive there very shortly, ahead of when our Marines will be ready for deployment."

"Not a problem, sir, but I did want to mention something that is way over my pay grade."

"Oh, and what is that?"

"I think we can get substantial support from members of the commonwealth such as Australia, New Zealand, and Canada. However, it will take someone with the necessary political horsepower to contact them."

"Valid point. I will bring it up to Slim, who I'm sure will ask Prime Minister Attlee. After all, the Prime Minister – in our meeting with him – seemed rather lost as to what he should be doing to help the military. This will give him a good, solid task."

"Good work!" Dunbar added as he walked to the door to leave. "Keep at it."

Dunbar walked the short distance to his own office, greeted his secretary, entered his office, and went to his desk. Dunbar sat down in his massive chair. *The paperwork never ends,* he thought as he viewed the stack of papers on his desk. He answered those of an urgent nature and put the rest in his In-basket. He viewed the time, and he saw that he just had time to get home and kiss his children before they went to bed. *Time flies when you're having fun and probably even when you aren't!* He turned out the lights, bid his secretary goodnight, and went to his car. The evening traffic was heavy, but it didn't bother him. After all, the objectives of the day had been accomplished!

Dunbar arrived home just as his wife, Carol, was tucking the children into bed. The youngsters were obviously delighted to see him, and Carol had trouble keeping them from jumping up! And Dunbar, of course, was no help. He started rough-housing with them, and all three were enjoying the playtime immensely. Finally, Dunbar noticed Carol's stern look, so he herded the children back under the covers.

"That's all, folks!" he said in his best cartoon drawl. Giggling, the children waited for the goodnight kiss from their parents. The lights went out, and the bedroom got quiet. *I wish I could get to sleep that easily,*

Dunbar thought. He took his wife's hand, and they went to the kitchen. She took up his dinner, and Dunbar recounted his time with the former Prime Minister.

"How is he?" she asked.

"Well, I think he's alert for his age," Dunbar replied between bites. *No use telling her about my unsubstantiated concerns.*

Dunbar finished eating and told his wife that he should get a quick note off to Jennifer. After all, it had been quite some time since he had written, and he was sure that she would like to know that he would be heading for Korea. Carol concurred, so Dunbar went to his study, sat down at the desk, and took out pen and paper.

Dear Jennifer

It has been some time since I have written you, so I thought I should give you an update. Carol and the children are fine, and the children are growing at an unbelievable pace. They are both walking, speaking, and (fortunately) learning at a rapid clip. Needless to say, I am very proud of Carol and the two of them.

You have probably guessed that I will be going to Korea. Field Marshal Slim, who is now head of the Army, has selected me to lead our ground contingent over there. It is probably more due to my rank than any of the talents that I may have. In any case, I am trying to get a representative group of fighters together that will do Great Britain proud. This is proving to be a not-too-easy task. As with your military, ours has been left adrift since the end of the last war.

I hope that you and Jack MacLaine are doing well. Carol and I greatly appreciated your informing us of your engagement. Personally, I think Jack will make a great husband for you, and he certainly has my approval!

We got a letter from Molly saying that she and Summerfield are new parents and that he was able to get a short leave to come home from Tokyo and see the baby. With the flare-up in Korea, it will probably be some time before he can return. I will hope and pray that the war there ends soon.

And what about you, dear Jennifer? I know that quality nurses are hard to come by and that the Army would love to have you back in uniform. Any chance of this?

All for now and my very best to you always,
Frank

Dunbar sealed the envelope, addressed it, and put a stamp on it. He slumped back in his chair. It is true that Bill Summerfield would miss a lot of his child's formative days. But so would Dunbar! Would the Korean War end quickly, or would China and the Soviet Union eventually enter in? Nobody knew. However, this little 'police action' had the potential to really expand, and certainly not for the better. Dunbar knew this, and he was convinced that his superiors did, too.

Chapter 12

Otto

Otto Bruner sat reading the morning paper and having a cup of coffee. As was his usual habit, he had gotten up well ahead of his wife, Kat, and children, Klaus and Liesl. Klaus, named after his deceased brother, was now 3. Liesl had been named after Otto's older sister and was a year younger at 2. Luckily for Otto, Kat went along with naming the children after two people who were very near and dear to his heart.

The paper was full of the North Korean attack on South Korea. Naturally, the paper took the position that the North Koreans were fully justified. After all, Otto and his family lived in East Berlin, which was nothing more than a puppet city for the Soviet Communists. While Otto wished that he had access to more objective reporting, he had to take what was available. And, as Kat kept reminding him, he would have to keep his criticism very muted. If he were open about it, he would not only lose his well-paying job in the STASI Secret Police. He could also be imprisoned and – worse yet – could lose his life.

Rubbish! Otto told himself as he threw the paper down. *The North Koreans had no justification whatsoever. Saying that they were simply trying to reunite the peninsula didn't make any sense. The people of the South were starting up a fledgling democracy, while the people up north were under the harsh rule of a tyrant and dictator, Kim Il-sung.* But Kim Il-sung was being backed by the Chinese Communists and the Soviet regime. Hence, the

North Koreans were definitely the 'good guys' according to the biased reporting that Otto was being subjected to.

Working for STASI does have its advantages, Otto mused. Having access to Intelligence documents did allow him to have a realistic view of what was actually happening in the world. But he doubted that it would have much impact on his fellow workers at STASI. After all, they were mainly ex-Nazis who were a brutish bunch who believed in dealing harshly with any dissent. *No wonder ordinary East Germans by and large hated STASI. Under any other government, these thugs would undoubtedly be in prison.*

"I heard your grumbling," Kat said as she walked into the kitchen, tying the belt in front of her robe. "What is causing your dissatisfaction?" she asked as she poured a cup of coffee for herself and refreshed Otto's.

Otto picked the newspaper up off of the kitchen floor. "See this?" He said, pointing to the headlines. "Our paper says that the North Koreans are right for attacking South Korea and that the peninsula should be one entity. I totally disagree."

Kat sat down at the table and started reading the column to which Otto was referring. Between sips of coffee, her expression became more intense. She finally completed the article after turning to page 2.

"I see what you mean," Kat said as she looked at Otto. "But remember, your bosses at STASI will expect you to back the party line, and that will mean to enthusiastically endorse what the North Koreans are doing."

"I know, but how long can I continue doing it?"

Kat put her hand softly on his. "For as long as you have to," she replied quietly. "After all, the animals where you work will kill you just as quickly as they would anyone else who disagreed with them. And I couldn't stand for that to happen."

Otto nodded. "I do have some potentially good news. I received word that Walter Ulbricht, the First Secretary of the Socialist Unity Party, wants to see me right away. He is the real power behind our government – the Soviets actually like him and trust him! Perhaps he has a job in mind for me, and I can get out of STASI before the East German people become fed up and overthrow the regime."

Kat shuddered. "If that were to happen, the Soviet tanks would come rolling back in as they did toward the end of the last war. It would be catastrophic." She grasped Otto's hands tightly. "I will hope and pray that you can get out of STASI. You are a kind and wonderful man in every way and don't belong there."

Otto was pleased but obviously concerned. "I just hope that I won't be jumping from the frying pan into the fire."

Kat smiled. "I think that God may be giving you a change so that you can exercise your real strength in life – standing up for what is good and right. You have done it in the past, and you must continue doing it in the present and future."

Kat and Otto hugged and kissed. *How wonderful it is to have a wife that thinks so highly of me. I mustn't let her down.*

"Do you think you should mention your association with Field Marshal von Paulus during the last war?" Kat asked.

"I've been wondering the same thing. Ulbricht certainly knows von Paulus, but, unfortunately, the Field Marshal has been spending all of his time and energy trying to justify why he surrendered the German Sixth Army at Stalingrad. After all, he is the only Field Marshal in German history to have surrendered an entire Army."

Otto paused for a moment, then continued. "And, of course, Ulbricht has been a communist for a long time. He actually lived in the Soviet Union from 1937 to 1945, and, after von Paulus surrendered the Sixth Army in early 1943, Ulbricht was in charge of the festivities in Moscow celebrating the defeat. Underneath, he may have a strong dislike for von Paulus, since von Paulus fought for the anti-communist Adolf Hitler."

"I see what you mean. It's just a thought that I had. I want you to succeed if at all possible."

"I sincerely appreciate that, and I don't want anyone to think that I don't appreciate what von Paulus did for me. If he hadn't sent me to Battalion Officers' School in France, I would probably have perished at Stalingrad."

"Just like my first husband did," Kat replied softly and somewhat morbidly. She momentarily showed sadness, which Otto was quick to notice. He hugged her tightly, recalling that her first husband had died on the Russian Front. *What a dummy I am!*

"It certainly isn't your fault," Kat said, recovering quickly. She looked at her watch. "My word, it's getting late. I have to start your breakfast, and the sooner the better." She went to the small refrigerator and took out eggs and sausage. "Unfortunately, I only have rather stale bread. I hope it will do."

"As long as it is brown bread," Otto replied smiling. He knew he could ply the bread with lots of jam to make it better. And he hoped his response would cheer his wife.

The smell of breakfast cooking woke the children. Klaus came out rubbing his eyes. He was followed shortly by Liesl.

"Guten Morgen," Otto said cheerfully. The two children hugged their father and went over to see what their mother was cooking. Kat greeted them warmly and went about the business of taking up the food. She had set four places at the kitchen table and placed a helping of eggs, sausage, toast, and porridge at each place. She then helped the children into their special chairs. Otto said a short prayer, and the four began to eat.

How lucky I am, Otto thought as he peered at the other three busily devouring the food in front of them. He couldn't help but think back to his futile situation of just a few years earlier. He never dreamed that his life would be so full after Jennifer had abruptly abandoned him in the hospital in Normandy. *It just goes to show that one should never give up hope.* He would have to remember this philosophy when he met later that day with Ulbricht. After all, what happened in the near term may completely camouflage what is to transpire later on.

Otto finished eating and looked at his watch. "Wow," he said. "I'm really going to have to hurry." He got up, kissed his children, and then turned to kiss his wife.

"Wait a minute," she said, swallowing quickly. "I'll get my jacket and walk you to the car." She got up and hurried out of the kitchen. The two children looked up with puzzlement on their faces, obviously not sure of what was happening. They quickly returned to eating.

"Good, but you'll have to hurry." Otto said to his wife. He took the suit coat off the back of his chair and put it on. He then started walking to the door. Soon, Kat was by his side, and the two went out, walking arm in arm.

"I can't tell you how much I hope you'll be getting a new job and transferring out of STASI," Kat said. "You're much too good a man to be associating with those people."

Otto sighed. "I thank you for your kind words. I feel deep down inside that I should be serving the people of Germany, and for that matter, the world. But I just don't know how to do it."

"Trust in God," Kat replied. "I believe that it is He who has led you through the chaos. I also believe he has big things in store for you."

"I hope you're right, and I hope He gives me a sign pretty soon. The waiting can be exasperating."

The two kissed, and Otto got in his car. He started the motor and slowly backed out of the driveway. He waved to his wife as he turned onto the street, and she soon disappeared from the rear view mirror as he drove away.

All kinds of thoughts raced through his mind as he drove into work. Even though he was very happy with Kat, his thoughts turned to Jennifer. *What was she doing now? Was she married? Did she have children? Would she be nursing wounded soldiers back to health – as she had been doing for him – now that America would be back in a fight?* He shook his head. *Why can't I just contact her? What right do the Soviets have to prevent people like me from contacting people on the other side?* It didn't make any sense, but that's the way things were. It would be up to people like him to right the situation. Just how they would do it was the big issue.

He came to a fork in the road and swerved to the right. He would go see Ulbricht now! After all, a time hadn't been set for their meeting, so it would be better to have it sooner rather than later. He would call his boss at STASI to let him know as soon as he arrived at Ulbricht's office. He had gotten a reputation at STASI as being very dependable, and he didn't want that to change. Thus, he should let his boss at STASI know right away that he was on official business and that he would be in to work as soon as possible.

Otto pulled into the parking lot at Ulbricht's office complex. He stopped the motor, got out, and went in. There was no doubt as to which way he should proceed to get to Ulbricht's office. After arriving at the outer office, he went up to the secretary, explained his situation, and asked if he could see Herr Ulbricht. He used the phone on her desk to call STASI while she went to check on the availability of her boss.

Otto finished his call and went to a chair. He had no sooner sat down than the secretary returned. "Herr Ulbricht will see you now," she said sternly.

Otto thanked her and went to the open door. He peered in before entering, and there he was. The great man was sitting at his desk, reading a medium-thick document. Finally, he looked up and motioned for Otto to come in.

"You must be Herr Bruner," Ulbricht said as he rose from his chair to come around and welcome his guest.

"Yes, sir," Otto replied. The two shook hands, and Ulbricht motioned for them to go to the table at one side of the room. Ulbricht plopped down in a chair at the head of the table, and Otto sat down next to him.

Ulbricht initiated the conversation. "I guess you wonder why I asked you to come over." Otto nodded, and Ulbricht continued. "I reviewed your background, and you seem to be just the man I'm looking for. You have a sparkling background, and I think the East German people would respect you in a position of authority. Do you have any hesitation to run for an office?"

Obviously, Ulbricht felt that the elections were rigged and the people would vote for whoever the party backed. Otherwise, they could expect the Russian T-34 tanks to roll in once again.

"I don't have any hesitation to run," Otto responded, "but I do want to help the people all that I can."

Ulbricht studied his guest for a moment as his face became flushed. "And you don't think I want to help the people? Let me tell you something! I was against Hitler from the start. I knew he would lead this country to destruction, and he certainly did. That is why I spent a number of years living in Communist Russia. Do I think the Communists – and Stalin in particular – have all of the answers? Certainly not! But we are stuck with them for now, and we will have to do our best to accommodate all involved."

Otto was taken aback by Ulbricht's outburst. "I'm sorry, sir. I didn't mean to imply anything. I think you are doing an outstanding job."

Ulbricht nodded and calmed down somewhat before continuing. "I have heard that you think Field Marshal von Paulus is a saint. Let me assure you he isn't. It was another of Hitler's monumental blunders to put him in charge of the Sixth Army. A more capable officer could have prevented the surrender, and it will help you in your career if you forget about him."

Otto was shocked. "But, sir, I do believe that I wouldn't be here today if the Field Marshal hadn't sent me to Battalion Officers' School in France."

"Let me tell you something, Bruner. You deserved to be sent to that school based on your performance. You owe von Paulus nothing."

Otto nodded. "What, sir, do you want me to do if I may ask?"

"Good question. I have set up an office for you right down the hall, and you will work directly for me. I will tutor and counsel you if you accept my offer. Do you?"

"Of course, sir. I will move today if you so desire."

Ulbricht smiled and nodded. "I hoped you would say that." He walked over, closed the door, and walked back over and sat down before continuing. "Bruner, we will have some conversations that are not meant to leave this office. I want you to know that the East German people are my first concern, and I will do my best to serve them."

"I feel much better hearing you say that, and I will work very hard to support you in every way that I can."

The two shook hands, and Ulbricht said that he wanted Otto to move into his new office today. "I will provide you with whatever help you need."

"I very much appreciate the opportunity," Otto replied.

Ulbricht went to his desk and picked up the phone. He ordered his secretary to get two men to help Otto with his move. By the time Otto left Ulbricht's office, the men were waiting in the outer area. Otto introduced himself to the men and thanked the secretary. "We will be seeing much more of each other," he told her as he left her office with the two helpers.

"I know," she replied. Obviously, her sixth sense had kicked in, and she believed Otto would be coming over.

Otto told his boss at STASI that he would be leaving. As expected, his boss was not surprised, nor did he try and convince Otto to stay. *Either he knows it would be futile to try and stop the move, or perhaps he just doesn't care. Probably the latter,* Otto told himself.

The two men quickly packed up Otto's belongings and waited for direction from him. "Just take the boxes to my new office," he said. "I'll meet you there."

Otto drove the short distance to his new office, got out of his car, and walked into the building. "Is he in?" Otto asked the secretary.

"No, he isn't, but he told me to tell you that you can use me for any administrative needs you have and that he will see you first thing in the morning."

"Good. I'll be here at 8:00 a.m. tomorrow, and I don't believe I'll need you the rest of the day."

The secretary nodded, and Otto walked the short distance to his new office. The two men were waiting for him with the several boxes they had collected from his STASI dwellings. He told them where to put the books and where the other items that he had brought with him would go. They finished up, Otto thanked them, and they left.

Not bad, Otto thought. His new office was good-sized, and the desk was about twice the size of his old one. He noticed that reading material had been placed on the desk. *Undoubtedly communist propaganda,* he mused.

The documents were well written but alarming. They relayed Stalin's plans for eventually incorporating Eastern European countries into the Soviet Union. The plans included East Germany.

Otto shook his head. *East Europeans are much too stubborn to accept a plan such as this. Stalin will be lucky if these people don't eventually break away and form their own sovereign state. I must do everything I can to ensure that these people are once again free.*

It was very evident to Otto that he must proceed with the utmost caution. It wouldn't do anyone any good for him to be considered a traitor and thrown into prison or possibly face a worse eventuality.

Otto looked at his watch, and he had to admit that the day had flown by. It was time for him to close his office and go home. He moved material into his desk drawers and locked up. The thought of telling Kat about his day excited him, so he quickly walked to the doorway and turned off the lights. He waved goodnight to the secretary as he walked past the entrance to her office. *She is obviously very dedicated, as she is working late. A good sign!*

Otto pulled into the driveway of his home. Kat was out playing with the children. She waved, and the children came running over as he stopped the car. He got out and kissed his children. Then he went over to his wife.

"You'll never believe what happened today," he said excitedly as he bent down and kissed her.

"Let's go inside, and you can tell me all about it." Kat motioned for the children to come over, and she grasped their hands. The four walked into the house and peeled their coats and hats. Klaus and Liesl ran into the living room to play some more, and Otto and Kat went to the kitchen table and sat down. Kat asked him if he wanted something to drink, and Otto shook his head.

"Now tell me all about it," she said as her eyes sparkled, "and don't leave out any of the details!"

"The bottom line is that I now work for Herr Ulbricht. I have an office right down the hall from him, and he will be coaching me to run for office! Apparently, he believes that my background will put me in good grace with the East German people."

"I couldn't agree more," Kat replied. "Your record is spotless, and, needless to say, I am very, very proud of you. You can count on my vote any time."

Sadness came over Otto's face. "If only the elections were free, they would mean so much more. I'm afraid that I'll never be anything more than a puppet for the Communists – at least in the foreseeable future."

"But you have to start somewhere," Kat countered, "and running for office in East Germany is as good a place to begin as any."

Otto nodded, but the sadness remained, and a distant look came into his eyes. Kat seemed to sense that something was still wrong.

"Okay, what is it? She asked. "I know that something is wrong."

"Nothing, really. It's just that I promised Jennifer –"

Kat cut him off. "Her again! I should have known! What is it now?"

"It's just that I promised that I would always be ready to help her, and I can't even contact her. It's now been several years since I've been in touch with her at all!"

Kat was obviously having trouble getting her emotions under control. Finally, she succeeded. "Okay, here is what I suggest. Write a letter to her telling her of your new position. Tell her that you will always be here for her in case she needs you. I'll start dinner now."

Kat was still obviously upset as she went to the small refrigerator. *Uh-oh. I've really done it now.* Otto got up and went over to his wife. "Thank you, as always. You have been a huge help." He kissed her softly on the lips.

"Go on, get out of here!" Kat said with mock anger.

"I'm going! I'm going!" Otto replied as he headed to his study. He kissed Klaus and Liesl as he hurried through the living room. He entered his study and he went to the small desk pushed up against a wall. He took out pencil and paper.

Dear Jennifer
I hope you haven't given up on me, as I think of you often. I am writing this letter, which is long overdue and at my wife's insistence. The reason that

it has taken so long is that – as I'm sure you know – I have to be very careful. If my bosses found out that I am contacting you, it would be the end for me.

I don't expect to hear back from you, and I hope you don't try. The reason is, of course, that it would be very dangerous for both of us. Your Senator McCarthy seems to be on a witch hunt, just like my "comrades" are looking for reasons to do away with anyone that they can.

I do have so many questions about you. Are you married? Do you have children? Are you working? And perhaps most of all, I am wondering if you will go to Korea to once again serve your country. Yes, the East Berlin newspaper has carried the story about North Korea attacking South Korea. The paper, of course, says that the attack was totally justified.

I am now married to a wonderful woman – Kat – that I think I told you about. We have two children – Klaus and Liesl – that fulfill our lives. I can only hope that you have been as fortunate as I have been. And, if I remember correctly, the young man that you were trying to save that fateful day would do great justice to my hope for you.

I also want to tell you that I got a new job today. It is possible that I will be running for public office in the future! If so, it may be more convenient for me to try and contact you in the future.

In closing, I want to reconfirm that I will always be here for you if you need me. Somehow, I will come to your aid if the need arises. Please always remember that.

All for now and my very best wishes always,
Otto

What a relief! Otto thought. He had felt guilty for a long time for not trying to contact Jennifer and to let her know that he was still here for her. With this burden lifted, he would be able to concentrate on getting ahead in his occupational field. If he accomplished this objective, it would be good not only for his family, but for those other folks who he had become attached to along the way. Primary in this latter category was his American nurse from World War II – Jennifer Haraldsson!

Part 3

Chapter 13

Buildup and Crossover

Colonel Chesty Puller and his battalion commanders poured over the maps of Korea, and in particular, Inchon. Puller and his men were in Kobe, Japan, but they were anxious to get what they considered the greatest amphibious landing in history under way. While General MacArthur was confident that the Marines could take Inchon, cut off the North Koreans, and have peace restored by Christmas, Puller wasn't so sure. After all, there wasn't a beach at Inchon. Rather, there were just sea walls and jetties, as the city of Inchon came right up to the water. Would the 250,000 people of Inchon be glad to see the Marines? Puller thought so – at least he hoped so. After all, some fine young men of the United States – as well as South Korea and other members of the United Nations – would give their lives to throw the invaders out.

Another perplexing problem was that, based on reports back from his sergeants, the news of the soon-to-be Inchon landings was all over Kobe, in bordellos as well as on the streets. Thus, there would be no element of surprise. The only doubt would be when the attack would occur, and that would be dictated more by tides than by skillful planning. Puller could only shake his head, knowing that there were a lot of issues in favor of the adversaries. But he knew that the United States Marines would have to be successful, as victory would be the only acceptable outcome. Semper Fi!

Puller's constant companion was Army Colonel Jack MacLaine. And there was now another player from the Army: Major Jim Sherman. While

Chesty openly detested the relationship, he secretly felt that they could be much more of a pain in the neck than they actually were. After all, neither MacLaine nor Sherman interfered. Instead, they seemed more in awe of the Marines than anything else. And they never gave advice unless it was requested.

Late one evening, Puller asked MacLaine if he and Sherman could join him for a drink at the Officers' Club. "Sure" was the response. The three headed for Puller's jeep. Puller got in front with the driver, and MacLaine and Sherman jumped in the back. Soon they were on their way. The jeep stopped in front of the club, and the three passengers got out. Puller returned the driver's salute. "Come back in about an hour and a half," Puller ordered. "Yes, sir," the driver said, as he drove off into the pitch-black night. The three walked to the front door and entered. Soon, they were seated at a table in the bar. A waiter came and took their orders.

"First of all, I want to thank you," Puller said.

"For what?" MacLaine asked curiously.

"For not interfering. I appreciate it."

Jim Sherman smiled, and Puller asked what was so funny. "Nothing," Sherman replied. "It's just that we know better than to interfere. Your reputation has preceded you."

All three laughed as their drinks arrived. After a few sips, all seemed to relax and become more open.

"I have to tell you," Puller said, "I'm very surprised that your big boss asked for us. He's been an enemy of the Marines for nearly all of his career."

"Yes," MacLaine responded, "but for him to be successful, he needs the best, and that is you."

"Thank you," Puller replied. The three clinked their glasses.

"Tell me about yourselves," Puller continued. "I know very little of your backgrounds."

MacLaine related his experiences in the Philippines during World War II and about his Intelligence work after the war ended. Sherman said that he had been in the Far East during the war and that he had gotten into Intelligence work after the war. MacLaine added that he was engaged to be married.

"Congratulations, old man!" Puller exclaimed. "Marriage has been the happiest part of my life." He took out pictures of his wife and three children. Both MacLaine and Sherman were duly impressed.

As the night went on, there was even more camaraderie. "I have to ask you," MacLaine said. "Why is it the Marines have gotten such a distaste for General MacArthur?"

"Two reasons, old man," Puller replied as he lit his pipe. "Number one, he is too fond of the "I" word. He didn't take anything – his troops did. And number 2, he convinced President Roosevelt that the Philippines should be taken toward the end of the last war. Our boss, Admiral Nimitz, felt that it should be bypassed."

MacLaine nodded. "But I must say that I'm glad MacArthur won. Otherwise, I would have been in the Philippine mountains for a much longer time."

Before MacLaine could continue, Sherman butted in. "I think a lot of Army men agree with your rationale on the "I" word. But as far as strategic planning, there is none better than MacArthur. He lost fewer men in his whole campaign than Eisenhower lost during the Battle of the Bulge. He really understood better than anyone how to use the Army, Navy, and Air Force in a coordinated manner. Few Army men actually realize that and are grateful that we had MacArthur to lead us over here."

"I can't argue with that, old man," Puller replied in his usual fashion. Here once again he was using 'old man' in generic fashion. After taking a puff on his pipe, Puller continued, looking directly at Sherman. "And how about you? Do you have any romantic interests at the present time?"

"No, not really. I like several of the Geisha girls, but nothing serious."

MacLaine winked at Puller. "He's known as a ladies' man to a number of the Geishas." The three laughed.

Puller looked at his watch. "Our hour and a half is about up, so my driver should be out there." The three reached into their pockets to pay for the tab, but Puller wouldn't hear of it. "This is my treat, as you are my guests." He took out some bills and dropped them on the table. The others thanked him, and they got up to leave. Soon, they were out in the night air, and Puller was correct. His jeep was waiting for them.

The next morning, MacLaine and Sherman attended the briefing that Puller was giving to his regimental commanders. "We will leave Kobe on September 12," Puller began. "This will give us time to rendezvous with the large naval ships and the aircraft carriers that will soften the enemy before we land at Inchon on September 15."

127

He then turned the briefing over to his Intelligence Officers to show the layout at Inchon and the defensive emplacements. He obviously thought the Intelligence folks were blowing the defenses out of proportion.

"Wait a minute!" Puller growled. "A lot of those will be taken out by the Navy warships and the Navy planes. I want you to be very positive when you talk to your troops. For God's sake, don't be negative. This operation will be a success – period!"

"Yes, sir" rippled through his command team.

The Intelligence Personnel finished their briefing, and Puller made some closing remarks. He told his commanders to make sure the troops stayed fit by doing running in place exercises among others. He also said to have the troops leave their leggings on, as the enemy would know by the leggings that they were facing the much-feared United States Marines.

"That is all," Puller barked as he closed the activities. His commanders popped to attention and left after they were formally dismissed. MacLaine and Sherman remained, and Puller motioned for them to come up.

Puller waited for his commanders to exit the briefing room. Then he started in. "I have to appear very confident to the men, but I do have reservations. Here we are about to start on the biggest operation of its kind, and we are doing it with some inexperienced men in key command positions. Don't get me wrong. These are outstanding men, but a number of them do lack experience. To my way of thinking, the Marine corps has made a big mistake in forcing officers to have staff assignments. These assignments are good in peacetime, but they don't hold up in combat situations. But now, you have the Secretary of the Navy – a good man I'm sure – telling the Marine Corps how to conduct its business." Puller could only shake his head.

Jack MacLaine tried to assuage Puller's concerns. "It may be true that some of the officers are inexperienced, but the Marine corps, fortunately, still has outstanding, experienced men like you. I'm sure that fact influenced General MacArthur to insist on having the Marines lead the Inchon landings."

Puller nodded. He was obviously pleased by the vote of confidence.

"Well," MacLaine said, "we better leave and let you get back to work." Pleasantries were exchanged, and MacLaine and Sherman walked to the door. "We'll be in our offices if you need us," MacLaine added as they departed. Their offices were only a short distance away in improvised quarters. Soon, they were at MacLaine's small post, and he motioned for Sherman to come in. MacLaine poured two cups of coffee from a small coffee maker that was on a table in a corner of the room. MacLaine sat at his desk, and Sherman pulled up the single card table chair that had been unceremoniously brought in.

Sherman took a sip of the black coffee and then looked at his boss. "I've heard all of Puller's strengths, but I haven't heard any of his weaknesses. Surely he has some."

MacLaine squirmed. "Mind you, I don't know if any of this is true, but the one negative rumor I've heard about Puller is that he acts more like a platoon leader than a regimental commander. That is, he establishes his command post right near the front lines."

Sherman grimaced. "Ooh. I guess that means we'll be in lots of danger if we have to hang close to Puller."

"Exactly," MacLaine replied. "By the way, Jim, I meant to ask you about your own Army background before now. We hit it off so well that I didn't do any homework on you. Can you update me, being more specific than you were the other night when Chesty asked?"

"Better late than never, and I certainly can," Sherman said with his customary grin. "I was with Merrill's Marauders in Burma and Asia during the last war. I spent my fair share of time behind enemy lines, so danger is certainly not new to me. Then, after the war ended, I got into the Intelligence business. And being in Intelligence is probably the reason I survived the massive cuts to the Army after the war ended. Well, that's about it – anything more you want to know?"

"That's all I need to know. Any thoughts on what we should be doing to prepare for the upcoming mission?"

"Sherman thought for a moment. "I guess not. Your reports to General Almond and General MacArthur have been very comprehensive on Puller's activities and the Marines in general. And I don't think there's a need to alert the bosses about some rumors of Puller's shortcomings. They probably know better than we do if they're true or not.

MacLaine nodded and pulled out pen and paper. He sighed and told his second in command to sit tight. He started to draft his next report and said that he might have some questions.

Time was getting short until the Marines boarded the ships for their appointment with destiny. It was now September 10, and the embarkation date was September 12. Chesty Puller and his battalion commanders worked tirelessly to prepare for the great event. They were working so hard that they didn't comprehend the weather reports and the possibility that a typhoon was approaching the east side of Japan. However, men in the lower ranks certainly did. These men had experienced the severe ocean storms coming to Japan from the western United States, and they weren't looking forward to a repeat performance!

As he worked with his staff and battalion commanders, Puller was notified that the Division Commander, Major General Oliver Smith, wanted to see him. He turned to his adjutant, Major Reeves, and gave his usual short, no-nonsense direction: "Old man, take over." Puller then strode down to the general's office, knocked on the door, and entered.

"You wanted to see me, sir?"

"Yes, Lewie. Have a seat. I'll be with you momentarily." The general finished signing the paperwork and looked up.

"Lewie, you may not like this, but I've assigned Murray's Fifth Marine Regiment to Red Beach in the heart of Inchon. You will go in to the south at Blue Beach. You are my best regimental commander, and I don't want to risk losing you up north."

Puller was thunderstruck. "General, I don't agree with your decision, but I'll follow orders. If you want me at Blue Beach, then that's where I'll go."

"Good. And I don't want you personally going in before the third wave. Do I make myself clear?"

"Yes, sir."

After the formalities, the conversation became more relaxed. Smith said that he was well aware that calling them beaches was a misnomer. After all, there were no beaches, just seawalls and the edge of an industrial city. The general offered Puller a drink, but Puller declined. "I better get back to work, General. I'll have to redirect my people down south."

Puller saluted and departed the general's office. On his way back to his own office, it dawned on him that his regiment would be in a better position to cut off the leading elements of the North Korean Army, which were now locked in bitter fighting around the Pusan perimeter. He would emphasize this point to his regimental leaders.

As Puller walked into his office, two of his battalion commanders were in a heated discussion. Puller asked the senior of the two what was up.

"Sir, we're wondering what to do about the men that are in the brig. Several of them are still in jail and scheduled for sentencing later."

"Don't worry about it," Puller replied. "I've found that trouble makers are often the best fighters. I'll talk to the judge and get them released. We'll need them where we're going."

Puller's response alleviated the fears. He told the others that they would now be landing at a spot called Blue Beach. He pointed to Blue Beach on a map that was hanging on the wall. He ordered the others to modify their plans accordingly.

Puller noted the disappointment on the faces of his battalion commanders. "I know you hoped we would be landing and going into the heart of the city. However, going in to the south also has its advantages. We will be in the prime spot to cut off the forward elements of the North Korean Army and destroy them. Please keep this in mind."

Puller's words did the trick. The others in the room understood that their newly assigned entry point had some very definite advantages. It would be up to them to make the most of the situation.

Puller adjourned the meeting so that his commanders could tell the others about their new attack point. He told them to report back as soon as they could.

Puller then walked over to MacLaine's office. It would be important to keep MacLaine and Sherman fully appraised of the latest plans. When Puller entered his office, MacLaine called down the hall for Sherman – who had returned to his own office – to join them.

"Old man," Puller said to MacLaine. "There has been a shift. We will now be landing here." He pointed to Blue Beach on a map that he unrolled. "And, as I told my regimental leaders, we will be in a better position to cut of the head of the North Korean Army."

MacLaine could see the advantages. "Do you think MacArthur is right and the war will be over by Christmas?"

Puller put tobacco in his pipe and lit it. "Old man, things never go as smoothly as planned. I have serious doubts."

Both MacLaine and Sherman nodded.

"I'm afraid you're right," MacLaine replied. "I heard Eisenhower say in a speech recently that plans are great until you put them in motion. Then they break down. But Eisenhower also said that he is a great believer in adequate planning. And one only has to review the D-Day landings in Normandy to understand all of the planning that was done before the day of execution."

Puller said he agreed and then continued. "But there are a number of positives regarding MacArthur saying that our troops should be home by Christmas. Our Marines are in fine form and should give the North Koreans more than they bargained for. MacArthur understands Marine strategy – I think – and how best to employ us, so, who knows, maybe he will be proven right. I sure hope so."

The Army men stated their agreement, and Puller departed. Soon, everyone would find out if the plan – designed by MacArthur himself – was a good one and if it would do all that it was supposed to do.

On September 13, 1950, General of the Army Douglas MacArthur boarded the command ship *Mount McKinley*. The ship, anchored on the southwestern coast of Japan at Sasebo, would travel through the Sea of Japan, the Korean straits, and finally the Yellow Sea to reach Inchon. There, MacArthur would have a bird's-eye view of the landings that were to take place.

MacArthur was in good spirits as he went to his small cabin. He had invited the Marine commanders – including Chesty Puller – to ride with him on the command ship. Puller had refused, preferring to be with his men, but General O. P. Smith, the Marine First Division Commander, had taken him up on his offer.

MacArthur exited his cabin and went to be with the others on the ship. He chatted amicably with his guests, both Marine and Army officers. But when the ship got away from shore, reality set in. Typhoon Kezia hit, and the ship started pitching and rolling. MacArthur, among others, became sick. It didn't faze him for long, however. Soon, he was back entertaining those whose constitutions were strong enough to weather the storm and who had not returned to their cabins.

MacArthur had hoped to get a good night's sleep the first night out. However, that was not to be. Wanting someone to talk to, he had a Marine sentry wake his aide, Courtney Whitney. "Court," MacArthur said, "thanks for coming down. I need someone to talk to."

MacArthur was in pajamas, robe, and slippers. As was his usual habit, he paced back and forth as he talked. Whitney sat in the chair at a small desk.

For the first time, MacArthur expressed doubts. "Court, I don't know if this plan will work. We lost the element of surprise, as news of the striking point is all over Japan. There are no beaches, and the tide comes in and goes out quickly. Everything will need to proceed perfectly if the plan is to work."

Whitney reinforced the strong points. "Sir, you have the best people involved, and your suggestion of the landing at Inchon is a stroke of genius. Anywhere else would not have near as strong an impact. Further south wouldn't have much of an effect at all, in my opinion. So, my advice to you is to wait and see how it plays out. My prediction is that this will be your greatest victory of all."

"Court, I always feel better after talking to you." MacArthur picked up his bible and sat down on his bed. Whitney nodded, saluted, and departed. By now, MacArthur was immersed in the book in his hand.

By September 13, the big ships had assembled off of the Inchon coast. Four aircraft carriers – two of them quite large – plus other ships were ready to start their attack on the mainland. The Naval bombardment began, and even Chesty Puller was duly impressed. "You see," he said as he turned towards MacLaine and Sherman as the three watched from the ship's deck, "I knew the Navy would come through for us. I think they will have knocked out a lot of those gun emplacements that Intelligence was so concerned about."

MacLaine had a worried look on his face that didn't go unnoticed by Puller. "Old man, have you written this girl you plan to marry? If not, I would suggest you do it now. I'll go and leave you alone."

MacLaine nodded, and Puller smiled and then walked down the deck.

"That man must have a sixth sense," MacLaine said somewhat in awe after Puller was out of hearing range. He then turned toward Jim Sherman. "I'm glad we're alone. I've been thinking of this all night, and I need to ask you a big favor."

"What is it?" Sherman replied.

"If something happens to me, I need for you to look after Jennifer and to make sure that she is all right. Will you do it?"

"Of course. I would have done that even if you hadn't asked."

MacLaine thanked his assistant and patted him on the shoulder. "I knew I could count on you. I'm going to our room and write Jennifer a nice letter. I hate to say it, but it is overdue. Puller undoubtedly knows more than I gave him credit for!"

Sherman smiled and turned back to watch the fireworks as MacLaine walked to the door leading to the inside of the transport ship. MacLaine arrived at their room, opened the door, and went in. He walked to the small desk at the side of the room, got pen and paper from the middle drawer, and thought for a moment.

I've got to make this the most meaningful letter I've ever written. He didn't believe in pre-destination, but it bothered him that he had this feeling that he wouldn't make it through this so-called police action. Was there any truth to it? He didn't know, but he definitely didn't like it. He started to write:

Dearest Jennifer

I will be going into harm's way once again, so it will probably be a little while until you hear from me again. My only regret is that I doubt that I have ever found the right words to let you know how much I love you. You are my whole life, and you always will be. Please know that you are always in my thoughts and prayers.

I can't begin to tell you how much I am looking forward to our wedding. When this present ordeal is over, I think it will be time for us to consider setting the date. I know that your life is in flux and that you are scheduled to come to Korea. That is wonderful news to me, as it means that we will see more of each other. But please know that I will let you steer the ship and set the date. After all, you deserve that and much more.

I am very anxious for you to meet my second in command, Jim Sherman. He and I are constant companions, and I know you will really like him. He grows on you!

I should close for now, as I am expected to be in a briefing shortly. Just know that I love you much more than I have ever been able to express to you. And, needless to say, I am counting the days until you arrive here and I can hold you once again.

All my love forever and ever,
Jack

MacLaine signed the letter, put it in an envelope, addressed the envelope, and took it to the mail slot. He felt much better as he walked out to meet up with Sherman. The Naval bombardment was proceeding, and it was a doozy! Time would tell if there were any North Koreans left to fight.

Chapter 14

Turning Point - Inchon

Douglas MacArthur peered over the rails of the command ship Mount McKinley at the activity in Inchon Harbor. The mainland was shrouded in dust and smoke from the naval bombardment, and it was impossible to see what was happening there. But the bombardment had lifted, and MacArthur knew that the Marines were headed in to disembark on the piers and seawall.

It was still way too early to know if the landings would be successful or a failure. However, he had a good feeling.

"Court, this reminds me of our landing at Lingayen Gulf in the last war," he said to his ever-present aide, Courtney Whitney. The landing in the Philippines had been a complete success. Right then, a seaman walked by, and MacArthur flagged him down. "Be sure to let me know as soon as reports from the landings start coming in."

"Aye, aye, sir," the seaman replied. He saluted smartly and hurried off.

Time passed excruciatingly slowly as MacArthur paced back and forth. "Court, when I think back to all of the trouble I had getting this mission approved, I'm flabbergasted that it's actually starting. Everyone in Washington was against me. General Collins of the Joint Chiefs wanted the invasion to be in Kunsan of all places. Kunsan is 100 miles south of Inchon and would be entirely ineffective to my way of thinking. Even my own Eighth Army Commander, General Walker, tried to talk me out of it."

MacArthur lit his pipe and continued. "I tell you, Court, the most important element is the element of surprise. Unfortunately, we may have lost it, and – I'll admit – Inchon is risky. It has no beaches, only piers and seawalls. So the attack will have to be launched in the heart of the city. And there are only about two hours in the day when we will be able to land the Marines and Army troops. And, yes, the harbor could be mined. But the Navy has never let me down, and I don't expect they will do so now. I believe in every fiber of my being that the Navy will come through for me."

Then word started making its way to them. Fighting in the northern part of the city was heavy, but the Fifth Marines were making good progress, and – best of all – their casualties were light.

"I knew it!" MacArthur bellowed triumphantly. "Court, I'm going to send a message to the Joint Chiefs. I'll write it down, and you can take it to the message center for transmission."

MacArthur took out pencil and crumpled paper from his pocket and wrote a short, to-the-point message:

Landing successful and casualties light
MacArthur

MacArthur had a satisfied look on his face. After all, there was nothing he cherished more than being right. He handed the message to his aide, and Whitney hurried off. Soon, the whole world would once again know of the magnificence of this talented leader.

By the time Whitney returned, MacArthur was still in a euphoric state. He had been joined at the railing by Admiral Doyle, the lead U.S. Naval officer, and General Oliver P. Smith, Commander of the Marine First Division. Doyle was seemingly hanging on every one of MacArthur's words, but Smith was more aloof.

"What's wrong, Ollie?" MacArthur asked the Marine.

"Nothing is wrong. I'm just worried about my men. We're far from the point of it being a mopping-up effort, and I feel for my boys who are bound to be lost."

MacArthur nodded. Smith was obviously referring back to the last war when MacArthur said that they were in a mopping up mode in the

Philippines when the troops doing the fighting knew it was far from over.

I guess I should have expected it, MacArthur told himself. *The Marines never liked me, and they will use everything they can find to put me down.*

But MacArthur wasn't about to let Smith's feelings get him down. The best way to handle it? Throw him a compliment!

"Ollie, I have ultimate confidence in your men. I know they will do far better than anyone else could."

"I appreciate that, General," Smith replied.

Chesty Puller was getting anxious to go in. General Smith had ordered him not to go in until the third wave, so he had no choice. But it didn't make him any less eager. "Check your men and make sure they're ready to go," he told his battalion commanders. Soon, they hurried off. He liked their enthusiasm.

Jack MacLaine and Jim Sherman were standing next to Puller on the ship's bridge. "You must have taken my advice and written your girl," Puller said to MacLaine. "You seem much more relaxed."

"That I did, Chesty. You know a lot more than I ever gave you credit for." MacLaine called Puller 'Chesty,' but Sherman was much more formal. He called the old man 'Colonel Puller.'

Puller nodded triumphantly and then went back to the business at hand. Regimental officers came up to him to get the latest information, and he readily obliged. While he still couldn't see the dust and smoke-covered mainland, he could see at least some of the small boats milling around in the harbor. Seeing them made him even more eager to land his own troops.

Finally, his own turn came. His battalions were already landed when he went in and climbed up on a seawall. His constant companions MacLaine and Sherman were with him.

"Where are you going to set up your command post?" MacLaine asked.

Puller pointed to the map in his hip pocket. "This is the only thing I need with me, so my command post will be very informal and more-than-likely near the front lines."

MacLaine and Sherman nodded. "Just like we've been told," Sherman said under his breath to MacLaine. His boss nodded.

Puller had taken out his binoculars and was looking up and down Blue Beach. He noted that his men were hunkered down near the exits to the beach. "It looks like the naval bombardment has blocked the exits. We'll have to fix that." He had an aide hand him a field telephone. He cranked it, and when the operator answered, he told him to have the engineers dynamite an opening. Soon, his troops were moving out.

Puller was ecstatic about the light casualties. "I was really concerned," he relayed to MacLaine and Sherman, "that our casualties would be heavy. After all, I expected our young, unpracticed troops to be confused. However, they have performed magnificently."

An aide walked up to Puller and gave him the field phone. Puller seemed elated as he took in the news. He turned to MacLaine and Sherman. "Well, I'll be darned," he said. "One of my battalions has moved about a mile inland, and the men have taken a ridge. They overran the enemy and booted him out of the emplacements without sustaining any casualties."

MacLaine and Sherman were as impressed as Puller was. "Before we hit the sack, I want to visit the troops," Puller said. They both nodded. "I can hardly wait to relay all of your good news to General Almond," MacLaine said. "It should make his day."

"Old man," Puller replied to MacLaine, 'Please thank Almond for me and tell him that the Army has done exactly as they should have. And that is they stayed out of our way."

The whirring of a jeep was heard coming toward them, and soon Puller's driver, Sergeant Jones, was seen. "How did you find me, old man?" Puller asked when the driver came to a stop.

"Easy, sir," Jones said with a grin. "I just whistled "Dixie" and asked the sentries where you were."

As was the normal configuration, MacLaine and Sherman got in the back, and Puller got in the front. They headed off to visit Puller's men, especially those who had overrun the North Koreans and taken the ridge that was inland by a mile!

On September 16, 1950, Inchon was secured, and General Almond, X-Corps Commander, came to brief General MacArthur. He reported to CINCFE on the *Mount McKinley.*

"Sir," Almond replied, "Inchon is in our hands, and we can now start proceeding to Seoul."

"Good. Seoul is only about 17 miles away, so it should be liberated quite quickly. General Walker is now moving up from the Pusan perimeter, and we will be trapping the North Koreans in a giant pincer movement."

"Once again," Almond added, "your insight has been perfect, and we should be finishing off the North Koreans in short order."

MacArthur suddenly was in a pensive mood. "Yes, if the Chinese don't enter the war."

Almond appeared stunned. "Your Intelligence Head, General Willoughby, has been adamant that the Chinese won't enter the war. What makes you believe otherwise?"

"Mind you. I wouldn't say this to anyone else, but the officer who is second in command of my Intelligence Unit – General Summerfield I believe his name is – thinks differently. If he is right, this war could be long and drawn out."

"What are your plans then?"

"I am still tasked – by the President – to rid South Korea of the North Korean's presence. But I am also under the auspices of the United Nations, and those people are interested in a united Korea. Thus, first of all, I will crush the North Koreans who are in South Korea. Next, I will think of crossing the 38th parallel and going clear up to the Yalu River. The Yalu is where Communist China starts and North Korea ends."

Almond whistled softly. "It's a lot more complex than I thought it was."

"Yes, it is. But don't worry about anything right now but clearing the invaders out of South Korea."

Almond nodded and replied. "Sir, I've always realized that Chinese intervention was a possibility. But we could use an atomic bomb in case they did. Has that been considered?"

"I doubt that it has, Ned. Anyway, it would take the approval of the President of the United States to use this weapon. And I doubt that we would ever get it."

"What good does it do to have this weapon if you can't use it?" Almond moaned.

MacArthur smiled. "My sentiments exactly, but right now, you have other things to worry about."

Almond stood up, saluted, and went to board a launch that would take him to Inchon. His work was still cut out for him, and he realized it.

By September 17, 1950 – the landing day plus two – General MacArthur was adamant that he wanted to be taken ashore. After all, the Inchon landing was being advertised as the greatest amphibious landing ever, and he wanted his picture taken in the heart of the city. He also wanted to personally decorate Chesty Puller, one of his favorite officers from World War II. He had never personally met Puller, but the Colonel's reputation had been widespread.

When informed that MacArthur wanted to decorate him, Puller was his normal self. "If he wants to decorate me," Puller growled, "he'll have to come to the front. I don't have time for the usual shenanigans. After all, we're fighting for every foot of ground."

It was true that fighting was still very intense. Puller was on a hilltop with MacLaine and Sherman when MacArthur arrived. Artillery shells were reigning down, and it was no place for the light-hearted.

Six jeeps came to a stop, and General MacArthur got out of the lead jeep. He huffed and puffed to get up the hill. After all, he was seventy years old. But he did make it. He extended his hand, and the two men shook.

"Puller, I want to award you the Silver Star. You have done magnificently." MacArthur fumbled through his pockets but didn't find one. He told an aide to send the award when they returned to Tokyo.

"By the looks of things," MacArthur said, "you've encountered some pretty heavy resistance."

"It is heavy," Puller muttered, "but it's nothing like I encountered on Peleliu. I lost over half my men there."

MacArthur expressed his sympathy and asked how long it would take Puller to get into Seoul.

"About four days" was the response.

The reply was exactly what MacArthur wanted to hear. "Colonel, I want to award your regiment the Army Presidential Unit Citation. They have done extraordinarily well." MacArthur added this award almost as an afterthought. He then departed the area.

MacLaine and Sherman grinned after MacArthur had left. "Chesty, the big boss almost gave you full credit for your regiment's success," MacLaine said. "I'm glad he finally came to his senses and gave your unit an award. After all, they are the ones who are fighting and dying."

"You are absolutely right, old man." Puller lit his pipe, and away the three of them went in the Colonel's jeep. There was a lot of fighting still to be done.

As they drove along, Puller began to convey some of his leadership thoughts to MacLaine and Sherman. "I always try and figure out what I would be doing if I were in the enemy commander's shoes. Where would

I place my big guns? How would I deploy my troops? These are issues that can make the difference between winning and losing. And, perhaps most of all, you should never underestimate the enemy."

The topic of conversation then changed to a lighter subject. Puller talked about his wife and children, praising them profusely.

MacLaine smiled. "Don't tell me, Chesty, that even you get sentimental at times."

"Without a doubt, old man, without a doubt."

Fighting remained heavy for a number of days. On September 25, Puller's regiment was pressing into the heart of Seoul. It was two days past the estimate that Puller had furnished MacArthur on retaking the city. By then, Puller had raised an American flag over a schoolhouse in the heart of the city.

"Aren't you getting a little ahead of yourself, Chesty?" MacLaine asked. "After all, the Marines are still taking sizable casualties."

"Not at all, old man. But I do realize that it will require heavy fighting to get the job done."

MacArthur, as was his old habit, took the opportunity to say that Seoul had been secured. General Oliver Smith, Commander of the First Marine Division, was shocked at the proclamation. Marine casualties were still substantial, and Smith believed that Seoul was by no means secure. He sent a message to MacArthur so stating his position. He then set out from his headquarters, which was now on Korean soil, to talk to Chesty Puller. He finally caught up with Puller in intense fighting in the capital city. He jumped out of his jeep and ran up to Puller.

"Lewie, what's the meaning of this?" He waved a copy of MacArthur's statement at his First Regiment Commander and passed it over to him.

Puller looked at the communique and chuckled. "I see the big boss is up to his old tricks." He handed the message back to Smith.

Smith was not amused. "Did he get the idea that everything was secure from you?"

"Absolutely not. Those two can verify that I didn't say anything to that effect." Puller pointed to MacLaine and Sherman.

Smith motioned for the Army men to come over. He showed them the message, and both men were obviously disturbed by it.

"I don't know how he could say that," MacLaine said, pointing to the nearby engagement.

"I don't either," Smith replied. He turned back to Puller. "Lewie, tell your men that this statement does not reflect the position of the United States Marines. I'm going up to the Fifth Regiment to tell them the same thing." Salutes were exchanged, and Smith roared off in his jeep.

"It mustn't feel very good to get chewed out for something you didn't do," Sherman said to Puller as the three men stood in the battered roadway.

"It comes with the territory, old man. Let's get back to work." An artillery shell was incoming, and the three dove into a ditch. After the shell exploded, the men picked themselves up, dusted themselves off, and went over and climbed in Puller's jeep.

Lewie Puller was right. There was still a lot of work still to be done.

It wasn't long before MacArthur's words rang true. Seoul was secure, and MacArthur took it upon himself to escort and reinstate the nation's President, Syngman Rhee, into his offices in the nation's capital. After the ceremonies and on-board his airplane *SCAP*, MacArthur was feeling exuberant almost to the point of giddiness. As he stood at the back of the airplane, he was with the ones he trusted most: General Almond, Courtney Whitney, and, now, MacLaine and Sherman. The latter two were ordered by General Almond to attend the ceremonies, and they were aboard the plane for a quick trip back to brief their bosses in Tokyo.

MacArthur started espousing his general beliefs. "Gentlemen," he said, "I know that there are those in Washington – Secretary-of-state Acheson and Secretary-of-Defense Marshall, for example – who will criticize me for personally reinstating Syngman Rhee as President. However, I will also tell you that as long as I am winning, the criticism will be muted. And this Administration, as have ones in the past, will give very loose directives. This will let them wiggle out of any responsibility for failures that may occur."

Even the stoic Ned Almond seemed genuinely impressed. "General, you missed your calling. You would have undoubtedly been an Academy Award winner in Hollywood."

"Thank you, Ned. But I must say that there has always been only one career for me, and that is in the United States Army." MacArthur was looking as regal as ever. As he took a seat in the rear of the aircraft, the others took seats further to the front. MacLaine and Sherman sat next to each other.

"What do you make of all of this?" Sherman asked in a muted tone.

MacLaine shook his head. "As I understand it," he said softly, "MacArthur hasn't been told exactly what to do. However, he has been directed not to have American troops go north of the 38th parallel – only South Korean troops are to proceed up there."

"And did you notice all of the revetments at Kimpo Airport outside of Seoul?" Sherman asked his boss. "I think a modern air force – such as the Chinese – had intended to move in there."

MacLaine whistled softly. "God forbid. If the Chinese do enter this action, things will become a mess in a hurry."

Sherman nodded. "Do you think the old man has an inkling?"

"I think so. But he probably plans to ignore it and hopes it will go away."

Sherman laughed and put an imaginary pistol to his head. MacLaine could only nod.

The future wasn't nearly as bright as MacLaine had thought it was just a few minutes earlier. He hoped that his beloved Jennifer wouldn't be getting into a horrific mess, but only the future would tell.

Part 4

Chapter 15

MASH Unit

September, 1950 was nearing the end, and Brad Taylor, Jennifer Haraldsson, and the other doctors and nurses – having recently arrived in Korea – worked furiously to get their MASH unit operational. MASH was a new concept in the Army, designed to save the lives of wounded soldiers and make them more comfortable in the process. Soon, the Army would know if the concept had merit, as MASH would be taking over operational responsibility from the more temporary units that were developed and deployed during World War II.

MASH was meant to stay near the front lines of the war zone. Therefore, it had a very 'mobile' appearance. Instead of permanent structures, the hospital was constructed of tents. Power was supplied by movable generators on wheels. Hence, the hospital could be moved quickly as the situation dictated.

And, with the availability of substantial numbers of helicopters at the forward edge of the battle, patients could be transported to MASH units much more quickly. Thus, all of the various features gave the MASH concept the potential of being highly effective.

After a long day of setting up their MASH unit, Brad Taylor and Jennifer Haraldsson were having a nightcap in his patchwork office before turning in. "Tomorrow, our patients will start arriving," Taylor said as he peered at his watch. "I hope we'll be ready."

"We'll be ready, one way or the other," Jennifer replied. She made a quick glance down at the shiny new major's leaves on her collar. She still couldn't believe that she was now a major! Nor could she fathom that Brad Taylor was now a bird colonel! Not that both of them didn't deserve their new rank.

Jennifer recovered quickly from her euphoric state. "I checked the number of patients who will be transferred here tomorrow. It's well within our capability, and there is plenty of room to accommodate the wounded who arrive by helicopter or truck."

"Good. As long as there are no more new entrants in the war, then we should be okay."

A puzzled expression came over Jennifer's face. "What does that mean?"

Taylor shook his head. "Nothing, really. It's just negative thinking on my part. But I do hope MacArthur doesn't do anything to make the Chinese or Soviets mad enough to enter the war. It would be like stirring up a hornet's nest."

The light was dawning. "Oh, I see what you mean," Jennifer responded after thinking for a moment. "Do you think there's much of a chance of that happening?"

"I don't know, but I certainly hope not. We have to hope that MacArthur is wise enough and that President Truman is cautious enough to keep the situation under control."

At that moment, Sergeant Bear Carter, the non-commissioned officer in charge of administration, knocked and stuck his head in the office. "Sir, is there anything I can do for you before I turn in?" he asked.

"Not a thing, Sergeant. Tomorrow is an early morning, as our patients should start arriving about 0530."

"No problem, sir. My men will be through chow and will be ready to greet them when they arrive.

"Do your men know where to take the patients?"

"Absolutely. We have it all mapped out with Major Haraldsson."

"Great, Sergeant. In that case, get a good night's sleep, and I'll see you in the morning."

Taylor said goodnight and turned back to Jennifer. "Now I know why I brought you on as my head nurse."

"Thank you, kind sir."

The two finished discussing the plans for having their unit activated in the morning. "We better turn in," Taylor said. "Tomorrow is going to hectic, and – based on my past experience – it might even be frantic.

Jennifer nodded, and the two finished their drinks. She then headed to the nurse's quarters, and Taylor went to bed down in the commanding officer's 'bedroom.' Taylor looked around when he arrived. "Not bad," he said softly. It was definitely makeshift, but certainly more-than-satisfactory when the primitive circumstances were considered.

At dawn the next morning, trucks started arriving with the wounded. As Taylor had predicted, events were rather chaotic. Some patients were more seriously wounded than the new staff had expected, and there were more casualties than listed on the original ledger. *Oh well,* Jennifer thought, *these types of anomalies are to be expected. And the differences could have been a lot more severe.*

By the time the patients were situated, it was almost noon. Jennifer felt a tap on her shoulder. She turned around, and who was there but a smiling Monica Davis! The two squealed and hugged. Suddenly, Jennifer was self-conscious, as she saw the less-serious patients in the ward sitting up and grinning. They were obviously enjoying the show!

Monica also immediately recognized the problem. The two nurses backed up and became more formal.

"How was your trip?" Jennifer asked as she tried to walk a tight line between being adequately formal and showing her friend how glad she was to see her. "Your shiny lieutenant's bars look great on your collar."

"Thank you," Monica replied softly. "And I think your major's leaves are most attractive."

Jennifer thanked her. "I'll show you to the nurse's quarters and where you'll be bunking." Jennifer picked up one of Monica's bags, and the two walked outside.

Once out of sight of the patients, Jennifer sat down the bag and hugged her friend again. "I'm so glad to see you, and I know Brad Taylor has been anxious for you to arrive. You have no idea how good it is to see someone you know and trust."

"I can imagine, and I'm ready to go to work. Just tell me what you want me to do."

"First, we'll get you squared away in the nurse's quarters, and then we'll get some lunch. How does that sound?"

"Great! I'm famished!"

Jennifer introduced Monica to the other nurses that were in the nurse's quarters. Monica dumped her bags onto her bed, saying that she would move her belongings into her foot locker at a later time.

"There is one more person I must introduce you to – Sergeant Bear Carter. He's our administrative sergeant who controls just about everything around here. Without him, this place would fall apart."

"He does sound like a very good person to know," Monica replied. Shortly, they came upon Sergeant Carter. He was chewing out two men who had obviously put things where they didn't belong.

Jennifer waited until Carter was through redressing the young men. Then she approached the Sergeant. "Sergeant Carter, this is Lieutenant Monica Davis. She is one of our new nurses."

"Pleased to meet you, ma'am. I guess the Major has told you about me and my role here."

"Yes, she has. I understand you're the one I should see if I need anything."

"Absolutely correct, ma'am. You need anything, you just come see me."

Jennifer and Monica thanked Carter and proceeded to the mess hall. Brad Taylor was seated over at one side having his lunch with some other doctors. Jennifer pointed to him, and the two nurses walked over.

"I've got someone here I know you'll be very happy to see," Jennifer said, barely able to conceal her enthusiasm.

Taylor looked up and broke into a broad smile. He got up and hugged his newly arrived nurse.

"Boy, am I glad to see you. This place is getting very busy." Taylor introduced Monica to the doctors at the table and put in some sparkling words for her.

"Gents, Monica worked for me at Walter Reed, and I can tell you that she is top notch." A young doctor, Captain Mike Pulaskey, got up and extended his hand. Jennifer could tell that his interest was more than just professional!

The other doctors at the table nodded, and Jennifer said that she had to get her young ward something to eat. Taylor said that he would talk to Monica very soon, and the two nurses went to get in the chow line. Monica was not bashful in filling her tray!

The two nurses went to an empty table and sat down. "How is everything back home?" Jennifer asked.

Monica shrugged. "Okay, I guess. Todd is growing daily and seems to be doing fine. Molly likes her role of 'Mommy,' and she seems to be doing as well as can be expected without Bill there."

Better change the subject, Jennifer thought. *It doesn't seem to be one of Monica's favorite topics.*

"Brad was obviously as glad to see you as I was. I can guarantee that you will be well appreciated here."

"That's good," Monica replied. "I'm ready to go to work, and the busier I am, the better."

The two finished their lunch and took their trays to a sorting table. They separated silver ware, dishes, and cups based on the protocol that had been established. As they walked out of the chow hall, Mike Pulaskey approached.

"May I walk with you?" he asked.

"Certainly" was the joint response from the two nurses.

Pulaskey talked to both of the ladies, but it was obvious that he had eyes for Monica. Suddenly, the loud speaker system boomed: "Incoming wounded!"

The three took off in a dead run for the helicopter pad that was in front of the MASH unit. By the time they got there, the wounded were being offloaded from two helicopters. Brad Taylor was bending over the wounded soldiers, barking orders as to where to take each. Pulaskey bent down to help.

Taylor determined that two of the soldiers needed surgery. "You take that one, and I'll take the other," he said to Pulaskey. "Jennifer, you'll be my lead nurse. Monica, you assist Pulaskey."

Jennifer motioned for some of the other nurses to come to their aid. Soon, the two soldiers were on the operating tables, and the doctors and nurses scrubbed and put on the operating gowns. The surgery commenced in short order.

Pulaskey had drawn the more serious case, as his patient had an intestinal wound. He, Monica, and the other nurses labored intensely for over two hours. By the time the surgery ended, all were drenched in sweat.

Pulaskey expressed his appreciation to Monica as they walked out. "You were magnificent in there. You kept the fluids drained so I could see what I was doing."

"You were pretty good yourself," Monica replied. "I've never seen surgery done so smoothly."

It was obvious that the two were bonding!

That evening, Jennifer stopped by Monica's bunk. Monica was putting the last of her belongings in her foot locker.

"Brad Taylor has asked that we join him in the mess hall for dinner. Are you game?"

"Yes," Monica replied. "Just give me a second to put these last few items away."

Monica folded the last of her personal belongings and placed them in the locker at the foot of her bed. She closed the lid, and the two nurses departed for dinner.

Taylor was waiting at the entrance to the chow hall. He smiled as he saw his two nurses approaching. He motioned for them to enter first. They walked to the cafeteria line and filled their trays. They then went to a table at the side of the mess hall. It was the one that Taylor and the other doctors were eating at during their lunch meal. The three sat down and began to eat.

"I guess you know that Mike Pulaskey was highly impressed by you," Taylor said to Monica.

Monica nodded and continued to eat.

"He has requested that you work with him full time. Is that okay with you?"

"Yes. I think he is an outstanding doctor."

"Good. That's settled. By the way, Mike should be joining us shortly."

Jennifer thought she noticed a slight gleam in Monica's eyes. *Perhaps there is more than just a professional relationship developing here.*

It wasn't long before Pulaskey appeared in the doorway. He looked around and then spotted them. He smiled and started walking in their direction. He soon stopped and pointed to the chow line. His intentions were clear. He would get his food and then join them.

Pulaskey walked to their table with his tray in hand. He sat down and smiled at Monica.

"I can't say enough good things about this young lady," Pulaskey related with significant emotion. "Without her expertise, the operation may well have failed."

"You're too kind," Monica replied. "You were the only one who was totally indispensable."

Brad Taylor and Jennifer looked on with great interest. Taylor was obviously happy that the operation had been a success and that the patient was not only expected to live but to have a complete recovery. Jennifer was happy that her favorite nurse had exceeded all expectations.

"If I had a glass of champagne, I'd propose a toast," Taylor said enthusiastically. "This is exactly the tone that I like to hear – that everything is preceding better than expected."

"I'll drink to that," Jennifer said, raising her water glass. The four clinked water glasses and savored the moment.

"It's only a start," Taylor admitted, "but it's a great start."

The four finished eating and took their trays to the appropriate counter. After dividing the silver ware and dishes into the designated compartments, Jennifer and Monica departed the mess hall and walked toward the nurse's quarters. The two men headed to Taylor's office.

"By the way," Monica said as they reached her bunk, "how is Jack MacLaine?" None of the other nurses were nearby, so the two could talk freely.

"He's fine as far as I know. I hope to see him shortly."

"Does the guy ever write?"

"Yes. I got a letter from him just the other day. It was very emotional for him. It was also very loving. I was impressed."

"I'm glad," Monica replied.

"By the way," Jennifer added. "I couldn't help but notice the way Mike Pulaskey was looking at you. Is there any chance that the two of you may have more than just a working relationship?'

"Naw, I doubt it. I don't intend to get involved over here with anything but work."

Jennifer giggled. "You remind me more of your sister than you'll ever know."

"Thanks a bunch!"

The next day started off in frantic fashion. Helicopters continually brought in wounded soldiers, and Jennifer had her hands full just assigning nurses to the required medical functions. On a momentary lull, Brad Taylor came up to her waving a paper.

"This is from the aide to the British Commander, Major General Francis Dunbar. Dunbar wants to have dinner with you. Obviously, you know him."

"I sure do. I also know his aide, Brian Hawkins." Jennifer took the letter and quickly read it. She then handed it back to Taylor.

"Go ahead and keep it," Taylor said. "General Dunbar wants to have an agreement with us to have his wounded soldiers treated here. I've taken down the pertinent information and will send him a reply in the affirmative."

"Don't agree just because of me. Judging from how busy we were this morning, we might not be able to take on much more."

"I won't, but I really don't think I have a choice. The Brits are our allies, and we have to treat them as such."

Jennifer nodded.

"By the way," Taylor added, "have you heard anything from that man you're going to marry?"

"He said he would come and see me as soon as the fighting slowed down a bit, so I expect him any time."

"Good. Let me know if you hear anything definite. It is way too important an event to let it go unnoticed."

"Thank you, Brad. I certainly will." The two started moving in different directions when Jennifer called after her boss.

"Brad, if you have a moment, I would like to mention one other thing."

"For you, I have lots of time. What is it?"

Jennifer mentioned the letter that had finally reached her from Otto Bruner. She briefly covered the contents and that Bruner had mentioned that she should not try and contact him in return.

"I would really like to write him back," Jennifer explained, "but I am hesitant to do so. Do you have any advice?"

Taylor scratched his head. "It's a sticky issue, but I think your Jack MacLaine would be the best person to ask. If anyone could tell you how to do it, he could."

Jennifer smiled. "No wonder you have all that rank on your collar."

The time passed quickly, and Jennifer was feeling very tired. It had been a grueling day, as patients were flooding in. With her clipboard in hand, Jennifer was updating patient status by personally checking on each individual. She had just finished taking a patient's vital signs when she looked up to see none other than Jack MacLaine standing in the doorway. She dropped her clipboard and rushed over to greet him. Her fatigue had disappeared!

"How are you, darling?" she said as she leapt into his arms. She was oblivious to the presence of Jim Sherman, who was standing beside him. Sherman had his normal smile plastered on his face.

After a long embrace, MacLaine introduced her to Sherman.

"He told me about you," Sherman said, "but his description didn't do you justice. You are much more striking in person than I would have thought."

"I can imagine. He is the master of the understatement." Jennifer nudged MacLaine in the ribs. "Let's find my boss. Also, Monica – Molly's sister – just arrived, and I want her to see you." She took MacLaine by the hand and led the two of them toward Brad Taylor's office. Taylor was approaching from the other direction.

"Well, I'll be," Taylor said when he saw MacLaine. "It's been awhile, Jack. How are you?" The two shook hands and expressed greetings. MacLaine then introduced Jim Sherman to Taylor.

"You two can have my quarters tonight," Taylor said to Jennifer and MacLaine. "Sherman and I can bunk with the other doctors. That okay with you, Jim?"

Sherman nodded.

Jennifer thanked Taylor, and the three set out to find Monica Davis. "After we greet her, we can get something to eat," Jennifer said excitedly. She gazed at MacLaine. "Then we can start our nightly activities."

MacLaine winked at her as they started their search for Monica.

That night, Jennifer and MacLaine lay in Taylor's bed. It wasn't a very big bed, but at least the two of them had some privacy. Jennifer's head rested on MacLaine's shoulder.

"You remember Francis Dunbar?" she asked.

"Yes, of course. He's now a two star general and in charge of the U.K. ground forces here."

"Well, he wants to see me. He will be arranging to come over here for dinner in the near future."

"Great," MacLaine replied. "I know that the two of you go back quite a ways together."

"We do, but the one thing that bothers me is that he's always been around during my times of tragedy, such as when Dude was killed. I hope it isn't an omen that something bad is going to happen to you."

MacLaine was very dismissive. "I don't believe in that kind of thing. My suggestion to you is that you enjoy seeing your old friend."

"Good advice," she said softly.

Jennifer brought up her letter from Otto Bruner and asked if there was a way she could correspond with him.

"Let's address that the next time we're together," MacLaine replied. The two kissed, and Jennifer was very happy to oblige! They obviously had better things to do.

Jennifer awoke very early the next morning. It was still dark outside, and it felt wonderful lying next to Jack MacLaine. But how long would her state of bliss last? The world was a very dangerous place, especially for those on the Korean peninsula.

When MacLaine awoke, the two kissed. "Jack, I've been thinking," Jennifer said. "Why don't we get married here? I know that I'd talked about a big wedding back home, but that might not be possible for some time."

"Now you're talking," MacLaine replied. "My sentiments exactly."

"Getting a chaplain to marry us will not be a problem, as there are a number of them around here. The big question is this: Can you set a date with your schedule being what it is?"

MacLaine laughed. "I see what you mean. Traveling with Chesty Puller makes scheduling an event dicey. However, for something this important, I'll just tell Puller that I'm getting married. And I know that family life is very important to him and that he'll be very encouraging. So you schedule it when you want it and I'll be here."

"Good. Now I have to get you out of here, as I have a lot to do."

Chapter 16

Tragedy Strikes

The days flew by as Jennifer prepared for her wedding. She wanted to make it as elegant as possible, even though it wouldn't be held in the states with her parents and four siblings in attendance. After lining up a chaplain to perform the marriage ceremony and getting Monica as her maid of honor, she procured the services of other nurses as her bridesmaids. Now it was time to break the news to her family. She decided to write her parents and let them disseminate the news to her brothers and sisters, since half of the siblings no longer lived at home. Instead, they were married, and one of them was even a parent! She would try and make this letter the best one that she had ever sent to her family:

> *Dearest Darling Mommy and Daddy*
>
> *It is dreadful being so far away from you. I can't begin to tell you how much I miss being able to jump on a plane from D.C. to come home to Idaho to see you. I hope and pray with all my heart and soul that this terrible war ends soon, and I will be able to come to Idaho and see you regularly.*
>
> *I am so happy that I got to bring Jack MacLaine, my husband-to-be, home to meet you before he left to go to Japan. I think I told you that he is now in Korea and that I got to see him recently. It was absolutely heavenly! I probably didn't tell you that he brought his aide and traveling companion, a Major Jim Sherman, with him. I must say that Jim seems like a nice-enough fellow.*

While Jack was here, we decided that we might as well go ahead and get married in Korea. I am crushed that you and my brothers and sisters won't be at my wedding, but it just can't be helped. No one knows for sure just how long the war will last, and coupled with my advancing age, we decided that we should go ahead and tie the knot. I hope and pray you understand.

I will say that you all will certainly be here in spirit. I have kept you close to me during all of the trials and tribulations that have occurred in my life, and I will certainly do so now and forever after. Please pass this information to Billy, Buck, Kristen, and Kali.

Oodles and oodles of love,
Jennifer

Jennifer was very happy to have this unpleasant task out of the way. She addressed the envelope and took it over to the MASH post office. After putting the letter in the mailbox, she walked over to Sergeant Bear Carter's office. He would be the one that she would rely on to get the flowers, space, and refreshments for the ceremony. He was indeed worth his weight in gold.

In the hubbub of activity, Jennifer had forgotten that her old friend, Francis Dunbar, was in Korea. Word had come that Dunbar, now a major general in the British Army and head of Britain's ground forces in Korea, would be joining her for dinner that evening. She wanted everything to be perfect, so she had arranged for the chef to prepare a special dinner. Her old friend and boss, Brad Taylor, had agreed to set up a dining table in a vacant part of the camp. Since the area was supplied with heat, light, and running water, everything was falling into place.

At precisely 1755, five minutes before he was to arrive, Jennifer and Taylor were standing out front waiting to greet him. Standing with them and slightly to their rear was Sergeant Bear Carter. Taylor had the foresight to have Carter with them, adding assurance that everything would go smoothly.

Sure enough, at 1800, a British car bearing a two star flag at the front came to a stop. Major Brian Hawkins got out and came quickly around to open the door for the General. A smiling Francis Dunbar got out as the Americans saluted. He came over and gave Jennifer a big hug.

How are you, my dear?" Dunbar said. "It's so good to see you."

"And you too," Jennifer replied. "Sir, I'd like you to meet my boss, Colonel Brad Taylor, and our administrative sergeant, Bear Carter. Sergeant Carter is the one we see if we need anything."

"I know what you mean," Dunbar said as he shook hands with the other Americans. "Jennifer, I believe you know my aide, Major Hawkins." She nodded, and the two greeted each other warmly. Hawkins was then introduced to the others.

"Taylor," Dunbar added, "I'll have to talk to you before I leave, but for now, I place myself in Jennifer's capable hands."

Taylor replied in the affirmative, saluted, and broke off with Sergeant Carter. The Colonel motioned for Major Hawkins to come with them. "Your general will be well taken care of," Taylor whispered. Hawkins looked relieved.

"Right this way, sir," Jennifer said as she led Dunbar to their dining area. "I imagine you're hungry, so we'll go right to dinner."

"That I am," Dunbar replied.

The mess sergeant had laid out the dinner area beautifully. A nice tablecloth along with fancy silverware, fine dishes and glasses, and candles adorned the table. *I'll have to remember this for the next time Jack comes down,* Jennifer thought. She had no idea that the mess sergeant was so creative!

The two were seated, and dinner was served shortly. It consisted of a New York steak, baked potato, and asparagus. Each was also offered a salad, and both accepted. For dessert, ice cream was served along with assorted cookies.

"That meal was delicious," Dunbar exclaimed. "By the way, would you mind if I smoked my pipe?"

"Not at all. Please do."

Dunbar took out his pipe, filled it with tobacco, and lit it. Soon, the room was filled with a very pleasant aroma.

"Before I forget it, Winston Churchill wanted me to relay his regards."

"And please tell him hello for me. By the way, how is he?"

Dunbar thought for a moment. "I think he's okay, but what concerns me is that the people seem to be getting nostalgic. I think they'll want him back in as prime minister within a year. He's now 75, and I hope it won't be too much for him."

"That is sobering. Is there any way he can turn it down?"

"I don't think he ever would. He believes that one should serve if they're called on to do so."

Jennifer was speechless for the moment. What could she say? Obviously nothing. Men like Winston Churchill were meant to serve. He would obviously give his all for his country.

Francis Dunbar changed the subject. "How is your young man, Jack MacLaine? I want you to know that I like him very much, and I wholeheartedly approve of your decision to marry him."

"Thank you very much. Your opinion means a lot to me. And by the way, Jack and I have decided to get married here, as no one can be sure exactly how long this war will last. So you will be getting a wedding invitation very soon."

Jennifer related that MacLaine was just down to see her, and that they had a wonderful time together.

"That's great," Dunbar replied.

Dunbar updated Jennifer on the status of his family. He proudly took out pictures of his wife and children and showed them to her.

As dinner was winding down, Jennifer mentioned that she had heard from Otto Bruner and that Bruner was happily married with children. She also said that Bruner had said that she shouldn't try and contact him back, as it would be very risky if his superiors found out about it.

"I suggest you talk to Brian Hawkins if you want to correspond with him," Dunbar said. "Brian is a master at these clandestine issues."

"I'll do that," Jennifer replied. "Jack MacLaine is also looking into how to do it."

"Good. Between the two of them, they should be able to get it done."

"I'll talk to Taylor while you broach the issue with Brian," Dunbar added.

The two got up from the table and told the waiter attending them to be sure and tell the chef how good the meal was. The man was obviously delighted, especially after they told him how great the service was!

Jennifer and Dunbar went to Brad Taylor's office. Taylor and Brian Hawkins were talking. Both came to attention when Jennifer and Dunbar entered.

"As you were, gentlemen," Dunbar said. He then told Hawkins that Jennifer had a question for him that the two could discuss outside. In the meantime, he would talk to Brad Taylor about getting British soldiers treated at the American facility.

Jennifer and Hawkins went outside, and Jennifer said that she had heard from Otto Bruner but he had said that it would be too risky for her to contact him. Her question was direct: What should she do if she wanted to write him back? She said that Jack MacLaine was also working on the problem.

"Ah, good old Jack," Hawkins replied. "I can certainly work the issue with him, and it will be good to see him. What's it been, about four years since we've been together?"

"1950-1946 equals four years. Your math is perfect."

"By the way, congratulations," Hawkins added. "You two will make a perfect couple."

Jennifer thanked him, and the two went back into Taylor's office. Dunbar and Taylor were just finishing their conversation.

"Did you get something to eat?" Dunbar asked Hawkins.

"Yes, sir. It was delicious, and the driver also got to eat."

"Great," Dunbar replied as he looked at Taylor. "We're going to have to have our chef talk to yours. Your eats are definitely better."

Hawkins seconded Dunbar's comment, and the four walked out to the general's staff car. The driver was waiting and opened the door for the general.

"Remember," Dunbar said to Jennifer, "I'm right down the road. If you need anything whatsoever, just ask."

"Thank you." Jennifer and Dunbar hugged, and the Americans saluted.

"I'll be back to you shortly," Hawkins said to Jennifer as he scurried around to the other side of the car. He got in and shut the door. The car with the two British guests became smaller and smaller until it was out of sight.

Jennifer and Taylor stood there as if they were transfixed.

"You have a true friend in General Dunbar," Taylor said. "He thinks the world of you."

"And I think the world of him. He's always been there in my hour of greatest need. I would have never survived in Norway if it hadn't been for him."

Jennifer couldn't help it. Her thoughts went back to Norway and of Dude lying there in the snow, dying. If Dunbar and Lars hadn't dragged her away, she would have never made it out. Instead, she would have remained there with her first love.

Taylor obviously sensed that Jennifer was wracked with emotions. "I'll leave you here to sort out your feelings," he said softly. He touched her shoulder and went back inside.

Taylor didn't really understand the emotions that were wracking Jennifer. *Seeing Dunbar was certainly wonderful,* she thought. But she couldn't help but think that Dunbar had been there when Dude died. Was there significance in her seeing him again? Could something disastrous be in store for Jack MacLaine? She certainly hoped and prayed not, but she couldn't be sure. *I've got to get over this,* she told herself. *Otherwise something bad could happen just because I'm thinking so much about it!*

Jennifer went back inside and went to her quarters. She had a small desk at the side of her room and went over and sat down. She started concentrating totally on her wedding plans when someone was heard clearing their throat. It was Monica Davis.

"Come in. I'm very happy to see you." Jennifer went over and gave Monica a big hug.

"How are the wedding plans coming, and is there anything I can do to help?" Monica inquired.

"They're coming along beautifully, and no, there's nothing you need to do to help. I just need you as my maid of honor."

"That is my great honor and privilege."

Jennifer thanked her and changed the subject. "How is everything with Mike Pulaskey? Rumors persist that you two are getting along quite well."

Monica blushed slightly. "I guess denying it won't do any good. Mike and I are hitting it off well, and I would be less than candid if I didn't admit that things might be getting a bit serious."

"I'm delighted for you," Jennifer gushed. "Maybe the plans I'm laying for me might help you in the not-too-distant future."

The two hugged again, and Monica left the room. Jennifer went back to her desk.

The United Nations troops, under General of the Army Douglas MacArthur, were on the move. The Eighth Army had broken out from the Pusan perimeter and was moving north. The X-Corps troops, including the U.S. Marines, were coming down from Inchon, having liberated the capital, Seoul, in the process. The North Koreans were definitely on the run, and it was just a question of how far north MacArthur would push. Would he go clear to the Yalu River, or would he stop short of that geographical location? The big question in the minds of many Americans would be the trigger point at which the Chinese Communists would enter the war.

The MASH unit, headed by Colonel Brad Taylor and Chief Nurse Jennifer Haraldsson, was moving almost constantly to keep up with the advancing troops. It was a grueling task, but it was paying substantial dividends in terms of lives saved.

Jennifer had postponed her wedding date twice to accommodate the moves. Finally, she complained to Brad Taylor. "How am I ever going to get married if we keep moving?" she moaned.

"Now don't you worry," Taylor said soothingly. "We will stick with your next date even if we have to hold up a move. Put in a call to MacLaine and tell him it's definite!"

"That's what I like to hear!" Jennifer said. She raced over to Bear Carter. "Bear, can you get me Colonel MacLaine on the phone?"

"Absolutely, Ma'am. Just give me a minute."

Carter had rigged a setup so that Jennifer and MacLaine could be in direct contact. Jennifer paced around the room as Carter put in a call. Soon, Carter held up the phone, and Jennifer walked back over. The connection was not very good, but it was a lot better than anyone had a right to expect. The communication faded in and out, so Jennifer had to time it correctly. *This is frustrating,* she thought. But she knew better than to say anything to Carter. After all, she was very fortunate just to be able to hear MacLaine's voice.

"Jack, darling, is that you?"

"Yes, it is, my sweet. What can I do for you?"

"Is that gunfire I hear in the background?" Jennifer asked. "Fighting up there is a lot heavier than I thought."

MacLaine laughed. "Anytime you're with Chesty Puller, you know the fighting is not very far away."

"You be careful! But the reason I'm calling is to see if you can marry me this Saturday. Brad Taylor promises that this time it will be a go."

"That's music to my ears. I'll be there!"

Time flew by for Jennifer. It was now Friday, the day before her wedding! But she had this uneasy feeling. Something didn't feel right. Part of it was that Jack had been calling her every day. But she hadn't heard from him in a while. Nor had she been able to get ahold of him. Maybe he was on a secret mission and couldn't tell her about it. She hoped and prayed that this was the case.

Then it struck. She looked up to see Jim Sherman standing in the doorway. He wasn't his normal, cheerful self. Instead, he had a look of deep sorrow and anguish on his face. She knew immediately what it was. She didn't have to ask. All she could do was bury her face in her hands. Seconds – minutes – went by before she could regain her composure. All the while, Sherman just stared at her. He couldn't bring himself to come over. Perhaps he knew better. Or perhaps he was feeling his own grief for his fallen best friend and perhaps he was simply unable to move.

Jennifer looked up, her face wet with tears. Sherman was finally able to move and rushed over to her. "I'm so terribly, terribly sorry," he croaked as he fought to hold back his own tears. The two embraced, softly sobbing. By now, Brad Taylor and Monica had rushed in. They stood close by, offering their condolences and hugging the two tightly.

"What have I done to deserve this?" Jennifer wailed as she asked no one in particular.

"You have done nothing," Taylor replied emphatically. "Neither of you has done anything to deserve this. These things happen in war, and only God knows why they do."

The speech helped both Jennifer and Sherman pull themselves together. Sherman wiped his face and then gave his handkerchief to Jennifer. She quickly dried her tears.

"Thanks, Brad," Jennifer said as she touched Taylor's arm. "As always, you know just the right thing to say. And thanks to you, Monica, for being here." Monica nodded and gently stroked her friend's cheek.

"Jim, are you okay?" Jennifer asked as she looked back at her fallen fiancé's best friend.

"For having lost the best friend a man could possibly have, I'm okay," Sherman replied. "But you're the one who should get the most concern. I want to say again how very sorry I am."

Jennifer and Sherman embraced again. This time, though, both were trying to console the other.

"I promised Jack that I would always be here for you if anything happened to him," Sherman said, "and I intend to do just that."

"That's very kind of you," Jennifer replied. "Right now, though, I have to quit thinking of myself and concentrate on others who are still alive. His parents are quite elderly, for example, and this will be a huge shock for them. He was their only child."

"I know, and I intend to write them. But to be quite honest with you, it will be very difficult."

Jennifer put her hand on Sherman's shoulder. "Why don't you let me do it? I'll be sure to mention that you had planned to write them but I said I would do it for the both of us."

Sherman seemed quite relieved. "No wonder Jack was in love with you. You are a living, breathing angel!"

"You're much too kind, but I hope to see you again soon and to see you very often."

"You won't have to worry about that. I'll be around here so much that you'll probably grow sick and tired of me."

"No chance of that," Jennifer said as she walked Sherman to the door.

The two were arm in arm as they proceeded to Sherman's jeep. "Call me if you need anything whatsoever," Sherman said. His voice was filled with emotion.

Jennifer waited until Sherman's vehicle was out of sight. As his jeep became a speck on the horizon, another car came into view. There was something familiar about it. Yes, as it got closer, the two-star flag on the front identified it as the staff car of Francis Dunbar! Word of her great loss had apparently reached him.

Tears welled up in her eyes as the staff car came to a stop. Dunbar didn't wait for his door to be opened. Instead, he popped out and raced over to her. *Here I go again,* she thought as the two embraced. She sobbed uncontrollably.

"Let it all out," Dunbar said softly. Jennifer complied!

After she regained control, the two went to the cafeteria for a cup of coffee.

"I don't know how he died or if I ever want to," Jennifer said. "All I know is what his aide, Jim Sherman, told me."

"I understand," Dunbar replied. "War is a terrible business, and somehow we have to figure out how to end it so future generations aren't subjected to this misery."

"I agree."

As they were talking, the nurses, doctors, and administrators came by to express their sympathy. Brad Taylor and Monica came by at regular intervals to see if there was anything they could do.

"Just take good care of the patients," Jennifer would tell them. "I'll be back on duty very shortly."

Jennifer and Dunbar walked back to his staff car. The driver opened the door, but Dunbar was in no hurry.

"It means so much that you came," Jennifer said as she looked up at him. "You have always helped me in my darkest hours, and it means more to me than I can ever tell you."

"If I can do anything whatsoever," Dunbar replied, "all you have to do is ask."

"You better get out of here," Jennifer said with a laugh. "Otherwise, I'll break down again."

The two embraced once again, and Dunbar got in his car. She threw a snappy salute, and the general gave a half-hearted response. Military bearing was obviously the last thing on his mind at this precarious moment.

Jennifer went back in and threw herself into her work. It was surely the best thing to do at another terrible moment in her life.

Chapter 17

Someone to Watch over Her

Jennifer spent the rest of a day working very hard. She tried valiantly to get the terrible loss out of her mind. It was no use, though. Visions of Jack MacLaine kept popping up. Several times, when it became too much to bear, she had to leave her duty station and go outside. Her world was definitely crumbling, and there was nothing she could do about it. Thankfully, Monica Davis and the others around her understood the situation and did as much as possible to help. But all Jennifer could really do now was hope – hope that time would heal the great wound she felt deep inside.

Got to get my mind off myself, she told herself repeatedly. Finally, the work day came an end. Several of the doctors and nurses had invited her to go to dinner with them. She graciously declined. She couldn't eat a thing in her state of emotional distress. And she had to write a letter to Jack's parents. It couldn't wait any longer. She went to her quarters and sat down at her desk. She got out pen and paper.

Dear Mr. and Mrs. MacLaine
By now, I am sure you have heard the terrible news. Your son and my sweetheart – dearest Jack – is dead. I don't know if I can make it through

*this devastating loss, but I am going to try. I will undoubtedly need your help
to survive.*

*And I can assure you that you will have my support. Together, I have to
believe that we can make it. I'm sure that Jack would want it that way. He
was that kind of man – always thinking and caring about others. He was
wonderful in so many ways, and that is the reason I fell deeply in love with
him. You can be very proud of yourselves for the way you raised him!*

*I got the terrible news from Major Jim Sherman, whom I'm sure Jack told
you about. Jim was planning to write you right away, but I persuaded him to
let me do it. I am sure you will hear from Jim in the near future.*

*I think Jim was almost as crushed as I was with this terrible event. This
fact also speaks to what a fine man Jack was. I think it is correct to say that he
will be dearly missed by everyone who came into contact with him.*

*I have to close for now, but I want you to know that I consider you as my
parents. You are indeed stuck with me forever!*

Lots of love,
Jennifer

Jennifer walked to a nearby reproduction machine and made two
carbon copies – one for Jim Sherman and one for herself. She would
give Jim his copy the next time she saw him. She folded the letter to the
MacLaines and put it in an envelope. After addressing it, she walked down
to the mail station and deposited the letter.

When she got back to her room, Brad Taylor was waiting for her. The
two hugged momentarily.

"I thought you may want a sleeping pill," Taylor said.

"That's very sweet of you, Brad, but no, thanks. I have to learn how
to get through this without the aid of a crutch."

"I thought that's what you'd say, but it was worth giving a try."

The two hugged again, and Taylor left. Jennifer stretched out on her
bed, knowing that sleep was a lost cause.

Jennifer thought the night would never end, but eventually it did. It
was a blessing when the sun finally appeared. She got up, showered in
the facility that was temporary at best, dressed, and went to the mess hall.
She was sure she couldn't eat anything, but the thought of a cup of coffee
was very pleasing. Standing at the entrance to the mess hall was a crusty
Marine colonel, with an unlit pipe wedged between his fore- and middle
finger. After seeing her nametag, he came up and introduced himself.

"Hi, I'm Lewis Puller." He stuck out his hand.

"Colonel Puller, it's very thoughtful of you to come."

"Nonsense," Chesty replied, "I wouldn't have it any other way. MacLaine was a fine man, and I owed it to you to come and give you my personal condolences."

Jennifer thought she had regained her emotional control, but the kind words were too much. The tears began to flow again. Puller was quick to recognize her grief.

"There, there, my dear," he said softly. "I know how difficult it must be for you." He pulled out a handkerchief, handed it to her, and then gave her a hug.

"Thank you, sir," Jennifer said as she wiped the tears away. "By the way, have you eaten?"

"Yes, but I'll have a cup of coffee while you eat."

"That's very nice of you," Jennifer replied, "but I'll probably only have coffee, too."

"I don't want to tell you what to do, my dear, but you must keep your strength up. And eating solid food is the best way to do that."

"I'll try."

Puller got some coffee while Jennifer went through the food line. He got a table for them and sat down. Shortly, she joined him. He was obviously happy that she was taking his advice.

"That's the ticket," he said. "Food will make you feel better."

Jennifer was surprised. The food actually tasted good to her. Having missed eating her main meals yesterday left her hungrier than she imagined. She was able to clean her plate, much to the delight of Chesty Puller.

"May I smoke?"

"Please do."

Puller placed tobacco in his pipe and lit it. Soon, there was a very pleasant aroma in the air.

"Do you think the war will be over soon?" Jennifer asked.

"In all honesty, I don't know," Puller replied. "It really depends if the Chinese enter the war. I think they could give us all we could handle, especially if their territory remains a refuge and we're not allowed to attack it."

"Do you think there's a good chance they'll enter the war?" Jennifer asked.

"I think it all depends on how far north we go. If we stop at the 38th parallel, then no, I don't think they'll come in. If we cross into North

Korean territory, then all bets are off. Personally, if I were the Chinese Communists, I wouldn't let an outsider such as Uncle Sam conquer my ally."

Jennifer was amazed at how much Puller was up on the politics of the situation. She also realized that the intense discussions had gotten her mind off of her personal problems.

"Colonel, I want to thank you for bringing me up to speed on this crisis. I also want to thank you for getting my mind off of my own tragedy."

"That's quite all right, my dear," Puller replied. "I consider it my obligation to help you in any way that I can. " He then changed the subject entirely by reaching into his pocket and pulling out his wallet. He opened it to show Jennifer pictures of his wife and three children. He had sparkling things to say about all of them.

"In the end," Puller continued, "It's all about family. Between you and me, I hope my boy has at least two sons. That way, the family name will almost certainly be continued. I plan to tell him this when he gets a little older."

And what about his daughters? Jennifer wondered. *He'll probably want them to take care of him in his old age! Oh well, this isn't the time to confront him about this issue. He has a lot of other worries to contend with.*

Jennifer and Puller finished their second cup of coffee. He took out his watch. "Look at the time," he muttered. "I have to be going."

"I'll walk you to your jeep." Jennifer said. She put his cup on her tray, stood up, and took the tray to the unloading rack. By now, she was very familiar with where to unload the silver ware, dishes, cups, and glasses.

The two leisurely walked to the colonel's jeep. "If you need anything whatsoever, all you have to do is ask me," Puller said.

Jennifer felt the emotions once again swelling up inside her. "I can't thank you enough for coming," she said. "I needed to hear all those good things you said about Jack."

"I only said them because they are true." The two hugged, and Puller got in his jeep. The two waved as the jeep sped off.

Jennifer threw herself into her work over the coming days. She was invited to dine with doctors and nurses, but often she refused. Instead, she would take a tray back to her quarters and dine alone. She even refused when she was invited by Monica to eat with her and her newfound boyfriend, Mike Pulaskey. Even though Jennifer had refused, she had to admit that Monica had become like a sister – a true sister. Monica had spent long hours consoling her over her devastating loss – a function that Jennifer desperately needed.

As she lay in her bunk at night, Jennifer couldn't help but wonder about Jim Sherman. She was sure that he was feeling great anguish over the loss of his best friend. She needed to see him and the sooner the better. Should she contact Colonel Puller and request that he get Sherman down to see her right away? Puller had said to contact him if she needed anything. And without a doubt Puller could get Sherman down there to see her right away.

Jennifer had a field telephone on her small desk, and she knew Puller's number. But she hesitated to make the call. After all, Puller was head of the First Marine Regiment of the First Marine Division. As such, he had lots of demands on his time. And maybe she should hold off and just give Sherman a chance to come down on his own. If he felt desperation over the situation, he would be down as soon as he could get away.

After another night of tossing and turning, Jennifer welcomed the arrival of the sun. She got up and took her personal gear to the women's latrine area. She showered, dressed, and put on some makeup. She was actually a bit hungry this morning! *Perhaps there was some truth to the saying that time heals all wounds.*

When she got to the mess hall, a number of doctors and nurses were already there. At one of the tables was her friend, Monica, with Mike Pulaskey right next to her. Monica motioned for Jennifer to come over as soon as she saw her. Jennifer lipped that she would be over as soon as she got her breakfast.

"Well, I'll be," Pulaskey said. "Maybe she's on the road to recovery."

Monica nodded and got a chair for her friend and boss. "I hope so," Monica replied. "She's been through hell."

Jennifer came over with a plate full of chipped beef on toast, eggs over easy, and two strips of bacon. She also had a cup of steaming coffee and a glass of orange juice. She set her tray down on the table and pulled out the chair. She sat down and commenced eating.

"Well look at you," Monica said enthusiastically. "It appears that you've got your appetite back."

"More self-defense than anything else," Jennifer replied. "I was famished after missing dinner last night. You may recall how busy we were."

"I certainly do," Pulaskey piped in. "The incoming wounded on those helicopters kept me operating until the wee hours."

"How are they doing?" Jennifer asked Pulaskey between bites.

"They were all still breathing when I left about 2:00 a.m. If you'll excuse me, I'll go check on them now."

Jennifer and Monica both nodded, and Pulaskey gave a wink to Monica as he got up to leave. Monica smiled and blew him a kiss that was barely perceivable to anyone but the two of them. Jennifer, however, was not fooled.

"You don't have to hold off showing affection because of me," Jennifer said to her friend after Pulaskey was out of earshot range. "That won't help anything."

For once, Monica didn't have a jaunty response. Instead, she measured her words carefully. "Okay, I thought it would help if we didn't show our feelings toward each other. But now I realize I was wrong. You know, I have grown very attached to you, and I wouldn't do anything to hurt you."

Tears welled up in Jennifer's eyes. "I know you wouldn't, and I shouldn't have been so terse. I have become very attached to you also. You are about my dearest friend in the whole world."

The two patted each other's shoulder briefly and then went on to the business at hand. Jennifer marveled at Monica's efficiency as her subordinate reviewed patient status and who the attending doctors and nurses were.

"I'm impressed," Jennifer said as Monica finished. "As a matter of fact, I'm going to put you in for a commendation and a promotion."

Monica only slightly objected. "There are other nurses around here that deserve promotion more than I do."

"Don't worry about them. They will be taken care of. But, right now, you're the one I'm thinking of."

"Thank you."

Jennifer nodded, and the two nurses got up and took their trays to the appropriate counter. They separated the dishes, silverware, and glassware and exited the mess hall. As they walked out, Jennifer recognized a tall, dark figure in an Army uniform standing in front of the nurse's quarters. It was Jim Sherman, who was now sporting the silver leaves of a lieutenant colonel!

"I'll let you two talk," Monica said as she hurried off. Jennifer nodded, only slightly aware of what her friend had said. Her full concentration was on the man who had obviously come to see her.

"Hi Jennifer!" Sherman said in a loud voice as he picked up a duffel bag and rushed down to see her. The two embraced briefly.

Jennifer could hardly believe the change that had taken place in Jim Sherman since she had last seen him. He was now extremely well groomed, with a sharp crease in his uniform pants and his hair neatly combed and freshly shorn. He had obviously just shaved within the last few hours.

He's a lot more handsome than I recalled, Jennifer thought. *No time to be thinking of that right now, though.*

"Congratulations for your change of rank," Jennifer said after a slight pause while she shook off her trance-like state.

"Thank you very much. One of the reasons I came was to bring you some of Jack's personal belongings. But I must admit that the main reason for my being here is to see you and to find out how you're doing."

"That's most kind of you, and I have to confess that I really had hoped you would come. I've desperately needed to see you, as you were very close to Jack."

Jennifer felt the emotion building up inside her, but there was nothing she could do about it. Sherman was most understanding, and he put his arms around her. "Let it all out," he said softly. She did just that.

"Look at your nice uniform!" Jennifer said after she had regained her composure. "I'm getting it all wet!"

"Don't worry about that. Just feel better."

Let's go where we can talk," Jennifer said as she took Sherman's hand. She wiped away her tears, and Sherman picked up the duffel bag. She led her guest to the empty area where Francis Dunbar had been hosted. The table with two chairs had not been removed, so the two sat down.

"Where are my manners?" Jennifer asked. "Can I get you coffee or something to eat?"

"Not a thing," Sherman replied. "I just want to see you and find out how you're doing."

"That's very kind of you."

Jennifer related the hard time she was having getting over MacLaine's death and how everyone at her unit had been exceedingly nice to her. She also mentioned that she was very happy to see that Sherman was recovering from the huge blow.

"I must tell you that I'm still torn up on the inside," Sherman said. "Jack was the finest man that I've ever known, and I miss him like I would a brother."

"These are the words I need to hear," Jennifer replied softly. "What's most important to me now is to know that he was appreciated for being the fine man that he was."

"I assure you that everyone who knew and worked with Jack held him in the highest regard. By the way, I have a letter for you from someone you know." Sherman reached in his pocket, pulled out the letter, and handed it to Jennifer.

She looked at the return address and found that it was indeed from an old friend. "My word! Bill Summerfield!" Jennifer gasped. "I thank you so much for bringing it."

"No problem, and please read it if you like."

"I'll read it later. Right now, I want to hear all about you, what you're doing, the risks you're taking, and so forth."

"Not much to tell, really. Jack and I were the interface between the First Marine Regiment – Colonel Puller's – and X-Corps. As you probably know, X-Corps is the Army Unit headed by General Almond that MacArthur put in charge of ridding South Korea of the Communists. Our job was to move with Colonel Puller, reporting back to X-Corps."

"And that's how Jack was killed," Jennifer said sadly.

"Yes. Colonel Puller believes in staying close to the fighting, and Jack was in the wrong place at the wrong time when an artillery shell landed."

"And you're moving up to take Jack's place?"

"Exactly. I'd much rather have it the way it was, but that's not possible."

"Well you be careful. I don't want to hear of you getting hurt."

Sherman nodded. "Not to change the subject, but a British major – Brian Hawkins – contacted me about your desire to respond to a letter you received from that German fellow, Otto Bruner."

"You know about Otto?" Jennifer asked inquisitively.

"I know a lot about him, as Jack discussed him on several occasions. I know he's on the other side of the Iron Curtain."

"If I write a letter, can you get it to him?"

"I think General Summerfield can. I've contacted him about the issue, and he's working on it."

"In that case, I'll get the letter written tonight after I'm off duty."

The two got up from the table.

"Thank you for bringing the duffel bag," Jennifer said. "I'll go through Jack's things tonight, keeping some of them and sending the rest to his parents."

"That's a good plan."

Jennifer gave Sherman a copy of the letter she had written MacLaine's parents. The two hugged, and Sherman carried the duffel bag as they walked out of their meeting area.

"Where would you like me to put the bag?" Sherman asked.

"We'll be passing the entrance to the nurse's quarters. If you set it there, I'll carry it the rest of the way."

Sherman nodded and set the bag down at the appropriate spot. The two then proceeded to Sherman's jeep. He got in the driver's seat and started the motor. The two waved as the jeep sped away.

Jennifer watched as the jeep disappeared over the horizon. Oddly enough, she was beginning to feel a definite attraction to Jim Sherman. Perhaps it was because of his closeness to Jack MacLaine. It certainly couldn't be anything more, as the time delta since Jack's passing wasn't that great.

Chapter 18

Getting Serious

The day went by quickly for Jennifer. There was a continual stream of wounded soldiers flown in by helicopter, and word had come that their MASH unit would be moving tomorrow. Apparently, people were taking the word 'mobile' in the MASH title seriously. They would indeed move as the front lines repositioned.

That evening, after, chow, Jennifer went to her quarters and opened the letter from Bill Summerfield. She read it sitting on her bed. It said essentially what she thought it would say. Summerfield expressed his sympathy for her great loss, and he reiterated the many fine points of Jack MacLaine's character.

Jennifer could also tell that Summerfield was hurting from this loss. After all, he had worked with Jack for a long time, and it was evident from his writing that he would not be over the loss in the immediate future. What did surprise Jennifer a little bit is that Summerfield said that he would hold off telling Molly about the loss. He thought that Jennifer would want to do it.

Jennifer checked off the people that she had notified of Jack's death. So far, it had just been his parents and hers. Now she would have to write both Summerfield and Molly as well. And, of course, she would have to notify Jacob and the Partudes. They were now part of her extended family. But first she would have to respond to Otto Bruner's letter. She had received it some time ago, and while Bruner had encouraged her not to write, she knew that a non-response from her was now out of the question. After all, people in American and British intelligence were now actively working on a way to get her reply to Bruner in a clandestine manner. Therefore, she felt that she must work on a letter to him immediately and have it ready in case Jim Sherman or Brian Hawkins thought the time was right to send it. Therefore, she went to her desk and started writing.

> *Dear Otto*
> *I can't begin to tell you how good it was to receive your letter. It means more to me than you will ever know. I realize that there is danger for you if I respond, but people in both the U.S. and British Intelligence organizations are working to ensure that you will get this letter in a way that is safe for you. Therefore, I have to trust that you will be okay.*
> *I am so happy that your life is working out well. Your children are adorable, and your wife is obviously the perfect one for you. You deserve all of this and much more, as you are a fine man.*
> *I got a terrible shock the other day. Jack MacLaine, who you met and who you helped get to the American hospital, was killed here in Korea. He and I were going to be married, and the shock of losing him has been almost too much for me. I am carrying on, but just barely.*
> *Yes, I am once again in a war zone and working in what's called a Mobile Army Surgical Hospital (MASH). We will be moving as the Army changes the position of its forward lines, staying very close to the front. That way, we will supposedly save more lives. It seems to be working, as the Army uses helicopters to transport wounded soldiers here. We are, to say the least, very busy.*
> *Word came that we will be moving tomorrow, so I must close for now and try and get some sleep. Please do try and write if you get the chance and can do it safely. I will eagerly look forward to reading anything you can send.*
> *Love always,*
> *Jennifer*

Jennifer put the letter in an envelope and sealed it, laying it on her small desk. She then changed into her nightclothes and stretched out on her bunk. It would be a long night, but hopefully she would be able to get at least a couple of hours of sleep. She would need it, as the next day's move would be trying and hectic.

After tossing and turning for what seemed like an eternity, Jennifer finally dozed off. She had no sooner conked out than the dreams started.

There was a man standing in the mist. She couldn't make him out clearly, as the scene was sketchy. Was it Dude, her first love? It certainly looked like him. The man was tall, dark, and handsome. But as the man came closer, Jennifer realized that it wasn't Dude. Perhaps it was Jack MacLaine. The man continued walking toward her, and now she realized that he had a faint smile on his face. But as he got even closer, she realized it wasn't Jack. It was Jim Sherman! Jennifer bolted upright in her bed. She was now wide awake.

She had to tell someone about this dream, so she went out to where Monica was sound asleep. She gently rocked her, grasping her at the shoulders. When Monica stirred, Jennifer put one hand over Monica's mouth so she wouldn't wake the other nurses. She put the index finger of her other hand to her lips to alert her friend to not make any sound.

Monica was obviously still half asleep when she looked up at Jennifer. She started to talk, but Jennifer's hand over her mouth muffled the sound. Jennifer motioned for her to come outside. By now, Monica was awake. The puzzled look on her face indicated that she knew something was up. Monica reached for her robe, which was dangling at the end of the bed. She put it on, and the two walked quietly outside.

When they reached the outside area, Jennifer started in. "I had the strangest dream, and I just had to tell someone about it."

"Well, I'm glad it was me" was the retort.

Jennifer related her dream, and Monica chuckled. "You really have a thing for tall, dark, handsome men, don't you?"

"I guess so. But I'm wondering what it means. Do you think I secretly want Jim Sherman to pursue me?"

"I wouldn't be surprised," Monica responded. "But just make sure you don't want him out of desperation. That could lead to a very bad situation."

"You're right. I do have to be very careful."

"Now can I go back to bed?" Monica asked.

"Yes, you may. And I have to add that you've sure grown up in the time I've known you. That's why I sought your counsel."

"I'm glad," Monica replied.

The two nurses hugged, and Monica headed back to get some much-needed sleep. But Jennifer was wide awake, and she decided to go to the mess hall and get a cup of coffee. Fortunately, the coffee pot was 'on' all through the night.

As she sat drinking her coffee, Jennifer couldn't help but think about Jim Sherman. He was undoubtedly tall, dark, and handsome. But more importantly, he seemed to have many fine personal qualities. He was reliable, for sure. When he said he would come to see her often, he undoubtedly meant it. After all, he had already seen her twice since Jack MacLaine's death. While it was way too soon after Jack's death for Jennifer to develop romantic feelings, she knew that she would have to be alert to this possibility. Maybe he would be the one for her. In any event, Jim Sherman was giving her a reason to live!

"May I join you?" Jennifer heard as if the words were being passed through a long tunnel. She looked up, and it was none other than Brad Taylor. She looked at her watch. "My word, its only 4:30 a.m. I knew you were an early riser, but I didn't realize just how early."

"We have a big day today, with the move and all. So I decided I better get an early start. But what about you? Why are you up so early?"

Jennifer explained her dream to Taylor. All he could do was whistle softly and shake his head.

"I've heard of people being contacted from beyond the grave, but I've never experienced it personally. In your case, however, it seems to me that MacLaine may be contacting you – trying to tell you that you have a lot to live for."

Jennifer sighed. "You may be right. I know that something – whatever it is – is helping me get over Jack's death. I'm beginning to realize – not that I didn't already know it – that we will all die someday, and that we have to make the most of it while we're here."

"That's my girl," Taylor replied, obviously pleased. "I need my head nurse to be at her best, and I now know that you will be."

"By the way," Taylor continued, "I probably shouldn't be telling you this, but Jacob Partude called yesterday. He talked to General Summerfield, and Summerfield told him about your great loss. Partude plans to come and see you in the next few days."

"That's wonderful. I knew he was coming to Korea to fly F-51's, but I've kind of lost track of him. It will be great to see him."

"Taylor smiled. "I envy you for your support network. It's the best I've ever seen."

Jennifer concurred. "I'm very fortunate."

The two finished their coffee and went to put the day's planned activities into motion. Jennifer saw Sergeant Bear Carter as they walked out of the mess hall. He was very business-like with a clipboard in his hand. She flagged him down.

"Bear, I'm at your disposal all day regarding the move. Just tell me what you want me to do."

"Thank you, Major. By the way, you seem more like your old self."

"Thanks, Bear. With the help of my friends, I'm beginning to feel like my old self. And it certainly helps to have people like you to lean on."

Carter nodded and smiled. "Now let's go to work."

Carter gave Jennifer two menial tasks and headed off. Jennifer looked at her watch, and it was now 6:00 a.m. *Won't be long until this place is a beehive,* she told herself. She went to make sure the patients were okay before attacking the tasks Carter had given her.

Jennifer went to take the vital signs of the most critical patients in the hospital. After taking them, she made small talk with the patients who were awake. Each of them expressed their sadness over her great loss. *Apparently, word has gotten around. Not a bad thing,* she told herself.

Jennifer was finally to the point where she could carry out Bear Carter's instructions. She counted beds and the number of tents, including the ones that were folded up and lying in the supply area. She saw Carter in the assembly area and once again flagged him down. He was busy giving orders to the men who would load the patients into trucks and take down the standing tents.

"I hope the Army knows what it's doing," he fumed. "Moving patients and facilities so often doesn't make any sense to me."

Out of the corner of her eye, Jennifer saw Brad Taylor rushing up to them. He was waving his arms wildly.

"Hold everything!" he yelled. "Our orders are changed. We're to leave the patients here and the tents standing. The only things that go with us are the doctors, nurses, and medical supplies."

"That's an improvement," Carter said under his breath.

But Jennifer questioned the decision. "What about the doctors and nurses who are intimately involved with the patients. The doctors who operated, for example."

"That's a good point," Taylor replied. "Headquarters has given me permission to leave one doctor and one nurse. I've chosen Mike Pulaskey to stay behind, and I'm leaving the nurse selection up to you."

Jennifer shook her head. "You know as well as I that the nurse will be Monica. I hate to lose her, but I don't have a choice."

Taylor nodded. "I agree with your decision, both professionally and personally."

"I better go tell her," Jennifer said with a sigh. "Now is as good a time as any."

Sergeant Carter was already off, supplying new orders to the workers. Brad Taylor told his head nurse to not be long as he needed her to help with the decision on medical supplies to be moved with them.

"I'll be back very soon," Jennifer said. "By the way, Brad, thanks for everything."

"You don't owe me thanks for anything."

"Yes, I do. You've been the best friend and boss that a girl could possibly have."

Jennifer patted her boss on the shoulder and went to find Monica. She found her just heading for the mess hall.

"I need to talk to you for a minute."

"What about?" Monica asked inquisitively.

"Brad Taylor just got word that patients and facilities are to be left here."

"Oh? What about the critical patients who have put their trust in a certain doctor and nurse?"

"You've gotten to the heart of the matter, and Brad has been told that he can leave one doctor and one nurse behind. The doctor he chose is Mike Pulaskey."

"What about the nurse?"

"He's leaving that decision up to me, and – unfortunately – I think it has to be you."

Monica thought for a moment. "I think you're right. I've gotten very attached to some of these guys, and I certainly don't want to be separated from Mike. But what about you? I don't take our relationship lightly, and I don't want to leave you in a bind."

"It won't be easy, but I'll manage somehow. And I promise that I'll have Brad get you and Mike back with us as soon as possible."

"Do you have an estimate of how long that'll be?"

"Not really. But Brad tells me that it shouldn't be more than a few days – only long enough for the new staff to get to know the patients and feel comfortable with them. And I'll remind Brad of that – daily!"

"Good. By the way, I'm really going to miss you," Monica said.

"And I'll miss you. But you haven't seen the last of me. I'll come see you before we go."

"I'm counting on it." The two nurses hugged, said goodbye, and went their separate ways.

The day was even busier than usual for Jennifer. She had nurses to supervise, patients to check in on, and the move to prepare for. She checked regularly with Sergeant Carter, who said repeatedly that he was glad the Army had come to its senses and decided to leave patients and structures alone. It not only made absolute sense, but it made his job a lot easier.

Once Jennifer was satisfied that the necessary items were being packed and that the applicable medical personnel would be transported satisfactorily, she went back to the business of nursing. As she gave orders to the nurses and checked on patients, Jennifer couldn't help but think of Jacob Partude's impending visit. It would be great to see him. From his fairly recent letter, Jacob seemed to have regained confidence in his life and a satisfaction that was missing when she had last seen him in Europe. She was very happy for him – happy that his life with Sandy was working out. And perhaps he was meant to be a fighter pilot. He seemed to do much better in this role.

Jennifer was yanked back to the present, as Brad Taylor called her name. "Say your goodbyes, and let's go," he said. Looking outward, Jennifer saw a number of vehicles strung out in a single column. These vehicles were obviously meant to take them to their new location. Sergeant Carter was with her boss, standing almost directly behind him.

"Bear," she asked. "Are there enough spare tents, tables, and other supplies going with us to set up a new hospital?"

"Yes, ma'am. We had essentially twice as many of everything. The new hospital won't lack for anything."

"Good."

Taylor said that she would ride with him in a staff car. The other personnel – including doctors and nurses – would ride in the trucks."

Sergeant Carter grinned. "Now they will see how the other half lives."

"I just have to say goodbye to Monica, and I'll be right with you," Jennifer said to Taylor as she hurried away. Her boss nodded. It was obvious to her that Taylor was somewhat impatient, so she would have to make it a quick goodbye.

Jennifer found Monica re-wrapping a soldier's wound.

"I don't want to rush you, but I have to say goodbye. Our transportation is here and waiting."

Monica stopped what she was doing at an appropriate point, and the two nurses walked outside. "There are two corpsmen that will be staying with you," Jennifer related to her friend. "The replacements – doctors and nurses – are scheduled to arrive here in the morning. Bear Carter has promised me that he will get transportation here for you when you are ready for it. But it will be up to Mike and you as to when you feel you can leave.

Monica smiled. "As usual, you've thought of everything."

"What was it Eisenhower used to say?" Jennifer quipped. "That a plan sounds perfect until it is put into action, and then it falls apart?"

"Obviously, Eisenhower never had you in on his planning."

The nurses said their goodbyes, and Jennifer hurried to the staff car that would take her and Colonel Taylor to the new location. She got in, closed the door, and the car launched forward. One after the other, the trucks behind them started to move. The convoy was on its way!

The next two days flew by. Jennifer marveled at Sergeant Carter's stamina. The sergeant worked non-stop through not one but two nights. By the end of the second day, they were ready to accept patients. And it was none too soon, as helicopters ferried in a new batch of wounded soldiers and one airman. The airman was none other than Jacob Partude! Jennifer went over to him and grasped his hand. Fortunately, the wound didn't appear too serious. While Jacob had lost a considerable amount of blood from the shoulder wound, the wound was clean. From her initial assessment, Jennifer saw that the bullet had passed on through.

Partude looked up at her and smiled through the winces. "I really wanted to see you, but this is ridiculous."

"Don't try to talk. There will be plenty of time for that later."

Glad that he's kept his sense of humor, Jennifer thought. *I wonder how he got that wound. Probably from flying too low! I'll have to find out.*

"You know him?" Carter asked.

"Yes. We go back a long way together. I'll tell you about it when we have time."

Brad Taylor came up and inspected Jacob's wound. Jacob had slid into unconsciousness.

"We won't need to operate on him, but we'll have to clean and bandage his wound. And we may have to give him a transfusion. He's lost a lot of blood."

"Yes, sir," Jennifer replied. "I'll take care of it."

"Get Tom Smith to help you. He's our newest doctor, but very competent."

Jennifer saluted as Taylor walked off. She then called a nearby nurse to watch over Jacob while she went to hunt down young Dr. Smith. She found him hunched over a nearby patient.

"Dr. Smith, Dr. Taylor told me to have you assist on an Air Force Major who was wounded and now under our care. He's got a shoulder wound that won't require surgery, but he's bled a lot. He may need a transfusion."

"Where is he?" Jacobs inquired. "I'll take a look."

"Right this way." Jennifer led Smith the short distance to where Jacob was on a stretcher that was placed on the ground. Smith kneeled down to check the wounded aviator.

Jacob had regained consciousness. "What's the verdict, Doc?"

"Well, I think you'll live. With appropriate rest and recuperation, you may even fly again."

Smith turned to Jennifer. "Let's hold off on a transfusion for now. He appears healthy as a horse. Just wash the wound out and get it properly dressed."

"Yes, Doctor. I'll get right on it."

Smith went back to the other patients.

Jennifer quickly checked on the other patients to ensure they were getting the right care. She then returned to Jacob's side with the bandages and medications. She gingerly lifted Jacob's shoulders and slid off his upper clothing. He grimaced but didn't make a sound.

"You're very brave," Jennifer said. "I know this hurts like the dickens."

"Only when I smile," Jacob said, trying to make light of the situation.

Jennifer finished dressing his wound. "I'll talk to Sergeant Carter, our administrative sergeant, about moving you to a bed. You'll be a lot more comfortable there. And don't worry – I'll be checking on you regularly. And I also want to hear all about Sandy and Jenny."

Jacob smiled and thanked her as she stood up from her crouching position. She reached down and grabbed his extended left hand.

"It's good to see you," she said.

"And you, two. Here I was planning to come here to help you over a rough patch, and you end up helping me. I'm just so sorry – . "

Jacob couldn't finish as Jennifer cut him off. "I know you are, "Jennifer said, "but the important thing now is for you to get well. So please don't think about anything but recovering."

Jacob nodded and the two let go. Jennifer felt warm inside as she went to find Sergeant Carter. It was good, indeed, to see her old friend Jacob at a time of great crisis in her life.

Jennifer was up bright and early the next morning. The night before had been a very late night, as the staff had to get all of the incoming patients squared away. That didn't matter, though. Today was a new day, and there were a number of patients to be checked on. She also had to get a new duty roster prepared to assign nurses to patients. Finally, she was eager to see Jacob Partude.

Jennifer couldn't help but recall when she had first met Jacob. It was at the Mayflower Hotel in Washington, D.C. She, Dude – her first love, and Dude's brother, Jacob, were heading off to serve in the last war. She and Dude were going on a secret mission to Norway, and Jacob was going to flight school in Texas. They couldn't be sure that they would ever see one another again, and, in Dude's case, the prophecy became fact. Dude lost his life in Norway.

I've got to get my mind off that and off Jack's death, she told herself. *Otherwise, I'll sink into a deep depression.* She put on her robe and took a towel as she walked to the nurses' shower area. She showered, dried off, dressed, and put on some makeup. She felt much better as she headed to the new mess hall. After all, she had a lot to live for!

After breakfast, she went back to her quarters and to the small desk that Sergeant Carter had insured would be in the new area. She made out the nurses' duty roster and posted it in the proper place. As the nurse in charge, she had a great deal of flexibility as to the patients she would see. Tops on her list was – of course – Major Jacob Partude. She would see him first.

As she walked to where Jacob was located, she noticed a handsome Army officer off to the side of the activity. It was Jim Sherman – again! And Jennifer was duly impressed. Once again, Sherman was spic and span in his uniform. Her heart pounded. Surely it was nothing more than a feeling of comradeship for the man who had been so close to her fiancé. Or was it? She rushed over to greet him.

"Jim, it's so good to see you!" The two hugged, and Sherman said that he felt the same way about her.

"Let's go where we can talk." Jennifer led a very willing Jim Sherman by the hand. Bear Carter's office was empty, and Jennifer said that they could stay in it until the sergeant returned. Sherman pulled two chairs close together, and the twosome sat down.

"I want to hear how everything is going, and don't leave anything out," Jennifer said as she fixed her gaze on her guest.

Sherman objected. "But that's not why I came. I want to hear how you're doing – and in the words you used – don't leave anything out."

The words poured out of Jennifer's mouth. How good it was to know that someone outside of her very close circle actually cared about how she was doing! She told all about the move and how Jacob Partude, the brother of her first love, was now a patient here.

"I'm not sure I like that," Sherman replied. "Is he married?"

"Yes, silly. And he has a little girl that they named after me. They call her Jenny."

"That's a relief!"

For the first time, Jennifer had an inkling that Sherman might be interested in her romantically. Or was he? In any event, it was much too early to think of romance when the man she was going to marry – Jack MacLaine – had just been killed. She would have to put romance out of her mind completely, or at least keep it submerged for a while.

"How rude of me," Jennifer said. "Would you like a cup of coffee or something to eat?"

"Nothing, thanks. I'm just here to see how you're doing."

"I appreciate that greatly," Jennifer replied. It means a lot to me."

After a short pause, Jennifer continued. "Would you come with me while I check on Jacob Partude? He has a fairly nasty shoulder wound."

"Absolutely. I'll follow you."

The two walked the short distance to where Jacob was berthed. He was awake and sitting up in bed when they arrived, and Jennifer introduced the two men. She checked Partude's vital signs, and he was doing okay.

"So you were with Jack?" Jacob asked, implying that he meant at the moment that Jack succumbed.

"Yes, I was," Sherman said, looking at Jennifer, "and I really don't want to talk about it."

"Good," Jennifer said, trying to control her emotions. "There are a lot of other things we can talk about."

Jacob and Jennifer talked about their time in Europe together, and Jacob showed Sherman a picture of his wife and little girl. "That's Jenny," Jacob said proudly.

"She's adorable," Sherman replied. "You're very fortunate to have a child, particularly one as cute as she is."

"Don't I know it," Partude replied proudly. "I'm so very fortunate to have both Sandy and Jenny in my life."

Jennifer smiled. She was delighted to know that everything was working out well for Jacob.

"We better let you rest now," Jennifer said to Jacob.

"And I've got to get back," Sherman said as he looked at his watch. "Colonel Puller is probably wondering what is taking me so long."

"The famous Chesty Puller?" Jacob asked.

"The one and only," Sherman replied.

"I'm impressed."

The two men shook hands, and Jennifer and Sherman walked out.

"I'm really glad you came," Jennifer said as she peered up at Sherman.

"I wouldn't have missed it for anything."

The two gazed in the other's eyes for a moment, and then they simultaneously broke it off. Both seemed to realize that their relationship would last for a long time, perhaps for the rest of their lives.

Jennifer waved as Sherman roared off in his jeep. She was transfixed on the jeep as it disappeared over the horizon. She was baffled. Did Jim Sherman represent the next big event in her life?

Chapter 19

Smooth Sailing (almost)

Colonel Lewis "Chesty" Puller was talking to Lt. Colonel Jim Sherman as they went northward across the 38th parallel. He was obviously worried about the change of seasons.

"I've tried to tell your General Almond that we need to be concerned about logistics. You feel the nip in the air? Now is the time to get those logistics types moving! I've seen the weather change here overnight. One moment it's shirt-sleeve weather, the next minute it's freezing. I'm not sure he realizes that logistics can be a nightmare."

"I see what you mean. Do you want me to alert the Army brass?"

"Yes. Talk to anyone who can get the ball rolling. I know Almond and MacArthur both think young Marines are very tough. And they are. But I refuse to have my men go into battle without proper clothing, ammunition, and food."

"I agree, and I'm very happy that you look out for your troops. I've been told that I have to report to Tokyo toward the end of this week, so I'll bring it up."

Puller lit his pipe. "Good. I hope you're more successful than I was talking to Almond. To tell you the truth, Almond kind of reminds me of stories I've read about von Paulus, the German General who surrendered close to 100,000 German troops to the Soviets at Stalingrad during the last war."

"Oh?" Sherman asked, feigning ignorance. "Why is that?"

"The German troops were starving and running out of ammunition. And, of course, they had to fight in sub-zero weather without adequate clothing."

"That is shocking." Sherman shook his head.

Puller was obviously feeling somewhat melancholy. "Some people say I love war, but I'm actually very much against it. Did you notice who was mainly buried at the ceremony outside Seoul? It was mainly young Marines! And your Army bigwigs – MacArthur and Almond – didn't give the Marines any credit in discussing who had thrown the North Koreans out of Seoul and the South. It appears that they're going to put us in the back seat for now, but, believe me, if the going gets tough in the drive up north, they'll be clamoring for the Marines."

"I can't argue with that."

This was the first time Jim Sherman had heard Puller elaborate on his feelings. Obviously, MacArthur knew that it would take the Marines to pull off something as big as the Inchon landing. But, as he had done many times in the past, MacArthur took the lion's share of the credit. Still, he could have given the Marines their just due. After all, Puller was right in that the Marines had paid a substantial price for throwing the North Koreans out of the south.

"Well, I've gone on probably longer than I should have," Puller declared. "Now let's change the subject. How's that young lady – Jennifer I believe her name is – doing?"

"She seems to be doing okay. When I saw her the other day, she seemed to be getting back to normal. But it will take some time before she's totally back. Losing Jack has been a huge shock."

"I'm sure it has," Puller said, taking a puff on his pipe. "And how are you doing? I'm sure it hasn't been easy on you."

"I'm doing okay, but losing Jack was the worst thing that's ever happened to me. He was a super person, and he sure taught me a lot about surviving in this man's Army."

"I know what you mean. At times I try and picture every Marine who's served with me, dating back to the banana wars in Central America. It's an awesome task, especially remembering the ones who are no longer with us."

Sherman nodded.

As if he were being pulled out of a trance, Puller looked around and put out his pipe. "Enough of this gibberish. We have work to do."

Puller waved at his jeep driver, who was about a block away at the side of the road. The driver jumped up and got in the jeep. He started the jeep and headed toward the two officers.

Lt. Col. Jim Sherman arrived at Brigadier General Bill Summerfield's office on Thursday of that week. It was early October, 1950, and the day was bleak. *Chesty was right,* Sherman thought as he peered in at Summerfield studying a document. *It was getting cold, and Almond better get the Logistics guys on the ball. Otherwise, the troops won't have the right clothing to wear.*

Sherman knocked, and Summerfield looked up.

"Am I glad to see you!" Summerfield got up and came over to give Sherman a bear hug. There was none of the usual military bearing, and it was obvious to Sherman that his boss and newfound friend was in a very tense situation in a no war zone!

"I don't need to ask," Sherman said. "I can tell that things aren't all rosy here."

"You don't know the half of it, but I'll fill you in shortly. First, though, I need to know how Jennifer is."

"She's doing remarkably well. I can't say she's back to normal yet, but I think she's getting there. I do need to see her regularly just to make sure she's doing okay."

Sherman saw Summerfield's raised eyebrows and knew he needed to clarify that last statement. "Of course, I feel more like a brother to her than anything else right now."

"You don't owe me any explanations, Jim. I know that Jack MacLaine couldn't have had a better friend than you, and I leave it entirely up to you as to what you do in the future."

"Thank you, sir. I appreciate that."

Summerfield then turned to the business at hand. "I probably don't have to tell you this, but MacArthur and Willoughby don't want to consider the alternative that the Chines may come into the war if we go north of the 38th parallel. Does your boy, Chesty Puller, ever say anything about this?"

"Puller is a fighter. He doesn't worry about the politics, just the outcome of the war. He did tell me to remind General Almond that the weather is changing and to make sure winter clothing gets here on time."

Summerfield looked as if a light bulb had turned on. "That's an excellent point. We at the top here in Tokyo don't think of some of these practical aspects. I'll make sure that you get to bring the subject up where it will do the most good."

Before Sherman could respond, Summerfield went back to discussing the strategic aspects of the Korean conflict. "I tell you, Jim, I'm very concerned. If we continue to proceed northward, I think the Chinese will eventually enter the war. So far, I haven't gotten Willoughby or MacArthur to listen to me."

"I sympathize with you, sir. But I think MacArthur is once again only thinking about how he will go down in history. I don't believe he'll be satisfied with just freeing South Korea. Instead, he'll want to unify the whole peninsula."

"I'm afraid you're right, but I have to keep trying. After all, a lot of young American boys will lose their lives if they have to fight the Chinese."

True to his word, Summerfield enabled Sherman to talk to people high up in the logistics chain of command. Sherman thought he had gotten the point across that now was the time to get proper winter clothing in. Was he successful? The proof would be if heavy coats and other warm clothing arrived in short order.

"Your talk to the logistics commanders was quite impressive," Summerfield said after Sherman concluded his briefing. "I especially liked your discussion of how the Germans in the last war were fighting on the Russian Front in shirtsleeves when it was snowing!"

"Thank you, sir. I must now ask you how soon I can return to Korea. I'm sure Colonel Puller will want me back as soon as possible."

Summerfield thought for a moment. "I think you can go any time, and, if you don't mind, I'll go with you. My wife, Molly, would never forgive me if I don't check up on Jennifer and see how she's doing. And I can check on her sister, Monica, at the same time."

"That's fine, sir. I'll be glad to have your company."

Jim Sherman knew that there was some hypocrisy in his reply. He didn't really want General Summerfield going to Korea with him. After all, he suspected that Summerfield would want him to arrange a meeting with Jennifer. And, while it was too early to develop a romantic relationship with Jennifer, the inkling was definitely there. Thus, Sherman feared, Summerfield could only get in the way.

Two days later, Summerfield and Sherman were in Korea and searching for Chesty Puller. They found him – as usual – near the front lines. This time, however, he was talking to General Smith, the two-star general in command of the Marine First Division. He was also Puller's boss. Introductions were made, and Smith passed on the good news.

"Lewie was just selected for brigadier general. It was a long-time coming, but it is a richly deserved promotion."

Puller showed off the new star that Smith had presented him, and congratulations were passed from Summerfield and Sherman.

"When will you pin on the new rank?" Summerfield asked.

"I don't know," Puller replied. "Probably not until I've done something significant here." Puller, as usual, was minimizing his own accomplishments.

"Not to change the subject," Smith said, "but I'm glad to see you two. I think your big boss, General MacArthur, is getting too complacent. General Almond tells me that MacArthur wants to slice my troops into small entities and send them north. Marines have never fought this way, and I'm afraid it will lead to disaster. I need you to tell MacArthur, as I doubt that Almond will."

Summerfield shook his head sadly. "General Smith, I agree with you wholeheartedly, but I'm afraid my boss, General Willoughby, and MacArthur won't listen to me. I've talked to them until I'm blue in the face about the dangers of the Chinese coming into the war, but they just waved me off. I will do what I can, but I'm afraid it won't be much."

"I hear you, and I appreciate anything you can do. Thank goodness, I have good men like Puller with me. It will be up to them to get us out of the mess that I'm afraid our leaders will get us into."

Puller thanked Smith and said that he had to get back to his men. Sherman asked Puller if he could have some time to take General Summerfield down to see Jennifer.

"Of course you can," Puller replied. Then he turned to Summerfield. "So you know this young lady?"

"Yes. She was in Intelligence with me in Europe after the war. She is also my wife Molly's best friend. And, on top of everything, my wife's sister is serving in a MASH unit along with Jennifer."

General Smith grinned. "Sounds like you can kill two birds with one stone on this trip. But don't forget what we talked about when you get back to Tokyo."

"No, sir. Indeed I won't."

Goodbyes were said, and the four men broke into three groups. Summerfield and Sherman headed south, while Puller, of course, headed north.

After the MASH unit's recent move, it was fairly close by. Sherman, believing that Puller would approve his brief absence, had arranged for the two of them to be transported by helicopter to the MASH location. They drove to the helicopter pad, and Sherman stopped the jeep. The two got out and boarded a waiting helicopter. Soon they were in the air.

"Have you ever been on a helicopter?" Sherman asked Summerfield over the roar of the helicopter engine.

"Once or twice," Summerfield answered back loudly. "To tell you the truth, I'll be glad when we're back on the ground."

Sherman nodded, and the two rode the rest of the way in silence. They landed in the MASH area normally reserved for incoming wounded. Looking out, Sherman could see Jennifer excitedly waving at them. The two exited the aircraft and went over to see them. Jennifer saluted, and then she hugged Summerfield.

"Oh, c'mere you," she said to Sherman. She gave him a big hug, and he no longer felt left out.

Jennifer and Summerfield brought each other up to date, and Summerfield asked how she was doing after her great loss. She said that she still had her ups and downs, but overall was on the upswing.

"Colonel Taylor, our Commanding Officer, would have been out to greet you, but I convinced him to let me be out there by myself. He agreed, but I did promise to take you by before you left."

"It will be good to see Brad again," Summerfield replied. "I haven't seen him since Washington."

The three headed to the mess hall. The mess sergeant yelled 'attenhut' when he saw the star on the General's uniform. The few people in the room jumped up, with one of them knocking over his chair as he came to a rigid standing position. Summerfield shot back 'at ease,' and the soldiers sat back down.

The mess sergeant came up to take orders, and the three each ordered coffee and told whether they would need condiments.

"I wrote Molly last night," Jennifer said, starting the conversation. "I tried to be as upbeat as possible, but I may have gotten a little melancholy at times."

"And rightfully so," Summerfield responded. "One thing about Molly – she's very understanding. I'm sure she'll be very sympathetic toward your problem."

"And how about your situation?" Jennifer asked Summerfield. "Is working for General MacArthur everything you hoped it would be?"

Summerfield chuckled. "In the beginning, I reported directly to MacArthur. But I guess I wasn't enough of a 'yes man' for him. He's brought in a two star – General Willoughby – and I now report to him."

Jennifer was somewhat stunned. "That doesn't sound good. I thought at your level, you'd be kicked upstairs, not downstairs."

"I don't really think it's a matter of being kicked in one direction or the other," Jim Sherman said, breaking into the conversation. "You can't believe how difficult the politics are in Tokyo. I think General Summerfield deserves a great deal of credit for just hanging on."

"Thank you for your support," Summerfield replied. "I have to level with you two. I have even been threatened with being shipped home, so I can't be sure how long I'll be in my present position."

"This is even more serious than I thought," Jennifer said, frowning. "May I ask, Bill, what exactly is it that your bosses don't like you saying?"

"This is strictly off the record, but I've voiced my concern about the Chinese entering the conflict. General MacArthur doesn't want to worry about that aspect. His only desire is to reunite the Korean rule under a democratic regime."

"And you can't really blame him," Sherman said, breaking into the conversation once again. "He obviously wants to go out with a total victory under his belt. After all, he's now 70, and this will more-than-likely be his last hurrah."

Summerfield shook his head. "I know, but just think of the casualties that young American boys – and others for that matter – would suffer. Looking around here, there appear to be plenty of casualties without the Chinese in the conflict. I think it would be a terrible price to pay for one man's reputation."

Jennifer and Sherman both nodded. At that moment, an Army Colonel walked up to their table. It was Brad Taylor.

"General Summerfield, how are you?" Taylor stuck out his hand and the two men shook.

"Fine," Summerfield replied, "and you, Brad?"

"The same, sir. I would have met you at the helicopter pad, but Major Haraldsson assured me that you were here on a social visit."

"That is correct. As you know, Jennifer and I go back a long way together, and my wife, Molly, would never forgive me if I didn't check up on her to make sure she was okay."

Taylor chuckled. "How well I know, and I certainly wouldn't want to get on the wrong side of Molly. She was with me for a good deal of the last war, and she bailed me out on numerous occasions. But I knew better than to cross her."

"You're right, there," Summerfield replied. He pulled out pictures of Molly and his new-born son.

"He's sure grown since the last time I saw him," Jennifer said.

"Just like a weed," Summerfield responded.

Jennifer, Taylor, and Sherman oohed and awed over the new-born boy, and Summerfield couldn't help but reflect being the proud father. He finally put the pictures away, and the conversation returned to the situation at hand. Taylor had pulled up an empty chair, sat down, and listened intently.

"Brad?" Summerfield asked in a questioning tone, "if the Chinese enter the conflict, can you handle more wounded?"

"As we did in the last war, we'll do the best we can. We'll need help, but I think the Army will get it for us."

"Good answer. Now if I can see my sister-in-law, Monica, we'll be on our way.

"She should be arriving shortly," Jennifer replied, "but she isn't here yet. She's back at our last position breaking in the new doctors and nurses. Can you wait a little while?"

Summerfield looked at Sherman, who shook his head.

"I'm afraid not. We're tying up a helicopter that is due elsewhere."

"I'll leave you folks," Taylor said. "General, it was great seeing you." Summerfield nodded, the two shook hands, and Taylor departed. The other three then got up, and Summerfield waved off the mess sergeant, who was about to call the room to attention.

On the way to the helicopter, Summerfield was very serious.

"Jennifer, if you need anything, don't hesitate to contact me. But you'll have to do it soon, as I don't know how much longer I'll be in Tokyo."

Jennifer was horrified. "Bill, is your situation that serious?"

"I just don't know. I do know that MacArthur views loyalty as being the most important ingredient, and I don't think I've convinced him on this issue."

The next morning, Summerfield and Sherman attended General MacArthur's staff meeting. The General was very pleasant and greeted them both warmly. As General Willoughby gave the Intelligence Briefing, Jim Sherman was alarmed.

"He's sure sugar-coating it," Sherman whispered to Summerfield. Summerfield nodded.

At the end of Willoughby's briefing, Summerfield raised his hand.

"What is it?" MacArthur asked.

"Sir, General Smith, the Commander of the First Marine Division, asked me to tell you that he feels uncomfortable about the Marines being broken up into smaller groups. He said that the Marines had never fought in that manner."

"I'll take that under advisement," MacArthur replied. He then gave an almost imperceptible nod to Willoughby.

That can't be good, Sherman thought. *No use alarming General Summerfield, though.*

The meeting came to a close, and MacArthur cheerfully said goodbye to the group. Willoughby approached Summerfield.

"I need to see you in my office," Willoughby said.

"Yes, sir."

Willoughby and Summerfield walked into Willoughby's office. He told Summerfield to have a seat as he went behind his desk and sat down in the swivel chair.

"I might as well get right to the point," Willoughby said. "You're being relieved of your present position and sent back to Washington. You will keep your one-star rank."

"Have I done anything wrong?"

"No. General MacArthur just feels that it is unnecessary to have two General officers in his Intelligence Unit."

Summerfield slowly rose. "In that case, I'll start clearing out my office."

Willoughby extended his hand and wished his subordinate good luck.

Summerfield walked out of Willoughby's office in a daze. He had never been relieved before, and it didn't feel good. On the other hand, though, he was happy to be going back to be with his wife and infant son.

He walked past his own office and down to Jim Sherman's. "Jim, I've been relieved. I'm going back to Washington. Do you want to go with me?"

Sherman thought for a moment before giving his response. "I would, sir, but I feel a responsibility to Jennifer. I have to be close to her."

"I understand."

Summerfield and Sherman talked for a while. Summerfield gave him the advantage of his experience with the top brass. At the end, Sherman could only say that he was very sorry for what was happening to a truly outstanding man. Summerfield thanked him and went to his office to pack. He only had a few personal items, and it didn't take long.

As he flew back to the states, Bill Summerfield had a bad feeling. Not only had he been relieved for the first time in his long career, but he had the feeling that the Chinese would enter the conflict before long. If this did occur, the U.S. would pay a very high price for a little parcel of land.

Chapter 20

The President and the General

It was early October, 1950 when General of the Army Douglas MacArthur arrived at his office in the Dai Ichi Building in Tokyo. He was feeling quite upbeat. U.N. forces were pushing northward, and the North Koreans appeared on the verge of total defeat. The newspapers were heaping praise on him, and everything was proceeding as planned. As he went into his office, his long-time staff member, Colonel Sid Huff, was there to meet him. The expression on Huff's face alerted the General: He was going to hear something that would not be pleasing.

"Good morning, Sid. By the look on your face, you have some news that isn't necessarily good, so let's have it."

"Sir, President Truman wants to meet with you, either in Hawaii or on Wake Island."

MacArthur was puzzled for a moment. "Probably just a political junket, that's all." He took off his overcoat and hat and went over to the chair behind his desk. He sat down.

"I can't afford to be gone too long, Sid. Tell them I'll be delighted to meet with the President on Wake Island." MacArthur pulled over a calendar and glanced down his list of upcoming events. "You can also tell them that I will meet with the President on October 15."

"I'll get right on it, sir." Huff walked swiftly out of the office.

In Washington, D.C., President Harry S. Truman was meeting with members of his cabinet when word came of the proposed time and place of his meeting with General MacArthur. He looked at his Secretary of State, Dean Acheson, and asked if he would accompany him.

"I would like to beg out of it, sir. I'm up to my neck in paperwork and meetings."

Truman looked at his Secretary of Defense, George Marshall. "How about you?"

"The same with me, sir. I'm just too busy. Besides, with MacArthur away from his office, I should be at mine."

The President was obviously disappointed, but he wasn't about to let the absence of these two men stop him. He told an aide to get the Secretary of the Army and the Chairman of the Joint Chiefs of Staff on a secure line.

"If necessary, I will order those two to accompany me," Truman growled. As it turned out, there was no need to consider such a harsh alternative. Both men readily consented to go. With a triumphant look, Truman hung up the phone.

"It's all set," Truman said to his aide. "Wire MacArthur that we will meet him on Wake Island on October 15."

"Fine, sir," the aide replied. "I'll also make your preliminary flight plans and firm everything up as soon as I know how many will accompany you."

"I'll make that information available to you very shortly."

The aide thanked the President and hurried out of the room.

Word came to General MacArthur that President Truman would meet him on Wake Island on October 15. The General took the information in a nonchalant fashion. He obviously felt that he was on a par with the President of the United States!

"Sid, I'll tell you shortly who is to accompany me to Wake Island."

"Yes, sir," Huff replied. "In the meantime, I'll have your staff ready your aircraft and make other necessary preparations."

MacArthur nodded. It appeared that everything was proceeding like clockwork.

President Harry S. Truman's DC-3 touched down at about 6:00 a.m. on October 15 on the Pacific real estate called Wake Island. He could see bullet holes in the structures that dated back to the intense fighting in the early days of World War II. *What a pity,* he thought, *that there wasn't better U.S. Naval leadership back then in this area of the world.* From reports he had read, he knew that the U.S. may well have won the battle for Wake Island and repelled the Japanese attack if only the U.S. Navy had provided better support.

As the DC-3 taxi'd to a stop, Truman looked out the window and saw him. There he was, five-star General of the Army Douglas MacArthur, with his open collar and well-worn Army hat, waiting to meet his boss. "Doesn't that man own a class A uniform?" Truman grumbled to no one in particular. "If he had been a lieutenant in World War I under me, I would have reamed him good for looking like this when his superior arrived. Oh well, I have to keep the meeting cordial."

Truman picked up the gifts they had brought for MacArthur's wife -- boxes of her favorite candy. He walked to the airplane door and waited for it to open. Then he walked briskly down the gangplank. He stuck out his hand as the General approached.

"I have waited a long time – too long – to meet you," Truman said cheerfully. "I hope our next meeting will be much sooner."

"I do, too, Mr. President." MacArthur gave the President a very enthusiastic handshake but didn't salute him. It was a very noticeable departure from established protocol.

Got to watch myself, the President thought. *This man obviously believes that he is my equal, which he isn't!*

A beat-up automobile pulled up to take them to their meeting destination. An aide tried to open a rear door, but both were stuck.

"Let's just get in the front," Truman said, somewhat irritated. The two men climbed in, and off they went. The others accompanying the two leaders had to fend for themselves in getting to the meeting place.

The President presented the General with the boxes of candy, and MacArthur was obviously moved that a man of the President's stature would be so considerate. MacArthur gave his heartfelt thanks.

The elderly men made small talk for the rest of the ride.

"Would you like to freshen up before we start the meeting?" MacArthur asked.

"It will only take me a minute," was the response. "But I would also like to have some time alone with you."

"That is very understandable, Mr. President, and I will see that you get it. Would you like the meeting between the two of us to take place at the start?"

"That would be fine. I would also like to have a little ceremony in which I give you an award. I need to do it while we're here, as it may be awhile before we're back together."

MacArthur just nodded. He had received so many decorations in the past that the thought of receiving another didn't seem to peak his enthusiasm.

The car stopped at the building in which the meetings would take place. MacArthur pointed to where the President could freshen up. The President nodded and walked off. MacArthur then motioned for an enlisted man to come over. Instructions were given, and MacArthur walked into the conference area. He went to a chair and sat down.

The President arrived after a few minutes. He had obviously washed his face and put a comb through his neatly groomed hair. He pulled out a chair and sat down.

"Is it okay if I call you Douglas?" The President asked.

"Certainly, Mr. President. I would encourage you to do so."

"Good. Douglas, the first thing I want to ask about is the possibility that the Chinese will enter the war. As you can probably guess, a lot of world leaders are warning me of this possibility. Why, just the other day, I got a message from Nehru saying that I should proceed with caution, as the Chinese are massing their troops for an incursion into Korea. What do you say about this?"

"My Intelligence Officer, General Willoughby, doesn't think there is much chance of this happening. And, if by some remote circumstance it does happen, we have atomic weapons to hurl at them. Thus, I think we should proceed to advance to the Yalu River and get rid of the North Korean threat once and for all."

"You make it sound simple, Douglas, but the truth is that I have to consider world opinion. And the world would be against our using atomic weapons."

MacArthur seethed. "Mr. President, I feel like I will be fighting with both hands tied behind my back if the Chinese do enter the conflict. As I understand it, I will not be allowed to bomb the Chinese on their side of the border. They in essence will have a sanctuary. And now you tell me that we can't use atomic weapons. What good does it do to have them if we can't use them?"

"I am tired, Douglas, and you are tired. Therefore, I don't think now is the time to debate the issue. Just proceed with caution. That is all that I'm saying."

"I don't mean to cause you extra problems, Mr. President. But I must tell you that I need to use American Forces to proceed northward. I know that you have established a line beyond which Americans are not to proceed, but I don't believe the South Koreans – or the other U.N. Forces for that matter – can go it alone. They will need the U.S. Army and the U.S. Marines."

Truman thought for a moment. "Douglas, I must word this very carefully. If you need to use American boys beyond the previously established line, then tell me through the chain-of-command. But try not to incite the Chinese. And by no means are you to take the conflict beyond the North Korean border with China."

MacArthur reluctantly nodded.

"Good," Truman replied cheerfully. "Now let's invite the others in. And I do have a decoration for you. Do you have time for a short ceremony after we talk some more business?"

MacArthur looked at his watch. "Mr. President, if I am to get back to Tokyo at a decent hour, I will have to leave pretty shortly."

Truman was obviously disappointed. "Oh well, I'll work on the fly if I have to."

The staffs of the President and the General were brought in, and lighter subjects were discussed. The stickiest of the issues was whether or not Chiang Kai-shek's troops would be brought in if the Chinese Communists entered the fray. Both Truman and MacArthur stayed out of the discussion, and the two staffs reached agreement. Chiang Kai-shek's troops would not be brought in even if the conflict did heat up.

At the conclusion of the meeting, President Truman announced that he would pin a medal on General MacArthur. It was the Distinguished Service Medal. The General looked pleased, but he would obviously have liked a more prestigious medal.

At the end of the ceremony, Truman bid farewell to MacArthur, and he and members of his staff jumped in the beat-up automobile. They sped off to their air transportation, leaving the General to fend mainly for himself. Finally, the General was able to flag down a pickup truck, and he and a staff member were off to the air terminal.

MacArthur was infuriated. "Imagine!" he grumbled. "The President of the United States didn't have the decency to share his transportation with me."

After traveling thousands of miles in a little over 30 hours, MacArthur was back at his desk in the Dai Ichi Building.

"How did your meeting with the President go?" an aide asked.

"About as well as could be expected," MacArthur groused.

General Walton "Johnnie" Walker and Lieutenant General Ned Almond were called in, and MacArthur told them that he wanted the Korean conflict to be finished soon. "I am going to show the President," he snarled. "We are going to finish this thing before the Chinese have the chance to move in."

Walker and Almond looked at each other but didn't say anything. Then Walker spoke up. "Sir, I hear that the Chinese have crossed into North Korea in large numbers. They apparently are in the mountains just over the border."

"Nonsense, Johnnie. If they were in North Korea, my Intelligence people would know about it. But just to put your mind at ease, I'll fly up there and take a look for myself."

Both Walker and Almond objected, saying that it was too dangerous. But MacArthur wouldn't hear of it. He rang for an aide and told him to get the flight set up.

MacArthur, with Almond and other top aides, flew along just south of the Yalu River. MacArthur couldn't see any Chinese down below, and he was in high spirits.

"You see, Ned," MacArthur said. "It's just as I expected. There are no Chinese down there. And this flight has taken the enemy completely by surprise. That's why there are no fighter aircraft up here to give us problems. As I've always said, surprise is the best element one has in combat.

"Sid, take a note to the Joint Chiefs," MacArthur said to his aide, Colonel Sid Huff. "Tell them that I'm flying just south of the Yalu River, and I don't see a single Chinese soldier. Tell them also that I expect our boys to be home by Christmas."

"Yes, sir," Huff replied. Huff made some notes on paper and walked up to give it to the radio operator.

"Sid," MacArthur yelled after his aide. "You can also tell the pilot that we can head for home. I think we've seen enough."

MacArthur's state was almost euphoric. The General liked nothing better than to be right.

As October, 1950 approached an end, MacArthur's plan was bearing fruit. A South Korean Army unit was close to the Yalu River. It appeared that the North Koreans were finished. Then it happened. A large Chinese force moving seemingly out of nowhere attacked the South Koreans and almost wiped them out. Everyone but MacArthur was stunned. MacArthur didn't seem to pay any attention to it. Instead, he was more concerned about Communist aircraft attacking from over the border in China and then returning to their sanctuary.

I have told the Joint Chiefs and even the President that this is no way to fight a war," he fumed. "But will they listen? No! In a war, you can't let the enemy have any sanctuaries if you expect to win. Thus, I'm afraid we're destined to tie at best."

MacArthur sunk into a near depression. It was as if he realized that his great victory at Inchon was about to be neutralized. He desperately needed total victory as he headed into his sunset years. It now appeared that he would be denied.

There was equal concern in the nation's capital. Truman met with Secretary of State Dean Acheson and Secretary of Defense George Marshall. Neither of these top cabinet officials had gone with him to meet with MacArthur. For this, he was none too happy. But there were now other concerns, namely the fact that the Chinese had readily defeated the South Koreans near the Yalu River. But then they disappeared, and Truman needed an assessment of just how serious the Chinese were. To get the assessment, he needed to talk to the two people nearest the top — Acheson and Marshall.

"First of all, I'll ask you, Dean. Just how serious do you think the Chinese threat is?"

"I don't trust MacArthur's opinion one bit, Mr. President. And part of the reason I didn't go to Wake Island with you is that I didn't think any good would come of it."

"Now hold on," Marshall said in a combative tone. "You're talking about the man I consider our most brilliant General of World War II. And don't forget his Inchon landing. I believe that will go down as one of the most magnificent moves of all time."

Truman was amused. "Gentlemen – gentlemen. I like your passion, but my question remains unanswered. Do either of you feel that MacArthur's assessment is right?"

"Mr. President, I have sent MacArthur an "eyes only" document," Marshall said. "It gives him complete strategic and tactical freedom in Korea. I don't like the man, but I do trust him and his opinion."

"That settles that," Truman replied. "How about you, Dean?"

"I have to admit that the CIA thinks as MacArthur does – that the Chinese won't enter the war, at least not in a big way. But I believe they are both wrong."

Truman stoked his chin. "It appears that we have a split decision and that there is not a consensus. Oh, well, as I have always said, if it is too hot by the stove, then one should get out of the kitchen."

Truman thought for a moment and then spoke again. "I'll let MacArthur proceed onward for now, but if things get any more terse over there, then I'll have to reconsider. That is all."

Acheson and Marshall nodded to the President and got up to leave. Marshall momentarily forgot that he was no longer in the military and started to salute. Then he remembered.

Truman sat at his desk pondering the situation. What a mess! Did Mao Tse-tung and Josef Stalin feel the same way? He couldn't be sure, but he thought so.

Half-way around the world, Jim Sherman had stopped off to see Jennifer before proceeding on to catch up with Chesty Puller. He kept telling himself that there was nothing other than friendship attached to these meetings. But there was no doubt that the two really enjoyed seeing each other.

At the end of their meeting, Jennifer walked him to the helicopter pad. There was a helicopter waiting to take him to his rendezvous with Puller.

"You be very careful," she said softly. "I couldn't stand it if anything happened to you." She softly kissed him on the cheek.

"I'll be very, very careful," Sherman replied. The two remained in an embrace until they mutually broke it off.

Jim Sherman looked at Jennifer out of the helicopter window until she was nothing more than a speck on the horizon. What did the future hold for him? Uncertainty for sure. With the Chinese now making hit-and-run attacks, all bets were off!

Chapter 21

Hordes Cross Over

L t. Colonel Jim Sherman caught up to Brigadier General Select Chesty Puller as Puller was heading north. The terrible news had come in that the South Korean unit approaching the Yalu River had been roundly defeated by the Chinese. Sherman knew that Puller would not be in a good mood.

"Oh, there you are," Puller exclaimed as Sherman strode up after having trudged a good way through the snow. "I've been wondering where you were."

"I had to stop off and see Jennifer. How are things up here?"

"Not good. Your boss Willoughby said we Marines were telling a fib when we said we were engaging Chinese troops. I aim to show him proof that we're telling the truth."

Sherman shook his head. "How are the Chinese as a fighting force?"

"A lot better than they're given credit for," Puller replied as he lit his pipe. "And I'll tell you another thing. Their General – Lin Piao – is quite a good officer. He's cagey and he cares about his troops. That's a very dangerous combination."

"I have to agree with you," Sherman responded. "I've tried to tell anyone that would listen that it took a lot for Lin Piao to fight the Japanese and then turn to routing Chiang Kai-shek's forces after the last war ended."

Puller nodded and motioned for his jeep driver to bring their transportation over. "We have to get going," he said. "Our work is cut out for us."

Puller was right. The Marines were now being thrown into the battle full-force. The problem was that they were split. Marines were not used to this mode of fighting, and their First Division Commander, General Smith, had complained. But it had not done any good, and, for now, the Marines would have to be content with the Eighth Army fighting next to them.

As their jeep proceeded northward, Sherman noticed that Puller's teeth were chattering. He also noticed that Puller wasn't wearing a topcoat.

"Colonel, shouldn't you have a topcoat on?"

"One of my men didn't have a coat, so I gave him mine. He needed it a lot more than I did. Particularly because I have access to a warming tent."

Puller took a puff on his pipe and continued. "Genghis Kahn supposedly said that no one could win a battle against the natives in cold weather around here. I just hope he was wrong."

"I just don't see how MacArthur could have missed a lot of Chinese soldiers when he flew just south of the Yalu River," Sherman said, reflecting his amazement.

"Readily explained, old man. The Chinese cover their uniforms with white cloth. From an airplane, you could easily miss the presence of whole Divisions. And then, of course, they like to hole up in the mountains."

So that's it! Sherman thought. *There could be hundreds of thousands of Chinese troops waiting in the mountains. Then, at the right time, they could come out and fight. What if they split the Marines and the Eight Army? This could spell big trouble for the Americans. Better ask Puller.*

"Colonel, now I'm worried. What if the Chinese split the Marines and the Eighth Army? Couldn't they then overwhelm them individually?"

"Exactly. My boss, General Smith, tried to tell Army people clear up to MacArthur that it was a bad situation. But I'm afraid MacArthur is more interested in personal glory than anything. Thus, he is having the Eighth Army move right next to us up to the Chinese border."

"I'm afraid he's forgotten what he should have learned from Bataan," Sherman lamented. "From what I've read, he didn't think the Japanese would come down the mountains in the middle, and he let his troops get split. Then it was an easy task for the Japanese to force the surrender."

Puller smiled. "There's hope for you yet, old man."

"Incoming!" the Jeep driver shouted. He pulled into a ditch, stopped the jeep, and the three jumped out and hit the ground. Suddenly, there was a huge explosion nearby, and the ground shook. After lying perfectly prone for what seemed like minutes to Sherman, Puller got up on his elbows, looked around, and signaled that it was okay for them to get up. They shook the dirt and snow off and re-composed themselves. Momentarily, Puller grinned at Sherman. "That incoming shows we're getting close to the front."

"Too close," Sherman grumbled. It was much like the incident that had killed his good friend, Jack MacLaine.

The jeep driver tried to get Puller to stop and proceed no further, but Puller was adamant. "No, damnit. Take me to the front!" The driver had no alternative but to comply.

After riding a short distance over bumpy roads that were heavily scarred by heavy artillery rounds, the three were obviously at the front. Marines were crouched down, firing at the well-camouflaged enemy. Puller jumped out of the jeep and ran to a foxhole where two Marines were firing at enemy troops hiding behind a hastily set up barricade. Puller jumped head-first into the foxhole.

The Marines kept firing, not realizing who the visitor was.

"How many are there, old man?" Puller asked as he kept his eyes glued on the enemy position.

"Too many for my taste," one of the Marines answered, still not realizing who the visitor was.

"I'll get you some help," Puller remarked as he scrunched up to make a dash back to the jeep. He patted the Marine next to him on the shoulder as he prepared to leave. One of the Marines looked around. "Do you know who that was?" he said with amazement. "That was Colonel Puller!"

The other turned to watch the middle-aged man zigzagging toward the jeep that was in the gully and only slightly exposed. "Well I'll be! And here I was beginning to think I'd never see him."

"How far should I fall back, sir?" the jeep driver asked his commander.

"Not far at all, old man." Puller replied. "I still want to hear the artillery blasts loud and clear."

"How's this, sir?"

"Fine. Pull over anywhere along here and throw up my tent. Get some help to do it."

The driver waved at several Marines walking slowly along the side of the road.

"You Men!" the driver shouted. "Give me a hand."

The sun was going down, and the temperature dropped dramatically. The Marines helped the driver get the tent out from the back of the jeep. The tent had been resting precariously in the space next to Jim Sherman. As usual, Sherman was sitting in the back of the jeep in a space normally reserved for the Commander. However, as was his normal practice, Chesty Puller didn't waste time on protocol. He sat in the front next to the driver so he could jump in and out of the jeep as the situation dictated.

"Let's go!" the driver growled at the other Marines. Soon, the tent was upright, and the Marines were packing snow around the base of the tent, making the structure air-tight to a large extent. The jeep driver started a roaring fire in the pot belly stove, and soon Puller and Sherman were in out of the cold. Cots were quickly erected, and the tent took on an appearance of home.

"Want a nip?" Puller asked Sherman as he pulled a flask of whiskey out of his pocket. "It's great for fighting the night air."

"That's an offer I can't refuse," Sherman replied. He took a cup out of a mess kit that was lying nearby and thrust it outward.

"Say when," Puller said as he poured.

Sherman waited until the cup was generously supplied before he gave the signal.

As the two relaxed and took swigs of their liquid refreshment, Sherman finally asked if Puller thought his men were fighting North Koreans or Chinese today.

"No doubt in my mind," Puller replied. "Those were Chinese. Did you see the white cloth draped over the uniforms of the guys my men were engaging? Tomorrow morning, we'll collect some insignias off their dead. That will be the proof I need, and I hope your man Willoughby is big enough to admit he's made a tragic mistake."

"I hope he is, too," Sherman replied softly.

What a pickle! Sherman said to himself. *I have to agree with Puller, even though I haven't seen definite proof that the Chinese are now in the fight. But I can't afford to offend General Willoughby, either, because he is my boss and the one who will write – or at least sign – my efficiency report. I have to be extremely careful.*

"Here, old man," Puller said as he tossed Sherman a package of C-rations. "We'll have to eat these tonight."

Sherman opened his package, and, to his satisfaction, he had gotten ham and lima beans. While they weren't the best, they were reasonably tasty and filling. He ate with gusto, as he had gotten hungry – almost famished – since he had last eaten.

They ate and then turned in, as Puller said that the next day would be very busy.

Jim Sherman was awakened early the next morning as he heard movement in the tent. He looked up, and there was Chesty Puller getting dressed. He looked at his watch, and it was 3:30 a.m.!

"What are you doing up so early?" he asked. His eyes were only half open, and his facial features were distorted.

"War waits for no one," Puller replied as he tied his shoelaces. "My battalion commanders will be here very shortly to give an update, and we will have to eat first."

Sherman expected to eat more C-rations when the entrance to the tent opened. There was Sergeant Bodey, Puller's aide, with two piping hot trays of food and a smile plastered across his face. He handed a tray to Puller and one to Sherman.

"This is a miracle," Sherman stammered. "I expected cold C-rations. Instead, I'm treated to a breakfast that one would expect from the finest restaurant."

"Bodey here is a genius," Puller replied. "He is always surprising me with what he cooks up."

Sherman picked up a fork and started to dig in. He had eggs over easy, toast, and grits.

"I wish I could have given you some Virginia ham," Bodey said almost dejectedly. "However, there is none available right now."

"That's quite all right, old man," Puller replied. "You've prepared a real feast."

Sherman seconded Puller's statement between big bites of food.

After finishing breakfast, both Puller and Sherman needed to shave. Shortly, Sergeant Bodey entered the tent with two helmets filled with hot water.

"I hope this will do," Bodey said as he handed each a helmet with steam rising from the top.

"This is fine," Puller acknowledged. "Tonight, though, we'll need a bath. Try and find us a bath house with plenty of hot water."

"Yes, sir," Bodey replied as he exited the tent.

The two men finished shaving just as the three battalion commanders reported in.

"Sherman," Puller said, "I think you know Jack Hawkins, Allan Sutter, and Tom Ridge."

"Yes, sir, I do."

Sherman shook hands with the three commanders, and the meeting commenced. All three said that their units had incurred heavy fighting. Puller was not surprised.

"I thought this little 'police action,'" Puller noted, "would be nothing like what MacArthur would have people think. The fighting from here on in will be intense, whether or not the Chinese come out in the open."

Puller shook his head as his three officers recounted their casualties.

"Gentlemen," he said, "before you go back to your units, we have to consider the consequences of the Chinese crossing the Yalu River in massive strength. Our boss, General Smith, has considered this possibility, and he's told me that our regiment will form a rear-guard action if this does occur. As you know, the other two regiments of the First Marine Division are farther north than we are, and we will have to ensure their safety."

Puller laid out how the task would be accomplished and asked if anyone had any questions.

"Sir, I have one," Sutter replied. "If the Chinese do enter this struggle in massive numbers and we're forced to retreat, I believe a lot of civilians will clog the roads moving southward and impede our movement. What would we do about them?"

"Good question. Unfortunately, Chinese troops would more than likely take advantage of the situation and blend in with the civilians. They could then slaughter our troops at will. We can't let this happen. Do I make myself clear?"

The three battalion Commanders nodded.

"And one more thing," Puller added. "I need insignias off those dead Commie troops to show we're fighting the Chinese. I'm tired of the Army bigwigs saying we're lying, and I want to prove them wrong once and for all."

"That'll be easy," Ridge replied. "I've already got a fistful of insignias, and there's no doubt about it. We're fighting the Chinese."

"Good," Puller said. "I'll ship them right up the line. I hate to say it in front of my good friend, Sherman, but we're going to shut his boss up once and for all."

Puller grinned and put an arm around Jim Sherman's shoulder. Sherman could only smile, as he knew Puller was right.

The day was fraught with danger, as many times Puller, Sherman, and the jeep driver had to dive for a ditch or gully after the jeep had almost come to a stop. The artillery fire exchange was intense and brutal. In between, Puller would order the jeep driver to stop any time they came to a group of fighting Marines. Puller would jump out and run in a crouching position to his troops, giving them words of encouragement.

"Remember, men," he would say, "you are the world's best fighting troops in the greatest fighting force in the world. Never forget that and give 'em hell!"

Puller would then run to the jeep and the three would move on to the next firefight. Jim Sherman was impressed!

That evening, Sergeant Bodey had found them a bath house. Bodey and another Marine brought in lots of hot water, and Puller and Sherman greatly enjoyed this newfound luxury. Puller smoked a cigar as he lounged in the heavenly hot water.

"I'll tell you, old man," Puller said to Sherman. "It doesn't get any better than this – at least not in war."

Puller took a puff on his cigar and continued. "My big regret is that my wife and children are very worried about me. My wife tells me in her letters that the papers make it sound like we're up against more than we bargained for over here. I tell her not to pay any attention to the news media and that we're doing fine. However, I know that she still worries."

"Not to change the subject," Sherman injected, "but I need your advice on a critical issue."

"Oh? What's that?"

"Well, as you know, I considered Jack MacLaine to be perhaps my very best friend. For that reason, I've been very hesitant to go after his girl romantically. But now I realize that I could very well be in love with her. So I need to ask your feeling as to whether it's too soon to pursue her."

"Old man, I'm flattered that you asked for my opinion. All I can do is give you my best input based on my own experience, so here goes." Puller took a puff on his cigar and continued. "My wife is the most important

---

thing in my life, and I wouldn't trade her for anything. Therefore, if you love this girl, to hell with artificial time constraints. Go after her – now!"

"Thank you, sir. I think your advice is perfect. I'll plan to write her and tell her my feelings right now."

Sherman got out of the tub, dried off, and dressed. He put on his clothes – including his coat and hat – and readied himself to go out into the cold night air.

"Our tent should be ready by now," Puller said, "so go to it."

Sherman nodded and threw a salute as he hurriedly exited the bath house. Snow was coming down, and he shivered as he walked hurriedly to the newly erected tent. He threw open the flap and went in. There was a glow from the pot bellied stove, and the tent was relatively warm. He took off hat and coat, laying them on a cot, and went to the small makeshift desk at one side. A kerosene lamp on the desk was lit and putting out marginally satisfactory light. He sat down and took out pen and paper from a drawer. He started writing.

Dearest Jennifer

I've hidden my true feelings from you during our recent meetings, but I can't do it any longer. I haven't told you how I feel because of Jack being probably my very best friend. But the truth is that I have very strong romantic feelings for you, and it could very well be that I love you. I just had to let you know this very moment, as I plan to see you as often as possible from now on.

I know that you are very busy taking care of our wounded, and I can't begin to tell you how much I admire you for taking on this most important duty. Without you and people like you, we could not possibly undertake missions like this one in which we free people from the domination of wicked and ruthless dictators.

To say that you are on my mind every conscious moment is an understatement. You have all of the qualities that I have dreamed about and that I would want in my wife. You are dependable, caring, and very loving. I don't know how Jack was so fortunate, but he picked a real winner in you. And, yes, it sure doesn't hurt that you are beautiful!

My bunkmate – Colonel Puller – will probably be coming in shortly, so I better close for now. I will come see you just as soon as I possibly can. Right now, though, the fighting is more contested than many folks probably realize.

Thus, I can't say exactly when I'll be able to see you, but I promise that it will be soon.

Love always,

Jim

Sherman folded the letter and put it in an envelope. He addressed the envelope, sealed it, and stuck it in the temporary mail slot that Sergeant Bodey had erected. How would it get delivered? He didn't know, but he also knew that the letter would somehow get to Jennifer. Needless to say, he felt a great sense of relief, as Jennifer would know shortly how he felt about her.

Sherman went over, moved his coat and hat, and stretched out on his bunk. He dropped into a very sound sleep – better sleep than he had gotten in some time. Soon, though, he was awakened by some soft chuckling. Chesty Puller, sitting on the other bunk, was taking off his hat and coat and looking over at Sherman.

"From you being in a deep sleep, I would suspect that your letter told the young lady everything that you needed to tell her."

"I think it did. Thanks to you, I can now relax."

The next morning, Puller, Sherman, and the jeep driver headed for the front lines, where fighting was intense. As was their usual placement, Chesty Puller was in the front seat beside the driver, and Jim Sherman was in the back.

As they drove along, Puller turned to Sherman. "Do you see any supply dumps along here?" Puller lamented. "I swear to you that this is no way to fight a war. If I were the Chinese, I would sure take advantage of what I believe to be a lackadaisical attitude of our high command."

At that moment, Lt. Col Tom Ridge approached from the other direction in a jeep. He waved for Puller's jeep to stop and pulled up beside them.

"Colonel, the Chinese have come out of hiding, and it's a real mess. They're not only pouring across the border, but they're coming out of the mountains in large numbers. We're greatly outnumbered."

"Just as I thought," Puller replied. "General Smith told me that my regiment will provide rear guard action. So that's what we'll do."

Ridge saluted, turned his jeep around, and took off at a frantic pace. Puller's jeep was not far behind.

In Tokyo, General Douglas MacArthur was holding a press conference. He was on an emotional high, telling those in attendance that the Korean War would soon be over. Suddenly, his aide, Colonel Sid Huff, came up and whispered in the General's ear. The General's mood darkened. "Gentlemen," he said, "if you'll excuse me, something has come up that demands my immediate attention."

The General departed the room with his aide a short distance behind.

Chapter 22

The Reservoir

"How could this happen?" MacArthur fumed when back in his office. He was obviously in agony, knowing that his place in history had been jeopardized by the Chinese onslaught.

"Sid," he said, "take a message to the Joint Chiefs. Tell them that the Chinese have stormed over the border en masse, and that we're in real danger of getting swept out of Korea."

"But, sir," Huff objected. "Isn't this contradictory to everything you've been telling them up to now?"

MacArthur waved his hand, and Huff knew that he was wrong in bringing up the subject. "I don't give a damn about the Joint Chiefs," he bellowed. "It's the President I'm concerned about. I was adamant – I almost gave him my word – that the Chinese wouldn't become involved. I'm afraid I will look like a complete fool to him."

"Sir, you will never look like a fool," Huff countered as he got back onto MacArthur's good side. "If it hadn't been for your magnificent thrust at Inchon, the peninsula would have been lost to the North Koreans, even without the entrance of the Chinese into the war."

"You're absolutely right, Sid." His aide's words were undoubtedly comforting to him.

Chesty Puller had to see for himself, so his trusty jeep driver drove the Colonel and Jim Sherman up to the Chosin Reservoir. Even though he would be providing rear-guard action, Puller nevertheless needed to see what it was like up at the northern tip. As they reached the 'frozen Chosin,' Jim Sherman noted how desperate the fighting was. The Chinese were out in overwhelming numbers. They were on horseback as well as on foot. They had modern rifles and machine guns as well as old-fashioned swords. And he had come to believe what Chesty Puller had been espousing – the Chinese were a damned good fighting outfit!

Moreover, Sherman saw that Puller was in his element. Puller would tell the jeep driver to stop periodically. He would then run over to a group of Marines to give encouragement. He would ask the right questions, such as 'What's your field of fire?' or 'Are you getting enough hot chow?' If the report came back that the food was substandard, he said he would do something about it. It didn't matter that some of these troops didn't work directly for him. They were his because they were U.S. Marines!

At one point, Puller was told by a Marine that they were surrounded. He hollered back, "Good. Now you can fire in any direction!"

As Puller set up rear guard action to ensure a successful retreat, Sherman could tell that the no-nonsense Marine was feeling a great deal of pain. "I tell you, old man, we're getting the hell beat out of us, and it's not a good feeling. We're going to have to get a lot tougher as a country if we're to remain free and keep our status in the world."

Sherman could only agree. *What was wrong?* he thought to himself. *Was it Walker, the Eighth Army Commander? Was it Almond, the X-Corps Commander? Or was it MacArthur?* Whatever the problem was, Sherman knew it had to be fixed. There was no way that the United States could let an upstart like Communist China ensure the expansion of a Communist regime. But who could fix the problem? He decided to ask Chesty Puller.

"Colonel, you are undoubtedly right. But what can be done about it?"

"Good question, old man." I believe it will take the President of the United States to make things right. In my opinion, it's the Pentagon that has royally messed things up, so the Joint Chiefs can't be depended upon. They treat MacArthur in too deferential a fashion."

Sherman was shocked. "So you think MacArthur is to blame?"

"Not exactly. I have to admit that his Inchon Landing was a brilliant tactical move, but he seems to have become complacent after that. This is off-the-record, of course."

Sherman nodded. *Maybe Puller is right,* Sherman speculated. *After all, MacArthur was in complete denial about the Chinese entering the conflict.*

"And, of course," Puller continued, "MacArthur is correct about the Chinese having a sanctuary. You can't fight a war to win if the enemy can withdraw into a safety zone, which is what the Chinese are allowed to do. I believe that we shouldn't be fighting with one hand tied behind our back and that we should attack China – perhaps even using atomic weapons."

"But wouldn't that bring the Soviets into the struggle?" Sherman asked.

"I suppose it would, and we wouldn't want that to happen."

Puller gazed outward, obviously deep in thought.

The environment was not calmer in Washington, DC. At the White House, President Harry S. Truman paced in the Oval Office as his two trusted secretaries –Dean Acheson and George Marshall – looked on.

"How could this have happened?" Truman moaned. "MacArthur at our meeting on Wake Island almost guaranteed me that the Chinese wouldn't enter the war."

"As I've said before," Acheson reiterated, "he can't be trusted."

"And as I've said before," Marshall said tersely, "General MacArthur is one of our most highly respected Generals. And I have to say again that I've given MacArthur almost cartablanche authority to do whatever is necessary – limited of course to the Korean peninsula – to quell the trouble and bring peace to the region. MacArthur obviously felt it was necessary to use United States troops right up to the border with China."

"And that's one problem, George," Truman said as he retook the initiative. "It was my understanding – and I thought I had given the order – to only allow South Korean troops to go all the way up to the Yalu."

Marshall waited only a moment and then replied. "With all due respect, Mr. President, I thought your orders were somewhat ambiguous. Since the Chinese have their own country as a sanctuary, I thought it only proper and defensible to give General MacArthur broad latitude to accomplish his mission."

Acheson then spoke up. "Mr. President, I think your only option is to relieve General MacArthur of his command. I know it will be very painful for you, but I see no other way out of this mess. I have spent countless hours trying to convince the Chinese that their country won't be attacked, but I am not sure that MacArthur won't proceed as he sees fit. He seems to have done this in the past."

Marshall didn't say anything; instead, he just shook his head.

Truman spoke after a long pause. "Dean, I need you to continue working with the Chinese. Try to get them to back off. I won't fire MacArthur for the time being, but I might have to do it in the near future."

Marshall seemed uncomfortable. "George," Truman continued, "I need you to get MacArthur under control. I want a report on my desk by tomorrow evening stating what you intend to do. That is all, gentlemen."

Truman went back to studying documents on his desk as Acheson and MacArthur got up and walked out of the room. The two walked shoulder to shoulder as they departed the White House.

"I'm sorry to have been so blunt," Acheson said to Marshall as their limousines approached.

"You said what you had to say," Marshall replied. "I respect you for that."

The two Secretaries shook hands and walked to their respective cars.

Back at her MASH Unit, Jennifer had barely enough time to read Jim Sherman's latest letter. She was thrilled, though, that he was developing special feelings for her. She definitely had them towards him! But she also had the same problem. Had enough time elapsed since Jack MacLaine's death to move on to the next phase of her life? She wasn't sure, but she figured that she better get advice from people she knew very well and respected. On top of the list was her boss and long-time friend, Brad Taylor. And, of course, there was Monica Davis. She hadn't known Monica for as long as she had known Brad, but she had developed a deep respect for Monica. Perhaps it was because she depended so heavily on Monica, just as she had done previously with Monica's sister, Molly. In any event, these were the two that she would ask for their guidance and counsel.

Jennifer, though exhausted from assisting in many surgeries, had to find Brad Taylor and then Monica Davis to get their input on her very personal and very important problem. She knew that she couldn't rest until she did.

Jennifer walked hurriedly towards Brad Taylor's office and found him coming out of surgery. He was covered in sweat and looked on the verge of collapse. The day had been very rough on the doctors and nurses that were on duty at their MASH unit. Helicopters, it seemed to Jennifer, were coming in continually to unload the wounded. It appeared to her that they wouldn't be able to keep up with the load much longer. She would talk to Brad about this issue after unloading her personal problem on him.

"Brad, are you okay?" Jennifer asked. "You look as if you're about to keel over."

"I'll be okay after I have a tall, stiff one. Will you join me?"

"Of course."

Jennifer knew that this was the best way to get some personal time with her boss.

They entered Taylor's office, and he walked straight to the cabinet that contained his sipping whiskey. He pulled out two glasses and poured a generous amount into each of them. He handed Jennifer a glass and motioned for her to have a seat on a beat up couch that had been moved into his office. He then went and sat down behind his desk, putting his feet up amidst a pile of paper in the center of his desk. It appeared that he no longer cared if paperwork going up to the Generals would be a bit crumpled!

Taylor took a couple of swigs before talking. "I guess you know that I have to get us some help. We're going to break under this load."

Jennifer nodded. She too had taken several large sips and was beginning to feel relaxed.

"But," Taylor continued, "I know you well enough that you have another topic to talk over with me. So shoot."

Jennifer quickly summarized the letter she had received from Jim Sherman and reported that he was developing romantic feelings for her.

"To tell you the truth," she said, "I'm developing the same feelings toward him. But both of us feel somewhat guilty, thinking that we should honor Jack longer before getting romantically involved. Thus, I need your opinion. What do you think?"

Taylor thought for a few moments, taking another sip of whiskey. "Well, if war has taught me anything, it's that life is very short. Therefore – and I believe Jack would wholeheartedly agree – I think you should press on with your life."

"As always, you give very wise counsel," Jennifer replied. "Now, what are we going to do about our overload situation?"

Taylor relayed that he would write the Army General in charge of their MASH unit, and he requested that Jennifer write someone with influence in the nursing corps.

"Together," Taylor continued, "I think we can convince the powers that be that we are severely understaffed and that something has to be done. After all, nobody at the top – including MacArthur – expected the Chinese to jump in. And our casualties are very quickly going to swamp our capabilities."

"I agree," Jennifer replied. She finished her drink and said that she would write the letter this evening. She bade her boss good night and got up to leave his office.

"So who is it you'll write?" Taylor called after her.

"I'll write Ruby Bradley. She's the top nurse in Korea, and I know she has influence with the top people."

"Good idea," Taylor replied as Jennifer disappeared from his office.

I'll find Monica and ask her opinion, Jennifer thought as she went back to the nurses' quarters. *Then I'll write the letter to Ruby. I believe Ruby's a reasonable lady, and I don't think she'll need much convincing.*

Sure enough, Monica was sitting on her bunk putting on makeup when Jennifer walked over.

"I really need to talk to you," Jennifer said as she put her hand on Monica's shoulder. "Can we go outside?"

"Sure. Just give me a minute. I have to look nice for Mike, you know."

Monica finished putting on her makeup, and the two walked outside.

"Okay. What is it?" Monica asked.

"I need your input on a personal issue. You know Jim Sherman – Jack's former deputy or whatever you want to call their relationship – well, Jim says he's developing feelings for me. I need to know if you think it's too soon for us to be involved. After all, Jack and I were very soon going to tie the knot."

"Of course I don't think it's too soon. You have to go on with your life, and I'm sure Jack would feel the same way. And come on now – didn't you know what my answer would be before you asked?"

"I suppose so," Jennifer replied, "but I guess I did need the positive reinforcement."

Monica invited Jennifer to have dinner with Mike and her, but Jennifer declined.

"I have to write the head of nursing here in Korea to get us more help. We're drowning under the increased patient load."

"I couldn't agree more. Let me know if you need any help."

Jennifer expressed her appreciation, and the two headed in opposite directions. Jennifer went to the desk in her small quarters and pulled out pen and paper.

Jennifer sat at the desk for a few minutes almost in a trance. She had gotten advice from the two people she trusted most on her personal problem: Brad Taylor and Monica Davis. But she would still have to be careful. After all, she had thought previously that the man she would marry was, first, Jonathon "Dude" Partude and then Jack MacLaine. But these two had been killed in action. And a third, Otto Bruner, hadn't worked out. Jim Sherman would be her fourth attempt. Thus, she would have to be careful – quite careful. Frankly, she wasn't sure she could go through a similar situation with Jim.

And she didn't want to do anything that would demean Jack MacLaine's time on Earth. After all, he was a wonderful man and should be shown adequate respect. *How fortunate I've been,* she told herself. *I've had three very fine men in my life – Dude, Jack, and of course Otto. It's true that Dude and Jack were both killed, but I've always got to count my blessings. How many women would count themselves lucky to be in my shoes – probably a lot!*

Right then, a nurse stuck her head in and said "Incoming!" Jennifer automatically jumped up from her table and went running out. The letter would have to wait.

Jennifer couldn't help but think of Ruby Bradley as she ran to the helicopter landing pad. Ruby had been a prisoner of the Japanese, having been captured when Japan invaded the Philippines. For three long years, Ruby had been interned by the Japanese. But, during this time, Ruby had done an immeasurable amount of good. She had provided medical care to anyone in her area that needed it.

And now Ruby Bradley had headed to the northern-most reaches of the Allied advance in Korea. "Safety be damned!' Jennifer could almost hear her say. Jennifer was sure that Ruby was surrounded by hundreds of thousands of Chinese by now, but knowing Ruby, Jennifer was sure that she was giving the utmost in medical care. Jennifer was greatly looking forward to writing this very courageous lady to ask for the much-needed help!

Chesty Puller shook his head as he looked down at the Marine dead and wounded.

"You see this, old man?" he said to Jim Sherman. "They've bayonetted some of our men while they were still in their sleeping bags. I tell you, they'll pay for this."

"And they should," Sherman replied.

By now, the Allies were getting organized. A British commando unit had been furnished to Puller as well as South Korean and U.S. Army units. Puller was becoming more optimistic that U.S. Forces could be withdrawn from the reservoir and would live to fight another day.

"By golly," Puller said, "I believe we're going to pull this off. And that British Major General – Dunbar I think his name is – has been a big help. Have you met him?"

"No," Sherman replied, "but Jack used to talk about him some, and I know Jennifer has met him. I also know that she thinks very highly of him."

Puller nodded. By now, his battalion commanders were arriving, and Puller let it be known to each of them the terrible price that the First Marine Regiment had paid for the Chinese onslaught. He also relayed the high price that the other two Marine Regiments – the Fifth and Seventh – had paid. He then laid out their plans for serving in the rearguard role and how they would extract vengeance on the Chinese and North Koreans.

Puller had no sooner finished giving instructions to his battalion commanders when his own boss – General Oliver P. Smith – arrived.

"Lewie, you're doing a wonderful job, and, as always, I'm very proud of you. I'm going to recommend you for the Navy Cross. I believe it will be your fifth, making you the most highly decorated Marine – ever."

"I appreciate that sir. I really do. But what about my men? They're the ones who have really made this work."

"I know that, Lewie. And I'm not forgetting them for one second. I'm putting them in for the Unit Presidential Citation."

"Thank you, sir. I should have known that you wouldn't leave them out."

Smith pulled out his cigarettes, and after offering Puller and Sherman one, he lit up.

"Lewie, I've been asked to take General Almond's place for a while. And I need someone to fill in for me at the First Marine Division. I would like you to take that responsibility if you feel you're up to it."

"Yes, sir!" Puller replied. "I've been shooting for this my whole career. I'll have one of my battalion commanders take over for me."

"How long will it take?"

"Oh, about an hour."

Smith took a final puff and put his cigarette out. "Good. I can wait that long and then I'll brief you on our drive to my headquarters."

"Can I bring this man along?" Puller asked, pointing to Sherman.

Smith looked at Sherman and nodded. Smith then turned back to Puller and asked if there was a place where he could get warm.

"Absolutely, sir," Puller replied. He turned to his aide, Sergeant Bodey, and told him to take General Smith to a warm area out of the cold. It was now about -25 degrees, and everybody was shivering.

Bodey smiled and requested that General Smith follow him.

"Come get in my car," Smith said to Bodey. "That way, Lewie will have his jeep when he needs it."

Smith got in the back of the car, and Bodey sat up front with the driver. And off they went. Meanwhile, Puller had his radio man contact Lt. Colonel Allan Sutter.

"Hi, Al?" Puller said. "I've got some big news for you. How long will it take you to get here?"

"About ten minutes" was the reply.

"Good. Come on the double. We'll meet at my old headquarters, where it was yesterday."

Sutter arrived at the tent that had been previously erected. By now, there was a roaring fire in the pot-bellied stove, and the warmth felt good to everyone. Puller and Sherman shook hands with Sutter, and Puller told him that he would be acting commander of the First Marine Regiment while he – Puller – temporarily filled in for General Smith as Division Commander.

"And Al," Puller said. "I'll write a memo to the officers and men asking them to give you the same cooperation and support that they've always given me."

"Thank you, sir," Sutter replied.

Very interesting, Sherman thought. If he stayed with Puller, he would learn how the Marines operated from the Division standpoint. He would, of course, have to get General Willoughby's permission to stay with Puller, but he thought that it would be doable. And, if it did go through, he would get to see more of Jennifer!

Chapter 23

The Air War

Jennifer Haraldsson was coming out of surgery. It had again been a very busy day for the medical staff. Jennifer knew that her boss, Brad Taylor, had written the medical staff commander to ask for more support in terms of the medical personnel that were available at their MASH unit. And she had written Ruby Bradley, the legendary nurse from World War II who was serving in Korea, to get her support. While neither had received an answer to their urgent request, Jennifer felt that it was only a matter of time before they received an answer. Anyway, she hoped this was the case.

As she wiped the sweat from her brow, Jennifer looked up to see a familiar face approaching. It was Jacob Partude. Accompanying Jacob was a man she had not seen before.

Based on Jacob's jaunty gate, Jennifer could tell that his swagger had returned. She had not witnessed this since their party in San Francisco at the end of the last war. She was delighted to see that Jacob was feeling good about himself once again. *It's important,* she thought. *Certainly the commander of an Air Force squadron should have positive feelings. It could be vital in combat.* The two of them hugged.

"Jennifer," Jacob said as the two released their embrace, "I thought I better stop in and make sure my wound has properly healed. By the way, this is Captain Zach Barton. He often serves as my wing man."

Jennifer and Barton shook hands, and Jennifer could tell that the young man was mesmerized by her. *Should I tell him right now that it is out of the question for me to get involved with him? No, that would be a bit premature.*

"How is the air war going?" Jennifer asked Jacob.

"Pretty good actually. We had a P-80 – I mean F-80 – shoot down one of their jets for the first time. And we're going to be getting the new F-86 Sabre jet very shortly. We'll need it to take on their latest jet."

"Oh? And what's that?"

"The Mig-15. It's a classy plane that can climb and turn at phenomenal rates. Luckily, Zach here has already been checked out in the F-86, so we will get our training from someone within our squadron."

"And what about you, Zach?" Jennifer asked. "What do you think of all of this?"

Zach cleared his throat before responding. "Well, Ma'am, I think we'll be in okay shape once we get our Sabre jets. The Sabre is a great airplane, and from what I know about it, the Sabre is a lot tougher than the Mig."

Jennifer was curious. "Why is that?" she asked.

Zach was now in his element. "The reason is that our folks worry a lot more about aircraft survivability. For example, we have self-sealing fuel tanks. This means that our planes won't run out of gas if a bullet penetrates the fuel lines. If that happens to the poor guy on the other side, he is out of luck."

"That will be for air superiority," Jacob interrupted. "We still have our air-to-ground role, and there's this Marine Colonel – a guy named Chesty Puller – who's always on our case about doing more. We can't seem to please him."

Jennifer giggled. "I know Chesty, and I'm not surprised."

Jacob shook his head. "How do you know him?"

Jennifer explained that Jack MacLaine had been assigned to work with him, and when Jack was killed, Puller came to see her to give his condolences.

"I'm so sorry," Jacob replied softly, obviously having forgotten for a moment that Jennifer had lost her fiancé.

"You don't have to be. I'm sure Jack would want me to go ahead and have a full life, and that's what I'm trying to do."

Jennifer couldn't help but notice that Zach hadn't taken his eyes off her. *I could do worse – a lot worse,* she thought. Zach was tall and thin with a thick head of blonde hair. He had almost movie-star good looks.

Jennifer turned her attention back to Jacob. "Tom Smith was your doctor, wasn't he?"

Jacob nodded.

"I'll have to get you someone else, as Tom is no longer at this station. Why don't you two wait in the mess hall, and I'll see if I can get another doctor to take a few minutes to check you over."

"Great," Jacob replied. "I could sure use a cup of coffee."

Partude and Barton went in one direction, and Jennifer went in the other. Shortly, she came upon Monica and Pulaskey as they exited making patient rounds. Jennifer observed that the two had become almost inseparable.

"Hey, you two. I've got a former patient who's come by for a checkup."

"Who, may I ask, is that?" Pulaskey queried.

"Jacob Partude, the Air Force squadron commander."

"Jacob Partude," Monica butted in, "the brother of the man who was going to marry you?"

"One and the same. I would have introduced you when he was here before but the two of you were taking care of patients at our former locale."

"I remember that," Pulaskey said. "I would be happy to check him over, and I've got a few minutes right now."

"Good. He and a young captain are down getting a cup of coffee."

The three walked to the mess hall in rapid fashion. Jennifer looked around and spotted them sitting at a table in the corner. She pointed at them, and the three started walking in the appropriate direction. When they arrived, the two men stood up, and introductions were made.

"Jacob, you know Monica's sister, Molly."

"Molly Davis? I sure do. As a matter of fact, I worked closely with Molly in Europe."

"And she never bit your head off?" Molly asked somewhat facetiously.

"I plead the Fifth Amendment."

Smart, Jennifer thought. Jacob obviously didn't want to get into the sordid details of their relationship. She quickly changed the subject.

"Jacob, Mike has generously offered to check you over. As soon as you've finished your coffee, we can go to an examining room."

"Roger that," Jacob replied. He quickly finished his coffee, and Jennifer, Jacob, and Mike Pulaskey headed for an available space where Jacob could be examined. Monica and Zach stayed behind.

It was nothing more than a cubby hole that Jennifer found, but it would have to do. There was an examining table, which was all that was really needed. Pulaskey told Jacob to take off his upper clothing, baring his chest. Jacob shivered as he stripped.

"This won't take long," Pulaskey said. He put his stethoscope on and moved it over Jacob's chest and back.

"Well, I can say without reservations that you're in excellent health. Your wound has completely healed, and I would say you could run a marathon if you so desired. You can put your shirt back on."

Jacob dressed quickly.

"By the way," Pulaskey asked, where are you stationed?"

"My squadron is currently at Taegu Air Base, but we're getting ready to move to Kimpo – just as soon as we get the new F-86 Sabre jet."

"Do you know how to fly the Sabre?"

"No, but the young man I introduced you to – Captain Zach Barton – is going to teach us as soon as we get our allotment."

Jennifer was curious. "Do you think it will be hard for you to learn?"

"No, not really. But I have to tell you that our leading propeller-aircraft ace of World War II – Richard Bong – was killed taking off in a jet. So the speed factor will probably have more of an impact than I currently believe."

"You be careful," Jennifer replied. "I wouldn't want Sandy and Jenny to have to go through life without you."

"Now I'm curious," Pulaskey said. "Who are Sandy and Jenny?"

Jacob laughed. "Sandy is my wife, and Jenny is my little girl, named after you-know-who." Jacob pointed at Jennifer.

"It all makes sense now," Pulaskey replied.

"Seriously, though," Jacob added as he turned to Jennifer, "is Monica as good as her sister?"

"Be careful," Pulaskey cajoled.

"Actually, I only have good things to say about Monica, so I don't have to be careful," Jennifer replied. "Yes, I think she is as good as her sister. But, Jacob, you have to be careful and not bring up the comparison. There is some sensitivity there that I don't understand."

"I've noticed the same thing," Pulaskey said. "So, as I've gotten to know Monica better and our relationship has become closer, I've avoided the topic."

Jacob nodded. "Wise move, and I'll do likewise."

The three entered the mess hall and walked over to the table where Monica and Zach were seated. They were unaware of the three approaching, as they were in a detailed discussion. Zach was motioning with his hands, and Monica was paying close attention.

"I hope we're not interrupting something important," Jennifer said as they reached the table.

"Zach was just explaining how airplanes work," Monica said enthusiastically. "I now understand why the Sabre jet has wings that are swept back.

Monica suddenly looked dejected, and Zach asked why.

"I was born too early," Monica moaned. "I want to be a fighter pilot, but women aren't allowed to fly in combat. Oh well, if I'm lucky enough to have a daughter, maybe by then things will have changed."

Jacob gave Pulaskey a playful nudge in the ribs.

Zach looked at his watch. "Boss, we better get ready to go. They'll expect you back shortly."

"Ah, the trials of being a squadron commander," Jacob lamented. "But you're right, Zach. We better head out."

"I'm impressed, Zach," Jennifer said. "You're obviously a very responsible and caring individual."

Monica and Zach got up from the table, and the five walked out of the mess hall. Monica and Pulaskey bade the visitors farewell and headed back to the patient area. Jennifer walked out with them.

Jacob and Zach headed to their helicopter that was parked on the pad outside the MASH entrance. The pilot started the engines when he saw them. But before getting in, Zach turned to Jennifer.

"Ma'am, would it be okay if I wrote you or planned to come see you?"

Jennifer was somewhat taken aback, but she recovered quickly. "Certainly, Zach. I would be very happy if you did. But I have to warn you if I read your intentions correctly. You will be facing stiff competition."

Zach nodded enthusiastically, but Jacob had a curious look on his face. "I better tell you that we're moving bases in the next few days," he said to Jennifer.

"Why?" she replied in surprised fashion.

"We're transitioning from propeller airplanes to the new Sabre jet, and our allotment should be arriving in the next couple of days. The Sabre requires a longer take-off field, so we're moving from Taegu to Kimpo Air Base."

Jennifer nodded. "Your explanation really helps."

Jennifer and Jacob hugged, and then she hugged Zach.

"If we're going to be good friends," she said to Zach, "then a hug is certainly more appropriate than a handshake."

"I certainly agree with that," the young Captain replied.

The two Air Force officers boarded the helicopter, and soon it was in the air.

"You don't think I was too forward, do you?" Zach asked his boss.

Jacob just laughed. "No, not at all. In fact, I think you will need to be quite aggressive if you are serious about Jennifer."

"I certainly am. She has all of the qualities in a woman that I'm searching for. She's kind, considerate, smart, and very sophisticated. I think she would make an outstanding wife. And I know your brother thought so, too."

"He certainly did. And you forgot to say that she's beautiful. That certainly doesn't hurt."

"I can't deny that, and, while I hadn't really thought about it, I have to agree – it certainly helps."

After a bumpy and seemingly long flight, they landed at Taegu Air Base. There was a lot of activity at the base, meaning that members of Jacob's squadron were preparing to move to Kimpo.

"It won't be long," Jacob said to Zach, "before you're training our guys on the Sabre. Are you ready?"

"Absolutely, sir. I can't wait."

Jacob and Zach climbed down from the helicopter and walked over to Jacob's jeep. Zach got into the driver's seat, and Jacob walked over to the passenger side and climbed in.

"Let's stop by the squadron," Jacob said. "I'll see if there are any directives that have come down."

Zach nodded, and soon they pulled up in front of the squadron headquarters. Zach stopped the jeep and they got out and went into the building.

"I'm going to miss this place," Jacob said under his breath.

"I agree," Zach replied.

They greeted the sergeant outside of Jacob's office and went in. Jacob turned on the lights. When he did so, he saw an official looking packet sitting on his desk. He went over and opened it.

"Wow," he said after reading the document. "We're to move to Kimpo immediately and begin training on the F-86."

"That will be your show," Jacob added as he looked over at Zach.

"I look forward to it," Zach replied.

The next two days were a blur as the move was completed. Jacob was satisfied with the new quarters, thinking that they were somewhat improved over the old ones. Now they were ready for Zach to start training people on the new jet fighter. His training started bright and early the day after the squadron was re-situated in its new quarters. At precisely 0600, Squadron Commander Jacob Partude gave his introductory remarks. His audience was the pilots that were seated in the briefing room.

"Gentlemen, you are about to begin your training on the new F-86 jet fighter. You will need this airplane if you are to successfully compete against the enemy's jet fighter, the Mig-15. Captain Zach Barton will be your instructor, and he will teach you how to fly this jet. I encourage you to learn all you can from Zach and to not be over-confident. Being too cocky can get you killed. On the other hand, I want you to be aggressive and assertive. You will need to be if you are to successfully compete against the Mig-15. That is all I have to say, and, at this time, it is my pleasure to bring on Zach Barton. Listen to him and do exactly as he says. It could save your life."

Zach Barton walked to the podium, and he shook hands with his boss.

Trying to make light of the situation, Barton mentioned that Jacob would also be a student. The audience – made up of fighter pilot students – howled at this information. One of the students quipped that it would be good to be on equal footing with their boss. The students laughed heartily again. *This is good,* Jacob thought. *It is helping the students to relax.*

The students became very quiet as Zach started his lecture. "You may wonder why the wings are swept on the Sabre. It is because of compressibility effects. In other words, it keeps the speed of the airflow over the wings at subsonic speeds under normal conditions. Now, if you go into a steep dive, the speed over the wings could reach supersonic magnitudes. If this happens, all bets are off. But I can tell you that the

Sabre is a very tough airplane. You should come out of this scenario in satisfactory shape, but you should realize that the Sabre is not designed for supersonic flight under normal conditions. This is coming down the road, but nominal supersonic flight is not yet here."

Zach then laid out the following days' schedules. The pilots would have two days of InClass instruction followed by flights in the two-seater Sabre jet fighter.

"At the end of this time," Barton continued, "those of you who are deemed to have passed the training regimen will be allowed to take the Sabre jet into aerial combat. Those of you who are thought to need more training will be held back. Are there any questions so far?"

One of the students asked if they would be allowed to use the Sabre jet in an air-to- ground role. "No!" Barton answered emphatically. "The F-86 is here to take on the Mig-15. Remember that."

"But what about that Marine Colonel," the student continued. "Puller is his name. All he cares about is support of the ground troops. He got some of us in trouble for not being aggressive enough in the air-to-ground role. He wanted us to dive down and support them in bad weather."

"If he rears his head again, you let me know," Barton replied. "I'll go to the top if I have to. I'll get him off your backs."

Barton looked at Partude, who gave him a nod. Barton smiled. "It's great to have a boss like Colonel Partude. He's very supportive."

Barton continued his briefing. "Let the Air Force pilots who still fly the F-51 worry about the ground support role. Also, the Navy is bringing in the F9F Panther, which has quite an air-to-ground capability. Those folks can worry about Puller and the other ground-pounders. Your role will be to neutralize the Mig-15. Remember that."

The pilots – who filled the room – clapped. *Nice to have a group such as this,* Partude thought. He smiled and gave the group a 'thumbs up.'

The in-class training was intense. Barton had two other officers helping him with the lecture material. The three of them went over the flight characteristics of the F-86, emphasizing the strong points as well as the weaknesses. By the end of the two days, pilots felt very comfortable with their transition into the latest fighter aircraft of the U.S.

As he wrapped up the ground portion of the training, Barton cautioned the pilots: "Remember, the Mig-15 will be able to climb faster and turn faster than you. It also has a higher ceiling. But it is not perfect, either. For one thing, its rate of fire is too slow. This means that, in combat against it, you don't want to be moving in a straight line. Keep jinking or whatever."

Barton paced back and forth, his hands clasped behind his back. "Before we start giving you aerial training in the two-seater F-86, I have one more piece of advice to give you. Remember, although the Mig-15 can outperform the F-86 in an aerodynamic sense, their pilots aren't as smart or as well-trained as you. Therefore, talk to your wing-man. Develop your own tactics. Go out there and win!"

The pilots gave Barton and the other instructors a standing ovation. They were now ready to get their hands on the yoke and start flying this 'faster-than-greased-lightning' airplane. They hurriedly exited their classroom.

The flight training schedule had been posted on the bulletin board outside the classroom. Jacob Partude already knew that he would be the first one to go up with Zach Barton. He waited for Barton to arrive at their aircraft.

"All set, skipper?" Barton asked as he approached the plane.

"You bet I am," Partude replied, donning his helmet.

The two officers climbed into the seats, Partude in the front and Barton in the rear.

"I'll take the controls for the first takeoff, letting you get the feel of it," Barton said. "Then I'll let you take over during our 'touch and go' after you've gotten a feel for it."

"Aye, aye, sir," Partude replied. He realized that his response was corny, but he couldn't do anything about it now.

Partude was amazed at the power of the plane during takeoff. The jet lifted effortlessly into the sky with a speed that was breath-taking. But all that Partude could muster was "wow," another corny response from the squadron commander!

During the first two 'touch and goes,' Barton maintained control of the stick. But before holding it longer than originally planned, he had received the consent of his student.

On the third go-around – where they momentarily touched the runway and then climbed into the air right away – Partude was feeling a lot more comfortable. He said that he was ready to take the controls.

"Great, sir," Barton replied.

They made the approach to the runway in routine fashion. As they came in to touch down, the runway came up faster than Partude anticipated. He made a hard touch-down and then started climbing right away. The plane awkwardly twisted and rotated upward. Finally, Partude got it under control.

"That wasn't so bad, was it?" Barton said reassuringly.

"Oh, no?" Partude replied jokingly. "How many years did it take off of your life?"

On each pass, Partude got better. By the time they finished, it was if he was an old pro.

As they taxi'd down to the parking area, Barton was very complimentary. "You'll soon be ready for combat."

The next days went by quickly, and it was soon time for members of Jacob's squadron to take part in the air superiority mission. Initially, Jacob was to fly as Zach Barton's wing man. Zach and Jacob developed tactics that they would employ if they encountered the enemy.

"We'll employ the same tactic as our guys did in the last war," Zach told Jacob. "If the enemy is on your tail, swing by in front of me, and I'll take care of him."

"So you think this tactic will work with the F-86 as well as our old War II propeller planes?" Jacob said to Zach.

"Absolutely. I don't see why it won't. The F-86 is still a plane. The only real difference is speed."

Jacob smiled. "I think you're right."

Jacob and Zach sat on the runway ready to take off. The okay came, the engines of the two planes roared, and soon they were in the air. Jacob and Zach circled the field until the other two pilots were in the air and ready to join up. Zach was flight commander, and the foursome headed north when everyone was ready.

Zach and the others flew to an area called "Mig Alley." The nickname came from Migs being spotted in this region on numerous occasions.

"We'll loiter in this area for a while to see if they show up," Zach said over the radio. "If they don't come in a little while, we'll go home."

"Roger that" was the uniform response.

No sooner had their communication ended then a reflection was seen on the horizon. As the four intently looked in this direction, one of them suddenly yelled "Bandits straight ahead!" The four dropped their wing tanks and prepared to engage.

The engagement was quite spirited, but the Americans prevailed. A Mig got on Jacob's tail, and Jacob led him right in front of Zach. At the appropriate time, Zach opened fire, and the Mig burst into flames. The Migs broke off the fight and headed for the Yalu. They were obviously going back to their sanctuary.

When they got back on the ground at Kimpo Air Base, the other three pilots congratulated Zach on getting his first kill in the F-86.

"I'll write you up and put it on the bulletin board," Jacob said.

"Thanks, boss," Zach replied. Jacob was glad that the notoriety hadn't gone to Zach's head.

"Did you hear that chatter from the Migs?" one of the pilots said to the others. "It sure didn't sound like Chinese to me."

Jacob laughed. "It's probably Russian. We'll engage a lot of those fellows before we're through."

The others nodded.

"Can all of you go to the Officers' Club for a drink?" Jacob asked. "Since this is our first mission, I'm buying."

All but Zach answered with an enthusiastic "Yes!"

Zach looked at his watch. "I can go for a little while, but I've got a very important letter to write."

Jacob patted Zach on the shoulder and grinned. "I'll bet you do."

The four got in a jeep and headed for the club. No one knew what the future held, but the first day had been a success. They would drink to that.

Chapter 24

Change of Command

General of the Army Douglas MacArthur was poring over documents at his desk when he was told that General Ned Almond was on the phone and wanted to talk to him. *Can't be good news,* MacArthur told himself. *My run of luck has been all bad lately.*

"What is it, Ned?" MacArthur said as he put the phone to his ear.

"I've got some very bad news, sir. Johnnie Walker was killed in a jeep accident today."

MacArthur was stunned. While he had differences with Walker, he liked the man. Walker was a fighter, and MacArthur very much admired this trait. And, as Commander of the Eighth Army, Walker had time and again told the bigwigs in Washington that the Chinese and North Koreans seemed to know his every move. This was a view that MacArthur had come to share with him. MacArthur stated that there was obviously a Communist spy hidden somewhere in Washington who was passing key information to the enemy. Time and again, MacArthur raised the spy issue for explaining the setbacks he had faced in Korea. Now he would have to go it alone, as the new head of the Eighth Army would more-than-likely be someone who was forced on him by the Joint Chiefs.

"General, are you still there?"

"Yes, I am, Ned. I'm just thinking about a number of issues. I'll, of course, notify Johnnie's family and pass on our condolences."

MacArthur hung up the phone and leaned back in his chair. He then straightened into a writing position and drafted a short, terse note to the Chiefs of Staff telling them of the accident. He handed the message to an aide and told him to send it immediately. He then went back to a state of near-paralysis. He stared at the wall in front of him with a far-away look.

MacArthur was brought back to the present by his aide, Colonel Sid Huff. Sid told him that the message had been sent to the Joint Chiefs, and he asked if there was anything else his boss wanted him to do.

"No, Sid," MacArthur replied. "The thing we have to do now is wait and see who my bosses in the Pentagon send out here to take over Eighth Army. I just hope it won't be someone who makes me appear irrelevant."

"That's impossible, sir," Huff responded. "You have a better military reputation than anyone – bar none."

"It's good to hear you say it, Sid, but the truth is I'm getting old. I think I have some good years left, but you never know."

Huff shook his head, braced into a military posture, and gave a brisk salute. MacArthur gave a half-hearted salute in return, but one could readily tell that his mind was on other issues.

Chesty Puller shook his head at the state of the ground war. "This is what MacArthur did on Bataan," he bellowed. "Our troops got split, and the Japanese came right down the middle. The Chinese learned the lesson and did the same thing to us." Puller turned to Jim Sherman. "I tell you, old man, this is one reason the U.S. Marines don't like to be split up and fight in small units. It is too easy for the enemy to divide and conquer. I hope someday you Army boys will learn."

"I'm sure we will, sir," Sherman replied. But, underneath, Sherman wasn't sure at all. The situation had seemed chaotic, at least up to the present time.

But now the United Nations troops were being withdrawn from North Korea in masterful fashion and retreating to the South in a very orderly fashion. And much of the credit goes to Marine Colonel – Brigadier General select – Lewis "Chesty" Puller, Junior. Puller had been placed in charge of the tactical retreat, and he was carrying it out brilliantly. He gave orders and expected them to be carried out fully. When the head of an Army Unit – a bird colonel – came over to ask Puller about retreating, he called his Artillery officer over and said to him – in front of the Army Officer – "If this bird retreats one inch from where I tell him to be, wipe out his whole unit." The Artillery Officer grinned, and the Army man got the drift!

Word reached Puller and Sherman about Johnnie Walker's untimely death. "I'm truly sorry this happened, old man," Puller said to Sherman. "But I hope the Army will replace him with a man that is a real fighter. God knows we don't want egg on our face that would result from us losing this war. We would never recover from it."

"I agree with you, sir," Sherman replied. "And I believe the Joint Chiefs realize just how important Korea is. Therefore, I would be very surprised if the Army didn't select its most capable General and send him."

Puller lit his pipe and pulled the tattered map out of his rear pocket. I hope you're right, son."

Sherman almost fell over. *Did he just call me son? That's what I call real progress!*

Communications between MacArthur and the Joint chiefs became even more brittle. MacArthur would routinely ask the Chiefs for permission to strike the enemy in Manchuria, and he would get a standard retort of "Permission denied" from them. When he asked for clarification, the response came back that no one from the Joint Chiefs on up desired that the war be expanded. This reply only infuriated him, and he would go into a tirade in front of Willoughby – his Intelligence Chief – and Sid Huff and anyone else who he deemed appropriate.

"How can we fight a war in which the enemy can run to his side of the border and we can't pursue him? It's ludicrous, I tell you. Ludicrous! If it weren't for the fine men in my command, I would retire and go home. But I refuse to leave them in a mess that they didn't create."

At this point, MacArthur was interrupted by a sergeant who brought him a message marked "High Priority." The sergeant asked if it had been okay to interrupt him, and MacArthur answered in the affirmative. "You were absolutely right to do it," MacArthur replied to him. The five-star General then opened the packet and read the message.

"Well, I'll be," MacArthur said with a look of amazement on his face. "General Omar Bradley – who heads the Joint Chiefs – says in the message that he is sending Matt Ridgway to take over the Eighth Army. I have to admit that Ridgway is probably the best that the Army has."

"Are you pleased with the selection, sir?" General Willoughby asked.

"From a professional standpoint, yes. From a personal standpoint, it's too early to say one way or the other. Time will tell if I can trust Matt totally."

MacArthur stood up and began pacing. He lit his pipe as he stopped walking momentarily. "What surprises me," he said to no one in particular, "is that they would take Ridgway away from his position very high up in the chain of command to come here. Maybe they expect that Ridgway will eventually replace me."

MacArthur was interrupted again by the sergeant who had brought the first message. This time he had a second message, but he was much more assured in bringing it to the General. MacArthur opened it and read it.

"It's from Matt Ridgway. Matt says he is going first to the front and then he will come see me."

MacArthur shrugged and continued pacing. "If he had come to see me first, I would have just told him to do as he saw fit. And I'll tell him that if he does bother to come see me in the future."

For the first time, MacArthur looked as if he were tired. "I don't want my last combat command to end in stalemate, but that appears to be what is happening. If the enemy can hide in a sanctuary when things go bad for him, there is no way that I can attain victory."

The mood in the room was somber. MacArthur thrust his hands into his rear pants pocket and stared out the window. No one in the room moved.

Puller and Sherman looked with interest as a jeep with the flag of a four-star General came barreling up the road. The jeep came to a stop a few feet away from where the two officers stood. General Ridgway climbed out, and Puller and Sherman came to attention and saluted. The four-star returned the salute and stuck out his hand.

"Hi. I'm Matt Ridgway."

Jim Sherman couldn't help but notice the similarities between Puller and Ridgway. Both were crusty old veterans, and both had a no-nonsense look about them.

"I've heard about you," Ridgway said to Puller. "And I like what I've heard."

"You probably won't like my thoughts on what's wrong with the way we're conducting this war," Puller replied.

"To the contrary, I want to hear your thoughts. Things will have to change if the tide is to be reversed."

Puller and Ridgway had a spirited, no-holds-barred exchange. At the end, Ridgway seemed definitely impressed.

"I'll consider everything you've said very carefully," the new head of Eighth Army stated. "Right now, I want to go up to the front. I've never been one to trust briefings. I prefer to see everything for myself."

"My sentiments exactly, sir," Puller replied.

Puller and Sherman saluted, and their boss returned the salute. "Reorganize the retreat as you see fit," Ridgway yelled to Puller as he got into the jeep. "We'll set up a counter-attack soon and drive the Communists back where they belong."

"Will do, sir," Puller replied with a grin.

"Little does he know I'm already doing it," Puller added softly.

Soon, the jeep carrying the four-star was heading north.

"Now there's an Army General I can respect," Puller said as the jeep was now a dot on the horizon. *He's actually beaming,* Sherman noticed.

"Let's get back to work," Puller said to Sherman. "There's a lot of work still to be done."

The temperature was bitter cold – 25 degrees below zero, and Chesty Puller was worried about frostbite and other maladies attributable to the weather. The fighting was intense, as the Chinese would surround Marine units and try to obliterate them. Fortunately, the Marines fought heroically, and the enemy was by and large unable to accomplish their objective.

Everything was looking rosy based on Jim Sherman's vantage point. He even asked Puller if the Colonel thought that the tide was again to be turned in favor of the U.N. Forces.

"No," Puller replied, "not at all. The Chinese Communists and North Koreans have about 500,000 men under arms. We have a little less than that – about 400,000 men. Their force is too large not to do something fairly dramatic. I would say that they have something big in store for us. If I were them, I would want to discredit Douglas MacArthur, and I think that's exactly what they'll try and do."

Puller was soon proven to be right. At the end of 1950, the Communists attacked U.N. Forces with a fury not seen before. They not only overwhelmed the U.N. Front, but they were able to recapture – at least temporarily – the capital city of Seoul. It was time for a further retreat by Puller and his allies. This was most distasteful to all of them.

Puller was furious at the turn of events. "Thank God Ridgway is now in charge. I think he'll make those birds pay for what they've done. And

I'll bet folks all the way up to the President will be very happy that they now have the right man in charge of the Eighth Army."

Puller's consternation was shared by President Truman. As the Communists rolled down the peninsula and took control of Seoul, Truman ordered his aide to round up top cabinet members and General Omar Bradley for a crucial meeting. "Get Acheson, Marshall, Bradley, and Snyder here. Don't let them give you any excuses," Truman stormed.

"Mr. President," the aide asked curiously, "are you sure you want Secretary of the Treasury Snyder here?

"Of course I do!" Truman bellowed. "How do you think we're going to pay for this war?"

"You're absolutely right, sir. I'll get them here on the double." The aide hurried to the door and disappeared.

The meeting convened early the next morning. All four of the men that the President had specified were in attendance.

"I assume you can guess why I called this meeting," Truman began. "Korea is now a real mess. The Chinese have taken Seoul. And here MacArthur almost guaranteed me that the Chinese wouldn't enter the war. So I ask you – what are we going to do?"

Dean Acheson shook his head. "I warned you about taking MacArthur's word, Mr. President."

"I know you did!" Truman replied testily. "But that isn't going to solve our present problem, is it?"

"No, it isn't, Mr. President," Bradley piped in. "But what I just did may help out. I sent Matthew Ridgway over to Korea to be in charge of the Eighth Army. While I sincerely hate that Walton Walker was killed, I do believe that Matt – if anyone – can get the situation over there straightened out."

"I believe that General Bradley is absolutely right," George Marshall added. "Matt is the Army's most capable senior officer."

"How long do we give him?" Truman asked.

"I would say no more than three weeks," Acheson replied. "If he can't do it in that time, he probably can't do it at all."

"What do you think, Brad?" the President asked his head of the Joint Chiefs.

"I would hate to impose a time limit. But I would say that we should expect progress in the near future in stabilizing our lines."

"That sounds like a wise solution," The President replied. "What do you think, Dean?"

Acheson shrugged. "We will have to see very substantial progress. Otherwise, our Allies will begin to lose faith in us."

The President scanned the others, and everyone appeared to be in agreement.

"That just leaves two more items on our agenda," the President said. "One, of course, is what do we do with his Majesty, Douglas MacArthur?"

George Marshall answered. "Mr. President, I suggest that we leave him in his present position for the time being. He says that he is going to let Matt run the show in Korea – and if he does – then I believe everything will be okay."

Truman again scanned the group, and the people seemed once again to be in agreement.

"My final question, then," Truman continued, "goes to the Secretary of the Treasury. Are we going to be able to pay for this war without raising taxes?"

"I think so, Mr. President," Snyder replied. "I have my people working on the issue day and night to get it figured out."

"Good," the President said, obviously relieved. "That is all, gentlemen."

The four participants headed for the door, eager to get back to their own offices.

After reading the message from General Ridgway, MacArthur tossed it into the air. "How dare he!" the five-star general roared. "He's fired another one of my commanders. How many has he fired – six? He doesn't seem to care that I hand-picked these men myself!"

"But, sir," Sid Huff interrupted. "Didn't you give him authority to do has he saw fit?"

"Certainly, but I didn't foresee that he would fire all of my commanders. What is he trying to do – put me out of a job?"

"Maybe he's just trying to stop the progress of the Communists," General Willoughby said.

"Well, do you think he's succeeding?" MacArthur shot back.

"Yes, sir, I think he is. Little by little, our lines are tightening. I wouldn't be at all surprised if General Ridgway takes Seoul back in the near future."

"Maybe so," MacArthur countered, "but he'll never be able to unify Korea as long as the Chinese are allowed their sanctuary."

No one had a rebuttal to this input, and MacArthur was satisfied.

Chesty Puller chuckled as he read the latest communique from Ridgway's headquarters. "He's fired another Army Commander. About time."

"May I see it, sir?" Sherman said.

Puller handed the message to Sherman, who quickly scanned it. "It really is Ridgway's Army now," Sherman said. "He will be responsible for what happens in the future."

"Exactly, old man," Puller replied. "And that's the way it should be."

Nightfall was coming, and Puller and Sherman were inside the tent that Sergeant Bodey had supplied for them. The pot-bellied stove was glowing, and the temperature was very comfortable compared to the outside frigid air. Sherman sat on his bunk and took out pen and paper. He needed to write Jennifer and re-confirm how he felt about her. It had been gnawing at him.

Dearest Jennifer

As I'm sure you know, the fighting here has been brutal. The Chinese have attacked in overwhelming strength, and our lines have caved but, thankfully, they have not broken. All of us here are heartened that our new leader – General Matthew Ridgway – is a soldier's soldier. We are sure that he will figure out a way to get us back on the right track.

In spite of the fierce fighting, I have to admit that I think of you all of the time. I am so relieved that my feelings for you are out in the open and that you have agreed to my courting you. You are a very wonderful and special woman, and I assure you that I will not take anything for granted.

I will plan to see you soon. Just when depends on the enemy, but please know that I will be there just as soon as is humanly possible.

All my love forever,

Jim

Sherman put the letter in an envelope and sealed it. Chesty Puller, who was reading a book, looked over at him. "Well, old man, you look as if you have had a heavy load lifted from your shoulders. I hope it all works out."

Sherman thanked Puller and went to the tent entrance. He opened the flaps and called for Sergeant Bodey. The sergeant double timed it over.

"Sergeant, please get this letter out right away. It's very important to me, so please take very good care of it."

"Yes, sir!" Bodey replied. He saluted and disappeared in the night.

Chapter 25

Recall

It was spring, 1951, and President Harry S. Truman once again called in his trusted advisors: Acheson, Marshall, Bradley, Snyder, and, new to the group, Averill Harriman. "You probably know what this meeting is about," he said in an almost subdued tone.

"Yes, we do, Mr. President," Dean Acheson replied, "and it sounds like you have your mind pretty well made up."

"I do, but I wanted to see what you people had to say."

Acheson went first. "I know I've always sounded like I wanted General MacArthur fired, but I think we have to be careful, Mr. President. After all, the General is thought of very highly by the American people."

"I know," Truman replied, "but now we're in a mess because the man wouldn't take orders. And he keeps sending requests up the line to bomb Manchuria and God knows what else. If something isn't done right away, we're going to be in an all-out war with the Chinese and Soviets. And I certainly don't want that to happen."

Truman looked around the group. "What do you think, George?"

Marshall answered without hesitation. "I think the General should be fired, Mr. President. He wouldn't hesitate to fire anyone underneath him who had disobeyed an order, and he has continually disobeyed yours."

"You've changed your thinking, George. That's fine. What about you, Brad?"

Omar Bradley shook his head. "Mr. President, I have to disagree with General Marshall. Over the years, no one has served this country more honorably than Douglas MacArthur. For this reason, I believe we should call him to Washington and lay the facts on the table. We could give him one last chance to conform, and if he doesn't, then I believe you should fire him. He would also have the option to retire if he isn't satisfied with the stalemate."

"That's what I don't want to happen," Truman retorted. "I don't want him to retire. He deserves to be fired, and that's exactly what I intend to do."

Truman thought for a moment and continued. "Gentlemen, as always, I find your recommendations most helpful. However, as I indicated previously, my mind is made up, and nothing anyone has said here has convinced me to do otherwise. Thus, I feel it is my duty – as hard as it may be – to fire General MacArthur. Does anyone else have anything he wants to add?"

Snyder and Harriman shook their heads.

A slight buzz went up, and attendees looked in shock – even those who had recommended MacArthur's termination.

"I know it's hard for at least some of you to fathom my reasoning," the President continued, "but time and again the General has defied my orders – and he has to be made to realize that he is accountable – even in his lofty position over there – to the President of the United States."

After the commotion ended, Truman asked Bradley to tell him who the Joint Chiefs would recommend to take over for MacArthur as SCAP – the Supreme Commander Allied Forces in the Pacific.

"We would recommend Matt Ridgway. He is certainly the most qualified."

"I agree," George Marshall added. He obviously didn't want to be left out of this very important discussion.

"Gentlemen, that makes total sense," the President replied. "General Ridgway is doing a fine job over there. As I understand it, Ridgway is firming up our lines and preparing to drive the Communists out of South Korea."

Bradley affirmed that the President was right. "You are correct, Mr. President. And I'll have the recommendation of the Joint Chiefs to you in writing within 24 hours,"

Truman nodded. "If there is nothing further, this meeting is over. I've got the unpleasant task now of writing down what I'm going to tell the American public."

Acheson spoke up immediately. "If you need any help with that, Mr. President, please let me know."

Others in the room quickly offered their assistance.

"I've got speech writers for this purpose," Truman quipped. "And I'll probably give them the opportunity to earn their salaries."

Chuckles were heard, and the members departed the President's office. Out in the hall, Marshall spoke in a subdued tone to the Chairman of the Joint Chiefs. "Bradley, I've got to speak a minute with you."

Marshall had done what he always had done: He called an underling by his last name, no matter high how up the chain the underling was. He had done this when Dwight Eisenhower was Supreme Allied Commander in Europe, and he was doing it now with the Chairman of the Joint Chiefs. When they got out of earshot of the others, Marshall told him to send over a name for the recommended Commander of Eighth Army as soon as he had it.

"I can do you one better, Mr. Secretary. I can give it to you now. We've anticipated that we may have to come up with the recommendation."

"Well, don't keep me in suspense, man. Who is it?"

"James Van Fleet. We think he's the best fit for the job."

Marshall almost choked. "Van Fleet? You must be joking! He hates stalemate even more than MacArthur does!"

"Politics aside, sir, we believe he's the best man for the job. Besides, I know he's a favorite of the President's. James was sent to Greece to implement the 'Truman Doctrine' back in 1946. It was during the Greek Civil War, and James provided advice to the Greek government and administered $400 million in military aid. I know Truman considers him his fair-haired boy."

"You may be right," Marshall replied in his usual no-nonsense manner. "Send me over the material you used for the recommendation. I'll back you up." He then walked off.

As usual, Marshall was a man of few words. Bradley, however, knew that he could count on the Secretary of Defense to be in his corner.

Douglas MacArthur was enjoying his mid-afternoon rest in bed when his wife, Jean, shook him by the shoulder. She told him that his aide, Sid

Huff, wanted to come over. However, she had discouraged him from doing so. She handed the General a message from the Joint Chiefs.

"You look very serious, Jeannie," the General said to his wife. "It must not be good news."

The General's expression became more somber as he read the message.

"Well, Jeannie," he sighed, "we're finally going home."

The General got out of bed and put on his robe and slippers. He began to pace. "The message says I'm being relieved of command. They aren't even going to give me the opportunity to retire first."

"Despicable," his wife Jean muttered. "And after all you've done for them and the country."

"Don't worry about it, Jeannie," the General replied. "We can hold our heads high when we return, but I better get ahold of Sid and tell him to start arranging for our trip back."

"And I have a lot to do, also," his wife replied. "I guess we don't have time to do any fretting."

"That's my girl," the General said. He went to the closet and pulled out a clean uniform. His wife started making notes as to what would have to be done – and it would have to be done in very short order.

At his headquarters in Korea, General Matthew Ridgway poured over the message that announced MacArthur's dismissal. It also informed him that he would be taking MacArthur's place as SCAP and that General James Van Fleet would become Eighth Army Commander.

"I can't believe it," Ridgway said to an aide. "The President actually fired the old man. It's true that I'd said they should fire General MacArthur when I was a member of the Joint Chiefs, but I never thought it would happen."

"Yes, sir," the aide said in an almost mechanical tone. "I'll start preparing for your move."

"Good," Ridgway replied. "I've got to write MacArthur and convey what an outstanding soldier he has been over the years and how much he will be missed."

The aide grinned. "Do I detect a bit of sarcasm, sir?"

"Absolutely not!" Ridgway said as he took out pen and paper.

He had no sooner finished penning the note than Major General J. Sladen Bradley, 25th Division Commander, came in.

"Ah, Slay, good to see you," Ridgway said, looking up. "I was just getting ready to notify Division Commanders that I will be replacing General MacArthur and that you have a new boss, effective immediately."

"First of all, congratulations, sir, and, second, may I ask who our new boss is?"

"You certainly may. It is Jim Van Fleet."

Bradley chuckled. "Somehow I can't see him enjoying this war very much. He's a lot like you – very capable and not liking to accept anything short of total victory."

"If anything," Ridgway replied, "this war is pointing out how times have changed. We are giving the Chinese a sanctuary so as to not get engaged in an even bigger war. In the last war, each side was doing its darndest to win at any cost. That is not the case now."

Bradley was puzzled. "So how do you see the war ending?"

"I think we will drive the Communists back to the 38th parallel, where the war started. Then the politicians will take over, and we'll see where it goes from there."

Bradley was obviously sad. "To think of all of the fine young Americans who have suffered immensely and even lost their lives. It's a shame."

"I agree. All we can do now is make the other side pay. And with our B-29s dropping tons of bombs, they're paying dearly."

"But I have to admit," Ridgway continued, "The Marine Colonel – Chesty Puller – may be correct. He says that it isn't a stalemate, but instead that we're actually getting roundly defeated here in Korea. I don't see it that way. After all, we are somewhat outnumbered on the ground. But in the air, we have complete tactical superiority with our B-29s. We can pound them at will on the ground and they don't have a retaliatory capability. But maybe Puller is right. Who knows?"

"I hate to disagree with you, sir, but I have to. The Communists fade back into the hills when they think they're going to be bombed. So it is questionable as to just how effective the bombing is."

Bradley was obviously incensed and Ridgway could barely hide a smile. "I can't say enough good things about my boys in the 25th," Bradley continued. "They have fought under terrible conditions here in Korea: – 25 degrees below zero and deep snow in places. They've done everything I've asked them to do and more. It is my sacred duty to stick up for them. "

"I agree, Slay," Ridgway answered. "I wouldn't expect anything less of you, and you have given me some good ammunition in case I have this discussion with our Marine friends."

"Incidentally, sir," Bradley said. "If I can give you one piece of advice – at least when you're talking to General Van Fleet – please remember that his son is a B-26 pilot. Therefore, you shouldn't forget to mention that the B-26s are playing a big part in neutralizing the Communists on the ground."

"Good point," Ridgway replied. "I'll be sure and do that."

Bradley gave a status report, the two Generals shook hands, and Bradley departed.

Ridgway prepared to move to Tokyo. He was satisfied with the progress he had made. The Communists were being slowly but surely pushed back to the 38th parallel, the United Nations forces from a number of different countries were now fighting effectively, and the war had been contained to the Korean peninsula. While Matthew Ridgway didn't like stalemate any better than Douglas MacArthur did, he was at least willing to accept it.

But in the way that MacArthur had treated him as a subordinate, Ridgway knew that MacArthur was right. MacArthur had told him to do as he saw fit. He would have to remember this and treat Jim Van Fleet the same way when Van Fleet arrived in Korea and physically took over Eighth Army.

At Taegu Air Force Base, Lieutenant Colonel Jacob Partude prepared to give his morning briefing to members of his squadron. "As you were, men. Please be seated."

Partude stood at the lectern and looked over some notes. "First of all, I think you've already heard – but in case you haven't – General MacArthur has been relieved of his command, and General Ridgway is moving up to take his place. And, certainly just as important, General Van Fleet is coming in to take over Eighth Army. Now, in spite of what you think, whether you hate seeing General MacArthur go or whether you're glad of it, I still expect you to carry out your duties to the fullest. And I'm sure you will."

Partude took a sip of coffee and continued. "From my personal perspective, I think the move could be a good thing. General Ridgway has been most impressive, in my opinion, in stabilizing the United Nations lines. And I expect big things from him in the weeks and months ahead. But now to what is most important to you – our mission. Today, you will have escort duty, so to speak. Your mission will be to keep the Migs off the backs of our B-29s. For one, I can't imagine a more important mission.

Talk to your squad leaders, and they will give you the specifics of your mission. They have already been briefed. Are there any questions?"

Captain Zach Barton stood up. "I just have one, sir. Do you think General Ridgway moving up will have any impact on us?"

"Good question. The only impact I would foresee is that General Ridgway is more of a 'hands on' leader. Therefore, I think he may expect more out of us. Along these lines, I have noticed that the base is making sure that urgent calls get through in a more timely fashion. So far, that is the only difference I have noticed."

Partude asked if there were any more questions. There were none, so he directed pilots to meet with their squad leaders. He once again was to fly as Barton's wing man in a group of four. Barton was the squad leader.

In the air, Barton was the first to see the B-29s. "There they are," he said. "Let's protect them while they carry out their orders."

Sure enough, the bombers were soon descended upon by Mig-15s. "Enemy straight ahead, boys," Barton said into his microphone. "Let's get 'em."

A frantic dogfight broke out, with the Americans in their F-86 Sabres taking on the Mig-15s. Once again, Barton and Partude used the tactic of one leading a Mig-15 into the gunsights of the other. The tactic was once again successful, with Barton getting a kill. Shortly thereafter, The Migs broke off and headed for Manchuria. They had obviously had enough.

"Thanks, Skipper," Barton said as the four Sabres formed up.

"You're welcome," Partude replied. "One more and you'll have five. That will make you an ace!"

The other two pilots cheered.

Back at Taegu Air Base, the pilots were debriefed. Partude sat in as the other pilots related what had happened in their skirmish with the Migs. All of the pilots commented on how rugged the Sabres were. One even said that he had taken several bullets in the fuselage, and his plane hadn't gone down. Partude was happy that his pilots were paying tribute to the design methodology that had gone into the construction of the American fighters. Ever since the start of World War II, American fighter planes had built a reputation based on their ruggedness and durability. Partude, as squadron commander, was happy that the designers still realized just how important these characteristics were.

"Those self-sealing fuel lines are worth their weight in gold," Partude said to the others. "If it weren't for them, our losses would be a lot greater."

Others in the room corroborated his statement.

At the end of the debriefs, Zach Barton came up to his squadron commander. "Boss, would it be okay with you if I saw Jennifer this evening? I don't think there's anything around here that needs my input."

"Sure," Partude replied. "Please pass on a 'hello' from me."

Barton nodded. "If I hurry, I think I can get an airlift to her area."

The young Captain dashed off towards Base Operations.

"Let her know you're coming!" Partude yelled in Barton's direction. Barton waved back, letting his boss know that he'd heard.

Zach Barton walked toward the Nurse's quarters at the MASH Unit. Thinking back, Jennifer sounded as if she would be glad to see him when he talked to her earlier. He certainly hoped so! His heart pounded as he neared his destination.

Outside of the nurse's quarters, there was a tall Army officer pacing around. He had a Lieutenant Colonel's rank on his military blouse. He was well-groomed from head to foot. *He must be courting one of the nurses,* Zach thought. *I sure hope it's not the one I've come to see!*

"Hi. I'm Jim Sherman," the Lieutenant Colonel said, sticking out his hand.

"I'm very pleased to meet you, sir. I'm Zach Barton."

Jim Sherman. I've heard that name. Oh my God! Now I remember. He was the best friend of the man Jennifer was going to marry. He must be here to court her!

"Good, you two have met," Jennifer said as she came out of her quarters. "Should we go to the mess hall? They always have a pot of coffee perking there."

"Sounds good to me," Sherman said.

"Me, too," Barton added.

"Good," Jennifer replied. "We're in total agreement, and we can't ask for more than that." The three walked to the mess hall.

Barton couldn't help but notice that Jennifer looked especially beautiful tonight. In fact, she was prettier than he had remembered. But now he knew who the competition for her was. It was in the form of an Army Lieutenant Colonel. While he suspected – okay, knew – that he wouldn't be alone in pursuing her, he had no inkling that the competition would be so stiff. Oh well, what was worth having was worth fighting for. And it would definitely be the fight of his life!

The three got coffee and went to a table at the back of the mess hall. No one was nearby, so they had a very pleasant conversation. Sherman updated them on what it was like to move with the Marine Colonel Chesty Puller on the ground, and Barton updated them on the air war. He gave examples of combat against the Mig-15. His fondness for the F-86 Sabrejet was obvious.

Finally, it was Jennifer's turn. She told them about the wounded they had served and how busy it had become for them after the Chinese had openly started fighting.

"I don't see how you manage," Sherman said shaking his head.

"I'll tell you," Jennifer replied. "We couldn't have done it if Brad Taylor, my boss, hadn't gotten more surgeons. And I contacted Ruby Bradley, the head nurse here in Korea, and she put her weight behind getting more nurses here at our MASH unit. So now we're actually holding our own."

"I met Ruby," Sherman stated, "and she's really something. She backed Chesty Puller off when he didn't want any women up at the front. She is a super nurse, and she did wonders for morale."

Jennifer looked admiringly at Sherman. "I'm glad you met Ruby. It gives us something else in common."

She's obviously referring to her old beau, Barton thought. *I've certainly got my work cut out for me, but I certainly won't give up. It's not in my nature.*

The rest of the conversation was very pleasant, as each one related more of a personal nature. Sherman looked at his watch. "It's getting late, and I better get going. Chesty will be expecting me."

"It's so nice that both of you came," Jennifer said. "It means a great deal to me. I'll walk you out."

The three handed their cups to a dishwasher as they walked out. They reached the Nurse's quarters very shortly.

"I'll say goodbye here," Jennifer said, "as I've got some paperwork due first thing in the morning. It's been great to see you."

Jennifer hugged both of her guests and went into her quarters. Sherman and Barton walked to the transportation area.

Sherman broke the silence. "I don't know what your intentions are, but, to be honest, I am out to win Jennifer's hand."

"I gathered as much. And, since you have relayed your intentions, I feel that I have to do the same. While I don't know her as well as you apparently do, I am quite taken with her. Therefore, my objective is the same as yours."

Sherman's expression reflected the grimness of the situation. "I suspected it when I found that you were waiting for the same woman. So all I can do now is wish you good luck."

Barton smiled as he thrust out his hand. "It sounds like we're going to have a good ol' fashioned Army-Air Force competition. I wish you the best also."

Inside the Nurses' quarters, Jennifer stopped at Monica's cot. Fortunately, the nurses right around her were out.

"You'll never guess what happened," Jennifer said to her young confidante. "I actually had two suitors tonight. I think things will get quite interesting."

Jennifer described her two 'guests.' "They're both handsome, and they both have admirable qualities."

"What are you going to do?" Monica inquired.

"Enjoy the moment, I guess. But I'll probably play it by ear for a while. I think Jack would want me to do that."

"Personally, I think Jim Sherman would be awfully hard to beat," Monica replied. "But the choice is yours, and I can only hope that you do what's right for you."

Jennifer thanked Monica, and she walked over to her own area. *Monica is right,* she thought. *The choice is mine, but it won't be easy. I too have to hope that I'll make the right decision.*

Chapter 26

New Commander

Matthew Ridgway went to his office in the Dai Ichi Building in Tokyo at a very early hour – 0500. It was his first day as Supreme Commander Allied Forces in the Pacific (SCAP), and he wanted to get an early start. He looked around the office. *Not bad,* he thought. *The office is comfortable, but it is certainly not extravagant. I'll keep it!*

He walked over to table that served as his desk. In the center of it was a letter with the Presidential seal. *Oh – oh. Better read it.* He sat down, wheeled the chair up to the desk, and opened the letter:

Dear General Ridgway

First of all, I want to congratulate you on your promotion to SCAP and on the fine manner in which you have stabilized our lines in Korea. I have no doubt but what you will push the enemy troops out of the Republic of Korea. They do not belong there and should never have invaded in the first place.

As I am sure that you are aware, I am very concerned that a small war in Korea can escalate into something that none of us want. Therefore, I am directing you to stop your Force movement at approximately the 38th parallel. You are to proceed no further.

Both the Secretary of Defense and the Chairman of the Joint Chiefs of Staff understand this direction. Please contact either of them at any time if you have any questions.

Once again, I pass my heartiest congratulations for the magnificent work you have done in the Korean peninsula. Every day I become more convinced that you are the right man for the position of SCAP.
Sincerely,
Harry S. Truman
President, United States of America

Ridgway put the letter down and pushed back in his chair. *I'm to proceed no further than the 38th parallel. That puts everything in concrete – it will be a stalemate at best. Oh well, that's a lot better than all-out war. I'll have to make sure that Jim Van Fleet understands this direction. And he certainly won't like it.*

Rushing in at this moment was Major General Doyle O. Hickey, Ridgway's Chief of Staff. "Sorry, sir!" Hickey said in a blustered fashion. "I didn't think you would be here this early." The clock on the wall showed that it was a little after 0600.

"That's quite all right," Ridgway replied. "I'm here a little earlier than will be the norm. I wanted to get a jump on everything. By the way, do you have a list of appointments for the day?"

"Yes, sir. Your first appointment will be with your new Eighth Army Commander, General Van Fleet."

"Good. I need to talk to him about this letter I just received from the President. Our Forces are to advance to the 38th parallel and go no further."

Hickey whistled softly. "Jim isn't going to like that. He hates stalemate."

"I know he isn't, but there is nothing any of us can do about it. The President has made up his mind, and between the two of us, I believe he is correct. We certainly don't want an escalation into all-out war with the Chinese and the Soviets."

"I see your point, sir, and I'll do my utmost to see that your orders are clearly and concisely carried out."

At 1000 hours that morning, Lieutenant General James Van Fleet arrived at General Ridgway's office. He was ushered in by General Hickey.

Ridgway and Van Fleet shook hands, and Ridgway told Hickey to stay. Ridgway then initiated the dialogue. "I'll call you Jim, and you can call me Matt. How's that?"

"Fine, sir" was the response.

Ridgway pushed the letter from President Truman over to Van Fleet, who had now pulled a chair up to the desk that was the centerpiece of the room. "Please read it," Ridgway instructed.

Van Fleet read the letter several times in a somber fashion before speaking. "I certainly don't like it, but I'll abide by it. After all, our President is our Commander – in – Chief."

Ridgway smiled. "I knew I could count on you."

"But I'll say it again," Van Fleet reiterated. "I don't like stalemate, and the 38th parallel is not good terrain to defend. It's too flat and too open."

"Yes," Ridgway countered, "but you notice that the President did use the word 'approximately.' We do have a little flexibility, though I grant you it's not much."

"I'll need you to find out from the Secretary of Defense or Joint Chiefs just how much flexibility we have."

Ridgway nodded. "I plan to do that, and I'll get back to you very shortly."

"By the way, Matt, what is your true feeling about MacArthur's firing? I will, of course, keep this conversation to myself."

'I know you will, Jim, and my feeling is that MacArthur should have been relieved, but I think the way it was done was quite tacky. Personally, I Think General Omar Bradley should have come out here and warned him. Bradley could have told him to either follow orders or retire, or he would be relieved."

Van Fleet thought for a moment. "That makes complete sense."

"You know," Ridgway replied, "MacArthur and I go back a long way. As a Captain, I was up at West Point when he was Commandant. I have a lot of respect for him, although I admit that he was dead wrong in not following direction."

"Maybe the President should have sent him definite orders, such as he did you in the letter you just showed me. I think there was a lot of pussy-footing around, from the Joint Chiefs up to and including the President."

Ridgway sighed. "You're right, Jim. Looking back at my own performance on the Joint Chiefs, perhaps I should have been more adamant that the Chiefs take a stronger role in how the war was conducted. Perhaps historians will be very critical of how the Joint Chiefs responded during this critical period of our country's history."

Van Fleet nodded, and Ridgway changed the subject.

"Jim, I think the Eighth Army I'm handing you is in good shape. I have replaced a number of the leaders MacArthur put in with those that can get the job done. While your job won't be easy, I think you will be able to drive the enemy back to the 38th parallel."

"And what about the Marines?" Van Fleet inquired.

"They have done an admirable job, from the Inchon Landing to the present. The only qualm I have about them is that their fine First Regiment Commander – Chesty Puller – has been promoted to brigadier general and is rotating out. It remains to be seen if his replacement will be as good."

Van Fleet smiled. "I'd heard that you really liked Puller, and I can understand why. Puller is a crusty old veteran who believes in only one thing – victory. He isn't afraid to say what he thinks, which is another very admirable trait in the military. And his track record has been outstanding, particularly in Korea."

Ridgway nodded. "Before we get into any more detail, you need to go to Korea and evaluate the men I have put in charge. If you don't like them, kick them out."

"Yes, sir," Van Fleet replied. "I plan to leave as soon as we're through."

"Go to it," Ridgway directed. "The sooner you get the Communists out of the south, the sooner we can bring this war to a conclusion. Just keep me in the loop and contact me if you have any problems."

The two shook hands, and Van Fleet walked to the door of SCAP's office.

"Remember, Matt, I need that definition of how far off the 38th parallel we can be as soon as you can get it."

Ridgway nodded and waved.

Chesty Puller prepared to depart Korea for his new assignment in San Diego. He now wore the star of a brigadier general. While he hated to leave his men in the still tenuous situation in Korea, he was glad to move up in rank. He was now alone with Jim Sherman in their quarters.

Puller pointed to the star on his collar. "I would never have gotten this rank if it weren't for this war," Puller confided.

"That may be true," Sherman replied, "but you are a magnificent officer, one who truly deserves to be a general."

Puller acknowledged the kind words and asked Sherman what he would do now.

"If your replacement will have me," Sherman answered, "I will ask my boss if I can stay here and interface with him."

"Shouldn't be a problem," Puller replied. "Allan Sutter is taking over the regiment, and I know he likes you."

Puller grinned. "But are you sure there isn't another reason for you wanting to stay, old man?"

Sherman's face reddened as he obviously felt some embarrassment. After all, he had never been married, and he was in uncharted territory.

"You've hit the nail on the head, sir. Yes, it's true that I have another motive. I think I'm in love with Jennifer Haraldsson, and I should get to see her more if I stay attached to the Marines."

Puller chuckled. "I appreciate your honesty, and I wish you good luck in your endeavor."

Sherman thanked him and then removed all of the stops. He told Puller about the new competition from the Air Force Captain. Puller listened intently, and it became obvious that Sherman wasn't at all sure that he would win!

"If you're going to win," Puller cautioned, "you've got to proceed with confidence. Don't for a minute think you'll be anything but victorious. This is the best advice I can give you."

Sherman thanked him. *Think positive. I've got to remember to do that.*

"Now let's get to bed," Puller said. "General Smith will be here bright and early in the morning to see me off."

Sure enough, a jeep with General Smith's three-star flag pulled up at Puller's headquarters tent the next morning at the break of dawn. General Smith got out and went to the tent. He pushed open the flap and entered. Both Puller and Sherman came to attention.

An aide and a Marine Corps photographer were directly behind General Smith. The two subordinates moved over by Sherman as Smith and Puller greeted one another.

"Lewie," Smith began, "I wanted to come and tell you what an outstanding job you've done. Naturally, I hate to lose you, but I'm glad to see that you're getting the recognition that you deserve."

"By the way," Smith continued, "I hear your men threw you quite a party the other night."

Puller chuckled. "They did give me a tremendous sendoff – one that I'll never forget."

Smith turned serious. "Lewie, you did a heck of a job in getting my regiments safely down from the Chosin Reservoir. Your rear guard action from Koto-ri to Hungnam should be studied by Marine units for years to come."

Sherman jumped into the conversation, his enthusiasm getting the better of him. "General Smith, I think the most impressive thing was that General Puller got the Marines boarded on ships at Wonsan to head south. These men will be available to fight in the future."

Smith nodded. "I agree, and I just got approval to give Lewie another Navy Cross. How many does this make – five? If so, you're the most decorated Marine – ever!"

"It wasn't me," Puller protested. "It was the enlisted men, the NCOs, and the junior officers who did the work, sir. I just gave them the opportunity to excel."

"And I'll make sure they get their recognition," Smith replied, smiling. "But right now, I want to recognize you for your magnificent performance. I heard how you would sneak out at night to visit your front-line troops. You asked them about their field-of-fire and said you would try to get hot chow up to them. Your encouragement was exactly what was needed. Now I want to reward you with this decoration."

Smith turned and nodded at his aide. The aide read the citation, and the photographer snapped pictures of General Smith pinning the award on Puller and shaking his hand. By now, Sergeant Bodey had entered the tent. Sherman and Bodey shook hands with Puller and offered congratulations at the end of the ceremony. Bodey had brought in a cart with hot coffee and pastries, and the attendees circled around it.

With a cup of coffee in one hand and a cherry pastry in the other, Smith went over to Sherman. "Tell me," he said, "have you decided to quit the Army and join the Marines?"

"No, sir, but I have decided to stay on with this regiment after General Puller rotates out. That is, if Colonel Sutter will have me and if my Army boss – whoever that turns out to be – will authorize it."

"A wise decision," Smith replied. "A Marine regiment is where the most action is. Also, Colonel Sutter is a good man. I'm sure he will take you, and he will see to it that you're well taken care of."

"I can vouch for that," Puller chimed in.

The ceremony ended, and Smith and his two staff members departed.

After finishing his coffee and sweet roll, Sergeant Bodey cleared the cart out of the tent, and Puller and Sherman were left alone.

"I greatly appreciate you sticking with me," Puller said. "If there is anything I can ever do for you, just let me know."

"I really appreciate that, sir. I recognize that in future years I will look back at my service with you and realize that it was a highlight of my life."

"Humph!" Puller replied gruffly. It was obvious that Puller didn't want the moment to turn too nostalgic!

"I'm taking Bodey and my driver with me. Otherwise, my unit will remain intact."

Puller and Sherman shook hands, Sherman saluted, and Puller exited the tent after returning Sherman's salute.

Sherman would soon be meeting with the new Regiment Commander, Colonel Allen Sutter. He liked Sutter, and he thought everything would work well. But it was still Sutter's decision. If Sutter okays him staying on, he would contact the new Chief of Intelligence in Tokyo to see if it would be okay. With MacArthur's hand-picked Chief – General Willoughby – stepping down, there was a lot of uncertainty.

Jacob Partude and Zach Barton were in the Officers' Club bar at Taegu Air Force Base. Partude had held a squadron staff meeting earlier that day in which he told squadron members of General MacArthur's relief as SCAP and General Ridgway's promotion into the position. He tried to be as upbeat as possible, but he knew that some officers were skeptical. After all, some squadron members held MacArthur in high regard and hated to see him go.

"Tell me boss," Barton said. "What is your true feeling? Do you think Ridgway's promotion will make things better or worse?"

"Well, Ridgway will probably toe the line and do what the President wants. From that standpoint, I think things will be better. I'm afraid MacArthur was dangerously close to get us into an expanded war, which nobody really wants."

Barton nodded, thought for a moment, and decided it was best if he changed the subject. "Can you tell me again, sir, how is it that you know Jennifer Haraldsson?"

Partude laughed. "So we're now back to the subject of Jennifer? I guess she's certainly as good a topic as any."

Partude took a sip of his drink and continued. "I met her at the start of the last war. She and my brother Jonathon – or Dude as we all called him – were on their way to Norway on a secret rescue mission. I flew to Washington from Texas – where I was to start pilot training – to see my brother one last time before they left on their mission. I could tell that they were in love even then. As it turned out, my brother was killed on the mission. But I stayed in touch with her ever since, and we even named our little girl after her."

"You must have thought very highly of her."

"I did – and do. If I weren't married to Sandy, she would definitely be the woman for me. Therefore, I admire your choice of women and wholeheartedly encourage you to try and win her. I have to warn you, though, it won't be easy."

Barton smiled. "I know it won't, sir, but I believe she is well worth the effort."

Partude nodded, and Barton could tell that his skipper had drifted off – thinking about his long lost brother.

Jim Sherman waited patiently outside the Nurse's quarters at the MASH Unit. He had contacted Jennifer Haraldsson, and she told him that it would be quite all right if he came to visit her. He had flowers in one hand and a box of candy in the other. He knew that he would have stiff competition for Jennifer's hand from the young Air Force Captain – Zach Barton. He planned to go all out to win her hand. Jennifer was the right woman for him, and he was sure of it.

Soon, Jennifer walked out of the Nurse's billeting area. She was so beautiful and radiant that it took his breath momentarily away. He could tell that she was largely over Jack MacLaine's death – a very good sign. He gave her a soft kiss on the cheek and then handed her the flowers and candy.

"Where in the world did you get these?" It was obvious to him that she was almost in a state of shock over the gifts.

I've got to remember this, he told himself before answering. *The gifts obviously made a big hit with her.*

"I have to be honest with you," Sherman answered. "The candy was given to Mrs. MacArthur by President Truman. He had heard that she likes this particular type. She obviously didn't want it after her husband was fired, but it is very fine candy. As you can see from the label, it comes from Blum's in Los Angeles."

"So how did you get the candy, and where did the flowers come from?"

Sherman laughed. "It's a long story about the candy, but suffice it to say that I was in Tokyo at the right time to get it. As for the flowers, Chesty Puller had an aide who could get about anything you wanted. So I asked him if he could get some flowers fit for an angel, and he came up with these."

Jennifer was obviously flattered and assured Jim Sherman that she would really enjoy the gifts. She gave Sherman a soft kiss on the cheek. *Ah, progress!*

"I'll put the flowers in water and be right out," Jennifer said as she went back in the Nurse's quarters. When she returned, she was empty-handed.

The two walked to the mess hall, got a cup of coffee, and went to a table in an empty corner. Sherman related that Puller had pinned on his star and that he was rotating back to the states. He told her that he knew and liked Colonel Sutter, Puller's replacement.

Jennifer appeared somewhat perplexed. "Will you be able to stay in Korea as an interface with the Marines?"

"I think – that is I hope – I will. It depends on my new boss, the one who is taking over Intelligence from General Willoughby."

"When will you know?"

"I should know by the end of the week. I've put in an official request, and I've asked that it be expedited."

"If you need any help from my end," Jennifer said, "just let me know."

An encouraging sign, Sherman thought. *She likes having me around!*

The two obviously felt very comfortable being around the other. They discussed issues big and small about the conflict. As he got ready to leave, Jennifer asked him when he would return.

"Soon – real soon" was his reply.

Jennifer walked Sherman to his jeep. She thanked him for the candy and flowers and gave him a soft, meaningful kiss on the lips. He responded in kind, trying not to be overly enthusiastic. After all, he knew the other guy – Zach Barton – would be trying his best. And Jim Sherman didn't want to mess this up by being overly aggressive.

As he drove off, Sherman knew that he had made progress in his quest for Jennifer's hand. He just didn't know how much!

Chapter 27

Stalemate

United Nations troops, under the direction of U.S. Generals Ridgway and Van Fleet, had clawed their way back up to the 38th parallel. True to his word, General Van Fleet had identified terrain that would be more favorable to defend. He planned to continue fighting and to stop his troops at a point that met the spirit of the President's orders. Thus, to the best of his and General Ridgway's knowledge, he planned to be in complete agreement with President Truman's direction: to hold at approximately the 38th parallel.

The significance of the 38th parallel is that it divided what had been North Korea's southern border at the start of the war and Syngman Rhee's Republic of Korea, formerly known as South Korea. While Rhee desperately wanted a unified Korean peninsula, President Truman and members of his cabinet knew that this result would not happen on their watch.

Back at the White House, President Truman met with his Secretary of State, Dean Acheson. He would have invited his Secretary of Defense, George Marshall, to the meeting, but Marshall was getting ready to retire and spend the rest of his life at his Virginia home. Marshall had served his country for 50 years and had a remarkable record. Truman, therefore, resisted the urge to encourage him to serve on.

"Dean," Truman said, "I'm tired of this war. We need to bring it to an end."

"I agree, Mr. President, but it won't be easy. The Communists are a stubborn lot."

"Let's get the Communists to the negotiating table. I'll let you decide how best to do that."

"Yes, sir."

Acheson thought for a minute and then asked the President if he were going to run for re-election.

"It's 1951, and the election is next year. I guess I better make up my mind."

Both men chuckled. The President wasn't about to drop any clues about his future plans.

General Ridgway was working at his desk in the Dai Ichi Building when his aide, Major General Hickey, entered his office. Hickey was carrying an envelope.

"This just came in from the Joint Chiefs," Hickey said to his boss. He handed the message to Ridgway.

After reading it, Ridgway handed it to Hickey. His aide scanned it. Then he looked at Ridgway.

"So it's actually come down to this," Ridgway said sadly. "Now we're supposed to start peace talks with the Communists. Presumably, the lines will be at about the same place that they were when the fighting began. So you tell me – what did all of those American boys actually die for?"

Hickey thought for a moment. "Well, sir, the Communists will have been thrown out of the South, and the war didn't escalate from the Korean peninsula. I would have to say that a great deal was accomplished."

Ridgway nodded. "I suppose you're right. In any event, I need to send a message to Jim Van Fleet right away. We need to start the peace talks immediately."

"One question, sir. Do we stop the fighting while the talks are ongoing?"

"Absolutely not! Unless I'm ordered to stop the fighting, we will keep punching at them. We need to give them a reason for being cooperative. Make sure you put in the message to Jim that he is authorized to continue attacking. The scale of his attacks, of course, is up to him. And – as I'm sure he knows – he can't stray far from the 38th parallel."

"I'll get right on this," Hickey replied. "I'll have it back to you very shortly for your review."

Ridgway's aide got up and left the room.

Soon, Hickey returned with a draft of the document that Ridgway would sign and send to Van Fleet. Ridgway read the document, nodded his approval, and handed it back to Hickey.

"I've decided to hold a meeting with the Communist Army Generals," Ridgway said. "Tell Jim in the message that I want him there. No – tell him he shouldn't attend. We wouldn't want both of us to be eliminated in case the Communists are up to something. I'll suggest to them that we have this first meeting in Kaesong. I believe that will be to their liking."

"Yes, sir. I'll add this to the message going to General Van Fleet, and I'll draft a message to the Communists proposing this meeting. Do you have a preference on a date?"

Ridgway got out his calendar and looked it over. "Let's do it the middle of next week. Wednesday would be agreeable with me."

"Fine, sir."

Hickey once again exited the room.

The meeting at Kaesong started on time. The Communists were represented by General LI-SANG-CHO and Li Kenong and Qiao Guanhua. General Ridgway headed the delegation for the United Nations. The attendees introduced themselves to the others.

They're a terse-looking lot, Ridgway privately noted. *Oh well, I expected as much.*

With the aid of interpreters, the meeting started. Areas of interest were bought up by each side. The Communists wanted the boundary between North and South Korea to be set up at precisely the 38th parallel. This was unacceptable, countered the U.N. representatives, since there were portions of this artifice that were indefensible.

U.N. representatives brought up the repatriation of prisoners of war. Since some of the Chinese captives had fought the Communists, they did not want to return to China. This point of view was unacceptable to the other side.

Toward the end of the meeting, the Communists brought up that U.N. forces had moved against Kaesong. This move was in violation of the agreement struck between nation leaders.

General Ridgway could no longer contain himself. "Liars!" he blurted out. "There has been no such action by our troops."

The Communist representatives got up and abruptly departed.

General Ridgway left to meet with General Van Fleet, his Eighth Army Commander.

"How did it go?" Van Fleet inquired when the two were together.

"About as expected," Ridgway replied. "What really made me mad was when the Communists accused us of taking military action at Kaesong. Tell me it isn't so, Jim."

Van Fleet smiled. "As far as I know, it isn't. But you know how much Syngman Rhee wants a unified Korea, over which he would preside, of course. And I can't be sure that he hasn't ordered ROK troops to make probes such as this."

Ridgway shook his head. "Keep the ROK troops under control, Jim. I don't want to be the one who is lying."

"But how do we force the Communists to cave in?" Van Fleet asked. "I do believe Mao and Stalin want peace as much as Truman does. After all, they too are facing a big manpower and material drain. But I also think they will be just as uncooperative as they can possibly be."

"Here is where the Air Force comes into play. Have them bomb the Communists to smithereens. If that doesn't work, we'll attack them on the ground."

"Now you're talking my kind of talk, boss. I was hoping you would say that."

"One other thing," Ridgway added. "I think we're going to suggest that the peace talks be moved to Panmunjom. I think the Communists would like that location even better. After all, it is on the border of the two Koreas."

Ridgway thought for a moment and sighed. "I'm assuming that we can get them back to the negotiation table. But, I'm afraid, that remains to be seen."

The two Generals shook hands, and Ridgway departed.

The U.S. Air Force went into action with some of the heaviest bombing activity of the war. However, the bombing seemed to only increase the will of the enemy. They became even more strident in their demands. Thus, Ridgway met again with General Van Fleet, his Eighth Army Commander and unofficially the number 2 in command in Korea.

"I think it's time to resume the ground war – a very limited ground war," Ridgway said. "I've gotten permission clear up to and including the

President, so you won't get in any trouble. The President, just as we do, realizes that we have to give the Communists some incentive to return to the negotiating table. Just make sure you don't advance too far from the 38th parallel."

"My staff has been working on just such a plan. If you have some time, I'll go over the highlights with you."

Ridgway nodded, and Van Fleet started in.

"To begin with, there has been a lot of talk around here about troops being home by Christmas. These so-called peace talks have the folks back home, as well as the troops here, very excited. I've directed my Commanders to do their darndest to change this thinking. Time will tell if they've been successful."

"I'm glad you have your Commanders involved," Ridgway interjected. "I think it will be a lot longer than the Christmas time frame when we're able to send anyone home – if then.'"

"Before I get to the overview, I've got some things I really want to ask you. The questions involve our new Secretary of Defense, Robert Abercrombie Lovett. What is your take on him, and do you think he will be better or worse than George Marshall?"

Ridgway was caught somewhat off-guard, but he had obviously thought about the issues. "Well, to begin with, he followed Marshall over from the Secretary of State's Office to Secretary of Defense. So I think we can assume that Marshall and Lovett think quite a bit alike. And, from what I know about him, Lovett wants an increase in military spending, both to carry on with the Korean War and to rebuild the military. This is a very positive sign. Like Marshall, Lovett thinks the United States shouldn't have cut the military to the bone after World War II."

Ridgway paused for a moment before continuing. "Lovett is quite a bit younger than Marshall. Thus, I suspect he'll be a lot more involved in the execution of the Korean War than Marshall was. As long as he doesn't try to micro-manage us, this could be a good thing."

Van Fleet nodded and started his overview. "First of all, my staff knows the sensitivity of the issue. Therefore, our military thrusts will be made using the rationale that we are trying to shorten our lines and reach more defensible positions. We are not – repeat not – trying to gain new territory."

"Excellent. Continue."

"We are going to make thrusts into this area called the Punchbowl." Van Fleet walked to a map that was hanging on the wall and pointed to the area. "This is not only a Communist staging area, but it would put us on high ground. Any questions?"

"Your plan is a good one, Jim," Ridgway stated. "Go to it and good luck. Let's meet again in about a week."

The two men shook hands, and Ridgway departed.

The fighting at the Punchbowl was a lot more intense than either Ridgway or Van Fleet thought it would be. The initial actions of the U.N. Forces were limited in scope. Republic of Korea forces – the South Koreans – initially were able to take the high ground around the Punchbowl. Eventually, though, they were pushed out, and U.S. Army troops were used to attempt a retake of the high ground.

North Korean troops fought furiously to fend off the American assault. The area around the Punchbowl in which the fighting raged was appropriately renamed 'Bloody Ridge.' American forces, exhausted and low on ammunition, would take the high ground, only to be thrown off when the enemy counterattacked. The high ground changed hands often, and it became known as 'Heartbreak Ridge.'

After a siege at Heartbreak Ridge, an unhappy Matthew Ridgway met with General Van Fleet. "Jim, what the hell is going on here? I thought you would be successful, but it's doubtful that you have."

"The enemy has been a lot more tenacious than we thought he would be. He throws wave after wave of troops at us. He obviously wants us to give in to his demands just as we want him to give in to ours."

Ridgway stopped to reflect on the situation. "Do you need some new leaders in there? Maybe I didn't go far enough."

"I think I now have the right men in leadership positions. I have been very impressed with my new 2nd Division Commander, Bob Young. He has stopped the fighting at Heartbreak Ridge, calling it a fiasco. He wants to improve the tactics we're using before we resume the engagement."

Ridgway nodded. "I have to admit that your actions have gotten the Communists back to the negotiating table. And perhaps even more importantly, the Communists now know that the U.N. side will be every bit as resilient and stubborn as they are."

"Also Jim, I have been in close contact with the Joint Chiefs. With the Communists now back at the negotiating table, they want us to go in to a phase they're calling 'active defense.' They want our only military thrusts to be made to strengthen our lines."

Van Fleet looked distressed. "I thought that was what we were doing."

Ridgway smiled. "On the surface, yes, but you know as well as I that we had other motives in play. Going in to the active defense mode should cut way down on our casualties and our employment of manpower and material."

"Okay, Matt," Van Fleet replied, "but I have to tell you that I am becoming even more frustrated. I hate to be the first ground Commander in U.S. history to have to settle for a stalemate."

"I hear you, Jim, but you have to realize that the U.S. military works for the President as Commander-in-Chief. Thus, we have to do what he tells us to do. And I have to say that President Truman's goal of keeping this war from spreading is, in my opinion, a very honorable and worthwhile one."

"I agree," Van Fleet replied. His response was lacking any enthusiasm.

Back at the negotiating table, the Communists stuck by their original points of contention, as did the U.N. negotiators. It was becoming obvious to all concerned that the end of the conflict was not in sight. Unfortunately, for both sides, the fighting would continue into the foreseeable future, and men would lose their lives. However, there was a decrease in the fighting, and this allowed the United States to change the troop makeup on the front lines. Some National Guard Units were brought in to replace Army Units that had been there from the start. For the men at the front, this was good news. There was now hope that those who had sacrificed immensely would be relieved and could return home.

President Truman looked at his two most prestigious Secretaries – Dean Acheson and Robert Lovett – as he met with them in the Oval Office. The President appeared quite pensive. Obviously, he had made a big decision.

"Gentlemen, I've called you here to let you know before you hear it from anyone else. I've made a huge decision, and it wasn't made easily. I have decided not to run for re-election."

Acheson spoke for the two Secretaries. "Mr. President, I think I can speak for both Bob and myself. We are shocked."

"I'm sure you are, and I don't blame you. But the reality of the situation is that I don't think I could win. Even though I'm convinced

I was right in firing MacArthur, a large block of the American people disagrees. Also, I've gotten word that Eisenhower is seriously thinking of running for President. If he does, I think he would win hands down against anyone he faces. He is that popular."

Acheson spoke up again. "I hate to say it, Mr. President, but I think you're right. I also think you will be rated very highly by historians. It's unfortunate, but people in the near term tend to be much harsher critics than historians. It will be some years before you are given credit for all the difficult decisions you've had to make."

"Starting with your decision to drop the atomic bomb," Lovett added, "you've always had the best interest of the American people at heart. It's just a shame some of them can't understand this."

"Oh well," Truman replied, "such is life. And, as I've said before, the buck stops here."

"I want you two to know," Truman continued, "you have done a wonderful job. "Bob, from your time as an Undersecretary of State to your present tenure as Secretary of Defense, you have operated in superb fashion. And as for you, Dean, I couldn't have gotten by without you. If I can ever do anything for either of you, you only have to ask."

"That is most kind of you, Mr. President," Acheson said. "And, as I've said before, I don't think the Communists could have picked a worse spot than Korea to engage us. But they did, and years from now, I think historians will rightfully praise you for not getting us into a protracted war with the Communists."

"Mr. President, I agree with everything Dean said," Lovett injected. "And I want to add that I think you handled the Korean situation as best as anyone could. Thousands of American lives have been lost. Oh sure, some people think that we should have won over there. But most of those people never lost someone they loved in a war in a far-off place. It's too bad they can't talk to someone who has."

"Well put, Bob," Truman replied. "Maybe I should have talked to you before I made my decision."

The three laughed half-heartedly, and the meeting adjourned on a less-sobering tone.

In the fall of 1952, Dwight Eisenhower won to become the next President of the United States. While he won in overwhelming fashion, Eisenhower harbored no illusions. He knew he would inherit a very difficult job the following January. True to his word, he took the responsibility very seriously. After all, he wanted the United States to be very robust for his son, John Eisenhower, and any grandchildren that may follow. He called in his trusted advisor, John Foster Dulles, to talk over the situation.

"John," Eisenhower started, "I'm very concerned about how much the war in Korea is costing – both manpower-wise and dollar wise. I don't think our country can afford it. Do you have any suggestions?"

"I think you should go to Korea and assess the situation for yourself. I think you should do it now."

Eisenhower's eyebrows raised. "While I am still the President-elect?"

"Yes, sir. I think, based on your service to the country, no one would criticize you, not even President Truman."

Eisenhower thought for a moment. "I guess you're right, John. But I won't announce I'm going. I'll just go."

"That would be the correct way to handle it," Dulles replied.

Soon after, Eisenhower went to Korea and met with his two top Commanders, Matt Ridgway and Jim Van Fleet. After assessing the situation, Eisenhower told the two that he saw no reason why an armistice couldn't be signed. Neither objected, but Van Fleet asked if he could put in a request.

"What is that?" Eisenhower asked.

"First of all," Van Fleet replied. "I have cleared talking to you with General Ridgway. The point is that I have become very frustrated over here. As I am sure you know, I hate stalemate. Therefore, I request that you put in a new Eighth Army Commander shortly after you become President and assign me elsewhere."

Eisenhower looked at Ridgway, and SCAP nodded. "Okay, Jim. I understand your feeling, and I'll look into it. Mind you, though, I'm not promising anything."

"All I'm asking for, sir, is your consideration."

"Agreed," Eisenhower replied.

Before he left, Ridgway and Van Fleet made sure that Eisenhower understood that he, as President, could not accept the Communist's word at face value. On the flight back to the U.S., Eisenhower knew that, even if he planned to sign an armistice, he would have to make sure that the U.S. had a strong military presence in the Republic of Korea. *I hoped to have my cake and eat it, too. Apparently, that won't be possible.*

Part 5

Chapter 28

Civilians Again

Jennifer and Monica were stunned but very happy and excited.

"Peace at last!" Jennifer screamed.

Monica was almost as delirious but more cautious. "Remember, Jennifer. Ike signed an armistice, not a peace accord. The Communists have not surrendered."

"You're absolutely right. But an armistice means no more fighting and, hopefully, no more casualties."

"I'm glad you used the word 'hopefully.' I don't trust the Commies as far as I can throw them. My advice to Ike and the others is that we watch our backs very carefully."

"Your input is well taken," Jennifer conceded. "But I'm delighted that the heavy fighting is over – at least until one side breaks the rules, which is hopefully never."

Monica nodded. "By the way, what are you going to do about your dilemma – where you're pursued by two worthy courters?"

"You mean my happy dilemma?" Jennifer moaned. "Most girls would love to have more than one suitor, but I have to tell you – it's not all it's cracked up to be."

Monica was puzzled. "Why not?"

"Well, for one thing, they're both great guys. They're honest, dedicated, dependable, and have a great future, either in or out of the military."

"And it sure doesn't hurt that they're both handsome."

"That, too," Jennifer admitted. "I know I have to make up my mind soon, but what to do, what to do. I certainly don't want to make a mistake."

"Poor you," Monica said in a mocking tone. "I think every gal would like that chance."

Jennifer turned very serious. "Does that include you? I assumed you and Mike Pulaskey would get married and settle down in the near future."

Monica shrugged. "I don't know about Mike and me. I think we're mainly just going to be good friends. But who knows?"

Monica paused and continued. "What about you and Zach Barton? If Zach isn't the one for you, can I have him?"

Jennifer laughed. "That's what I like about you, Monica. You always speak what's on your mind."

"Just like Molly, right?"

Better be careful here, Jennifer thought. *I certainly don't want to open a can of worms.*

"What makes you bring up Zach?" Jennifer inquired.

"Oh, just a feeling I have. I think there's some chemistry between us. But I don't want to cut into your territory if he's still in the running."

"I appreciate your feeling that way. And you'll be the first to know when I make a decision."

Jennifer looked at her watch. "I guess we had better go back to work."

Monica nodded and started walking toward the patient's area. Jennifer watched her until she was out of sight.

Wow! Jennifer thought. *What a time bomb. Monica might be interested in Zach! I never dreamed I would be in this situation in a million years. I've got to be extremely careful.*

But Jennifer knew that she would have to determine who the best man for her was. She couldn't let Monica's statement impact her decision making. After all, she would be spending the rest of her life with the man she selected.

Jennifer decided that she should talk things over with Brad Taylor. He had always come through for her in the past, and she thought he would do so now.

It was evening, and Jennifer found Taylor in his office. He was having his usual nightly drink – a Jack Daniels. He looked up as she knocked on the open door that separated his office from the rest of the unit. He motioned for her to come in and have a seat.

"Can I get you a drink?" he asked.

"I need one," Jennifer responded. "I'll take whatever you're having."

Taylor smiled, fixed her drink, and handed it to her. "Sounds serious," he said. "Can I help you with whatever you're thinking about?"

"Yes, you sure can. I was just talking to Monica, and she asked if she could have Zach Barton if I didn't want him. I was shocked, but I said she could after I've made my decision and Zach isn't the one I've chosen."

Taylor looked puzzled. "Whoa. I thought she was going to hook up with Mike Pulaskey. Apparently, I was wrong."

"You and me both. I thought the same thing, but Monica informed me that she and Mike were more than likely just going to be good friends. So I need your wise counsel. Should I tell Monica to stay away from Zach or just let her have him if he falls out of my affection?"

Taylor whistled softly and took another sip. "I think you've handled it correctly so far. Monica's a big girl now, so she will have to decide for herself what she's going to do."

"I guess you're right," Jennifer said rather unenthusiastically. "It's just that I so hoped she and Mike would get together that I find this sudden turn of events disappointing to say the least."

"I know how you feel, but there's nothing you can do about it. So my advice is to just go with the flow."

Jennifer nodded and started to feel better. She slouched down in her chair and started to really relax for the first time since coming in her boss's office.

"Before you get too comfortable," Taylor said, "read this." He got up and handed her the directive from higher headquarters. She straightened up in her chair and read the document intently.

"Wow,"she said as if talking to herself. "It says to expect a large reduction in force and to prepare those patients needing more care for movement to a hospital facility in Japan."

Taylor shook his head. "We've got our work cut out, all right. Naturally, I'll want you and Monica to return to Walter Reed Hospital with me when we're back on civilian status, and I'll ask if any of the other doctors and nurses want to come with us."

"You really think we'll be civilians soon?" Jennifer asked.

"There's no doubt in my mind. Doctors and nurses will be among the first to be let out. That's why I'm staking my claim for you and Monica immediately."

Jennifer was puzzled. "But are you sure our jobs will still be available at Walter Reed?"

"Positive. I told my superiors before we came here that I intended to have my old job back after this conflict ended and that I would bring you two with me. They agreed, and I plan to hold them to it."

Jennifer got up and set her glass on Taylor's desk. "I better get going. If we're to move our patients to Japan, there's going to be a lot of preparation."

Taylor raised his glass and pointed it at Jennifer. "I knew I could count on you. By the way, I'll brief the staff tomorrow on these events. Sergeant Carter will post the specifics."

"Fine. Can I tell people I see to expect your briefing?"

"Absolutely. The sooner folks know about it, the better."

"I'll keep you up to speed on what transpires with Monica, and I'll inform her of your Walter Reed offer."

"Great," Taylor replied.

Soon, Jennifer was out of Taylor's office and on her way to start preparations for a patient move. She knew that she would have to coordinate closely with Bear Carter, but in the morning would be early enough to start working with him. She would go back to her quarters and start drafting initial plans now.

As she walked to her quarters, she saw a familiar face coming toward her. It was none other than Mike Pulaskey.

"Just the man I need to talk to," she said. "You have a minute?"

"I certainly do. Fire away."

"You will probably think what I'm about to ask is none of my business. And you'll be right. However, I'm going to ask anyway, so here goes. Are you and Monica no longer serious about spending your lives together?"

Pulaskey looked as if he were going to choke. "What in the world gave you that idea? I admit that Monica and I have been in a bit of a cooling period, but we – I that is – certainly feel that she is the right one for me. And I plan to marry her and spend the rest of my life with her."

"That's a relief, but Mike, I suggest you talk to her and renew your plans with her. I think she may feel that your relationship is not as definite as you feel it is."

"I appreciate your advice," Pulaskey replied. "I knew that something was probably remiss, but I ignored the warning signs. Thank you."

"You're more than welcome, but please don't tell Monica that we had this conversation. I don't think she would appreciate my butting in."

"My lips are sealed."

The two shook hands and went their separate way. Jennifer went back to Brad Taylor's office and gave him the details of her meeting with Pulaskey.

"Mike promised me that Monica would not know that we had our little conversation," Jennifer said. "So you must also be very clever if the subject ever comes up."

Taylor chuckled. "I certainly will. I don't want the little redhead to get all worked up over this. And I now recall why we called her sister 'Hurricane Molly'."

Taylor had finished his libation and was filling out paperwork. He got up from his desk and walked Jennifer out.

"Sleep tight tonight," he said. "You'll need all your strength in the days ahead."

The two hugged briefly and Jennifer headed back to her quarters.

The next morning, Jennifer told all she saw about Brad Taylor's upcoming briefing and said that they would be going through a period of transition. She told everyone to check the bulletin board for the time and place of the briefing. She then went down to check on the bulletin board herself.

Bear Carter was just posting the announcement of the briefing when she arrived.

"Hi, Bear. I see that I've come to the right place at the right time."

"Yes, Ma'am. The Colonel's briefing is going to be at 1730 today in the mess hall. I guess the Colonel felt that most people would be on their way to chow and that he might as well hold it there. As you see from the announcement, people pulling night shifts are excused, so I guess folks like you will have to pass on the information to them."

"Good point, Bear. I'll check with Colonel Taylor to see who all he wants me to give the information to. And naturally I'll have to work closely with you to see how we're going to pull this off."

At a few minutes before 1730, Taylor walked into the front of the mess hall. Sergeant Carter called the group to attention. Jennifer noticed that the doctors leisurely stood up. She smiled. *Their military bearing isn't the greatest. Oh well, what can we expect? They're medical doctors, for gosh sakes!*

"At ease," Taylor said. The occupants sat back down. "I guess by now you all know that there are big changes in the wind. For those of you anxious to get back to civilian life, your wish has been granted. Anyone wanting out can see me right away, and I'll sign your discharge papers. For those of you who want to continue working for me, I can almost guarantee that I can get you a job at Walter Reed. You folks should also come see me. For those of you wanting to stay in the Army, I'll see if I can get you assigned to where you want to go. Please check with me as soon as you can."

Taylor took a drink of water and continued. "Now about our patients. The ones who aren't well enough for discharge from the hospital will be sent to a hospital in Japan. I don't know exactly where yet, so please stay tuned. And please check – at least twice each day, once in the morning and once in the late afternoon – with the bulletin board. I will give Sergeant Carter updated information, and he will post it as soon as I give it to him. Are there any questions?"

Monica raised her hand.

"Yes, Lieutenant Davis."

"Will you need some of us to escort the patients to Japan?"

"Excellent question, and yes I will. I haven't thought about this very much, but I will have Sergeant Carter post the information as soon as I get it figured out. Are there any other questions?"

No one raised their hand, and the group was dismissed.

As they left the mess hall, Jennifer couldn't help but notice that Monica and Pulaskey were very chummy – even romantic – as they left. They gave each other a quick kiss as they went their separate ways. Jennifer hurried to catch up with Monica.

"I thought you said the romance was over," Jennifer said softly in a half-joking manner. Fortunately, the others coming out of the mess hall were not very close, and they were preoccupied with their own thoughts.

Monica shook her head. "I'm as surprised as you. I don't know what's come over him, but he has suddenly turned back to his passion and attentiveness of old."

"Are you still interested in me turning Zach over to you if I pick Jim Sherman?"

Monica thought for a moment. "I guess you can forget I ever said that. Mike is certainly the one for me. I just needed some assurance as to his intentions."

"Good. Let me know when you set up your wedding date."

Monica nodded as the two went their separate ways.

"Mike and I will have to talk to Brad about coming to Walter Reed," Monica yelled to Jennifer over her shoulder.

"Yes!" Jennifer replied. "It will be great to have the two of you there."

They waved as their separation distance increased.

There was a note from Jim Sherman waiting for Jennifer when she got back to her quarters. It said that he would be there tomorrow if she had no objections and for her to let him know. She quickly penned out a message saying for him to come by all means. It would be great to see him as always. She hustled over to Bear Carter's office to get it transmitted.

Sherman arrived at the MASH Unit bright and early the next day. He met Jennifer outside of the Nurses quarters. The two kissed.

"It's so good to see you," Sherman said quietly.

"I feel the same way."

They headed down to the Mess Hall. The two started to hold hands but then thought better of it. After all, they were in a military establishment, and military bearing was important. They got breakfast when they reached the mess hall and headed to a table in the back corner, figuring it gave them the best chance for a little privacy.

"How is your new Intelligence Chief working out?" Jennifer asked.

Sherman smiled, knowing that it was best to make small talk at first. "Okay, I guess. I was surprised that General Ridgway said that our former Chief – General Willoughby – was a fine Intelligence Officer. I personally thought that Willoughby left some things to be desired."

"Will your new Chief keep you in the Army with the Korean War winding down?"

"I think so. I've now had a lot of experience, both here in Korea and in the last war. And if he doesn't keep me, I'll just plan to go out in the civilian world. I think everyone at the top realizes that our military was shrunk too much after the last war, so I don't think they'll let that happen again. In other words, I think I'll be okay whatever the future holds."

Sherman took another bite and continued. "But let's talk about you. What are your future plans? After all, if you will have me, I want to be with you, wherever that is."

"You are most kind, sir. Right now, I plan to go back to Washington and work at Walter Reed. I'm building up federal retirement time – working both in the military and as a civilian – so I may as well keep that going."

"You have a good plan," Sherman replied. "If you decide that we have a future together, I can talk to my boss and put in a request that I get stationed in the D.C. area. But the sooner you decide, the better it is. Once the wheels start turning to get me sent to a certain locale, the harder it will be to stop the momentum."

"I understand, and I promise that I'll let you know soon. Just how soon I don't know, as I have an awful lot on my plate right now. We just learned that our patients who are not ready to be released will be sent to a hospital in Japan. I also have aging parents in Idaho and my move back to Washington coming up. So you see, I have a great deal on my mind."

"And that fellow Zach Barton? I guess he's a big reason why you're still undecided."

"And that, too."

Jennifer noted the dejected look on Sherman's face. *I can't let him get discouraged. After all, he may be the one!*

"Jim, please don't be discouraged. I assure you that you're right in there. I just want to make sure. After all, this is a huge decision, and now that I'm older, I know that I can't afford to make a mistake." She reached over and put her hand on his.

"I understand," Sherman replied. "I just need to be more patient and give you the time you need. After all, I know the trauma you went through with Jack's death."

I wish he hadn't said that, although it's certainly true.

"I'm sorry," Sherman said. "I shouldn't have brought up old wounds."

"It's okay. You have every right to have said it."

The two finished eating, and they took their trays over to the conveyor that was moving the dirty plates and silver ware to a back room. Soon, the trays were out of sight.

Jennifer and Sherman walked slowly out. Jennifer could tell that Sherman was feeling the uncertainty as much as she was.

"Jim, I will try very hard to come to a decision very soon. And I promise you that I will let you know just as soon as I make up my mind."

"I can't ask for any more than that."

The two kissed, and Sherman got in the jeep and started it. He was shortly out of sight.

On the way to her rounds, Sergeant Carter came running up.

"I've got another message for you, Ma'am. You're quite popular these days."

Jennifer saw that it was from none other than Zach Barton. She opened the envelope and read the message. He wanted to come see her tomorrow!

"Wow! Two courters in as many days," she said laughingly. "Bear, please send the message that I will be happy to see Captain Barton tomorrow."

"Yes, Ma'am!" Carter went speedily to send the dispatch.

The next morning, Jennifer arose early. She found herself wanting to look particularly nice for Barton. Was this an omen? Did she secretly favor Zach? She didn't know, but she had to admit that Barton was certainly in the running.

And Jennifer was happy that Monica was feeling romantically attracted to Mike Pulaskey once again. It would have been painful to see Monica and Zach together! Why? She wasn't sure. Perhaps it was just human nature.

As was the case with Jim Sherman, Zach would be arriving early. Thus, she would invite him to go to the mess hall. Fortunately, the cook was good, and the food was all right in every respect. She looked at her watch. *Better get out front,* she thought. *He might already be here.*

When Jennifer exited the Nurse's quarters, she found Zach talking to Monica. *Oh-oh,* she thought. *Not a good sign.* The two were laughing, and they looked very comfortable together. *Better not waste any time getting over there.*

"Hi, you two. I hope I'm not interrupting anything.

"Oh, no, you're not," was the almost simultaneous response.

"I've got rounds to make," Monica said. "Good to see you, Zach. Be careful going back to your base."

"Good seeing you, too, Monica. And I'll be very careful going back.

The two waved, and Monica was off.

This isn't good, Jennifer told herself. She followed Monica with her eyes as the young lieutenant entered the patient's area.

"A penny for your thoughts?" Barton said, a big smile breaking over his face.

Jennifer laughed. "I'm afraid they're not worth a penny. Are you hungry?"

"Famished."

"In that case, let's go to the mess hall and get some breakfast."

"I'm for that," Barton replied.

They filled their trays, and Jennifer nodded to a table in the back corner. It was the same one she and Jim Sherman had used yesterday.

"If we go to that one," Jennifer said, "we'll have some privacy and can talk."

"Sounds good."

Barton followed Jennifer to the table, and soon they were eating.

Jennifer started the conversation. "I couldn't help but notice that you and Monica were really hitting it off. Are you sure you want to continue a relationship with me?"

"I think so, but I sure feel better that you're so open about everything. I have to admit that Monica struck a chord with me, and I guess I need to do some real soul searching."

Jennifer nodded. "Yes, I think you do. And don't forget that Monica is in a relationship with one of the doctors here. So my best advice is that you don't start anything with her unless you're very sure you want to."

"I see what you mean. Life is complicated, isn't it?"

"I'll say it is!"

Chapter 29

Decision Time

J ennifer was now greatly perplexed. *The honorable thing to do,* she told herself, *is to tell Jim that his competition is decreased. However, I don't want him thinking that his competition is non-existent, because it isn't.*

She took out pen and paper and started writing. She had thought about starting with the term 'Dearest.' However she decided against it. *Got to be careful. I don't want him to be over-confident!*

Dear Jim

It was wonderful to see you on your recent trip. Your coming here means a great deal to me – more than you will ever know!

I am having to get used to the fact that I will be a civilian again. I still wear my oak leaves on my shoulder, but now it is truly just a matter of time. Needless to say, it will take some getting used to!

I must tell you that your competition from Zach Barton has decreased. Please don't be over-confident, but Zach may be interested in another Nurse here at MASH. I don't know for sure, but I wanted to tell you of the possibility.

Things here are now almost to the frantic stage. We have gotten the orders to prepare our patients for movement to Japan, but we don't know yet where they will be going. It is another case of 'hurry up and wait!' I know I shouldn't complain, because those of you who have risked your life know full well what it is to receive future orders that leave out crucial information. Oh well, from my perspective, I guess it's better to know some specifics than none whatsoever.

*I have to admit that I am thinking of you more and more. And I can't
wait to see you again. Please do come whenever you can.*
And I promise that I will make my decision soon.
Love always,
Jennifer

Suddenly Jennifer realized that she had accomplished the easy part:
Writing Jim Sherman. Pangs of conscience settled in, and she realized that
she must also write Zach Barton. Writing Zach would be more difficult
and would take more deftness on her part. *Oh well, may as well start in.*

Dear Zach
*Based on our last meeting, I realize that you may have eyes for someone
else. This is okay with me, although I want you to know that – as far as I
am concerned – you are definitely not out of the running with me. You have
many of the traits that I admire in a man. From what I know of you, you are
responsible, dependable, and – oh yes – your good looks don't hurt a bit! Thus,
I will be honored and delighted to have you in the running for my hand. I
don't want to mislead you, though, Jim Sherman – who you've met – is a very
strong candidate. As I've told Jim, I will plan to make up my mind soon. I
realize that it isn't fair keeping everyone in limbo.*
*As I'm sure it is with you, things here are in a rather uncertain state. With
the Armistice that President Eisenhower signed, we are in flux. We know that
our patients who are not ready to be released will go to a U.S. hospital in Japan.
We just don't know yet where it will be. After we get this issue squared away, I
will be leaving the Army once again and going back to my nursing position at
Walter Reed Hospital. I will be working for Brad Taylor – my boss here – so
it won't be a dramatic change. I have known Brad for a long time, and he is
great to work for.*
Well, I better close for now. I hope to see you in the near future.
Love,
Jennifer

Feels good having that out of the way, Jennifer thought. She put the
letters in envelopes, sealed them, and started the walk down to the mailing
area. She would give them to the ever reliable Bear Carter to mail them.
As she exited the Nurses' quarters, Monica Davis was just entering.

"We need to talk," Jennifer said. Unfortunately, the words came out
more icily than she had intended.

"I agree," Monica replied. "Shall we go to the mess hall and grab a cup of coffee while we hash things out?"

"Yes, let's do."

The two walked in silence down to the mess hall. They got a cup of coffee and went to a vacant table in the far corner.

Monica initiated the conversation. "It's your nickel, so I'll let you start.

"Fine," Jennifer replied. She started in very carefully, as she didn't want to lose Monica's friendship – particularly when she wasn't sure she could salvage or even want having Zach Barton in her romantic life.

"Monica, I hope you know that I consider you one of my very best friends. Your happiness means a great deal to me, and I welcome the fact that you want Zach back in your life. I don't know what transpired between you and Mike, but that is none of my business. I have to be frank with you, though, and tell you that I haven't yet ruled Zach out of my future."

"I appreciate your being straight forward with me. I'm in kind of the same situation as you are. I don't want to rule Mike out, but I have to tell you that there is a definite spark between Zach and me, and it's going to take some time to get it all sorted out."

Jennifer smiled at her young friend. "I guess we should start the competition and say 'let the best man – or woman – win.'"

"I'll drink to that," Monica replied enthusiastically.

The two clicked their coffee cups and changed the conversation to a more congenial topic.

"What can you tell me about where our patients will be going in Japan?" Monica asked.

"Not much. Are you volunteering to go with them?"

Monica shrugged. "It depends on what you and Brad want me to do. I definitely want to go back to Walter Reed, so if you want me to go there right away, I will. But if you want me to go to Japan first, just say the word."

"This is why you're so valuable to us," Jennifer replied softly. "Not only are you very competent, but you're willing to do whatever is necessary. I applaud you."

Monica was obviously a little self-conscious. "Thank you, kind ma'am."

The two nurses took their coffee cups over to the moving rack and placed them on it in a suitable position. They then strolled out of the mess hall.

"I'm so happy we cleared the air," Jennifer said. "I wouldn't want anything to come between us."

"Ditto for me" was the response. The two hugged outside of the mess hall and went their separate ways.

On her way to the patient area, Jennifer saw Brad Taylor approaching. He waved at her, and by the expression on his face, Jennifer knew that he needed to talk to her.

"I was just coming to see you," he said. "I just learned that our patients who can't be discharged will be going to Osaka Army Hospital in Japan. I've been bugging my superiors to let us know where our patients will be sent, and finally they came through. Bear will be posting this information very shortly, but I wanted you to be the first to know."

"I appreciate your thoughtfulness, Brad. And I am eager to tell you that everything is okay between Monica and me. I know it has been a concern to you."

Taylor nodded. "I very much appreciate your getting the problem resolved, especially since I'm having a little 'thank you' party in my office tonight. I'm inviting you and the others who have been here since the beginning. Not very many I might add. Just you – and I'm including Monica and Mike even though they weren't here quite from the start – and Bear Carter. The mess hall chef is fixing a little something special, so it should be very good."

"I'll be there," Jennifer replied. "What time should I come?"

"The festivities will begin about 1800, so any time around there will be fine."

Jennifer had trouble hiding her enthusiasm. "I can't wait," she said. She patted Taylor on the shoulder and resumed her walk to the patient area.

At promptly 1800 that evening, Jennifer walked into Brad Taylor's office. There was a small table with seating for four set up in the middle of the room. Taylor's desk had been moved back to make adequate room. Monica, Mike Pulaskey, and Bear Carter were already there, standing talking with Taylor. The Colonel had given each a glass, and it was evident that he had not stinted in the amount of Jack Daniels he had given to them!

The other four greeted Jennifer warmly, and Taylor handed her a glass with a generous amount of Jack Daniels present. As she entered in to the festivities, Jennifer couldn't help but notice that things were a little awkward between Monica and Pulaskey. *Uh-oh,* she told herself, *I guess Monica has relayed to Mike her new romantic interest. I hope it won't spoil the evening.*

Jennifer's fears were soon allayed. Dinner was brought in on a big cart by the chef, and Taylor relayed the seating assignments. Monica was seated next to Pulaskey, and the two soon let it be known that everything was fine between them.

Jennifer noted that the food looked absolutely scrumptious. The chef had somehow managed to round up filet mignon, and on the side of the filets were baked potatoes with all the fixings and fresh asparagus. Fresh asparagus! *How in the world did he manage that?* Jennifer smiled and only slightly shook her head. *He must be a magician, indeed.*

"Before we begin," Taylor said, "I want to thank you for your magnificent service. You indeed bring great credit to yourselves, your unit, and your country."

"Here, here," Carter said. All raised their glass and drank a toast. At the end, Jennifer proposed another toast. This one was to their boss, Brad Taylor. He beamed as each was highly complementary of him.

"Enough of that," Taylor said. "Let's eat."

They dug in, and all were very impressed with the feast that the chef had prepared.

"I don't think I've ever enjoyed a meal as much as this one," Jennifer said. The other three guests seconded her statement.

Dessert consisted of ice cream and fruit, and, by the end, it was obvious that all were full and content – very content.

"An evening such as this calls for a good cigar," Taylor said. He offered one to all, and Bear Carter accepted.

"The rest of you don't mind if we smoke, do you?" Taylor asked. In a joint response, the others said that they didn't.

Taylor started chuckling as he took a puff. "Jennifer and Bear, do you remember when we were fired at driving down to open our first MASH unit. Fortunately, Bear, you pulled immediately over into a ditch, and we jumped out and dove down. Bullets were flying all over the place."

"I remember that," Jennifer said wistfully. "It's something that I sure don't want to live over."

"I go along with that," Carter responded. "But the time that will stick with me the longest is when they brought those North Korean prisoners in. Our doctors and nurses took really good care of them, and I hope they remember that."

"They probably won't," Pulaskey replied, "but it doesn't matter. We took an oath to take good care of all of our patients, regardless of where they came from."

Taylor raised his thumb. "That's right, and I'm very proud of our doctors and nurses for doing it."

Jennifer raised her glass. "Don't forget to pat yourself on the back, Brad. You were right in there helping."

The others raised their glass to their leader.

"You've been a great boss," Monica said. "Brad, we salute you."

The four guests stood up and simultaneously gave words of praise.

"The evening went by way too quickly," Mike Pulaskey said after the toasting was finished. "But I have early rounds in the morning, so I had better go."

Brad Taylor shook hands with him and thanked him again for his outstanding service. The others said that they needed to leave, also. Taylor shook hands with each of them, offering his sincere thanks. The special occasion was concluded.

At the Officers' Club at Taegu Air Base, Zach Barton saw Jacob Partude on a bar stool at the end of the counter. Zach had made a monumental decision, and he wanted his boss to be the first to know. He went to the end of the bar and sat down on the stool next to Partude.

"Hi, Boss," Barton said. He motioned to the bartender that he wanted his usual.

Partude looked over. "Oh, it's you."

"That's right, sir, and I wanted you to be the first to know. I've made a huge decision regarding my love life."

"Oh? And what's that?"

"Well, you probably won't like this, but after putting a great deal of thought into it, I've decided that Monica is the one for me. I'm going after her with all I've got to offer."

Partude chuckled. "You've got to decide who you want to spend the rest of your life with, and, while I had hoped you would select Jennifer, the decision is totally yours."

"Whew. That's a relief. Thanks for your understanding, boss."

Partude nodded. "Perhaps of more importance where I'm concerned is what are your work plans are for the future? Do you want to stay in the Air Force or do you plan on getting out?"

"If I had my druthers, I would stay in the Air Force. I've become very attached to the lifestyle. But of course I'll have to take Monica's desires into consideration – that is if she'll have me."

After a moment, Barton continued. "But I suppose a lot of the guys would like to continue in the service."

"You're right," Partude acknowledged. "And I'll have to bring this up at staff meeting tomorrow. Obviously, since hostilities here are ending, there will be a big drawdown. But you shouldn't have to worry. Your status as an air ace should qualify you to go just about anywhere you would want to go, staying in the Air Force I might add."

"Even the Washington, D.C. area?"

"Yes. This is just my take on it, but with your record – and getting a great write-up from me – I think you should get the D.C. area hands down. The President will need top-notch people to fly cover."

"Thank you, boss. I would want to be close to Monica, and she will be going to Walter Reed. So D.C. would be the perfect assignment for me."

"I understand. Come see me first thing in the morning so we can get the show on the road."

Barton nodded, and the conversation changed to lighter subjects.

Dawn rolled around, and Jennifer awakened. The dinner the night before had been great, but now they had to get back to reality. There was a lot of work to be done. Patients that were not ready for release would have to be prepared for movement to Osaka Army Hospital in Japan. The others would have to be readied for out processing, a big task in itself.

Jennifer showered and dressed quickly and headed for Brad Taylor's office. She would see if he wanted to go to breakfast and would ask what her latest tasks were. When she got to his office, he was busily reviewing reports.

"Have you already eaten breakfast?" she asked.

"About an hour ago. How about you?"

"I'll go as soon as I found out if you have any new instructions for me. By the way, your party last night was super. I promise I'll never forget it."

Taylor was obviously pleased. "I thank you very much for your kind words. I don't have any new instructions for you, so go eat."

"Will do, sir," Jennifer replied. She walked out of his office and started for the mess hall.

Half way to her destination, Jennifer saw Bear Carter waving and walking toward her in a hurried fashion. He was holding what appeared to be two letters.

"Ma'am, these just came in," he said when he was close enough. He handed her the envelopes.

"Thanks, Bear," Jennifer replied. She tore open the envelope containing Barton's letter and started reading. Carter realized that it was a private matter and started walking away.

Barton's letter started "Dear Jennifer." She soon came to the gist of the message – that he had decided that Monica was the one for him and that he was no longer in contention for her hand. Jennifer felt a sense of disappointment. *Oh well,* she told herself, *you can't have your cake and eat it, too. But then one wonders what good it does to have the cake if you can't eat it?* That question would be one for a great philosopher to answer, she decided, not her.

Better read the letter from Jim to shore up my confidence. After all, as far as I know, I'm the only one he's interested in. She wasn't mistaken. He planned to see her tomorrow and didn't leave her any wiggle room. He was coming. Period!

I've got to tell him that his competition has vanished and that he is the only one still interested in me. It wouldn't be fair to let him think otherwise. Jennifer knew it would be difficult. But she also knew that it had to be done.

When Jennifer walked out of the Nurse's quarters early the next morning, there he was. Jim Sherman carried a bouquet of flowers and was perfectly groomed. She started to say something to him, but he waved her off. He got down on one knee and started in.

"Jennifer, my darling, will you save me from an empty and unfulfilled life by agreeing to marry me?"

For once, Jennifer was speechless. Finally, with tears rolling down her cheeks, she blurted out a highly emotional 'yes!' "Yes, my darling," she repeated. The two embraced and kissed passionately.

"This is the happiest day of my life," Sherman said.

"Mine, too," Jennifer replied. "And I don't intend to let you out of my sight for even one moment until after you're my husband."

"I hope that's a promise," Sherman said.

By now, doctors and nurses were crowding around the two and offering congratulations. Brad Taylor came up and found out what the commotion was all about. He couldn't hide his pleasure, kissing Jennifer and hugging Sherman. "What a great day!" he gushed.

"Gangway!" could be heard from someone at the back of the crowd. It was none other than Monica. She elbowed her way to the front and gave Jennifer a huge hug. "Congratulations, my friend," she said. Jennifer knew that her young friend was very sincere. She hugged Monica tightly.

"Okay, everybody," Taylor shouted over the noise that had erupted, "time to get back to work."

"I can't tell you how happy I am for you kids," Taylor continued. "Jim, if you don't select me for the wedding party, I will be terribly disappointed!"

"I can assure you that you don't need to worry, my friend. I will let you know your role very shortly."

Soon, Jennifer and Sherman were alone.

"In all of the excitement," Sherman said, "I forgot to give you this." He reached in his pocket and pulled out an engagement ring. It had a big diamond in the center. He reached for Jennifer's hand and slid it on her ring finger.

"How beautiful!" she said. "I assure you I will wear it most proudly." The two kissed again.

"I hate to interrupt the euphoria of the moment," Sherman said, "but I think we better plan approximately when and where our wedding will be."

"I hate to admit it, but you're right. I think we should have it in the Washington, D.C. area. Do you think your family and friends can make it there?"

"Absolutely. And I think we should just tell people when and where it will be. If they can make it, fine. If not, that's their problem."

"I mostly agree," Jennifer said. "But I need to make sure my family can come. If not, we may have to make some changes. After all, they live in Idaho, a considerable distance away. And I do need them there."

"I certainly understand," Sherman replied. "When do you think you'll know?"

"I'll write them today, and then it just depends on how long it takes their response to reach me. I'll more than likely be enroute to D.C. before it catches up to me, but I'll let you know just as soon as I know."

"I can't ask for more than that."

The newly engaged couple walked to the mess hall. Jennifer got the address of Jim Sherman's family, and she said that she would also write them that day. She brought Sherman up to date on Zach Barton.

Sherman chuckled. "It may be that we have a double wedding – Zach and Monica and you and me."

"I hadn't thought of that, but you may be right. I'll pose the question to Monica – that is, if she and Zach get serious."

"And don't count her Doctor suitor out. He may yet surprise you."

Jennifer thought for a moment. "You know, you're right. Mike Pulaskey might yet win her hand. I'll have to be very careful."

The two giggled. Nothing was going to interfere with this wonderful moment in their lives.

Sherman had departed and Jennifer had finished coordinating with Bear Carter on the patient moves when Monica appeared. Monica came up and hugged her boss and friend.

"I'm so very happy for you," Monica said. "No one deserves happiness more than you."

"That means a great deal to me," Jennifer replied. "By the way, did I see Zach Barton sneaking around a little while ago? He obviously doesn't want to run into me."

"Yes, you did, and I have some news of my own."

Monica thrust out her left hand, and there was an engagement ring on her ring finger.

Jennifer shrieked. "I'm so happy for you. Congratulations!"

The two hugged again.

"You can't believe it, but Jim and I were talking about the possibility of a double wedding. What do you think?"

"I would really like it if it were in the D.C. area."

"Great! I'll start coordinating with Jim's and my family. I'll let you know just as soon as I hear back from them."

"One thing, though," Jennifer added. "What about Mike Pulaskey? Does he know about Zach and you?"

"He sure does," Monica said sadly. "I told him this morning, and he said he understands. I'm not sure, though. And, to tell you the truth,

I'm really going to miss him. But I can't help it – I fell head over heels in love with Zach."

So much for Mike, Jennifer thought. *I sure hope she knows what she's doing. Oh well, I have other things to worry about.*
Would everything work out so that the two of them could marry together? She didn't know, but she could sure hope.

Chapter 30

Wedding!

Jennifer was now back in Washington, D.C. *How time had flown,* she thought. *Not only had time flown, but everything had changed dramatically.* Jack MacLaine, her betrothed when she left Washington, had been killed in action. Now she was set to marry Jim Sherman, his best friend in Korea. But Sherman was a great guy, and she might have married him anyway if things had been different. She would never know for sure. *Oh well, I've got way too many things to do to waste time thinking about what might have been.*

Jennifer had heard from both her family and Sherman's, and the key people could come to D.C. for the wedding. Now she had to decide who else to invite. The run-of-the-mill folks would be easy, as she would only have to send them an invitation. Others, such as Francis Dunbar, would be a little harder, as she would have to update them on what had been happening in her life. And then there were the really difficult ones like Otto Bruner. Otto probably couldn't come anyway, but none-the-less she wanted to invite him. For Otto's invitation, she would probably have to pass it through U.S. Intelligence. After all, she didn't want to get him in trouble, so the invitation would have to be handled very delicately. With her betrothed being in Army Intelligence, it shouldn't be a problem.

Jennifer had sublet her apartment to some nurses at Walter Reed. She had been unable – or unwilling – to terminate their lease. So she had to rent another apartment. It was for a short time, anyway, as Jim Sherman got his desire and was stationed in the D.C. area at Andrews Air Force Base. They would be finding suitable housing together.

Jennifer and Sherman were scheduled to go to Bill and Molly Summerfield's that night for dinner. Summerfield was now retired from the Army and was a civilian contractor. They had moved out of their old house and had bought a home in the posh MacLean, Virginia area.

Sherman had worked for Summerfield in Japan, so Jennifer was sure that the two of them would have a lot to talk about. While she had not yet seen Molly, she had talked to her several times. Molly said that her son, Todd, was growing like a weed and was now talking full –tilt. "What a hand-full!" Molly said. "And he's not yet 4!"

"I can hardly wait to see him," Jennifer told her good friend.

"Well, you can have him if you really want him," was the reply.

"I'll bet," Jennifer replied with a chuckle. She could tell that Todd was the apple of Molly's eye.

And Molly had confirmed in her conversations with Jennifer that relations with Monica had improved. This news was very welcome, as Monica and Zach Barton would also be at the dinner at the Summerfields the next night. Jennifer had not yet talked to Monica about specifics of their double wedding, so the next night might afford the perfect opportunity. *Have to be careful, though,* Jennifer told herself. The primary reason for the dinner was not to make wedding plans, so she would have to be careful not to let it dominate the evening.

But now back to the more pressing issue – who to invite to the wedding and how to inform them. As Jennifer had already decided, most of the queries would be very simple, just requiring the submission of an invitation. And even the invite to Francis Dunbar would be very straight-forward. She had seen him recently in Korea, and he was almost up to speed on events. In any case, she would just have to send him a short note with the invitation. She would also invite his wife, Carol, and two children, Jonathon and Molly. She really didn't expect that all of them would come, but nonetheless, she would invite them. *Oh, that reminds me, I must send an invitation to Winston Churchill. He may have his feelings hurt if I don't. I'll also have to bring him up to speed on all of the occurrences in my life. Perhaps Francis Dunbar would extend the invitation for me. I can ask him in my letter to him. It would certainly ease the burden on me – a lowly U.S. Army Major writing the Prime Minister of Great Britain. I'm not sure the word would even get through to him. If Francis Dunbar would contact him, it would certainly be good for me. I'll try it!*

Jennifer made a quick count of the invitations she would send. There were a total of 150. *And this doesn't include the ones Jim will want to send. And Monica and Zach will have a goodly number. Whew! I hope we can find a place that will hold all of them!*

Jennifer had initially thought that the wedding would be in about three weeks. But now she realized that three weeks might not be enough time. She would have to think about it and discuss it with Jim, Monica, and Zach. Perhaps the conversation could be worked in when they met the next night.

But perhaps the hardest part would still be the letter to Otto Bruner. She didn't have the invitations printed up yet, as she didn't even have a definite time and place. But she realized that she had to send him a letter inviting him. While she didn't expect him to be able to come, she really wanted him there. Why? She wasn't quite sure. She just knew that she wanted him in attendance. So she decided to start in on the letter.

My Dear Otto

Please don't be shocked hearing from me after all of this time. I have thought of you and your family a lot over the years, and I hope all is well with you.

The reason I am writing is that I am getting married, and I wanted to extend you and your family an invitation. If you can't come, I certainly understand. And please don't get in any trouble over this issue.

I am marrying someone who I don't believe you know. I was engaged to Jack MacLaine, the man you helped get to the American side after he was wounded in East Berlin. However, Jack was killed in Korea, and I am going to marry the man who was his best friend. However, please don't misunderstand. I am marrying his best friend – Jim Sherman – because Jim is a wonderful man who I have fallen head over heels in love with.

I have just returned from Korea, where I served in a Mobile Army Surgical Hospital (MASH) unit. I am now back at Walter Reed Hospital in the Washington, D. C. area. I am once again working for Brad Taylor, who you may remember from your time in the Normandy hospital. I am convinced that there are no better bosses around.

I will send you a formal invitation when we get the details worked out — unless, of course, I hear otherwise from you.

All for *now.*

Love,

Jennifer

Jennifer hesitated to sign the letter, 'Love,' but she decided to do it, anyway. *After all,* she thought, *the world certainly needs more love.*

Jennifer arrived at Walter Reed Hospital bright and early the next morning. As she walked into the building, it didn't seem like she had been away at all. *Funny,* she thought, *I've been through a great deal these past three years, but it is rapidly dropping into the background in my mind. I mustn't let that happen, and I must do all I can to restore the Korean conflict to its proper place in my memory. I must never forget our brave troops and the sacrifices they made to keep South Korea free.*

Jennifer decided that she would first stop at Brad Taylor's office and get the latest update on what was happening. On the way to his office, she saw familiar as well as new faces. The ones who she knew from the past welcomed her back in a hearty fashion. Some even gave her hugs!

Jennifer peered into Taylor's office as she reached the doorway. She couldn't help but smile. There he was at his old desk reviewing intently a document that he had pulled out of a stack of paperwork on his desk. *Some things just never change,* she told herself. Shaking her head in amazement, it appeared as if her old boss had not left, either!

Taylor looked up and then stood up. He smiled and walked over to his head Nurse and gave her a big hug. "I'm so glad to see you," he said. "You'll recognize the names of some of our patients. They're from our MASH unit in Korea. The poor guys are still getting over their wounds and trauma."

Taylor picked up a list and handed it to Jennifer. She scanned it quickly and handed it back. "You're right as always, Brad. I do recognize some of the names. I hope to see all of our patients today, and I'll make it a point to see these men."

Jennifer and Taylor discussed roles and responsibilities. Jennifer then departed to make her rounds. She also posted information on a

Nurse's meeting to take place later in the day. She posted the data on the appropriate bulletin board.

The day went by very quickly. Soon, it was time to break off for the day. True to her plans, she had seen all of the patients. And she had seen Monica during her afternoon rounds. What a pleasure it was seeing Monica, as Jennifer had come to rely on her very heavily. But in the back of her mind, she had come to the unpleasant thought that Monica might not be here forever. After all, she was getting married, and she might become a mother. Or Zach might get transferred out of the area. Either one of these possibilities might take Monica away.

But what about her – Jennifer? She was getting married also. And she might become a mother. If so, she would be gone from her job at least for her time on maternity leave. And what if she wanted to be a stay-at-home mom? Or what if Jim Sherman got transferred and she wanted to go with him? There were definitely more questions than answers. These issues never came up before, but it was very sobering thinking of future disruptions that may arise. *I can't put these issues off. In spite of all we have to do, Jim and I need to talk about them now. Otherwise, it will be too late.*

Jennifer was glad that she was recognizing some of the issues that many couples simply swept under the rug. As she walked to the parking lot to get in her newly purchased car, she felt a sense of relief. She would broach these subjects with Jim when he picked her up for the drive to the Summerfield residence. She knew that Jim probably wouldn't be happy talking about them, but he had proven surprisingly calm when she had brought up potentially divisive subjects in the past. Perhaps he would do so in the face of these issues. She certainly hoped so.

Jennifer parked her car and went into her apartment. It was small but very serviceable. She went to the closet and picked out a nice outfit to wear. She wasn't sure whether she was getting fixed up more for her betrothed or for the Summerfields. After all, she had seen Jim Sherman recently, but it had been a long time since she had seen Molly and Bill Summerfield. And she had only seen Todd when he was newly born. *Did it make a difference?* She wasn't sure.

Jennifer showered, dressed, brushed her hair, and put on her makeup. She planned to meet Jim Sherman at the front of her Apartment when he drove up. She looked at her watch. *I'm right on time. Better go on down.*

When she got to the front entrance, she was about five minutes early. And Sherman had not yet come. She thought about practicing how she would broach the subjects she wanted to talk about, but decided against it. *That's not a good idea. A marriage should be based on mutual trust. I'll just let it come out more naturally.*

Sherman was very punctual and drove up right on time. Jennifer went hurriedly around the front of the car and got in on the passenger's side. She sat down and closed the door. The two kissed, and Sherman slowly accelerated the car.

"Wow," Sherman said. "You look gorgeous tonight."

"Thank you, sir. And you look pretty nice yourself."

Sherman thanked her. He was in a blue pinstripe suit. While not perfectly coordinated with her pink dress, the two looked very nice together.

"I may as well tell you now," Jennifer said as they drove through the beautiful countryside. "I shouldn't have been doing this – I know – but I have been playing the 'what if' game. What if, for example, I decide to go back to work after I have a child – or what if I decide to be a stay-at-home mom?"

Sherman thought for a moment and then chuckled. "It's just like I thought when I asked you to marry me. You're well ahead of your time thinking out all of these potential issues. That's part of the reason I love you so much."

"Then you don't see a problem with all of these uncertainties?"

"Absolutely not. We'll work them out whatever you decide to do. And I'm certain that, being a nurse, you'll have no problem getting a job anywhere if that's what you decide to do."

"Do you have a preference as to what I should do?" Jennifer asked.

"No. That is entirely up to you."

This was a lot easier than I thought it would be. And he talks about me being ahead of my time? I think he's the one who's really advanced! She slid over to snuggle up to the man she was about to marry.

As long as she was on a roll, Jennifer decided to ask Sherman how best to get an invitation to Otto Bruner. In his usual unperturbed fashion, Sherman said to give him the letter as soon as she finished it. He would take care of it.

"I hoped you would say that," Jennifer replied. "She reached in her purse and pulled out the letter. She handed it to Sherman.

"Good," Sherman replied, putting the letter in his suit coat breast pocket. "Issue closed."

What a man! Jennifer thought. *I'm marrying a real gem!* She squeezed his arm and snuggled even closer. Sherman obviously enjoyed the attention.

Jennifer and Sherman arrived at the Summerfield residence at the same time that Monica and Barton did. The four exchanged greetings and hugs and went to the front door. Sherman rang, and soon the door opened. Molly was holding Todd as she pushed the screen door open. Enthusiastic greetings were exchanged.

"Oh my," Jennifer said. "You must be Todd!" She held out her arms and the boy reached out to her. Jennifer had obviously made a new friend for life.

"Come on in," Molly said as Summerfield approached from an area that was obviously the kitchen. Greetings and hugs were again exchanged.

The hosts and guests went to the living room. Jennifer – still holding Todd – and Sherman went to the couch and sat down. They slid to one end, and Jennifer motioned for Monica and Barton to join them. Soon, the four adults were squared away on the massive divan. By now, Todd had reached the end of his endurance. He scrambled off of Jennifer's lap toward a truck on the floor. He now had other things to do.

Molly excused herself to go take care of things in the kitchen. Both Jennifer and Monica offered to help, but they were turned down. Jennifer asked Summerfield how he liked being a civilian.

"It's okay, and it helps pay the bills," the former Army General replied, "but I guess I was in the Army too long. I miss the excitement, and I guess I always will."

The four agreed, and Summerfield said he better go out and help Molly with the dinner. He patted Todd on the head as he passed by. The youngster was too busily engaged to apparently notice.

Jennifer seized the opportunity and asked Monica and Barton if they had a date for the wedding in mind.

"How about two weeks from Saturday?" Monica said. Jennifer looked at Sherman, and he gave her a nod of approval. *It's a little sooner than I thought,* Jennifer mused, *but what the heck?*

"Sounds good to us. We'll have about 200 guests that we're asking," Jennifer said, putting in a figure for Sherman and some slack in case others came to mind. "But who knows? We might get substantially less."

"Same with us," Monica replied. "How about the Fort Myers Chapel? Zach was thinking that it would be a proper spot."

Jennifer looked at Sherman, and both nodded their agreement.

"I'll check Monday to see if we can get it," Sherman said. "This is a busy time for them, and I'm not sure they can work us in. But I'll try my best."

"Good," Jennifer replied. "We're counting on you."

Everyone seemed to be thoroughly enjoying the evening. Just as Jennifer suspected,

Bill Summerfield was intently interested in what her fiancé' had to say about the Intelligence Operation in the Far East after he had departed.

"I have to tell you, sir," Sherman said, "the Intelligence Operation got better after MacArthur and Willoughby left. Losing you, though, certainly wasn't a good thing for folks like me."

"I appreciate that, Jim," Summerfield replied. "I think Willoughby could have been more useful in another role. But MacArthur trusted him and wanted him to head his G-2. I wish I could have made it into MacArthur's inner circle, but I never could.

"You just met him too late, that's all," Sherman replied.

Summerfield nodded, and the conversation soon turned to a happier note.

Jennifer couldn't help but feel a sense of warmth as she looked around the group. She was with people who were very important in her life – her fiancé and her best friends. Seeing Todd playing with the truck on the floor was also very pleasurable. It reminded her of home in Idaho with her younger brothers and sisters.

At the end of the evening, the four guests thanked the hosts profusely. Jennifer giggled when she looked down and saw Todd sound asleep on the carpet.

"I was supposed to tell you that we'll always have a place for you if you want to come back to work," Jennifer said to Molly as the six adults walked to the front door. "Brad Taylor wanted me to mention that to you."

"Please thank him for me," Molly replied, "but, naw, for now I'm very content to stay with Todd."

"Why doesn't that surprise me?" Jennifer said, with a hint of jealousy in her response.

Goodbyes were said, and the four guests walked to the two cars. On the way, Monica pulled Jennifer to the side.

"Our upcoming weddings don't appear to be making you nervous," Monica said in a subdued tone. "But aren't you a bit nervous underneath? I know I am."

"On the one hand, I am. But on the other, I've been waiting for this for a long time. So, to be honest with you, I'll be very happy when it's all over and I'm Mrs. Jim Sherman."

"I understand," Monica replied. The two walked arm in arm to catch up with their intendeds.

The days went by rapidly, and their big day was here. Sherman had been very successful in getting the Fort Myers Chapel at the time that was mutually agreeable. The two women were in their wedding gowns and nervously waiting for the ceremony to begin. There was a knock on the door, and Monica went over to answer it.

"Frank Dunbar!" Monica squealed. "It's so good to see you, and we're thrilled you could come." The two hugged, and Dunbar carefully protected a letter in his right hand.

"Frank, it's so good to see you," Jennifer said as she hurried over to join the embraces.

"I wouldn't have missed it for the world," Dunbar said. "I'm just sorry I couldn't bring Carol and the kids, but you know how it is – school and other things. Mr. Churchill was also sorry that his duties as Prime Minister prevented him from coming, but he wrote you a nice, lengthy letter."

Dunbar handed the letter to Jennifer. She quickly opened it and started reading. Tears welled up in her eyes as she finished.

"He thinks a great deal of you," Dunbar said softly.

"And I of him."

"By the way," Dunbar continued, "there's someone outside who is very anxious to see you."

"Oh?" Jennifer replied curiously. "Who could that be?"

Dunbar grinned. "You'll have to see for yourself."

Jennifer walked to the door and slowly opened it. After all, there was a lot of activity in the Chapel, and she didn't want to contribute to the pre-festivity excitement.

Then she saw him over in the shadows. It was Otto Bruner! Somehow he had been able to slip out unnoticed by his superiors. She eagerly motioned for him to come over.

Bruner shook his head. "I'm very happy for you!" he mouthed. "I'll see you later."

Jennifer blew him a kiss. By now, Monica had come over and was standing on her tippy toes to get a look at the man she had heard much about. Frank Dunbar had also come over.

"So that's the famous Otto Bruner," Monica said to no one in particular.

"The one and only," Dunbar replied. "By the way, I should go out and be seated. I'll talk to you two later."

"Thank you so much for coming," Jennifer replied. "It means a great deal to me." She gave Dunbar a soft kiss on the cheek.

Jennifer peered out as Dunbar left. There was Brad Taylor, in his role as head usher, taking her family members down to be seated in the front. She also saw Sherman and Barton up there, both very handsome. Attending Sherman as Best Man was Chesty Puller, looking immaculate in his mess dress uniform with his rows of ribbons and decorations. Attending Barton as his Best Man was Jacob Partude. Pangs went through Jennifer as she looked at Partude. After all, Jacob was the brother of Dude, her first betrothed.

Soon, it was time. Jennifer heard a knock on the door and the door beginning to open. There were her Father and Brad Taylor. Her Father would escort her down the aisle, and Brad Taylor – doing double duty – would give Monica away. Would this event spell the end of the adventurous life for Jennifer and Monica? On the one hand, it would, but on the other it signaled the start of a new beginning.

Acknowledgements

When I started the original novel in the series ("Footsteps to Forever"), I never dreamed that I would write a trilogy and plan for one more novel beyond the third one. However, that is exactly what happened. I am now planning to take the series through the fall of the Berlin Wall (about 1991). Thus, I will introduce the next generation of the main characters as well as tell what happens to the original ones in their later years. Why am I doing this? In the first place, I believe that it is a very worthwhile endeavor to write historical novels. In the second place, I enjoy doing it and having the opportunity to interface with the readers. And, finally, I have become very attached to the characters and couldn't stand for them to languish.

As with "Footsteps," I owe a huge 'thank you' to my wife, Linda, for her continued support, encouragement, and suggestions. She has always been there for me, and I am indebted to her beyond words.

Marty Fleck has also been a great help. Not only did he write a super blurb that appears in the front of this novel, but he caught some typos and misprints as he read the draft. The end result is that this book is better because of his efforts.

I also owe a big thanks to Rosalie White, my main interface with my publisher (iUniverse). Rosalie worked tirelessly to turn out a great product in minimum time.

Finally, I want to acknowledge you, the reader. Without you, there would be no reason to write the books.